# The World as It Shall Be

*Translated by*

Margaret Clarke

*Edited with an*

*Introduction by*

I. F. Clarke

WESLEYAN UNIVERSITY PRESS

*Middletown, Connecticut*

# The World as It Shall Be

## ÉMILE SOUVESTRE

Published by

Wesleyan University Press, Middletown CT 06459


The Wesleyan Edition of Émile Souvestre's

*Le Monde tel qu'il sera*

© 2004 by Wesleyan University Press

Translation and critical materials

© 2004 by I. F. Clarke and M. Clarke

Printed in the United States of America

Library of Congress Cataloging-in-Publication Data

Souvestre, Émile, 1806–1854.

[Le monde tel qu'il sera. English]

The world as it shall be / by Émile Souvestre ; translated by Margaret Clarke ;

introduction and critical material by I.F. Clarke.

p.  cm. — (The Wesleyan early classics of science fiction series)

Originally published : Paris, 1846.

Includes bibliographical references.

ISBN 0-8195-6615-2 (cloth : alk. paper) —

I. Clarke, I. F. (Ignatius Frederick)    II. Clarke, M. (Margaret)

III. Title.    IV. Series

PQ2429.S7M713 2004

843'.7—dc22

2004041270


5   4   3   2   1

# Contents

# Preface

Émile Souvestre was a most enterprising and original writer. His tale of coming things—the first major dystopia in the new *roman de l'avenir*—was an innovation that owed everything to his narrative skill in showing fully formed in the third millennium those tendencies in his own society that he found most alarming and dehumanizing. His purpose was entirely serious. In the manner of the most competent satirists, however, he chose to entertain his readers through his use of the grotesque and the absurd. One way of engaging the reader's immediate attention was to present a text that would be visually arresting, and this Souvestre achieved by the use of most apposite illustrations and a number of typographic devices.

The most striking of these are the illustrations—eighty-three of them in all, full-page, half-page, vignette. The full-page illustrations, of the men in particular, make their point by showing the outward appearance of their subjects in absurd costumes that are true images of their inner pretensions. In his search after visual effect Souvestre employed variations in fonts and the sizes of type, italics, and capitalization. Since all of these devices are an important feature of the original, this first English translation of *Le Monde tel qu'il sera* reproduces the story as Souvestre wished it to appear.

Souvestre seems to have worked on the principle of a new character for every chapter, since his succession of allegorical *personae* adds greatly to the variety of the narrative: that *moulin à paroles* M. Atout, the well-named M. Omnivore, smooth-talking Abbé Coulant, and the bored Milady Ennui. Most of them are allegorical: the names signal the characters and propensities of their owners. A few, however, like Grelotin and Mlle. Spartacus, refer to actual characters. The decision was made not to anglicize them, so that they would all stay firmly anchored in their French context.

The next decision was the treatment of the verses that appear in the text. The quotations that Souvestre took from other French authors have not been translated. His quaint *vers de mirliton*, however, have been given an English form that seeks to capture something of the flamboyance of the originals.

We take this opportunity to thank all who have been so generous with their help. Our grateful thanks go to the staff of the Upper Reading Room of the Bodleian Library and of the London Library who furnished us with all the essential reading required in the translating and editing of this first English-language edition of *Le Monde tel qu'il sera*. We are particularly indebted to the help and advice of Dr. Arthur B. Evans of De Pauw University, a benign and most knowledgeable editor. We thank also those French friends who shone light in dark places, especially Bernard Cazes and Xavier Legrand-Ferronière.

Margaret Clarke
I. F. Clarke
Milton under Wychwood

# Introduction

Émile Souvestre, the author of the first major dystopia in the history of future fiction, was born in Morlaix on April 15, 1806, and died suddenly in Paris on July 5, 1854. During his short life he gained an international reputation for the originality of his fiction, the ingenuity of his plays, and the moral bent of all he wrote. It was early evident that Souvestre had achieved a *succès d'estime* with his many French readers: within three years of his death, the first study of his life and literary achievements had appeared. There, in the opening paragraph of the *Notice sur la vie d'Émile Souvestre* (1857), Eugène Lesbazeilles began by noting those factors that had made Émile Souvestre so popular with nineteeth-century readers:

> No one succeeds in obtaining a prominent place in literature, or in sur-
> rounding himself with a faithful and steady circle of admirers drawn
> from the fickle masses of the public, unless he possesses originality,
> constant variety, and a distinct personality. It is quite possible to gain
> for a moment a few readers by imitating some original feature in an-
> other; but these soon vanish and the writer remains alone and forgot-
> ten. Others, again, without belonging to any distinct group of authors,
> having found their standard in themselves, moralists and educators at
> the same time, have obtained undying recognition. Of the latter class,
> though little known outside France, is Émile Souvestre.[1]

The publishing records for the United States and the United Kingdom, however, run counter to Lezbazeilles's belief that Souvestre was "little known outside France." During the second half of the nineteenth century there were no fewer than fourteen translations of various works by Souvestre published in the United States and some sixteen in the United Kingdom. Indeed, a bad case of literary piracy suggests that Americans were greatly interested in Souvestre, and the editor of *Harper's Magazine* must have thought that *Le Monde tel qu'il sera* offered attractive material for his readers. In the January issue of 1856 he gave front-page placement to an anonymous twelve-page piece, "January First, A.D. 3000." This was a selection of passages from the Souvestre dystopia with eighteen illustrations copied from the originals, all held together in unnatural union by the narrator's commentary. Not a word about origins or sources, and no mention of the original language.[2]

Did the American editor know that Souvestre's publications had earned him a reputation as a writer of wholesome books for family reading? His concern for moral values is most evident throughout *Le Monde tel qu'il sera*, and it shapes his many Breton stories, which present acute observations on the characteristics and the habits of the people of Brittany, best examined in *Les Derniers Bretons* (1835–1837) and in *Le Foyer Breton* (1844). His most popular work was undoubtedly *Un Philosophe sous les toits* (1850), crowned by the French Academy for its "excellent moral tendency" and still in print. According to those who knew him, Souvestre was a modest man: unduly self-effacing some said, a man who never sought a commanding position in the literary world. He worked every day for most of the day—labors that were well rewarded. An English admirer pointed to "the immense sales of M. Souvestre's works" as evidence of the large number of readers "who appreciate the efforts of a brave, pure-minded man of genius to assert the beauty of goodness and truth."[3] His contemporaries thought so well of him that his widow received the Prix Lambert, given to "the families of authors who by their integrity and by the probity of their efforts have well deserved this token from the République des Lettres."

The appearance of Souvestre's *Le Monde tel qu'il sera*, in parts in 1845–1846 and as a book later in 1846, was a major advance in the development of future fiction.[4] As Pierre Versins remarked in his indispensable *Encyclopédie:* "A single work was enough to ensure a leading role for Émile Souvestre in the history of conjectural fiction."[5] That was a just estimation of a major innovator who has the distinction of producing the first *épopée de l'avenir* to appear in serial publication, the first major dystopia set in time-to-come, and the first handsomely illustrated tale of the future in which the images by Charles Albert d'Arnoux Bertall, Octave Penguilly, and Prosper St. Germain added a new dimension to future fiction. To judge from the four-page "Prospectus" for the serial (*On souscrit à Paris chez W. Coquebert, Éditeur*) the publisher evidently expected great things from the offer to subscribers of forty issues at twenty-five centimes each; for readers were promised that "the estimable author of *Le Foyer breton*" would entertain them with his "dream of a future time when Paris, like Babylon and Palmyra, would be a heap of ruins, inhabited by wild beasts. . . . He will relate the history of a world from which poetry, religion and love have vanished; and he will reveal a world that has its Sinai in a safe-deposit, that has made hard cash its only god. He will guide you through the ludicrous eccentricities of a perfect society, where all things obey the supreme laws of mechanism."[6]

Like his contemporary Honoré de Balzac in the *Comédie Humaine,* Souvestre found the France of Louis-Philippe (1830–1848) a dangerous and unfriendly place, animated by greed and ruled by *rentiers* and *propriétaires.* If the world was a bad place in 1846, Souvestre aimed to show how much worse it would be in the third millennium when self-obsessed grotesques like M. Omnivore and Madame Facile would be the most admired high achievers in their uncaring society. For the first time in the evolution of these future worlds, the narrative setting diverges from the ideal societies of Mercier's *L'An 2440* (1771) and Restif de la Bretonne's *Les Posthumes* (1802), where every prospect was designed to please. Moreover—another innovation—the reader is both told and shown the most undesirable condition of life in the far-from-brave new world of Souvestre's admonitory future.

Souvestre's *The World as It Shall Be* marked an advance into an unexplored area of time-to-come: a sign that the *roman de l'avenir* continued true to its origins and remained engaged with all the possibilities for change in the new industrial society of the nineteenth century. So, in his tale of consequences, Souvestre called for a radical reconsideration of ends and means that would take account of the mass society then emerging—the nonstop expansion of great cities, the steady growth of population, and the continuing explosion of powerful technologies. As a man with a mission, he used every means to reinforce his message. He took advantage, for instance, of the contemporary advances in typography to catch the reader's eye with often startling changes in font and frequent use of italics and capitals. Indeed, an examination of the eighty-three illustrations will show that Souvestre clearly sought to maintain a dialogue between word and image, especially with the full-page figures like those of M. Atout and Mlle. Spartacus. These make their separate entries in the story, as though controlled by a puppet master in this first theater of coming things; for it is apparent that the unsparing images of the illustrators belonged to, and gained from, the contemporary vogue for caricature.

That vogue had followed upon yet another change in the government of France. Fifteen years after the end of the Napoleonic Empire, the July Revolution of 1830 had terminated the long reign of the Bourbons and had introduced a new-style constitutional monarch in the person of Louis-Philippe, not king of France but *roi des Français.* The revolutionary *tricolore* replaced the fleur-de-lys, and the old Bourbon practice of muzzling the press was checked forever (so they thought) by the article in the Charter of 1830 that abolished all forms of censorship. The new freedom had coincided with advances in lithography that put illustrated papers and magazines within the reach of most citizens—an opportunity for Charles Philipon (1800–1862) to inaugurate a new and most powerful form of political and social satire. On November 4, 1830, the first issue of his weekly illustrated paper *La Caricature* appeared, dedicated to *politique, morale et littéraire*. It was the start of a series of papers—a departure in publishing—made memorable by the most original and compelling illustrations of artists like Honoré Daumier, Henri Monnier, and Grandville.[7]

Jean-Ignace-Isidore Gérard, known as Grandville, was an illustrator of genius and a most original caricaturist, a collaborator of Daumier in *La Caricature* and associated with Balzac in *La Caricature provisoire*. In 1844, when Souvestre had started work on his *Le Monde tel qu'il sera,* Grandville published (as Texile Delord) *Un Autre Monde*. This was the first major excursion into the many varieties of visual and verbal fantasy suggested by the new sciences and technologies, and it is a publication that has clear affinities with the Bertall illustrations in *Le Monde tel qu'il sera*.[8] In his other world, Grandville sought to give significant shape to all the possibilities—biological, technological, cosmological—perceptible in the first industrial revolution. The subtitle is the longest of its kind, for Grandville's imagination races through all things conceivable in the year 1844:

*TRANSFORMATIONS, VISIONS, INCARNATIONS*
*ASCENSIONS, LOCOMOTIONS, EXPLORATIONS, PÉRÉGRINATIONS*
*EXCURSIONS, STATIONS*
*COSMOGONIES, FANTASMAGORIES, RÊVERIES, FOLÂTRERIES*
*FACÉTIES, LURIES*
*MÉTAMORPHOSES, ZOOMORPHOSES*
*LITHOMORPHOSES, MÉTEMPSYCOSES, APOTHÉOSES*
*ET AUTRES CHOSES*

This most detailed catalogue offers supporting evidence for what Tocqueville had written about the imagination in his classic *De la Démocratie en Amérique*. In 1831 he had gone to the United States, that *Novus Ordo Seclorum*, to discover the "the image of democracy itself . . . in order to learn what we have to fear or to hope from its progress." And he found that democracy would inevitably change the condition of society as surely as it was transforming the immemorial links between past and present, generating new values and new attitudes: "Democracy, which shuts the past against the poet, opens the future before him." He had shown how the idea of progress and of the indefinite perfectibility of the human species is proper to democratic ages: "Democratic peoples scarcely worry about what has been, but they willingly dream of what will be, and in this direction their imagination has no limits; here it stretches and enlarges itself beyond measure."[9]

The prodigious workings of a most fertile imagination were apparent in the cosmogonies, phantasmagorias, and reveries of *Un Autre Monde*. In 292 packed pages Grandville played with the mechanical—a steam orchestra pumping out a melody for two hundred trombones; he sported with the new evolutionary ideas—hybrid creatures that are *mi-femmes, mi-poissons;* and then engaged with the severe logic of a society in which the wealthy and powerful are tall and handsome, whereas the proletarians are diminutive and ugly. And in his last pages he came to an appropriate conclusion in his forecast that "les machines remplaceront les créatures" and enjoyed a last fling in the final full-page color illustration of a *fin du monde* scene—a steam-powered Ark taking on the last animals on earth. It is the end of the world, chosen by heaven to punish "le genre humain et les vieux célibataires."

The liberties Grandville took with time and space were major entries in the book of the future. The succession of the new prophets had begun in 1771 with the utopian anticipations in Mercier's *L'An deux mille quatre cent quarante;* and in 1795 a new dispensation for humankind appeared in the confident predictions of Condorcet's *Esquisse d'un tableau historique des progrès de l'esprit humain.* Auguste Comte, Saint-Simon, and Charles Fourier followed, adding their formulations to the growing volume of observations on things to come. "Those idiots," as Souvestre called them. "If you listened to them, each one had the answer to the problem of Pandora's box; it needed merely to be opened to release universal happiness for mankind" (3).

So many had found so much to say on progress and the future that there had to be a book about the new literature. As early as 1834 a new term, *la littérature futuriste,* had come into circulation, coined by Félix Bodin, historian and parliamentary deputy, in his *Roman de l'avenir,* the first book ever written about futuristic fiction. In pious memory of *L'An 2440* Bodin began with a dedication—not to the future, however, but to the ancestors. In his address *Au Passé,* Bodin deliberately echoed Mercier's opening words—"Respectable and venerable year, destined to bring felicity to the inhabitants of this world"—for he looked backward across six decades of the new writing and found an evolutionary process at work: "Venerable Past, it is you who have provided all the elements for this book, for when you were the present, you were big with the future, as Leibnitz put it so neatly." The source of the new *littérature méliioriste* was the idea of progress. The future "appears to the imagination in a blaze of light" and

> progress, understood as a law of human existence, became in turn a clear demonstration and then a sacred manifestation of Providence. It was impossible that such a noble, such a great idea—distilled through the spirit of the age for half a century and illuminating it these last few years, when it had been proclaimed as a dogmatic certainty and with poetic enthusiasm—it was impossible that it could fail to flower in religions and in utopias. There has been no lack of these in recent days. However, I do not think anyone has so far tried to say anything about the future save by way of utopian theories and apocalypses.[10]

By limiting his survey to major works of future fiction, it seems that Bodin could not see how the idea of progress had become an Open Sesame, a deposit of faith in the future, from which all could borrow according to their interests. In 1810, for instance, Julius von Voss took the certainty of progress as the validation of his romantic tale of heroic adventures in *Ini;* for he wrote in his introduction: "As assuredly as the present is an improvement on the past . . . so with equal certainty a better future is coming; and we may at least be confident that we can expect our ever-developing civilization will be the salvation of all mortal creatures. What we cannot yet see, we dream of."[11]

These assertions were part of the common wisdom that would soon find expression in the stories of Jules Verne and in the progressive utopias of the 1870s. Progress provided the stuff of poetry; for it was good-bye to the past and ten thousand welcomes to the future in the ringing couplets of Alfred Tennyson's "Locksley Hall" (1841):

> Men, my brothers, men the workers, ever reaping something new:
> That which they have done, but earnest of the things that they
> shall do:
> When I dipt into the future, far as human eye could see,
> Saw the Vision of the world, and all the wonder that would be.

Similar certainties and expectations ran through Victor Hugo's poem, so aptly titled "Le vaste élan du progrès":

Oh! L'avenir est magnifique!
Jeunes Français, jeunes amis,
Un siècle pur et pacifique
S'ouvre à vos pas mieux affermis;
Chaque jour aura sa conquête
Depuis la base jusqu'au faîte
Nous verrons avec majesté,
Comme une mer sur ses rivages,
Montrer d'étages en étages
L'irrésistible liberté.

Like Tennyson, the French poet had "dipt into the future, far as human eye could see," and in *Plein Ciel* he foresaw humankind moving out from Earth. Another Columbus would one day make his way through deep space, and a future Vasco da Gama would round the "cap de l'abîme":[12]

Un Jason de l'azur, depuis longtemps parti,
De la terre oublié, par le ciel englouti,
Tout à coup, sur l'humaine rive
Reparaîtra, monté sur cet alérion,
Et, montrant Sirius, Allioth, Orion,
Tout pâle, dira: J'en arrive!

Across the Atlantic the manifest destiny of a new nation inspired Walt Whitman to write in the preface to the 1876 edition of his *Leaves of Grass:* "with such absolute certainty on the Great Future of the United States . . . I have always invoked that Future, and surrounded myself with it. . . . Of men, or States, few realize how much they live in the future. That, rising like pinnacles, gives its main significance to all You and I are doing today. Without it, there were little meaning in lands or poems—little purport in human lives. . . . All ages, all Nations and States, have seen such prophecies. But were any former ones with prophecy so broad, so clear, as our times, our lands—as those of the West?"[13]

By the 1870s the future—social, political, military and naval, mechanized, and industrialized—had become a publishing industry. The rapid spread of future-writing can be examined in the notorious episode of Chesney's *Battle of Dorking* (1871), which showed propagandists everywhere how to use fiction in aid of the military; and in the immensely popular stories of Jules Verne, which began with the initial success of *Cinq semaines en ballon* in 1863. In the years ahead, according to Verne, inventors of genius such as Nemo and Robur would transform the world into a paradise of marvelous machines. The idealized images of his favorite illustrators—Benett, Riou, Neuville—revealed the triumphs still to come in a succession of spectacular scenarios. These were invitations to contemplate a fault-free future.

In 1865, all but a century before the *Eagle* landed in the Sea of Tranquility, Verne made the first of many prophecies through the persona of his French hero in *De la terre à la lune*. Michel Ardan told the crowds at the launch site in Tampa Town that the journey to the moon "must be made sooner or later, and the mode of effecting it is only a simple consequence of the great law of progress." The images follow the main stages of the great enterprise, from the construction of the discharge chamber to "The Arrival of the Projectile at Stony Hill" and blast-off at "Fire!" when the *Columbiad* soars away from Terra, as "a pillar of flame darts up in to the sky, half a mile in height."

These stories and their triumphal images were a positive encouragement to look forward to a future of all-change for the technologies and no-change for the citizens. Encouraging, subliminal messages brought the comforting promise that, no matter how far science advanced, society in the twentieth century would be a continuation of the nineteenth century: same habits, same values, same social classes. This assumption is most evident in the remarkable anticipations of Albert Robida (1846–1926), "cette homme-orchestre de la conjecture," as Pierre Versins called him; for Robida has the glory of taking the image of the future far beyond the beginnings in *Le Monde tel qu'il sera* and beyond the reach of Verne's illustrators. The two were equal and opposite: Verne the word spinner and Robida the image builder. Where Verne told his tales of great innovators in dramatic episodes, Robida's images revealed the world of the future in panoramic views of a society at work and play in his *Le Vingtième Siècle*. That work began as a serial in 1882 ("50 livraisons à partir de janvier"), a nonstop display of life in the years 1952 to 1959: flying machines of all sizes, transatlantic air travel, the latest news on television screens, private communications by "téléphonoscope," underground transportation, submarine vessels, food factories, rotating houses, women advocates, women in knee-length dresses for air travel, women in business, chasing their percentages in "La Bourse des Dames." The march of progress has even reached the supreme level of government. Robida seems to have taken a hint from Souvestre and invented an incorruptible president of the Republic, an automaton made in two months by an inventor of genius, a supreme figure of wood who reigns but does not rule.

From the world at peace, Robida moved on to the world at war in *La*

*Guerre au vingtième siècle.* The first version appeared in issue no. 200 of *La Caricature* on October 27, 1883, and in a second enlarged album in 1887. In the calmest, most matter-of-fact way, Robida raced through the events of his Great War of 1945, using language that could not in any way match the extraordinary violence of his images. Aerial bombardments, submarine actions, gas warfare, germ warfare, enormous armored vehicles, underwater troops, and psychological assaults by hypnotists and mediums—Robida foresaw everything, except the atomic bomb.

Although the range of his visions of peace and war places Robida in a class of his own, he drew from the common pool of expectations that provided material for the new forecasts appearing in the 1880s. The first regular essays in futurology appeared in "The Prophetic Department" of the New York *Record and Guide.* David Goodman Croly was "Sir Oracle" and for some fifteen years he anticipated the onward movement of the human race in *Glimpses of the Future.* Science was the source of his vaticinations, as he explained in his piece on "What Science Can Do for Us": limitless in scope and fault-free in its effects. "It is hard to put any limitations to what man may do in the way of inventions and new discoveries. He is undoubtedly the god of this planet, and he will in time dominate the entire surface of the globe. Aëriel navigation will solve the mystery of the poles, and eventually there will be no 'dark region' on any of the continents. Waste places will be reclaimed, deserts made productive by irrigation, forests regrown where needed."[14]

This jubilant language would have confirmed Souvestre in his conviction that "le vaste élan du progrès" would be the dominant delusion of the nineteenth century. "Faith in the future," he wrote, is "that promised land for those who have no clear view of the present" (3). Those fighting words sounded the first wake-up call in the unrestricted war that Souvestre would wage against the Great Satan of the age—"the limitless progress of mankind." He wrote from the inside, a convert from early days in the ranks of the Saint-Simonians; and he told his tale of the dangers to come with all the accumulated experience of a successful author.

Souvestre is undoubtedly one of the great originals in future fiction. His command of his material shows in the extraordinary variety of the topics he introduces—from a shipwreck (whale-wreck?) to the hilarious play *Kléber en Égypte.* The quirks, oddities, grotesque characters, and haphazard events in Souvestre's future world are central to the development of his grand strategy: to warn against the abuses of technology, to foresee the social consequences of unrestrained capitalism and—most of all—to demonstrate the miseries that follow from man's inhumanity to man. The scenery is forever changing in the Tahiti of 3000—extraordinary educational establishments, hospitals that admit only after death, underground roads, palatial homes with automated dining rooms: all these supply the setting for dramas that reveal the wastelands of human behavior.

An idiosyncratic technology establishes the contours of coming things: air-conditioning, designer drinking water, giant vegetables, television, submarine transportation, bombards for crossing rivers, balloons everywhere. When Souvestre turns to the citizens of his brave new world, however, he writes like a latter-day Swift with the *saeva indignatio* of the moralist who fears that the acclaimed progress ("Oh! L'avenir est magnifique!") of his day would make for the worst of worlds: mind-annihilating prisons, venal lawyers, celebrity cults, children raised like battery hens, everywhere a frantic pursuit of profit and social position. This diversity works with great effect, especially when Souvestre concentrates on moments of surprise and laughter—a rarity in dystopian fiction. There are, for instance, frequent contemporary resonances. Behind the absurdities in the play *Kléber en Égypte,* the unnamed target is the extravagant melodrama promoted by Souvestre's contemporary Guilbert de Pixerécourt. The nineteenth-century passion for history, for instance, becomes a source of comedy when the Académicien plays the part of the expert and makes a splendid hash of the evidence in his lecture "On the Manners and Customs of the French in the Nineteenth Century." And the increasing centralization of government offers a target of opportunity that Souvestre turns into a comedy of bumbledom, when "the rotund traveler with the tiny nose" is trapped within twenty-three thousand regulations because he is no longer the thin, slightly built figure in his passport photograph.

There is a subtle strategy behind the play Souvestre made with the face that did not fit: it marks a giant leap forward in the *roman de l'avenir;* it owes everything to Souvestre's sharp eye for technological possibilities and to his close attention to their social consequences. He had come to his story in the first years of modern photography—the daguerreotype process of 1839—and he had gone straight to an appropriate conclusion in the tragicomedy of the little man with the wrong photograph. Consider, for instance, the affair of Madame Facile's corsets. One element in this knock-about farce of the man in the lady's bedroom went back to Goodyear's successful experiments with rubber in 1839; for that triggered another leap of the imagination in Souvestre. He had looked into the future, and he saw the "second skin," displayed for all to see in Bertall's illustration (45), the very latest figure-enhancing device: "the rubber palpitated; the material seemed to breathe."

The readability and the decided relevance of the narrative commend Souvestre's tale of the year 3000 to the general reader. The text of 1845 still speaks with clarity and force to the world of 2004. A mordant wit shapes and controls the story, especially in the one-liners that Souvestre scatters throughout the narrative. Talking of burial costs, Souvestre remarks: "It may cost a great deal to live in Paris; it is even more expensive to be buried there." And of customs officers: "Thanks to their ingenious and imaginative methods, fraud had become impossible for anyone but themselves." And of the children progressing through their eighteen years of steam-driven instruction: "They wanted for nothing, except their mothers."

Souvestre was his own man: an accomplished and original writer who owed nothing to his forerunners in future fiction. He turned from the dream-time recollections in Mercier's *L'An 2440* and from the outpourings of "the Celestial Spirit to whom the entire future is known" in Cousin de Grainville's *Le Dernier Homme*. Instead, Souvestre chose to open with the shock of the unknown: the sudden appearance of "the genie in the waterproof jacket." His facilitator is the first of the time lords, the little man who runs a transport service to the third millennium. The name of John Progrès, "the diminutive god," speaks of time-to-come: the English forename, his "machine of English make" enveloped in smoke, and his "leggings of English wool" were reminders to Souvestre's French readers of the recent origins of the steam engine then transforming the world of 1845. These are early examples of Souvestre's many talents that can be seen in his ear for individual diction (Blaguefort and the Abbé Coulant, for instance); his eye for characteristic behavior (Madame Atout and Mlle. Spartacus); and especially his gift for staging unexpected and dramatic episodes. In writing *Le Monde tel qu'il sera*, Souvestre moved easily from the domestic and personal matters that he had examined in his Breton stories. In fact, that experience was an invaluable apprenticeship for relating the varieties of behavior to be anticipated in the unrestrained self-seeking in his future world. Given the vigor and range of his imagination, Souvestre's story is the front-runner for nomination as the most varied and fastest moving dystopia of the nineteenth century. Indeed, the evidence suggests that in *Le Monde tel qu'il sera* Souvestre created one of the most remarkable dystopias in the history of future fiction: an all-talking, all-acting show, comic and tragic by turns. And yet, as this English translation shows, Souvestre remains the unknown prophet of the *roman de l'avenir*, ignored for the most part by his compatriots. Jules Verne has his societies and journals, a museum in Nantes and his name recorded in the *Université de Picardie Jules Verne*. Even Colonel Driant, who holds the world record for *guerres de l'avenir* (seven books, 7,616 pages), had a postage stamp of his own (*héro national*, 1936) in recognition of his contributions to world peace. *Hélas!* No monuments for Souvestre. The only remembrance for the author of *Le Monde tel qu'il sera*, it seems, is in Brest, in the rue Émile Souvestre, one of the permitted parking zones in that city.

His abilities are evident from the first pages. As soon as Marthe and Maurice have arrived in the year 3000, their dialogue becomes a nonstop talkfest. In the customary way of these other-time stories, Marthe and Maurice meet the top people in Sans-Pair—industrialists, academics, judges, publishers, doctors, artists—almost all of them allegorical characters with names that signal their assigned functions in this dramaturgy of coming things. Omnivore, Blaguefort, Milord Cant, Madame Facile, Mlle. Spartacus, and the rest of these talking heads appear in succession, make their revelations, and leave the stage to the next entrants. At times one suspects that Souvestre, a successful playwright, brought on characters in order to present ideas in direct speech. "The next day," for example, "when the young couple came down, they found their host with a relation of his, Doctor Minimum." The doctor urges them to visit the principal hospital in Sans-Pair where he talks at great length about their preposterous medical system. Enter Doctor Manomane and his "six hundred and thirty-three types of mental illness"; and he is followed by Pérégrinus, registered insane because he had traveled "the immense spaces of the old continent with no other motive than to visit peoples in decline."

At last, here was someone who had all the knowledge needed to give "a quick sketch of the world in the year three thousand." That was an opportunity that Souvestre seized to make a farce of the future by reversing the expectations of those many readers who would have echoed Victor Hugo's phrase "Oh! L'avenir est magnifique." Was it a punishment for proud nations? The world in 3000 turns out to be very different from the general expectations of 1845. The old order has passed with many whimpers: the Papal States have been bought by a Jewish banker; the English live on piracy, "eating their prisoners instead of the roast beef of Old England"; and the dilapidated Russia of the future in no way resembles the great power of Tocqueville's forecast. There is a world state, however, where the citizens of the République des Intérêts-Unis live by the profit motive and speak a mixture of English, French, and German. In his determination to suggest the bleakness of a mechanistic and utilitarian world, Souvestre piles up the negative images. The then-fashionable theory of Lamarck (that all living organisms are continually trying to improve themselves) is repudiated in the statement that "the least well-favored races had prevailed throughout successive generations" (51). Even worse is the cruel shift in historical perceptions. What did French readers make of the revelation that Tahiti (a far-off island that had just come under French protection in 1843) would be the center of world trade and industry in the third millennium?

Souvestre certainly made demands on his readers. He expected them to nod agreement at a quotation from Le Sage, La Fontaine, even Virgil; to perceive the connections between Comte, Charles Fourier, and Saint-Simon; to recognize snatches from popular lyrics and allusions to characters in major operas. This was the literary baggage he brought with him into his future world. In fact, Souvestre never moved very far from his baseline in the year 1845, certainly not in the way Orwell left 1948 behind him. For instance, he happily introduces contemporary figures (the chemist Jean Gannal, for example, and the librettist François Planard); the lunar discoveries of M. de l'Empyrée have links with the Great Lunar Hoax of 1835; and another publication of 1835—Lambert Quetelet's pioneering work on statistical theory, *Sur l'homme*—seems to have given him ideas about *l'homme moyen*. At times, it seems that Souvestre forgot where he was in his narrative. The administration of justice, for example, seems to be contemporary French practice: the barristers are "vultures serving no useful purpose" and the bailiffs are "lesser rodents." Again, the imaginative creator of passenger-carrying mortar projectiles, omnibus balloons, and winged tilburies suddenly returns to his own time when he talks of "thirty-two million civil servants, all occupied for eight hours a day in cutting quills for their pens and ruling lines on paper" (130).

Souvestre must have had his problems, since he had to maintain a narrative scored for many voices. First, there was the recording historian who tells the tale from the opening question to the reader: "Do you see them, leaning on their elbows at their attic window . . . ?" And twenty-two chapters later the unrelenting moralist begins the final coda with his summary conclusion that "Marthe and Maurice were left sad at heart. The two of them wept over this world where man was now enslaved to the machine; where self-interest took the place of love; where civilization had tried to make the mystical triumph of Christianity accommodate the three passions that drag the soul down into the abyss" (231).

That loving couple, Marthe and Maurice, "drawn together in their love of humanity," are innocents in a strange new future that has monsters in it. Maurice is young, generous, an idealist who hopes for the best of all possible worlds; Marthe is Souvestre's ideal woman: loving, devoted, maternal. They are well suited to maintain a running commentary on the mode of life in Sans-Pair, and their recollections of the good and virtuous give Souvestre an invaluable means of enlarging his narrative. There are six exemplary episodes, five of them are recollections from Marthe or Maurice that exist in the eternal present of the parable. The Spinner of Évrecy, Mademoiselle Romain, the old soldier Mathias, even that faithful horse Noiraud—their lives are revelations of self- sacrifice, fidelity, and goodness. They are touchstones of virtue by which to judge the false beliefs and perverted practices of life "tout à la vapeur" in the République des Intérêts-Unis. They are part of "those memories that melt the heart like the sight of the old hearth, where you listened to the stories told by your nurse" (67).

Souvestre was the first to reveal the profound convictions—social, political, moral—that have powered dystopian fiction from his calculated absurdities in *Le Monde tel qu'il sera* to the straitjacket world of *Nineteen Eighty-Four* (1949), the machine society of Vonnegut's *Player Piano* (1952), and the powerlessness of women in the man's world of Margaret Atwood's *The Handmaid's Tale* (1985). As it was in the beginning, so it is today: all these dystopias of the future are sermons dedicated to changing the ways of a society before it proves too late—tales of unprogress that have always had their starting points in the perceived weaknesses, failures, and disorders in contemporary society. Although they have that one objective in common, they have always gone their own ways from the first pages, separate navigations that make the landfall of their choice in the boundless ocean of time-to-come. For Souvestre, the message from the future said that we cannot live by the cash nexus alone. Twenty-five years later, in the first major English future dystopia of the nineteenth century, *The Coming Race* (1871), the high well-born Edward George Bulwer-Lytton (a most successful and inventive novelist) described a civilization light years ahead of Sans-Pair. The life of the subterranean Vril-ya "is immeasurably more felicitous than that of super-terrestrial races, and, realizing the dreams of our most sanguine philanthropist, almost approaches to a poet's conception of some angelical order." It will not work, says Bulwer-Lytton. Total perfection is not for mere mortals: "if you could take a thousand of the best and most philosophical human beings you could find in London, Paris, Berlin, New York, and place them as citizens in this beatified community, my belief is that, in less than a year they would either die of *ennui,* or attempt some revolution."[15]

Two decades later Americans had a choice between two options for the future. First, in 1888, there appeared the most successful utopia of the nineteenth century, Edward Bellamy's *Looking Backward, 2000–1887*, written with great assurance and filled with all good things for our world. And then in the following year there came the black opposite of those high hopes: John A. Mitchell's *The Last American* (1889). In this latter work, on May 10, 2951, in unwitting anticipation of Huxley's *Ape and Essence* (1949), an expedition arrives in the empty city of Nhū-Yok, desolate like the rest of the country. They "are astounded that a nation of more than seventy millions should vanish from the earth like a mist, and leave so little behind":

> There was nothing to leave. The Mehrikans possessed neither literature, art, or music of their own. Everything was borrowed. The very clothes they wore were copied with ludicrous precision from the models of other nations. They were a sharp, restless, quick-witted, greedy race, given body and soul to the gathering of riches. Their chiefest passion was to buy and sell.[16]

Finally, in the last decade of the century, there was still worse to come in Wells's *The Time Machine* (1895). His time traveler speaks the last possible words about the future, when he discovers that "Man had not remained one species but had differentiated into two distinct animals: that the graceful children of the Upper World were not the sole descendants of our generation, but this bleached, obscene, nocturnal Thing, which had dashed before me, was also heir to all the ages."[17]

*Marthe and Maurice dreaming about the future of the human race*

# §I—PROLOGUE

Do you see them, leaning on their elbows at their attic window, surrounded by gillyflowers in bloom and the air filled with the song of birds nesting in the eaves? Marthe's hand rests on Maurice's shoulder, and the two of them gaze down into the shadowy abyss. In the depths there first appears the dark blue of a star-studded sky; and then, lower down, the luminous darkness of Paris. Maurice contemplates Paris; Marthe sees only the sky.

"A penny for your thoughts!"

The eternal lover's plea; the anxious appeal of two souls seeking each other in the dark, like sisters lost in the night looking for reassurance with every step they take.

Maurice turned, and their two faces, glowing with youth and happiness, gazed long at each other.

A novelist would take the opportunity of this lengthy contemplation to paint two portraits for the reader. Thanks to the process of close analysis invented by the modern school, he would find in the blue eyes of Maurice, beneath their heavy lids, a reaching out toward the unknown; in his flaring nostrils a restless audacity; in his half-parted lips an abundance of tender feeling; and finally in his whole being a lively representation of his generation—questing, eager, uncertain—who *seek* they *know not what*. As for Marthe—her brow framed by waves of dark hair, with her expression at once loving, modest, and courageous—he would find in her the womanly beauty of the saint and the heroine: she would be a daughter of Julie de Saint-Preux, a friend of Claire du Comte Egmont, a sister of Jeanne *la grande pastoure*.[1] However, after these poetic descriptions, our readers could find themselves as embarrassed as the sergeant as he reads the passport of a citizen recommended by the king (for two francs) to the civil and military authorities of the kingdom. We think it simpler, however, to send our readers back to look again at the portraits engraved at the beginning of this chapter.

On the subject of Maurice's character it only remains to add some observations that even the most discerning intellect would have difficulty in deducing from this attractive thumbnail sketch.

Above all, we must declare that, although he is young and in love, he does not belong in the ranks of those fanciful young men who think of themselves as *charming egoists*. Maurice (it has to be said) was one of those rare spirits who are more interested in the destiny of the human race than in balls at the Opera House. Tormented by the sight of so much unrelieved suffering and of so much hopeless misery, he had come to dream of the happiness of humankind as a cause worthy of his endeavors, and to seek some means by which he could bring it about, although he had received no commission from the government for his actions.

In consequence, he began to study the works of those who laid claim to be serious thinkers—the wise men of the age. The first luminaries he consulted were the philosophers. They asserted categorically by means of formulae, which had all the elegance, but not the precision, of algebra, that it was merely a matter of the relative and the absolute, the self and the nonself, the causal and the phenomenal. As for any other concerns, they had not given them even a moment's thought! Philosophy was only concerned with first principles: that is to say, with those things that can make you neither happier nor better.

Somewhat dissatisfied, Maurice then consulted legal specialists, historians, jurists. They analyzed for him, one by one, the different constitutions, and they elucidated the various codes of law. But under all these systems of government, the vast majority of human beings died of hunger while a tiny minority died of indigestion. All these codes were treacherous seas where the poor barques of small-time smugglers foundered, while the big-time pirates swept on under full sail. Since Maurice had still not found what he was looking for, he then turned to the statisticians and the economists.

These gentlemen, who took the matter very seriously, led him on a six-month journey through their columns of figures; they ended up by telling him that everything was the way it had to be, and that the only thing to do was to leave well alone and let things take their course.

So he found himself precisely where he was before he started reading. In despair he had to turn to the idiots of whom Bérenger speaks.[2]

Maurice studied the Socialists: Robert Owen, Saint-Simon, Fourier, Swedenborg.[3] If you listened to them, each one had the answer to the problem of Pandora's box; it needed merely to be opened to release universal happiness for mankind; only despair would be left behind! Maurice tried each of the magic boxes in turn; he lifted the lids and looked inside. It seemed to him that, although there was some good in each of them, plenty of other things were mixed in: wheat came mixed with ryegrass; but, before a nutritious meal could be made, there had to be a lengthy process of winnowing and milling.[4] Unable to reject them all or accept them all, Maurice hesitated between half a dozen contradictory systems—an uncomfortable position to which M. Cousin gave a Greek name in order to dignify it with a semblance of philosophy.

All these studies had, however, strengthened his faith in the future—that promised land for those who have no clear view of the present. He believed in the limitless progress of mankind as ardently as some provincial, newly recognized as a *man of letters*, believes he has a future as a writer. Even the bewitching influences of his honeymoon had not altered his preoccupations; for Marthe had similar aspirations, and what might have been a barrier separating them had instead become a powerful bond between them. United in the one hope, their two souls met in a single flame whose radiance lit up the world around them. As Christian spouses, when they are in love, are drawn together in their love of God, they were drawn together in their love of humanity.

The reader will readily understand that these indispensable explanations are what grammarians call a *parenthetical clause;* and so we will close the parenthesis at this point in order to take up the thread of our story.

And so Maurice returned to Marthe's desire to know his thoughts; and the two of them looked into each other's eyes for a long time without saying a word, as young people do by the light of the stars when they are twenty years of age and sharing an attic.

Then, after a long silence occasioned by a lingering kiss, the young woman repeated her question.

"What are you thinking about?"

The young man put his arm around her.

"First of all, I was thinking of you," he replied; "then, with you in my thoughts, my solicitude gradually embraced the wider world in which we two love each other, and I asked myself what does the future hold."

"Do you remember the house where we met?" said Marthe. "There were newborn babies, young girls just starting out in life, and grandparents ready to leave it. Is that not the future of the world, just as it is now, and always was?"

"For individuals, but not for societies," said Maurice. "In addition to the physical life, which continues unchanging, there is the spirit, which does change. Men are living stones with which each century builds a different edifice according to its lights and its desires. Until the present day the edifice has been no more than an *encampment* of savages, a bivouac for warriors of warring factions, a caravanserai for merchants. But the great architect, who is one day to build the temple, will come sooner or later, since prophetic signs have heralded his arrival."

"Show them to me," said the young woman, whose cheek was touching Maurice's, as if she thought that one of these signs was a kiss.

"Look," said he, leaning out from the casement window. "What do you see in front of you?"

"I see little white clouds sailing in the blue, looking like guardian angels on the wing," replied Marthe.

"And lower down?"

"At the top of the hill I see a light in an attic—the one where we met."

"And lower still?"

"Lower still," echoed the young woman, "I see nothing but the dark."

"But this darkness enfolds a million watchful intelligent creatures!" said Maurice exultantly. "Ah! If you could only see all that is going on under the veil of this darkness! Those distant murmurings that sound like groans, those flickering lights, the haze rising in the air—all reveal a world in formation. It is just as it was on the first days of creation when all the elements were still in chaos; but give the sun time to rise, and the future will emerge from the darkness as the earth rose from the waters after the flood."

Marthe did not reply, but fascinated by the words of the young man, she leaned out over the dark abyss, hoping to see some magical transformation.

"Yes, I would like to see this wonderful future," she said with the wondering curiosity of a child. "Why can we not go to sleep for several centuries and wake up in a more perfect world? Oh! If only I had a fairy godmother!"

"The fairies have broken their wands and departed," said Maurice. "It is for the genius of men to find the pieces and put them back together again."

"Then whom should we ask for help?" said the young woman. "The angels no longer visit us, as they did in the days of Jacob and Tobias. Jesus, Mary, and the saints do not come down from heaven as they did in the Middle Ages to give strength to our souls or to comfort the afflicted. Have all the higher powers abandoned the earth? Is there no longer any god or spirit here below to serve as intermediary between the real and the invisible worlds? All countries and all ages have had their guardian spirits. Where and what is the one for our time?"

"Here!" came a brief and distant reply.

The two startled lovers looked up. Through the darkness, across the rooftops, a shadow came gliding rapidly and stopped in front of the open window with a burst of metallic laughter.

Marthe jumped backward in alarm; even Maurice took a step back.

"Here I am!" repeated the voice in sharp, rasping tones. "You called me, and I have come!" As he spoke, the newcomer moved into a beam of moonlight that shone on the roof and illuminated him completely.

*M. John Progrès*

{ 5 }

He was a little man wearing a short waterproof jacket, a metal top hat on his head, a ruff round his neck, and leggings of English wool. He had an enormous chain round his neck, gilded by the Ruolz process; in his right hand was a hollow metal cane, and under his left arm a briefcase from which protruded some share certificates. Every item of his attire bore the unmistakable stamp:

BY APPOINTMENT TO THE GOVERNMENT
Unofficially

As for his appearance, one would have said a cross between a banker and a notary. He was comfortably seated on a machine of English make, the smoke of which enveloped him in clouds of fantastic shape, and on the instrument panel there was a daguerreotype from the workshops of M. le Chevalier. Maurice, a little alarmed at first at this sudden apparition, was reassured by his mild appearance. He looked boldly at the little visitor and asked him who he was.[5]

"Who am I?" repeated the latter with a nervous laugh. "Dame Marthe ought to know."

"Me!" exclaimed the young woman, trembling like an author on the first night of his play.

"Haven't you just called me?"asked the little man.

Maurice gave a start. "Ah! I know who you are," he said. "You are the familiar spirit of attic dwellers, the ancient retainer of Don Cleophas Zambulo, the demon Asmodeus.[6]

The unknown visitor hammered on his machine with his fist. "I was sure of it," he said. "The reputation of that rascal has outlived him."

"Is he really dead?" asked Maurice in surprise.

"Didn't you know?" replied the little man. "Béranger made the announcement:[7]

> Au conclave on se désespère"
> Adieu puissance et coffre-fort
> Nous avons perdu notre père,
> Le diable est mort, le diable et mort.

"And yet," objected Marthe, whose courage was returning, "his *mémoires* have been published, and the account of his journey to Paris."

"Apocryphal works," observed the man in the waterproof jacket. "The devil never produced works like that. I knew him well; he was a good-for-nothing of the most sullen sort; but he had the same luck as his cousin Prince Talleyrand. He seemed to embody the spirit of the age. Happily, the spirit of gloom has had its day; his reign is ending, and mine is beginning."[8]

Fascinated, the two young lovers looked up.

"Your reign!" they exclaimed together, "Then you are . . . ?" They were hoping to know how they should address him. The man delicately slipped two fingers into the pocket of his French cashmere waistcoat and brought out a visiting card, which he presented to Maurice. It read:

---

### M. JOHN PROGRÈS.

Member of all the Utopian Societies of Europe,

of Asia, of Africa, of Oceania, etc., etc.

Rue de Rivoli

---

Maurice and Marthe bowed respectfully.

"I was on my way to visit the works for our new railways," said the genie in the waterproof jacket, "when I heard in passing the wish expressed by Madame Marthe. Then I heard her appeal. I turned back to reply to the one, and to respond to the other."

"Do you mean," exclaimed the young woman, "my wanting to leapfrog the centuries in order to find ourselves in that perfect future that we are promised?"

"I can do it," said the diminutive god, smugly touching her cheek with the knob of his hollow cane. "Just say the word, and you will fall asleep instantly—both of you—and you will not wake until the year THREE THOUSAND."

"In the year THREE THOUSAND," said Maurice; "and by then the seeds sown in our epoch will have borne fruit?"

"In the year THREE THOUSAND! And we shall be together when we wake?" Marthe added, one arm resting on that of her husband.

"In the year THREE THOUSAND, you will awake just as young, and just as much in love," the little man added, with the smile of an agent selling financial services.

"Ah! If it's true," said Maurice in great excitement, "do not delay a moment longer; show us the future with all its splendid promise. Who would choose to stay in the present where all is strife and uncertainty? Let us sleep while the human race goes forward painfully and by rough uncharted paths. Let us sleep, and only wake at the end of the journey."

He had clasped Marthe in his arms, holding her close to his heart in order to make sure of taking her through this sleep of many centuries. M. John Progrès leaned toward them and held out his hands like a mesmerist about to manipulate the marvelous fluid that links the visual nerve in the occiput and the sense of smell in the epigastrium; Marthe, however, drew back.[9]

"Ah!" she cried in terror. "Yours is the sleep of death; your world is the unknown. Oh! Maurice! Let us stay where we are and remain what we are."

"No!" cried the young man, spellbound. "I want to see what lies in store for us."

"But the path is so lovely! Look at the beautiful flowers we can gather! See the azure of the sky above our heads! Listen to the murmur of the streams and the sound of gentle breezes!"

"But Marthe; to know, to know!"

"But Maurice; to live, to live."

"Yes, but in a better world, and under more just laws. Rest your head against my shoulder, Marthe; hold me close, and don't be afraid. I am here, and I love you."

He had clasped his young wife in his arms, as the hands of the genie were still extended. Then the two of them instantly felt their eyelids growing very heavy. They made instinctively toward the large armchair where Maurice usually worked, and sank into a profound and death-like sleep.

The following day the newspapers carried, with slight variations, the following item of news:

An occurrence, as sad as it was unexpected, has greatly saddened the neighborhood of Batignolles. A young man and woman, who lived on the top floor of a house in the rue des Carrières, were found dead this morning. The authorities are at a loss to know how this tragic event happened, since it seems to be attributable neither to crime nor to despair.

The next day the *Moniteur Parisien* dedicated a new article to *The Lovers of Batignolles*. It stated that both had died of asphyxiation under the influence of a poetic inspiration to escape the disillusionments of life. On the following day, the *Constitutionnel* published intimate details of their last moments; and the day after that the *Presse* announced the issue of their unpublished letters assembled by a friend.

Furthermore, all the versifiers in the province *tuned their lyres* (for the lyre and the guitar were still familiar instruments in the provinces); and the result was twelve hundred stanzas in every verse form on the death of Marthe and Maurice. But the verses most often quoted were those of an employee of the associated workers of Bar-sur-Aube. He had just made a name for himself as a leading poetic dramatist, with a Greek tragedy playing with huge success at the Bobino Theater. The refrain was heard everywhere:

> Angel with black eyes, angel with blue eyes,
> Both now on your way to the skies!

A delightful verse. The first line, according to one celebrated critic, showed the influence of the romantic Shakespearian school, and the second the influence of the somber school of Racine.

The engravers exploited the two lovers just as much. The journal *L'Illustration* published a view of their attic window with a downspout in the foreground—a detail that lent a touch of pathos to the story of the two deaths.

Finally, to put the seal on their celebrity, M. Gannal wrote to the *Journal des Débats,* offering to embalm them free of charge and giving the address of his business premises.[10]

But a single word put an end to all this glory. Marthe's uncle, alarmed by all the public interest, and filled with indignation at the lies circulated by the papers, made a complaint to which he added in evidence:

1) The certificate from the local doctor stating that Marthe and Maurice had died suddenly, but from natural causes; and

2) The extract from the civil registry which proved that the two were married at the municipal offices in the fourth arrondissement.

So, the public who had believed that they had two lovers, and what's more, two suicides, found that they had only a married couple who died of natural causes. This news acted like a chill blast of wind that gave a bad cold to all the organs of publicity. The *Constitutionnel* went back to its account of the Jesuits, relieved by some anecdotes about sea serpents; the *Presse* discovered that the proposed correspondence was apocryphal and suspended publication. Finally, the *Gazette des Tribuneaux* came out with the story of the arrest of a poisoner—a woman of good family who had just disposed of all her relations, because our deplorable system allows us to inherit only from the dead.

This last affair engaged the entire attention of the public, and the names of Marthe and Maurice were consigned to oblivion.

Meanwhile, the two were laid together in the same coffin and carried to the cemetery. The simple hearse made its way through Paris, followed by an old man and a young woman and her children: the entire family of the dead couple. The sun was shining; the flower-sellers were offering the first violets to passersby; the trees were bursting into shimmering leaf; and the birds were chorusing all along the roofs, looking for places to build their nests. All was animation, the sky bright and the air full of sweet scents; and in the midst of this general reawakening the lonely coffin passed by unnoticed, for who can ask the living to spare a thought for the dead?

On returning, the old man, the young woman, and the two children climbed the stairs to the attic where those whom they had consigned to the earth had lived. On the threshold stood the employee of the funeral parlor, a handkerchief in one hand and his bill in the other. The handkerchief merely covered an eye; but the bill could have covered his entire person. It may cost a great deal to live in Paris; it is even more expensive to be buried there. In order to pay for the young couple's funeral, it was necessary to sell everything they possessed in life. Maurice's books paid for the coffin; Marthe's ring and her gold cross paid for the shroud; and their remaining possessions, the hole in the ground where they were laid. Finally, when the whole bill was settled, the undertaker put his handkerchief in his pocket and asked for his gratuity.

Meanwhile, the days rolled by, then the years, then the centuries, and all memory of Marthe and Maurice was lost. No one even remembered the verses of the employee at the associated workers' union of Bar-sur-Aube; but the genie in the jacket had not forgotten his promise. The death of the two lovers was but a sleep; and, from the depths of the tomb they followed the successive transformations of societies like the confused, shifting images of a dream.

It seemed to them that they were, at first, watching monarchies give way to constitutional governments, and constitutional governments to republics. Then the powerful races grew old and gave place to younger ones. Civilization, carried forward like the flaming torch of the Saturnalia, passed from hand to hand, moving ever onward from its point of origin. New interests attracted human activity to other lands. Europe fell victim to the neglect and inertia that overwhelm abandoned regions, while America, and then an even younger country, attracted to themselves all the vital elements of development. The old world became no more than a savage land, where modern societies plundered its ruins. All its buried treasures, toppled monuments, and forgotten tombs were appropriated by generations of tradesmen. Marthe and Maurice had the impression that the coffin that enclosed them was lifted from their burial place among thousands of others, put on board a ship, and transported to an unknown region—the center of a new civilization.

But here the mysterious intuitive sense that had so far revealed all these things to them grew very faint. Their dream was suddenly interrupted. Then a clear voice made itself heard, crying:

THE YEAR THREE THOUSAND!

At that very moment, the lid of their coffin flew off, and the two lovers, waking with a start, emerged from their shrouds.

At first they were aware only of each other. Then, on finding themselves still alive after a sleep of so many centuries, they both gave a cry of joy, held out their arms to each other, sighing each other's name as they kissed.

P.S.Germain.

A burst of rather grating laughter interrupted them.

They turned, trembling with fear to find their little genie perched just a few feet away on his fantastic machine.

Marthe cried out, blushed, and pulled the folds of her shroud round her shoulders.

"Well, I have kept my word," said the genie. "Thanks to me, you have traveled through eleven centuries without being aware of it."

"Can it really be true?" said Maurice, in amazement.

"And here you are, carried into the heart of the civilization you yearned to know," continued the genie. "Here we are on the island once known as Tahiti."

"The *New Cythera* of Captain Cook?" asked the young man.

"Today it is called *Charcoal Island,*" the genie explained.[11] "The country's great industrialists have combed the entire world to procure the materials for their commerce, and it is to their research that you owe your transportation here."

Marthe looked about her and noticed that they were in the middle of a huge building full of coffins and bones. Fearfully, she clung to Maurice.

"There's no need to be afraid," said the genie, with a shrill cackle. "They will not mistake you for one of the dead. You have arrived at the establishment of one of the most respectable merchants on the island, M. Omnivore, who will be delighted to find in you survivors from a barbarous age. He has been informed of your return to life, and is coming himself to see you."

But the young woman, still not reassured, wrapped herself more closely in her shroud.

"Don't worry about the flimsiness of your costume," observed the miniscule wizard. "Here we are no longer in that ridiculous climate of yours, where the sun is like a candle that gives light but no heat. On Charcoal Island the air serves as a jacket; and you will see that, by general agreement, clothing has been sensibly reduced to a minimum."

In fact, the two lovers noticed the transformation in M. Progrès: he was dressed only in a pair of shorts, a large-brimmed straw hat, and boots of plaited grass decorated with little bells. Maurice learned from him that this was the style of dress in general use for reasons of practicality and economy. The civilization of the year three thousand had turned its back on anything not immediately useful, and it had left fine clothes to women or to the frivolous: serious men were happy to wear shorts, letting a natural grace enhance their appearance.

As he finished these explanations, the sound of footsteps reverberated at the door of the building; the genie, digging his heels into his steam horse, disappeared in a flash.

# §II

*Diplomacy of Maurice—Perfect eloquence of M. Omnivore—*
*Dress of a successful man in the year three thousand—*
*M. Atout—Departure of Marthe and Maurice—*
*New method of crossing rivers—Underground*
*roads—M. Atout sets Marthe's mind at rest*
*with a statistical calculation—Marthe*
*falls asleep—A dream.*

M. Omnivore was followed by half a dozen servants who gave every sign of total astonishment. They all talked at once, as our deputies do when they wish to throw light on some important question. Maurice realized that their language was a mixture of French, English, and German; and he was able to understand it since he was familiar with those three languages. They repeated all together:

"Wonderful! Wonderful! Two people who died so long ago have been brought back to life. The engineer saw them emerging from the grave." But they broke off abruptly at the sight of the young married couple, exclaiming:

"There they are!"

They halted a little distance away, their curiosity tempered by fear.

Marthe, covered in confusion, was half-hidden behind Maurice. But the latter, eager to defend the honor of the nineteenth century, which M. Progrès had called barbarous a moment ago, drew himself up gravely, greeted the visitors, and addressed them in the following words:

"Gentlemen and honorable strangers!

"It is not mere chance but our own deliberate choice that has caused us to travel through almost two thousand years in order to return to life in the epoch of this powerful and enlightened generation—a generation which, by dint of making great advances toward perfecting the human race, has created a heaven on earth.

"We also consider ourselves most fortunate in being able to see for ourselves this race of demigods so nobly represented by my listeners at this moment."

(Here a murmur of approval greeted the speaker; and he continued in a stronger voice.)

"I have come to visit you, gentlemen, in order to warm myself at the sun of a civilization that burns more brightly than all others!"

(Loud applause.)

"To marvel at the miracles performed by an intelligent and generous nation!"

(Even louder applause.)

"To pay homage to a country that could be called the most glorious of all nations"

(Prolonged cheering.)

"Finally, to enjoy that noble union of order and liberty effected by the greatest people on earth."

(Thunderous applause: many voices crying, "Long live the dead Parisians!")

It took some time for the emotion released by Maurice's eloquent improvisation to subside; for the inhabitants of Charcoal Island could not hide their astonishment at finding a savage, buried for eleven centuries, with such refinement of thought, such subtle appreciation. The most informed listeners thought that they recognized in the young man's discourse a former president of a provincial government, or at least the secretary of a philanthropical society, no doubt embalmed by the Gannal technique. Finally, when silence reigned once more, M. Omnivore, wishing to make a fitting reply to his guest's speech, came forward in solemn manner, coughed three times while he put his thoughts in order, and said in an accent bearing traces of English, French, and German:

"Sir, in reply to yours of today, I hasten to inform you that the house of Omnivore and its staff will consider it an honor to be associated with yours, and that you will be received as favorably as if you had been formally introduced—the aforesaid house regarding it as an honor to preserve the good opinion you have formed of the society to which our house is privileged to belong."

His audience exchanged satisfied looks. Evidently they all approved of the clarity and the business acumen manifest in M. Omnivore's reply; and the latter, noticing the effect he had produced, put on a show of modesty by nonchalantly taking a pinch of snuff.

The ice was broken, however, and they continued in a less solemn vein. Maurice told the story of how he and Marthe had come to find themselves there, and expressed the hope that they could quit this funereal place as soon as possible, since it made his companion unhappy. M. Omnivore rushed off to arrange for clothing to be provided for them in the style re-

vealed by researchers into the world of the past. Then he retired, saying
that he would return for his guests.

He did, in fact, return after a quarter of an hour, and burst into help-
less laughter at the sight of the young couple's dress. He examined them
closely from top to toe with the same curiosity that a Frenchman of the
nineteenth century would have shown in studying the garb of a Hotten-
tot. He was at a loss to understand the practicality of the woman's long
dress, which made it difficult to walk; of the hat, which crowned her face
like a cornet; or of the man's outfit, which had skirts hanging down like
the wings of a sick mayfly; or of the trousers tugged apart by braces and
underfoot straps like a victim pulled apart by four horses. Marthe and
Maurice did their best to defend the dress of their epoch; but, after listening to them, M. Omnivore glanced at his own superior garments and could
not suppress a smile of satisfaction.

His dress had, in effect, brought the concept of utility to perfection: it
served not only as costume but also as an advertisement of current prices
and settlement dates.

On the belt of his shorts were written the words OMNIVORE AND
COMPANY, followed by very detailed commercial information about the
nature and excellence of the products made by their factory. The right leg
presented a complete price list designed to simplify even the longest calculations, and the left leg sported an official timetable of the departure
times for passenger and mail boats. On both sides there appeared—in the
form of ribbons—bows that displayed settled accounts, proclaiming at

one and the same time the scope of business in the house of Omnivore and the accuracy of its accounts. Finally, a pen behind the ear suggested that the worthy merchant had just been called away from the delights of his double-entry bookkeeping.

He began by leading Marthe and Maurice through an enormous warehouse crammed full of fragments his agents had taken from the ruins of the ancient world; for this was the specialty that had made the name and the fortune of M. Omnivore. He exploited past generations, just as others exploited carbonized vegetation in the form of oil and peat. Ancient sepulchers, broken pieces of monuments, precious bronzes, arms, medals, statues—all passed through his hands. His warehouse was the magnet for all the curiosities of the world. Thither came the collectors and the scholars—that indestructible race that the new civilization had been unable to eliminate.

The young couple met one of these gentlemen as they were coming out of the warehouse. It was the celebrated M. Atout whose specialty was to be competent in every field. In his own person he represented twenty-eight citizens; that is to say, he collected the remuneration of twenty-eight posts. The tally of his titles covered a quarto page, and he wore as many decorations as a Spanish mule has bells. M. Omnivore presented him merely as: the permanent secretary of the Historical Society, professor of literature, president of the University Council, director of all the teacher training colleges, and member of fourteen thousand seven hundred and thirty-four committees.

M. Atout had just learned that the young French couple had been restored to life and he greeted them with the dignity of a man who was affiliated with so many academies that nothing could surprise him.

After the first polite exchanges, he put to Maurice several questions that were designed to establish his credentials in the literary and historical fields. He asked if Maurice was familiar with Charlemagne, Madame de Pompadour, and M. Paul de Kock—three important figures in the history of the kings of France—and questioned him at great length on the High Constable of Louis XVIII, Napoleon Bonaparte, whose life history had been written by the reverend Father Loriquet.[1] Maurice, somewhat stunned at first, was trying to frame a response, but M. Atout did not give him a chance. In a series of short steps he rushed from the past to the present and launched into a lecture on the state of the world in the year three thousand.

The new arrivals from the past listened most attentively, since they had much to learn. The professor explained that they had arrived at the

**M. ATOUT**

*Académicien of the year 3000*

heart of the civilized world whose different peoples constituted a single state with the name of the *Republic of United Interests*. The center or capital of this republic was located on the ancient island of Borneo, now called *Budget Island*. Each nation sent a fixed number of deputies, and these together had the oversight of most affairs. As for the old world, the colonies maintained there received their instructions and guidance from the metropolis.

The cardinal principle of the division of labor had been established in the republic itself. Each state made a single product. Thus, one nation was responsible for pins, another for English wax polish, another for button molds. Every person worked exclusively at his own trade, and spoke of nothing else. That arrangement contributed only slightly to the advancement of ideas and to the charms of society, but it brought huge profits to the organization. Budget Island alone brought together all the different branches of arts and industry. There one could find the elements of an entire civilization, all methodically classified as they would be in a cabinet of representative specimens.

Maurice and Marthe immediately declared that they would like to visit Budget Island. The Académicien, who was going there, offered to take them; but M. Omnivore opposed the idea. He maintained that the young couple formed a part of the merchandise sent to his house and that they legally belonged to him like the other antiquities in his warehouse. A long debate followed. Finally, M. Atout, who was determined to present the resuscitated pair in the capital in order to claim the honor of their discovery for himself, agreed to reimburse the merchant from the funds of the Historical Society.

When it was settled, our young couple followed him to the shores of the bay they had to cross.

Batteries of passenger-carrying mortars had been set up on both shores to make the crossing. An operator opened the breech of the largest one and helped our three travelers inside, where they sat themselves down in the middle of a well-padded bomb. Marthe could not help feeling some emotion at finding herself ensconced like a projectile deep inside a cannon; but the Académicien launched into an explanation of the advantages of crossing rivers in this way. He was still in the middle of his exposition when Marthe heard the cry:

"Fire!"

At the same instant, she felt the blast-off and, after streaking through the air like lightning, she found herself on the other shore, surrounded by twenty or so smoking projectiles, which had just arrived in similar fashion.

M. Atout told them that they would continue their journey by one of the underground routes that crossed the island. He went on to say that, before the progress of civilization, the roads were built above ground; but eventually there were so many that they more or less took over the surface of the globe. The earth carried nothing but iron rails, and then it

*A new means of crossing rivers*

dawned on the people that although they had multiplied the means of transportation, there was nothing left to transport. Then the idea came to them to locate their routes not on the surface, but under the ground. Experience had proved the superiority of the new system. Thanks to the new arrangement, only the view was lost. One could travel undistracted, sleeping or thinking about one's business. Instead of the sun, by turns dazzling and dim, there was the steady illumination from the lights of the trains. There were no more curious people watching as you passed; no more shouts from traders; no more city noises. You traveled as comfortably as a parcel.

He then pointed out the underground routes and the entrances that appeared on the hillside like so many mouths of furnaces. Huge mechanical pickups disappeared ceaselessly inside, or pulled out trains of smoke-belching wagons. From deep in the mountain came a thousand rumbling noises, punctuated by the clanging of iron and the hissing of flames.

As she plunged down through these sinister shafts, Marthe, unable to suppress a cry, felt for Maurice's hand. The Académicien reprimanded her somewhat sharply and began to explain that the underground roads were not only the most convenient, but also the safest. In support of his contention he cited the numbers of people killed every year by different modes of locomotion. He went on to enumerate the number of people crippled; then he mentioned the number hurt, giving details of the nature and severity of their injuries. Finally, he added up all the figures and drew up a table of comparison providing evidence that the underground routes accounted for a mere thirteen hundred victims, or perhaps a few more.

At this demonstration, Marthe's unease changed to fright.

M. Atout then went on to the finer points. He asked her to consider that she was protected from all the minor inconveniences attendant on other modes of transport. She was not exposed to drafts, or to sunstroke, or to wind, or to the vapors rising from swamps, or to the impertinence of passersby. She was protected against everything except being killed.

At this Marthe's anxieties turned to terror.

Fortunately, at this point Maurice put his arm tenderly around her; and as she allowed herself to relax against his breast, she could feel his heart beating calmly and steadily. Her fears evaporated. Her entire being was permeated by the calm of the one dearest to her, and with a blissful smile she closed her eyes.

M. Atout, under the impression that she was thinking of his logical argument, admired the result produced by statistics. He went on to make a case for the various new vehicles, and to spell out their advantages.

He claimed that, given the average speed of locomotion, it now took no more than two hours to go buy one's sugar in Brazil, three to acquire one's tea in Canton, four to select one's coffee in Mocha. If need be, one could go further afield. Madame Atout had her fashion designer in Baghdad, her dressmaker in Timbuktu, and her furrier near the North Pole, just three stops from the Arctic Circle.

The Académicien produced figures to demonstrate the immense social benefits brought about by these improvements in the means of communication. He proved that, when one took into account all the hours gained for the citizens of the year three thousand by the rapidity of transport, the average length of life had been increased by twenty-five years and a fraction more. Thus they had solved the problem of locomotion without any of the fatigue involved in having to make conversation or to exchange confidences en route. One could depart without being seen; one could return without having had to say a word. All travelers were sealed off from the world and lived in an environment of their own. Traveling, in effect, no longer meant living on the road in the company of others: travel was a matter of departures and arrivals.

At first Marthe had listened to this exposition from M. Atout; but gradually her attention wandered, her eyelids drooped, and, lulled gently by the breathing of the one she loved, she fell asleep. At first, vague images from the past floated through her brain. Then a shining memory banished the other half-remembered scenes as it emerged from the confusion of images like a star from the storm clouds.

She was dreaming of the trip she had made with Maurice on the evening before their long sleep.

She seemed to see once more the last rays of the sun lighting up the hillsides of Viroflai and the edge of the woods. Once more she saw the hawthorn in flower forming a tapestry against the pale green of the hedgerows. She caught the scent of the lilacs whose cheerful sprays crowned the garden walls. On the roads, already lost in shadow, she heard the little bells ringing in time with the trotting horses.

Next to her was Maurice, his hand in hers; and next to Maurice there was an old coachman who looked very pensive. Sitting behind, there were other travelers: a rather loud-mouthed peasant; a young mother, anxious at every movement of her children; and an old soldier who sat without saying a word.

The carriage moved at a gentle pace on the soft ground; but as it moved more and more slowly, there were impatient cries.

"Whip that horse!" they all shouted.

The coachman merely shook the reins.

"Use your whip! Use your whip!"

"What a miserable creature!" said the peasant.

"A lazy thing!" added the mother.

"A good-for-nothing!" the soldier added.

The coachman shook his head. "No, no," said he, "Noiraud is no miserable nag. He has borne many hardships—more than the strongest—and for twenty years as well."

"Twenty years!" exclaimed the peasant in astonishment.

"Probably even more," replied the coachman, "and he is not lazy, because all this time he has provided for a man, his wife, and two children with his labors."

"As much as that?" said the mother, "Oh! He's a hero!"

"Not to mention his courage," continued the coachman. "Look at the two scars on his chest."

"Ah! Then he has seen service?" asked the old soldier in softened tones.

And as all eyes rested on Noiraud with keen interest, there were no more calls for the whip. The peasant was calculating the value of his labors over twenty years; the mother was thinking of the two children his work had supported; and the old soldier was reflecting on his scars. All

{ 21 }

their impatience had vanished. No one tried to hurry him along; instead, they were content to wait. Noiraud was allowed to take his time.

Later on when the going became easier, the mother wanted to let her children walk; the old soldier declared that he mustn't sit any longer or his wounds would grow stiff; and when they had both got down, the coachman began to call encouragements to Noiraud.

"Steady, old timer!" he said. "Just do your duty once more for Georgette, and tomorrow will be a day of rest."

Then, turning to Marthe and Maurice, he added with a smile:

"She's the daughter in the family is Georgette, and on Saturday she's getting married to our neighbor's son. Her mother and I have a surprise waiting for her—a bed, a writing desk, a chest of drawers, and ornaments for her mantelpiece. My child will only be married once, and I want everything to be perfect: a pretty nest and a fine bird! The bird is already found; but we still need a few shillings for the nest, and there's no rest for Noiraud until we've got them. Isn't that right old friend? You'll make sure that we have them by tomorrow?"

"He has already earned them for you," Maurice said, giving him the money. "You can make Georgette happy a daily earlier and bring forward the holiday for Noiraud too. On your way, my good man, and may God bless your young couple." He then jumped down and gave a helping hand to Marthe, and soon the carriage, much lighter now, disappeared into the night.

O. Pinguilly.

PISAN.

Paris was still a long way off; but the two of them walked on happily, arm in arm, talking quietly of Georgette, of Noiraud, and of the stars, enjoying that indescribable charm of sweet nothings, of fleeting impressions, of intuitive and wordless confidences. It was a dreamlike dialogue that faded from the memory but left behind a luminous wake to which the memory was forever returning.

It was the middle of the night when they arrived home, dropping with fatigue, streaming with perspiration, their blistered feet caked in dust, but with full hearts and light spirits. Never afterward could they forget this journey, because they had not only gone from one place to another: their eyes and their hearts had been opened. They had not only arrived; they had a souvenir of their journey. They would remember forever the old horse and his old master.

All these images had surfaced again in Marthe's dream, and she believed she had once more gained the threshold of her beloved attic when a great din made her wake with a start.

# §III

*Extraction of travelers—Model inns—A glass of spring water—
Departure of Marthe and Maurice on the express submarine
Dolphin—M. Blaguefort, commercial traveler in noses,
books, and colonial goods—A prospectus for industrial
enterprise in the year three thousand—Unfortunate
encounter with a whale—Lecture of M. Vertèbre on
cetaceans—Destruction of the submarine—
Its death certificate.*

The attendants escorting the member of the Academy and his two companions had just arrived at the bottom of a kind of chasm, and above their heads a patch of sky appeared crossed by the arms of an immense machine. M. Atout explained that they had arrived at their destination, and that each of the villages beneath which their carriageway passed had an exit shaft for travelers. In fact, their carriage had just been gripped by an arm of the mighty machine and, like a miners' cage, was starting on a rapid ascent.

As soon as they reached the top of the shaft, a thousand cries broke out around them, and hundreds of men, women, and children rushed toward the new arrivals. Marthe, thinking they were going to tear her to pieces,

retreated hastily toward M. Atout; but he explained that these were hotel keepers and local agents come to offer their services.

Some of them deluged the travelers with a rain of cards and addresses; others had great plates stacked with refreshments, which they pressed our travelers to accept. Some restaurateurs carried huge forks furnished with roast fowls, cutlets, and knuckles of ham, which they held up above the heads of the crowd as publicity for their establishments. There were also men with brushes and polish, guides, and porters, all fiercely determined to be of service. Maurice had hardly taken six steps before he found himself forced to accept two glasses of lemonade, and to hand his walking stick, his scarf, and his hat to three commissionaires.

M. Atout drew his attention to this zealous hospitality, this wealth of services, this cornucopia.

"Look," he said, "these are the blessings of civilization! An entire population is at the service of each one of us; everything the world produces is, as it were, at our fingertips. We have only just arrived, and already our smallest wishes have been anticipated; we want for nothing!"

In truth, Marthe and Maurice wanted for nothing—except that they could not breathe. They took refuge in the first hostelry they saw, as if seeking sanctuary.

At the door stood a concierge with a halberd, who saluted them three times and sent them on to an usher with a gold chain. He passed them on to a footman whose duty was to open the door of the salon.

It was an enormous gallery, the first sight of which astonished the young people. Their guide noticed it and smiled.

"You see before you the triumph of industry. Nothing that you see here is what it seems. This colonnade of carved marble is merely terra cotta. This brocaded tapestry is just a fabrication of spun glass; this parquet flooring of rosewood is made from blocks of colored asphalt. The velour that covers the sofas is made from cleverly processed rubber. Everything here will probably last for two years—that is to say as long as it takes for the hotelier to sell his establishment and retire a millionaire."

As he finished speaking, waiters arrived. They all had printed on their uniforms the signs of their particular duties: one had dishes, plates, cutlery; another glasses and bottles; still others meat, fish, or fruit. In addition they all wore a chain with the innkeeper's emblem that identified their establishment.

M. Atout invited his companions to dine, but after living all those centuries without eating, they had lost the habit. The Académicien, who was not very hungry, was happy to ask for just a glass of water.

The attendant in charge of orders went to a small bookcase and came back with a bound volume on which appeared in gold letters:

### LIST OF WATERS
SERVED AT THE HOTEL OF THE TWO WORLDS

1° Springwater:

2° Well water:

3° Brook water:

4° Streamlet water:

5° River water:

6° Carbon-filtered water:

7° Rock-filtered water:

8° Gravel-filtered water:

9° Water . . .

Maurice paused, turned thirty or so pages, and saw that the list went on to page 366. The Hotel of the Two Worlds had as many varieties of water as a leap year has days. M. Atout examined the list carefully, made erudite comments on the distinguishing characteristics and relative quality of the waters, hesitated, read it again, hesitated once more, and finally, after much deliberation, ordered springwater. The request was passed on by the servant in charge of orders. Five minutes went by; then the first waiter appeared carrying a tray. Five minutes later a second waiter brought a carafe; and in another five minutes a third waiter brought a glass.

The whole operation had taken no more than a quarter of an hour, thanks to the division of labor.

While their guide was drinking, Marthe and Maurice wished to go over to the window, but the footman who was standing there gave them to understand that, in order to do so, they must buy a ticket from the vista office. They refused, and tried to get to the door. Another attendant warned them that, if they went out without a ticket, they could not come back. Finally, much embarrassed, they went to sit down on a sofa by the wall, where a third attendant informed them politely that they would have to pay more for those seats.

So, repulsed on every side, they hurried back to the member of the Academy who had just finished his glass of water and asked for the bill.

A different servant immediately appeared bearing a magnificent sheet of velum, with a framed and illuminated text, and a tailpiece embellished with flourishes and shading. Over the guide's shoulder Maurice read:

### Account for Monsieur

*For three greetings from the concierge with the halberd* ........ *1 fr. 50*
*For the usher with the gold chain* ........................ *2 fr. 00*
*For the footman who opened the door* ...................... *0 fr. 50*
*For the use of the list of waters* ........................... *0 fr. 25*
*For one tray* ........................................... *0 fr. 30*
*For one carafe* ......................................... *0 fr. 35*
*For one glass* .......................................... *0 fr. 25*
*For springwater* ........................................ *5 fr. 00*
*For a table and stools* ................................... *4 fr. 00*
*For service charge* ...................................... *2 fr. 00*
*.... Total  16 fr. 15*

M. Atout pointed out that, thanks to the detailed nature of the bill, there was no need to worry about a tip for the servants. He then paid the 16 fr. 15 c. and left. Marthe could not help remembering the words of the Evangelist, for it struck her that the hotel keepers of Charcoal Island had found a way of making the promises of Christ come true on earth: *All who gave a glass of water would be repaid a hundredfold.*

The young couple's guide had accompanied them on the road to the port where they were to embark for Budget Island. When they arrived, the quayside was crowded with people landing or boarding, and the air was rent with cries:

"The steamship for Japan;

"The courier for the Red Sea;

"The omnibus for Brazil, with connections for the New World."

And, hearing these cries, the crowd rushed forward. There were news vendors selling their papers, and merchants weighing out their goods. M. Atout pointed out to his companions an official with a marking brush who was tracing on the chest or the back of each passenger the number identifying their luggage—a method, as simple as it was ingenious, of establishing the correlation between the passengers and their luggage. Finally, they arrived at a landing stage above which was written:

## DOLPHIN EXPRESS
FROM CHARCOAL ISLAND TO BUDGET ISLAND,
In fifty-three minutes.

"Here we are," said M. Atout.

Our travelers looked but could see nothing in front of them. "You're looking for the boat?" said the professor with a smile; "but it's there . . . in the right place for a Dolphin."

"What! Under the water?" Maurice asked.

"Under the water!" repeated M. Atout. "For a long time it was thought that a boat must operate on the surface; but new research has changed all that. Nowadays some of our ships travel underwater, just as some of our roads are underground. You will come to realize that there are advantages in both methods. The express Dolphins, when they are beneath the waves, fear neither the wind, nor lightning, nor boarding parties, nor pirates. As for their construction, you can judge for yourselves."

He led them to the end of the landing stage, where there was a diving bell to take them down to the submarine.

The shape was borrowed from the fish for which it was named. It was a huge Dolphin, whose tail and fins were driven by steam. Instead of scales, it had a gleaming row of little windows; and air was drawn into the interior through tubes, the ends of which floated on the surface of the sea.

A large number of passengers had come on board before the newcomers, so the Dolphin lost no time in starting on its journey through the waves.

M. Atout wished to use the time to prepare his companions for the sight of the capital of the *United Interests*; but he was immediately interrupted by a traveler who recognized him, and ran to him with open arms.

"Ah! It's M. Blaguefort," said the Académicien with a certain patron-

## M. BLAGUEFORT

*Traveling salesman from the year 3000*

izing air, as he responded to the eager attentions of the newcomer—"one of our best-known businessmen." And, indicating Marthe and Maurice, he went on to say, "May I introduce two people from ancient times."

"The Parisians belonging to M. Omnivore?" interrupted Blaguefort, who had already taken a close look at them. "I missed them by three minutes. I had heard of their return to life, and I rushed off to their owner with an offer to find a role for them. I would have made the most of this opportunity along with that of the lunar telegraph; but you have already made a deal there. Well done, sir; you could make six thousand percent."

M. Atout observed that there was no question of a speculation; that the reawakening of the young couple must benefit science alone, and that it was for this reason he had brought them to Budget Island.

Blaguefort winked broadly.

"Well, well," he said. "You have another scheme in mind. You're hoping to turn it to your advantage. Heavens above! You're entitled to. You must know that I shall not offer any competition. All the more so since I have expanded my business interests. Since we met at the Cape of Good Hope I have founded a limited company to exploit the invention of Doctor Naso. I believe you will have heard of this Peruvian who has just invented an orthopedic appliance to treat malformed noses. But excuse me; here is a traveler to whom I gave a prospectus and who now wants to speak to me." And indeed, another person had come up to speak to him.

He was a little man, and so fat that his arms were more like flippers, while his legs were so short that he looked like a roly-poly cartoon figure waddling along. His little eyes, buried in flesh, resembled bungholes, while his nose, wedged between the hemispheres of his cheeks, made one think of a pip in a Maltese orange.

He raised a foot in greeting, since he had not enough neck to incline his head. "A magnificent invention, sir," he managed to say in a strangulated voice, pointing with a flipper at the prospectus.

"Would you like to try one out, sir?" responded M. Blaguefort at once.

"Why not?" said the rotund little man, with a laugh that could have been mistaken for a fit of coughing. "Why not? I have always supported the progress of science."

"As we support progress in nasal technology, sir."

"So, you can now actually increase or reduce the size of a nose?"

"By means of an appropriate appliance. Look, sir, at the illustrations in our brochure. Thanks to our orthonasal device, everyone can now choose a nose, as he once chose his hat. Here you have models of every shape with the list prices."

The little man turned over the sheet that he held in his hand, and looked closely at a long catalog of noses, displayed according to price. For some time he wavered between Grecian noses and snub noses; but when M. Blaguefort commented that these were not very suitable, he looked at others.

The businessman immediately took a pair of compasses from his case and measured the wart-like thing that the doctor's appliance was to transform into a nose of antique proportions; then he entered the figures into a notebook with the name and address of the purchaser.

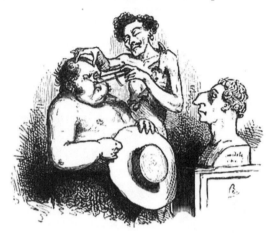

The young couple learned from this that the customer had arrived from Africa, where he had gone because he suffered from consumption, and that the cause of his obesity was a new dish—the racahout des Arabes.[1]

He had brought back the recipe and sold it to the Company of Public Hygiene, which had then engaged him to work as a living advertisement.

While he was explaining all this, M. Blaguefort had noticed some distance away a traveler whose bearing and long hair suggested a clergyman. He searched eagerly in his case of samples for relics, rosary beads and holy medals, and went up to him with a pleasantly deferential air, saying:

"Unless I am much mistaken sir, you have been ordained."

"Indeed," replied the traveler.

"I was certain of it," replied Blaguefort ingratiatingly. "A little voice tells you when you are in the presence of saints. But, since Providence has brought us together, I dare to hope that I shall be allowed to show you some articles designed for the edification of the faithful: *Ad majorem Dei gloriam.*"

And, immediately adopting the style of an auctioneer, he continued, presenting his samples one by one:

"Here is a relic of Saint Loriquet, certain to inspire a real interest in history! We are offering them for fifty cents a dozen—up to fourteen.

"Here is a medal dedicated to our patron saints. It is a shield against bankruptcy, the National Guard, and other earthly calamities. One franc for six or seven.

"And here we have a rosary . . ."

"One minute, sir," interrupted the long-haired traveler. "There must be some misunderstanding. I am not a Catholic priest."

"Oh indeed," cried Blaguefort, "do I have the honor of speaking to a minister of the Holy Gospel?"

He hurriedly opened his case again, picked out a Bible, and started again with the magisterial air of a schoolmaster explaining the nine parts of speech:

"How about this? For here we have the universal law, the Word itself, the living God. In it you will find nothing but the one true way . . . even though the apocryphal books have been added. Here you will find the prescription for spiritual and temporal health, and the way to attain it. It costs no more than ten francs—and that includes the case and the clasp."

"That really is very little to pay for so much," said the stranger with a smile, "and in the days when I was a pastor I would have taken advantage of such a bargain; but since then my convictions have changed, and the onetime minister of the Holy Gospel has taken refuge in philosophy."

"You're a philosopher," said Blaguefort, slapping his thigh. "Good heavens, I should have seen it straight away—that broad brow, that pensive look! Well, well! I'm delighted to hear it, sir. I too am a philosopher— a practical philosopher—and the proof of that is that I travel for the *Society for the Extinction of Creeds*. Here is the prospectus, and I am authorized to collect subscriptions."

He had been rummaging again in his bag, and offered his potential customer a brochure with an illustration at the front that showed the spirit of truth striking down the hydra of superstition. The spirit was the figure of the society's president, and the hydra's heads were the heads of priests.

Blaguefort left the ex-pastor examining the brochure and came back to the Académicien.

Maurice could not conceal his astonishment, and told him he felt he was looking at the quintessential commercial traveler.

"Ah! You want to flatter me," said Blaguefort with a smile. "Go on! I know my failings. I have a weakness in business dealings—a great weakness: I am too open! I have no idea how to put a proper value on my goods, to press my own advantage; but I keep to old-fashioned values; and I want everyone to feel comfortable when they deal with me. And then, everyone knows me. Sugar, chocolate, silks, honey, wine from Madeira—all these can be bought, sight unseen; and that's what I like. My reputation rests on the confidence of the public. That is the soundest and surest benefit for me."

While he was speaking, the businessman emptied his bag so that he could put everything back in order. Maurice caught sight of a paper which had just fallen open, and he read:

*Recipe for chocolate from the pure cocoa bean*: Take one-third kidney beans; one-third spoiled sugar; one-third suet. Flavor the whole with the husk of the cocoa bean, and you will have excellent chocolate.

*Recipe for honey:* Take some molasses, some rye flour, flavor with orange blossom, add a compound of salts of zinc, copper and lead; and you will have honey from Mount Hymettus.

*Recipe for white sugar:* Take some powdered alabaster . . .

Maurice could not bring himself to read any more. Blaguefort, who had now got everything back in order, took the piece of paper and filed it carefully among his business correspondence. Then, his attention was suddenly arrested by a letter that struck a chord in his memory: "By the way, I didn't tell you," said he, turning to M. Atout, "the Society for an Interplanetary Telegraph has just been inaugurated. Next year we shall be in direct communication with the moon."

"With the moon!" exclaimed Marthe and Maurice in astonishment.

"The recent experiments carried out at the observatory of Sans-Pair have made it possible," said M. Atout. "Thanks to the telescope built by M. de l'Empyrée, the moon can be seen close up at last."

"And soon she will yield up her secrets," added Blaguefort. "With the new electric telegraph it will be possible to speak to the inhabitants of the moon as quickly and as easily as I can speak to you.[2] Moreover, I have here the outline of a prospectus sent to me, which I can now let you see." He opened up a letter and took from it a signed sheet containing the following information:

# INTERPLANETARY TELEGRAPH

---

## TO INTERESTED PARTIES WITH FUNDS TO INVEST.

---

### Registered Capital : TEN MILLION.
### Profit assured : TEN BILLION

"An event, surpassing in importance all those which to date have changed the world, has just taken place in our midst. One of our scientists has revealed a hitherto unknown world. That world is the moon.

"A society was formed at once to exploit this new conquest, and all that remains is to take possession of it. Steps have already been taken to set up an interplanetary telegraph. This will allow us to get in touch with the inhabitants of the moon, and shortly after that it will make possible the establishment of a great communication system, built at public expense.

"The observations of M. de l'Empyrée have revealed that the moon contains incalculable wealth in slate, earth for brick making, deposits of granite, reserves of sand suitable for building, etc., etc., etc. The imagination reels in contemplating the benefits that the exploitation of such riches could yield. Yet we make no promise to the shareholders; even the most modest would appear exaggerated. We simply tell them that, according to the most exact and conscientious calculations, return from money invested in our undertaking must be, in the medium term, fifty thousand percent.

"Since nearly all the shares have been taken up in advance, we cannot accept applications until the thirtieth of the present month."

A list of signatures was appended.

Most of the travelers had gathered round Blaguefort while he was reading this announcement. The astonishing news had obviously made an impression. The most enthusiastic were already clamoring for information on how to acquire a share in the company. Blaguefort immediately proposed himself as agent and began to hand out promissory notes for shares with the right to commission for himself. The passengers who had managed to buy shares moved on into the other saloons on the boat, where they passed on the great news and sold their coupons, making a profit of two hundred percent. Maurice could not get over his surprise; and M. Atout took advantage of the occasion to deliver a speech extolling the advantages of associated funds. He had reached the twelfth aphorism of political economy when a terrible crash shook the Dolphin and caused it to lose buoyancy.

The terrified passengers, thrown against the windows, saw an immense cetacean rudely awakened from its sleep in the depths of ocean. At that very moment, when Marthe and Maurice were pressed against the window, it turned over. Marthe hardly had time to cry out. The waves, drawn in by the monster's breath, carried the vessel into the great chasm of its mouth, and it did not come to a halt until it arrived in the pit of the creature's stomach.

It all happened so quickly that there was no time for evasive action, and in the first minutes after the catastrophe the shrieks and groans were so loud that it was impossible to make oneself heard. Even the crew were in shock. It was the first time they had ever had to navigate in the belly of a whale, and the captain, old sailor though he was, was forced to admit that he had no idea how to proceed.

Consequently, everyone felt called upon to give advice; but all the methods they proposed seemed either dangerous or impracticable. In the end, they remembered the professor of zoology from the Museum, who happened to be on board, and all turned to him. Several voices shouted:

"Let's hear M. Vertèbre. He's made a study of whales. He could give us some good advice!"

M. Vertèbre replied with great gravity:

"I must admit, gentlemen, that this interesting mammal has been the object of my special studies; and, whatever my enemies may say, I believe I was the first to discover the true properties of the milk with which it feeds its young.

"The whale, gentlemen, is a cetacean—a name derived from the Greek word *kêtos*; it belongs to the family of the narwhal, the sperm whale, and the dolphin. It is a large mammal, pelagic, viviparous, pisciform, with two feet called fins, and breathes by means of lungs."

He was interrupted by a sudden jolt. The propellers of the vessel, which were still turning, had grazed the walls of the whale's belly and had set off a contraction that pushed the *Dolphin* toward the alimentary canal. The engineer, eager to take advantage of this development, went to full steam in order to break out—a move that made the monster so ill that it was violently sick and spewed forth the boat.

But the ejection was so violent that the *Dolphin* was hurled against a rock where it broke apart. All the passengers at the front of the boat were crushed by the impact, drowned in the sea, or burned by the exploding engine.

Fortunately, the stern of the vessel, where Marthe and Maurice were,

suffered less damage. Most of the passengers escaped the disaster and were assisted by people on shore who had come running at the sound of the explosion.

Finally, when they had sufficiently recovered their senses to look about them, they realized that the whale had very kindly not taken them off course, and that they were in the outskirts of Sans-Pair itself, just fifteen leagues from the town. The official in charge of the *Official Registry of Machines* was immediately informed. He arrived to record the disaster and he put up the following proclamation, on a preprinted form on which he needed only to fill in the blanks.

SANS-PAIR — OFFICIAL REGISTRY OF MACHINES.

DEATH CERTIFICATE.

We, the undersigned, declare that:

The express vessel *Dolphin No. 7*

Born at the *Black Isle*

Aged *eighteen months*

Value *four hundred thousand francs*

Perished in an encounter *with a whale*

This day May 17, 3000.

THE COMMISSIONER,

Hellement

Official report attached.

When it came to dealing with the passengers who had lost their lives, he took no action, since he would have needed to find out their names, their professions, and their ages. He was observing the principle of the Constitution which declares that *private life must be protected.*

# §IV

*Customs House of an ultra-super-civilized people — Disadvantage
of daguerreotype passports — M. Atout's model home —
Art of having service without servants — Supper
served by machines — An old way of life:*
***THE SPINNER OF ÉVRECY.***

The survivors continued on their way to the town of Sans-Pair. Maurice discovered that the town was surrounded by a double cordon designed to ensure the collection of customs duties and the examination of passports.

These last were not, as in former days, letters of safe-conduct with a description of the bearer, but daguerreotype portraits, stamped with the official police seal, bearing the likeness of the traveler. M. Atout was explaining to his companions the advantages of this new arrangement when he was interrupted by the sounds of an altercation. It was the rotund traveler with the tiny nose whom the officer refused to recognize from the passport photograph that showed him to be thin and slightly built. The little man was insisting in vain that his increased girth was caused by eating the racahout des Arabes; the gendarme, impassive and stupid, declared that he could allow only the original of the portrait to enter. The problem was referred to a controller, who passed it on to an inspector, who took it to a director. The latter gave it lengthy consideration, looked again at the twenty-three thousand regulations governing the matter, and decided finally that the fat man should be sent to a slimming establishment where the staff, after being sworn in, would work at getting him back to his former size. Then and only then could they verify his identity. The walking advertisement vociferously but vainly made the point that, if he lost weight, he would lose his job, that his rotundity was his fortune, that he lived by his size as others lived by their reputation. The director replied that these misfortunes were no concern of the law, and that his first duty was to protect society in general without worrying about individual members.

The young couple left the traveling advert for racahout in this rather awkward situation and arrived with M. Atout at the second barrier, where the customs officers were waiting. They too had kept up with the progress of civilization in perfecting their search procedures. Thanks to their ingenious and imaginative methods, fraud had become impossible for anyone but themselves.

Having finally escaped their clutches, Maurice and Marthe followed their guide to his home.

It was a huge parallelogram, whitewashed and pierced with narrow windows, which made it look very much like an enormous chicken shed. The Académicien saw the surprise of his guests and gave a smile of satisfaction.

"Perhaps you did not have houses like this in your day," he said, with just a hint of pride.

"Not exactly," Maurice replied. "However, we did have the Quai d'Orsai. . . ."[1]

"Yes, that was an advance," said M. Atout, "but architecture has moved on since then, and its practitioners have achieved the perfection of

the rectangular building. The house where I live was built by the most skillful among them, and it is regarded as a masterpiece. In all that you see before you there is no ornamentation—that is to say there is nothing that does not serve a useful purpose. As for the interior, you can judge for yourselves."

They had reached the flight of steps before the entrance. Hardly had Maurice stepped forward when the surface yielded slightly and set in motion a lantern, which advanced to light their way. His second step set a bell ringing; the third activated the door, which then opened of its own accord.

At that moment an inscription chiseled over the entrance caught the young man's eye:

EVERY MAN'S HOME IS HIS CASTLE.
EVERY MAN FOR HIMSELF.

"You no doubt recognize the precept of one of the seven wise men of your country," said the Académicien cheerfully. "It sums up the entirety of human law: *Every man's home is his castle*—that's the law; *every man for himself*—that's our duty. But, please do come in; there is much for you to see."

The young couple went through an anteroom in which there were various appliances whose functions were unknown to them. Atout first showed them a box into which his mail was delivered, and explained to them how large vacuum pipes made possible this distribution of letters to homes. He turned the levers that delivered water, light, heating, and air-conditioning. He showed them the conduit that would supply newspapers, the electric cables that made possible instantaneous telegraphic communication with outside suppliers, and optical devices that could bring distant objects into close view.

While this demonstration was going on, he had checked that Madame Atout was not at home, and by pressing various buttons he had given a series of orders. The ringing of a bell shortly announced that everything was ready; he ushered his guests into the dining room where their meal was set, and invited them to take their places.

Marthe and Maurice sat down and looked about them. They were waiting to see the servants appear; but the Académicien, who had guessed their thoughts, smiled to himself and, leaning to one side, pressed a button near the table. Immediately, everything on the table seemed to come to life. Bottles lowered themselves, their necks over the glasses; the soup spoons filled the bowls of each guest; the large knife by the leg of mutton began to cut slices, which little skewers immediately dipped into a gravy boat; the tortoiseshell tongs did a jig and tossed the salad; the fat chickens, already cut into portions, took station on the sides of the plates as if preparing for flight; the fish placed itself gently on the silver fish slicer that would carve it; the hors d'oeuvres began to circulate round the table like a carousel, making a scheduled stop before each guest; finally, even the mustard pot lifted its lid and presented its tiny ivory spatula.

Our two young people, after their sleep of centuries, could not believe their eyes. Atout explained how a series of ingenious inventions had made it possible for more perfect machines to do the work formerly done by human machines.

"You can see," he continued, "that in a really mechanized house like this one, there is no need for anyone else, and that adds delightfully to the sense of intimacy. Progress must aim to make life simpler, to ensure that each one lives for himself and by himself; and we have reached that point. In place of domestics who are at the mercy of a thousand infirmities and a thousand passions, we have servants of iron and copper, always robust, always reliable, always precise. Just a little more effort, and civilization will have achieved total individual freedom for everyone; every individual will be able to dispense with the services of the rest of mankind."

"Yes," said Maurice, who had become very thoughtful, "but what about the teaching of Christ that tells us to help and to love one another? Is self-sufficiency really the goal of our lives? Is it not rather to find our completeness as human beings in and through others? The human machine, as you call it, has a heart which beats in unison with our own, while iron machines mean nothing to us. In preferring them, you have sacrificed your soul to your convenience. You have broken the last link that connects the privileged classes with the disinherited. The wealthy cannot suddenly dismiss from their minds the people they take on as servants. These are like prisoners of poverty who by their presence remind us constantly of that poverty. We begin by engaging them out of necessity; and through familiarity we come to cherish them. Their sorrows become intermingled a little with our own; we have likes, dislikes, and weaknesses in common. The relationship, no doubt, is not perfect, but it is an association that promotes a sense of sympathy and encourages feelings of devotion and gratitude to grow in the mind. Ah! In fact, far from eliminating servants we should bring them closer to their masters. We should make them our humble friends, ready for any sacrifice and assured of our complete protection. We should enact the beautiful story of *The Spinner of Évrecy.*

The Académicien wanted to know about this story.

"A popular traditional tale told me in my childhood," said Maurice, "and one that will seem very strange to you."

"Let's see," said Atout, emptying his glass.

The young man seemed to hesitate, but in Marthe's eyes he read a request for the story. He made up his mind immediately and launched into the following tale.

### THE SPINNER OF ÉVRECY

Toward the end of the eighteenth century there lived at Évrecy in Normandy a gentleman whose only family was a ten-year-old daughter, and his only servant was an old woman. The little girl had received in baptism the name of Yvonnette, and the servant that of Bertaude; but the latter was known in the neighborhood only by the name of the Spinner of Évrecy, because she always had her distaff at her side. Indeed, Bertaude was spinning from morning till night, and often from night till morning, without managing to reduce the number of her master's creditors. And, it must be said, he cared little about them. The gentleman of Évrecy was one of those whose epitaph would read like that of the human race in general. Having eaten the best part of his estate, he had decided to drink the rest just to make things even, and went on even more resolutely because, according to him, he no longer had any fear of being ruined. Otherwise, he was an excellent man who would have given his daughter Yvonnette the sun and the moon, and one who always called Bertaude to drink the last glass of Marin-Onfroi cider or perry.[2] At last, when he had exhausted fortune and credit, he had the good luck to die almost immediately without the boring task of paying his creditors.

But, the coffin had hardly been taken away when those creditors came running, followed by officers of the law, to seize everything. The furniture was taken down into the courtyard and auctioned off; the meadows, fields, and orchards were parceled out, and a wealthy merchant of Falaise who had just recently bought a title came to live in the old family home.

Bertaude realized that she had to go. She took her distaff and spindle, packed her belongings and those of Yvonnette, and then went to take leave of the new master. He, seeing that she was holding a little girl by the hand, enquired if she was taking her to a relative.

"Alas! No," Bertaude replied, wiping her eyes with the corner of her apron." The poor innocent child has no family to look after her."

"Then, why not take her to the orphanage at Bayeux?" asked the new aristocrat.

"To the orphanage!" repeated Bertaude, overcome with emotion.

"It's not for illegitimate children only," objected the old merchant, "but also for abandoned children."

"By my Savior! She is not abandoned, sir," said the old lady, putting her arms round the child who clung to her in terror. "As long as I am alive, she has someone."

"Is she something special to you?" the bourgeois arriviste inquired, with sarcasm.

"She is my master's daughter," replied Bertaude with spirit. "For twenty years I was fed by her family; I took her in my arms when she was born; I carried her to church to be baptized; I helped her walk and say her first words. She may not be my own flesh and blood, but she is the child I have always loved and cared for. Ah! Lord Jesus! The orphanage! Don't be afraid, Yvette, as long as Bertaude can move one of her ten fingers, she will look after you."

She lifted up the child who clung to her, her head against Bertaude's shoulder, and then the two of them left, following the road to Falaise. She had thought of a plan, but said nothing about it to anyone.

There was among the Ursulines a sister she knew who, before being called by God to a life of holiness, had been much loved by men. Bertaude took Yvonnette to her, with a purse containing everything she possessed, and said to her:

"Bring her up as the daughter of a gentleman, and deny her nothing necessary to bring honor to the family name, because before the purse is empty, I shall return with enough to fill it again."

She embraced the child, shed copious tears, and departed. But three months later she reappeared with a greater sum of money than the original. She continued to return regularly every quarter, and on each visit she stipulated that Yvonnette should have more learned teachers and more beautiful clothes.

She herself looked just the same, wearing her old homespun skirt, the distaff at her belt, turning the spindle as she walked. People wondered in vain about the source of the money she handed over for Yvonnette. To every question she merely smiled and said:

"God has a savings account for orphans."

As time went by, the child became a young woman, so learned, so wise, and so beautiful that there was talk of nothing else throughout the Bessin region. The grandest ladies in the neighborhood wanted to meet her, and came to visit her in the convent parlor. The poets of Normandy wrote verses for her, young gentlemen fell in love and wore her colors. In the end there was a whole host of people who declared themselves kinsfolk or relations by marriage, and they came bearing evidence to prove it.

Madame de Villers was one of them. She insisted that the young girl should come and spend some time at her château; and it was there that Yvonnette met the Master of Boutteville, one of the richest and most accomplished gentlemen in the kingdom. He fell so desperately in love with the young lady that he asked for her hand in marriage; and Yvonnette, happy with what she knew of him, was dreaming of telling Bertaude the news when the latter came to present her with a number of outfits. Bertaude had not wanted her young mistress to marry like a girl with no dowry, and had brought her a complete trousseau.

The Master of Boutteville, who arrived just as it was being displayed in front of Yvonnette, did not seem to share the young girl's joy. He had already been told of the large sums of money brought by the old retainer, and of the question mark over their origin. He was afraid that this generosity might hide some shameful secret, and he could not help showing his reservations.

Bertaude went away without a word and did not return, much to the despair of Yvonnette, who felt that her flight confirmed the general suspicion. At last, the wedding day arrived. The bride, beautifully dressed for her wedding and somewhat tremulous, was driven to the chapel in the coach of Madame de Villers. As she was stepping down beneath the porch, she was surrounded by a crowd of beggars who had come, according to

custom, to offer their good wishes and to be rewarded with alms. Suddenly, her eyes fell on an old woman kneeling there. Her distaff and spindle were enough to make her instantly recognizable. It was the old servant: it was Bertaude!

Yvonnette ran to her, clasped her hands, and asked what she was doing there. "What I have been doing these last nine years," replied the old woman, who could not keep back her tears. And seeing M. de Boutteville, who hurried to her side, she continued:

"Yes," she said, "here is the great secret that has made your fiancé so uneasy. After leaving you at the convent I set off to travel throughout Normandy on foot, spinning as I went, and begging in the name of God.

My work produced very little, and that was for me; almsgiving brought in more, and that was for you. But your husband need not blush for what I have done: charity given in God's name can never shame anyone. The kindness of all men sustained you when you were a child; now that you are grown up, the kindness of one man will make you happy. Today I shall give up begging, because now that all your wants are supplied, I have nothing else to ask for."

Yvonnette, at first filled with astonishment, was overcome with the most tender feelings and embraced the old woman who was surprised at the strength of her emotions. But M. de Boutteville, whose eyes had filled with tears, took her hand and into it put that of his fiancée, saying:

"You have been a mother to her. It is for you to bring her to the altar and give her to me."

And all this was arranged immediately, to the great admiration of all the onlookers. Yvonnette, attired in silk, lace, and gold was led to the altar by Bertaude, still in her beggar's clothes and carrying her distaff and spindle. When the ceremony was over, the young bride went down on her knees before the old peasant woman to ask her blessing, as she would have done before her own mother. The congregation was in tears, and on all sides could be heard:

"God bless them! God bless them!"

That wish was granted; for the memory of that union lived on in the Bessin region for many years, giving rise to the proverbial saying: *As happy as the Bouttevilles.*

But even better was the fact that the couple never forgot their gratitude to Bertaude. Whenever the greatest gentlemen and the finest ladies in the land were invited into the salons of the château of Boutteville, the Spinner of Évrecy occupied the place of honor there. Moreover, every year at the parish church, a solemn mass was celebrated to which the old servant came in her beggar's clothes, holding her distaff and spindle, the Master of Boutteville on one hand and Yvonnette on the other. It was a moving ceremony that perpetuated the memory of devotion and of gratitude—an example to both masters and to those who serve them.

# §V

*Maurice's monologue while undressing—Disadvantages of high-tech bedrooms—An involuntary excursion—The drawing room of M. Atout; excessive multiplication of a great man's image—M. Atout presents his lawfully wedded wife, Milady Ennui.*

While he was taking Marthe and Maurice to their rooms, M. Atout lost no opportunity in pointing out a whole array of new improvements. The beds folded back to the wall in order to give more space; armchairs moved of their own accord; the windows opened without being touched; the floors were lowered or raised at will. There were pulleys and ropes everywhere. The whole apartment resembled a vessel with all its tackle that would respond in an instant, provided one knew how to operate it.

But the multifarious excitements of the day, along with the fatigue of the journey, had worn Marthe out. So she put off till the morrow her investigation of all these domestic gadgets, and in no time she was asleep.

Maurice, who was just as tired, went into the adjoining room, which had been put at his disposal, and started to get ready for bed; but as he undressed, he went over in his mind all the strange things that had happened to him, and engaged in a philosophical monologue common to the inebriated, to those who are half asleep, and to the heroes of tragedy.

"To come back to life again," he murmured, in the tone of Talma asking himself the famous question posed by Hamlet.[1] "To come back to life after twelve centuries! How can I be sure that I really am awake?"

At this point he pinched himself to make sure, and then went on:

"Yes, I am awake. . . . I really am in the world of the year THREE THOUSAND, living in a new society. . . ."

He paused to go on with his undressing. . . .

"So, my wishes have come true. Well, Maurice! You are going to see the future that your contemporaries were preparing. Ah! To judge it fairly, shed the prejudices of your youth . . . get rid of all the preconceptions that blind us . . . get rid of . . . ."

His mind, heavy with sleep, could think no further. He was content simply to shed his trousers and, with half-closed eyes, approached the bed that had been prepared for him.

But just as he was about to fall into it, he noticed that there was a window still open. Thinking to keep out mosquitoes and drafts, he seized a cord that he thought would close the window and pulled it.

The chandelier with its three globes was switched off suddenly, and he found himself plunged into total darkness. Instead of the cord for the window, he had pulled the cord of the light extinguisher.

It was not a dangerous mistake, however. So he decided to brave the night air and began to feel his way toward the bed. He was about to climb in when his outstretched hand encountered a button that yielded at his touch.

Immediately a squeaking sound of wheels was heard; and the bed, suddenly hoisted up, disappeared into the wall.

For a few seconds Maurice stayed there, one arm extended and one foot in front of him, in the pose of a conquering gladiator. However, since it was not a position conducive to sleep, he straightened himself up and, consigning to the devil all mechanical inventions, began to look for the button that would bring back his vanished bed.

Unfortunately, he could make out nothing in the darkness. His hands explored the wall without finding anything. Finally, one hand found a

{ 44 }

lever that turned. A jet of freezing water hit him in the face. He jumped back and collided with a partition close by. The floor gave way instantly beneath his feet with a groaning of pulleys, and he felt himself falling.

He barely had time to give a startled cry, immediately suppressed; for light had replaced the darkness, and he found himself in the boudoir of Madame Atout—only instead of entering at ground level, he had entered by way of the ceiling.

The first object that met his eyes was an elegant, half-naked figure, before which he bowed, murmuring excuses in his embarrassment; but on hearing a scream behind him he turned and saw the true owner of the boudoir wearing a very short garment that the most polite of French poets refers to as a *simple costume*.

When he turned, Madame Atout (for it was she) gave another scream and assumed the pose of the modest Venus. The young man turned quickly and discreetly away. The sight of that bony form that had just assailed his eye had awakened in him a chaste terror. He tried to pull down the only garment he was wearing that would keep him decent, and started to make his excuses.

But, alas! The most eloquent and inspired words availed little! It was the first time that Maurice had to speak with his back to anyone, and the unaccustomed situation robbed him of his confidence. In his present situation he tried desperately to find a suitable mode of accounting for what had happened; in his distracted state he could only think of the classical discourse between Telemachus and Calypso.

O thou, whoever thou art, mortal or goddess! Though looking on thee one could only take thee for a divinity . . . .

He was interrupted by the noise of a door banging, and turned around. The goddess had disappeared, and he could hear that she had taken the precaution of locking him out.

This sudden flight relieved him of the need to make a speech; for it appeared that the room had been abandoned to him. Fearful of any further adventures, he decided to stay there and take possession of the couch that occupied one end of the boudoir.

The latter was surrounded by movable mirrors that allowed every gesture and every attitude to be studied. The combined angles permitted different views—from the back, full-face, three-quarters, or profile. Like God when he created the human race, each person could thus have around him a society formed in his own image—a state of affairs that cannot fail to produce charming companions.

Near the couch stood a cabinet, the labeled compartments of which gave the lie to M. Planard's aphorism:[2]

Que toujours la nature
Embellit la beauté!

On some of the more conspicuous of these cubbyholes one could read:

## HIPPOPOTAMUS OIL
### FOR GLEAMING TEETH

---

### Essence of Gazelle
#### TO MAKE THE WAIST MORE SUPPLE

---

### SWANS' CREAM
#### TO WHITEN THE SKIN

---

### TURTLEDOVE MARROW
#### For that melting look in the eyes

---

### ELIXIR OF VENUS

Other compartments held false teeth that dangled and struck the hours, earrings that played a tune, and glass lenses that served as spectacles.

The dressing table too was covered with every imaginable kind of brush: for the nails, the hair, the eyebrows, the teeth, the ears. There were twenty soaps, all with different labels: soap flakes, honey soap, hard soap, butter soap, strong soap, sweet soap. Twenty sorts of cologne with Sessel or asphalt base; tobacco-scented balsam, essence of hydrogen gas, etc., etc., etc.

When he had finished admiring this arsenal of feminine coquetry, Maurice stopped in front of the figure that he had originally taken to be Madame Atout. It was no more than a mannequin carrying her "second skin." He admired the perfection of this artful contrivance that turned hollows into convex shapes and straight lines into pleasing curves. Like Pygmalion, the corset maker had breathed life into his statue: the rubber palpitated; the material seemed to breathe. Maurice could not turn his head away or shut his eyes. In spite of himself he kept calling to mind, like the hermit in the tale by La Fontaine, that rounded form[3]

> . . . Qui pousse et repousse
> Certain corset, en dépit d'Alibech,
> Qui cherche en vain à lui clore le bec.

The sight of the corset threatened to banish the chaste thoughts that Maurice ought to have felt on looking at a woman. He prudently turned away his eyes, lay down on the sofa, and was soon fast asleep.

# THE FIRST DAY
## §VI

*A Salon—Introduction of Madame Atout completed—
An aerial excursion—The Bois de Boulogne of
Sans-Pair, where the trees are chimney pots—
A lady of fashion—Motherhood.*

The following morning M. Atout came in just as
Maurice was opening his eyes. The Académicien
heard the story of the nocturnal misadventures
of his guest and burst out laughing. He led Maurice off to see Marthe, who had begun to worry
about his failure to appear; and he explained to
them again, in greater detail, the different mech-
anisms in their apartment.

He was well into his explanations when the
sound of a bell echoed through the whole house.
The demonstration came to an abrupt end.

"It's Madame Atout," he said, with a deference that suggested a certain trepidation. "We will continue this explanation some other time. She wishes to see you; we mustn't keep her waiting."

He rushed off, opened the door, led his guests through several rooms, and finally brought them into a large salon that they had not previously seen.

It was a picture gallery filled with many curiosities: paintings and watercolors representing different sections of machines. A very large frame enclosed all the academic awards given to M. Atout, arranged so as to radiate from his portrait and form around him a halo of glory.

This portrait, commercially reproduced, like that of all famous men in the year three thousand, could be found in twenty different forms. It grimaced from the moldings of ceilings; in the form of a caryatid it supported the pillars of a cornice; it was reproduced in relief on the carved arms of chairs. The need to adapt the image to these different uses had somewhat compromised the grave dignity of the model. Here he was represented at the base of a candelabra; there leaning forward with open mouth in the manner of a gargoyle; further on, doubled up beneath a door plate that he was supporting. No matter what the attitude and position, one would have recognized the illustrious M. Atout just as surely as the Paris urchin would have recognized the image of Napoleon, whether modeled in barley sugar or sculpted by a member of the Institute.

As the Académicien had guessed, Madame Atout was waiting for Marthe and Maurice; but although Maurice had met her the previous evening, he could not recognize her: the reality and the *appearance* were one and the same. The woman had disappeared into the encasing corset; the sculpted form alone was visible; Madame Atout was no more than the power-unit of the apparition!

Maurice bowed in confusion, and could not help murmuring under his breath, as he took his bearings:

"The corset maker is very clever."

As for Marthe, who was not yet in the secret, she trusted the evidence of her eyes and was filled with admiration.

Madame Atout had neglected nothing that would highlight the felicities produced by the hand of the best corset maker in Sans-Pair. Her dress of amaranthine silk came just to her knees, and her fine trousers of white muslin revealed a rosy limb of wonderful elegance. The thin and haggard face contrasted markedly with these splendors. Her skin was so white, her lips so fresh, her hair so black and lustrous! But it was the sumptuousness of her jewelry that caught their attention. Madame Atout wore on her head a small version of a machine for making the shanks of buttons—an invention of her father. On each arm she carried models of the wheel of a roasting spit modified by her great-uncle, and the hoop of a boiler perfected by her eldest brother. Maurice learned later that these were nothing less than armorial bearings indicating the titles of nobility in the family. On a clip she wore a miniature of M. Atout crowned with laurels and framed with a circlet of everlasting flowers. A locket hanging at her throat enclosed a statement of the sum she had received on marriage; in letters of gold it read:

## DOWRY OF THREE MILLION
### not including property!

Maurice immediately understood the deference that the Académicien showed to his corseted wife.

They were presented to Milady Ennui who nonchalantly peered through her lorgnette at the young visitors from the past with casual curiosity. She asked them a string of questions without waiting for a reply, then she suddenly declared that she would like to dine straight away so that she could then take them on an outing along the grand highway of the chimneys.

When they had risen from the table, M. Atout took his guests and Milady Ennui out onto the terrace of his mansion where an aerostatic barouche was parked and in which they embarked. In Sans-Pair the principal avenues of communication had been built, for greater convenience, in the space formerly left to the wind and the swallows. The roads were almost exclusively reserved for pedestrians. There were flying cabs, omnibus balloons, winged tilburies coming and going and crossing in every direction. The skies, finally conquered, had become a new field for human activity.[1] Here aeronautical stevedores were carving up the clouds to make rain or electricity. There rag-and-bone men were picking up flotsam and jetsam discarded in space; lower down some wretched flying chemists were collecting wandering gases and floating vapors; while nearby a good citizen in the lee of two dark clouds was "fishing" for passing birds.

After traversing the aerial plateau, the barouche dropped down toward a sort of avenue formed by the chimneys of the highest buildings. It was the Bois de Boulogne of Sans-Pair, and all the fashionable and elegant members of the aristocracy met there.

The Académicien pointed out, one by one, the carriages of the reigning beauties, the current celebrities, and the wealthiest bankers. He had his guests admiring the famous people of the day who were riding proudly by on their steam-aerostats and making eyes at the ladies perched on the balconies.

But the thing that struck Maurice the most was the range of facial characteristics in this select society. You could see hints of Mongol ancestry in some faces with their dark skins and shifty looks. In others there were hints of the Red Indian in the receding brows. Some had features that revealed the sallow Malayan, and the Negro with his hair tight-curled like an astrakhan coat. There were even Caucasians among them who conformed to the stereotype of their race with *the angle of the face at eighty degrees, and a long nose* . . . unless they were pug-nosed!

This blending of racial characteristics was the natural result of social progress. The blood of all the different races had been mixed. But, as in uncultivated ground where the coarsest plants immediately take over, the least well-favored races had prevailed through successive generations, and so universal brotherhood had brought universal ugliness.[2]

One singular exception struck Maurice. It was a woman reclining in an aerial chariot covered in mother-of-pearl. At the sight of her gliding gently through the air, one would have called to mind that goddess with the wonderful girdle whom Homer depicts borne through the air by her doves, who had only to smile to occasion a universal sigh of delight among men. Clad in a tunic of muslin striped with gold, she let one of her bare feet dangle from the chariot, as though it were bathing in the ethereal blue. Her chiffon dress floated behind her like a cloud, and her flaxen hair, held in a circlet of silver, rippled about her shoulders.

The young men of Sans-Pair pressed round her carriage like a swarm of bees round a spray of flowers.

Maurice pointed her out to the Académicien and asked who she was.

"Her name?" interrupted Milady Ennui. "Is there anyone who doesn't know it? It's Madame Facile, whose husband is always away on a mission six thousand leagues from Sans-Pair. Isn't that the president of the Chamber of Representatives following her?"

"Indeed, it looks like him," replied the Académicien.

Milady made an indignant gesture.

"What a disgrace!" she exclaimed. "An important man with such a weakness."

"As you say . . . a weakness," M. Atout repeated, although he did not look too strong himself.

"Daring to appear with her," continued Milady, "as she flaunts her well-known attractions for all to see."

M. Atout gave a sidelong glance, as if he longed for a closer acquaintance with those attractions.

"And not to show distaste or scorn!" intoned the corseted wife in conclusion.

At that moment Madame Facile sailed by the barouche. The air, set in motion by her passing, carried the perfume of her hair to M. Atout, and her bare foot almost brushed against him.

"Scandalous!" cried Milady.

"Scandalous!" repeated the Académicien, who was still quivering as he followed with hungry expression the voluptuous vision.

"Let's go," said the first indignantly.

"Let's go," said the second with a sigh.

The barouche altered course. Almost immediately Milady remembered the son she had sent out to nurse, and declared she would like to visit him.

Marthe was very much in favor, for although she was not a mother, her maternal instinct was well developed. The sight of an infant always roused tender feelings in her. She could not hear a baby gurgling without opening her arms; and when she had gathered it to her breast, she would be overcome with protective feelings. She would hold it against her shoulder, lay her cheek on the curly head, and sing a lullaby; and if the baby yielded to these caresses and fell asleep, she would close her eyes, her heart swelling with the happy illusion that she was its mother.

How many times had she been under the spell of this benign hallucination! How many times had she seen in her waking dreams all her fantasies and hopes translated into living images! At first, it was the child playing on the swing in the woods, or running with her pet goat in meadows filled with flowers. Then it was the young girl away at school, who had already said good-bye to those graces of early childhood that are the necessary prelude to the flowering of youth. Finally, there was the beautiful young woman dreaming on the shore of life, on the edge of a boundless sea. What secret thoughts could be detected in this reverie! What traces of tears discovered by a kiss! What kindly words given and received!

There was a powerful resurgence of forgotten emotions: a sweet enactment of the story of our youth when another being starts on the journey of life under the protection of our love. What does it matter that life fades in us, if it is reborn in our second self? Should those who inherit our blood and our spirit not inherit our happiness as well? Leave a place in the sun to the one who has taken your place in life. May the daughter you have nourished and guided find happiness without you, happiness with another!

Alas! From generation to generation ingratitude is an inherited bur-

den: we pay the debt owed to our fathers in caring for our children. Well, accept the new role you have been given; you are queen in this role, albeit as a devoted slave. Watch over and guide them unobtrusively. Give without asking anything in return. Never cease to be a mother to your child. You will live contentedly if she can be happy, for the happiness of those we love is like incense rising before the altar. It does not burn any longer for us, but we enjoy the perfume.

Then, will all the joys of motherhood not come flooding back for you when you see your daughter's children? Open your arms, press your white hair close to their blond hair, and you will hear once again those sweet sounds that reecho in the depths of a woman's heart. Once again your wrinkled cheeks will feel little hands demanding kisses. In the depths of their limpid eyes you can read everything. Take heart! Your task is not yet completed: there are still children to care for, to fear for, to watch over. And, grandmother, you do not need to fear that these little ones will abandon you, because when they are men, you will no longer be here. What would become of the human race without this sacred and generous love for children? Love passes, friendship fades. As the burden of the years weighs you down, the heart shrinks and becomes tainted like water exposed to the heat of the midday sun. All that remains unchanged is a tender concern for the child. That alone strengthens the declining spirit of devotion. Even if calculation dictates our actions, this love remains uncorrupted by self-interest. Because of it we accept disappointments, setbacks, sacrifices. Children not only ensure the continuity of the human race: they are also the guardians of our most precious and gentle instincts.

# §VII

*Feeding room—Mother's place taken by steam machines—Mother's milk improved—Means of recognizing vocations—Sans-Pair High School —Program for the baccalauréat in the arts—New teaching methods—Examination machine—Catechism for young ladies—Boarding school for the production of prodigies.*

So Marthe was lost in her dreams, sad and happy at the same time: happy at the thought of sacrifice; saddened by the thought of being forgotten.

But while she was calling up this fitful dream, the barouche landed, and M. Atout announced that they had arrived. Before them there was a building that looked like a cross between a barracks, a school, and a hospital. The Académicien informed them that it was a nursery.

"Do all the wet nurses live here?" asked Marthe.

M. Atout smiled.

"Wet nurses?" he said. "You are speaking of a custom from the dark ages."

"Then," Marthe replied, "the children are nursed by their mothers?"

"Good heavens!" was the instant response from the Académicien. "That would be even worse. Civilization has made us understand the folly of such a waste of time and effort. Here, as in all other spheres, the machine has replaced the human being. In your time the term "university" was limited to higher education; we have enlarged the system by creating an all-embracing institution: the newborn go to college on the day of their entry into the world, and they return home eighteen years later, their education completed. It would be difficult, as you can see, to loosen further the bonds of family. No more ties! No more anxieties! The child is as free as if he had no parents; the parents as free as if they had no children. They love one another just enough to get on together; they part from one another without any feeling of despair. One generation succeeds another in the same house, like travelers in the same hotel. In this way we have solved the great problem attendant on the perpetuation of the species by avoiding the strong emotional attachment of individuals.

As he finished speaking, the barouche came to a halt before a huge building, over the entrance of which was written in very large letters:

## UNIVERSITY OF UNITED PROFESSIONS AND TRADES

Institution for young ladies and gentlemen not yet weaned.

### MILK DELIVERED BY STEAM MACHINES

A machine with a carved pediment was surrounded by suckling infants, and toward them it extended its steel arms and its breasts of lacquered cork. Underneath appeared the words from holy scripture:

*Suffer the little children to come unto me.*

When he came into the office, M. Atout was required to give the number of the house in which his son was registered. The clerk leafed through the register of children, and said briefly:

"Jean-Jacques-Rousseau room, fourth line, compartment D."

The Académicien took the arm of Milady Ennui and ventured out along the vast corridors.

From time to time the warders, all dressed in their regulation uniforms, consisting of waterproof apron and cap in the form of a feeding bottle, pointed out the way to the visitors. Marthe and Maurice first went through a long room where workers in different crafts were making sets of baby clothes, then through a second where workmen were making small coffins. From there they went through a courtyard full of baskets on casters, in which children were learning to walk; and finally they arrived in front of a huge workshop lit by the flames of great furnaces.

M. Atout stopped to explain. "Here you see the kitchens where the feed is made for the infants. For many years it used to be thought that the most suitable food for the newly born was their mothers' milk; but chemical analysis has shown us that it is unwholesome and not very nutritious. Consequently, the Academy of Sciences appointed a commission that devised a more balanced formula. It is made up of fifteen parts gelatin, twenty-five parts gluten, twenty parts sugar, and forty parts water, the whole forming a compound known under the name *supra-lacto-gune* or *improved mothers' milk*. Moreover, an infallible test has proved the excellence of this beverage: all the newly born who refuse to take it—and there are many of them—go into a decline and without exception die after two or three days. As for the methods employed to distribute the *supra-lacto-gune*, you will be able to judge for yourselves.

{ 55 }

With these words, M. Atout opened a door, and the visitors found themselves in the feeding room.

It was an enormous gallery, furnished on two sides with what looked like bottle racks in which babies were sitting side by side. In front of each there was a serial number, and the patented feeding bottle that took the place of its mother. A steam-driven pump, positioned at the far end of the room, ensured the supply of the *supra-lacto-gune* to the tubes that delivered the feed to the babies. Feeding began and ended at set times—a proceeding that encouraged the development of regular habits. All had to have the same appetite and the same stomach capacity, on pain of going hungry or suffering indigestion. The same slogan that marked the doors of Republicans in 1793 could have been inscribed over the entrance here:[1]

*Equality or death!*

*Steam power replaces mother love*

M. Atout called on his companions to marvel at the details of this model establishment to which was attributable, in his felicitous expression, the ending of maternal superstition. He proved that the use of these machines had produced savings of three centimes a day per child, which added up in a year to 9 fr. 95 c.; and with ten million newborn babies, a saving of almost a hundred million. He went on to explain how the establishment was divided into nine rooms corresponding to the nine classes in society. Nourishment, care, air, and sunshine were distributed according to the principle of Roman justice: *Habita ratione personarum et dignitatum*. The children of millionaires received nine units, and the sons of beggars the ninth part of one unit—an apprenticeship that prepared both groups for the inequalities of society. One group would be accustomed from day one to demand everything, the other to expect nothing. A wonderful combination that would guarantee forever the stability of the republic.

While these explanations were being delivered, Milady Ennui was looking for her number—that is to say for her son, of whose infant charms she had boasted to Marthe. She finally found him in his pigeonhole; but the *supra-lacto-gune* was having its usual effect, and M. Atout's heir was writhing like a worm cut into quarters.

The doctor on duty was alerted, came at once, and declared that the contortions of number 743 were caused by sharp pains in the region of the colon, referred to in common parlance as colic; but the Académicien contested this etymology. He pointed out that colic had the same root as choler and could only come from the Greek χολη, *bile*. A long discussion ensued, studded with quotations from Madagascan, Syrian, and Chinese sources, while the suffering number was still agonized by the malady with the disputed name. Finally, the doctor and M. Atout, who could not come to an agreement, went their separate ways, each determined to write a paper on the subject.

As for Milady Ennui, shocked by the grimaces of her son and heir, she left with their two guests and was busily pointing out the luxuriousness of everything around them.

The walls were covered in hangings worked in expensive silks, the ceilings embellished with carved moldings, the windows draped with curtains in silk fringed with gold. The pigeonholes of the tiny babies were lined with soft materials; their numbers gleamed on enameled plaques; large fans of gauze with silver stripes ceaselessly kept the moving air fresh in the galleries. In short, everything possible had been done to ensure the comfort of the newly born. They wanted for nothing, except their mothers.

Next to the suite of feeding rooms came the second establishment, dedicated to infants who had been weaned. Here they took children from fifteen months, and from the start put them on a regime that consisted of a course of exercises designed to perfect different functions. There was a piece of equipment that taught them to look, a second which taught them to listen; and there were others to get them used to tasting, feeling, and breathing.

"In your time," said M. Atout to Maurice, "the child was left to himself; he used his lungs without knowing how; he acted without any apprenticeship; he learned how to live by living. What a barbarous system! Only the absence of enlightenment can excuse it. Today we have improved on all that. The human race is simply living matter to which we give a form and a future. Providence plays no part in it, for we have taken over the management of the world that Providence directed without any discernment. We produce men as we produce calico—by improved methods.

For the rest, these studies are merely a prologue to life; it is only on leaving the house of the weaned that each child takes the path that he will one day follow."

"And who indicates this path to him?"

"The doctors at the sorting bureau that you see before you."

In fact, they had arrived at a third building, smaller than the preceding ones, and they went in. It was a phrenological museum where they saw a dozen doctors busily recording different aptitudes. All the time the attendants working in the establishment were bringing in panniers of infants, whose heads they felt, and to whom they gave a name and a destined future according to the bumps observed. The notice hanging round the neck of those examined showed the result of the examination.

*Dr. Cerebellum decides the profession of every child according to its cranium*

There the child received his certification as a great mathematician, a great artist, or a great poet, and all he had to do was to fulfill his destiny. In this way, any uncertainty about vocation disappeared. Instead of setting off at random along twenty different career paths, like a stranger who asks the way from every passerby, you find the path laid out; you have only to set off, follow it, and you are sure to arrive at your goal . . . at least if you have not been shown the wrong path.

From the sorting bureau, Marthe and Maurice went on to the schools. M. Atout, who along with all his other titles held that of Inspector General of Studies, explained everything for them in great detail. The basis of instruction provided at the school in Sans-Pair was Tibetan, a language made more interesting by the fact that it had not been spoken for about a thousand years. The pupils gave four days out of five to it. The rest of the time was spent examining the hieroglyphs from the ancient pyramids of Egypt, of which only one of doubtful authenticity remained, and going more deeply into the difference between the complete absolute and the universal absolute.

The aim of these courses of study was to prepare the pupil for everyday life, and to be a stepping stone to a career in engineering, medicine, or business.

M. Atout, who was eager for his guest to appreciate the breadth of knowledge acquired by students at the establishment, showed him the program for the examination that all had to take before leaving.

### UNIVERSITY OF UNITED PROFESSIONS AND TRADES
## HIGH SCHOOL OF SANS-PAIR
#### SYLLABUS FOR THE BACCALAURÉAT IN ARTS

FOR TIBETAN:
1°   The thirty books of the *History of the Green Tortoise*, by Shah-Rah-Pah-Shah;
2°   The twelve books of the *History of the Black Elephant*, by Rouf-Tapouf;
3°   The six songs from the *Citernes du Désert*, by Felraadi;
4°   Treatise on the *Good Fortune of the One-Eyed*, by the same author;
5°   The speeches of Bal-Poul-Child against Chid-Poul-Bal.

FOR HISTORY:
1°   Give the succession of the kings of the Congo, Patagonia, and Hudson's Bay since Noah;
2°   Analyze the inscription of the Great Pyramid of Egypt, which no longer exists;
3°   Give an account of the expedition of Lord Ellenborough in India, with the number of cattle, sheep, and important persons killed by

the English army; and the campaigns of Marshal Bugeaud in Algeria, with the speeches, toasts, proclamations, orders of the day, to the number of twelve thousand six hundred and forty-three;[2]

4°   Give a list of marriageable princesses provided by Germany to other European states.

## FOR GEOGRAPHY:

1°   Name the different states of the four quarters of the world before the Flood, with their capitals;

2°   Cite all the rivers, lakes, seas, mountains, giving them the names no longer in use;

3°   Indicate precisely the borders of the ancient republic of Andorra, and the famous principality of Monaco;

4°   Discuss the population of the yet unexplored regions that stretch between latitudes 40° and 60°.

## FOR LITERATURE:

The candidate must give an account of different stylistic forms and the method of employing them; explain the idea of the sublime, the flowery, the graceful, and give a history of all men of letters known since the time of Solomon to our own day.

## FOR PHILOSOPHY:

Demonstrate the relationship of all things to the universal by the relationship of the whole to the sum of its parts. Find how the self differs from the nonself, and if the self as it is can become the improved self. Demonstrate the liberty of the plastic causal through its dependence on the concrete phenomenal.

## MATHEMATICS:

Show your knowledge of all the theorems without practical application that algebra, geometry, and trigonometry can supply, and solve all the pointless problems that could be put forward from them.

## PHYSICS:

Give the hypotheses for all the important laws that are the subject of ongoing investigation.

## CHEMISTRY:

Give an account, in the manner of recipes from the *Cuisinière bourgeoise*, of all the ingredients that make up each of the scientific compounds known under the name of *substance*.

Maurice was appalled at the amount of information demanded of the candidates; but fortunately he remembered that, even in his day, the syllabus and reality did not always correspond. For this examination, as doubtless for all the others, one needed only to go through the form—the supreme law for the Brid' Oisons in every age; for whoever asks the impossible knows in advance to expect nothing.[3]

M. Atout then told him about the ingenious methods for acquiring knowledge that were at the disposal of the high school students.

First of all he showed him the classrooms appointed for the study of history, where every wall represented a race, every bench a succession of kings, every beam a theogony. Every object bore a date or recalled an event. It was impossible to hang up one's hat on a peg without being reminded of a famous man, to wipe one's feet on a mat without walking on a revolution. Thanks to this system of mnemonics, as efficient as it was profound, universal history came down to a question of furnishings; the pupil learned in spite of himself, and merely by looking about him. If you were to ask him, for example, the name of the first king of France, he would remember the internal screw of a lock (*vis intérieur*), and reply: *Clo-vis*. If you wanted to know the date of the discovery of America, he would think of the four supports of the rostrum, each one portraying a different number, and answer: 1492. Then, if you wished to know the most important event after the coming of Christianity, he would see the two supporting *bars* that *intruded* into the lecture hall and reply boldly: *the invasion of the bar-barians*.

M. Atout did not neglect to point out to Maurice the advantages of this method, which had made any true understanding unnecessary, and thanks to which one had only to think of two things to remember one.

He then took him to the geography school where the world was sculpted in relief, so that the pupils could form a more exact idea of its beauty and grandeur. The mountains were represented by molehills, the rivers by barometer tubes, and virgin forests by labeled seedlings of watercress. There were cardboard towns, and little tin volcanoes in which very low night-lights were smoking.

A neighboring room contained the entire planetary system, made from plaster of Paris, and set in motion by a two-donkey-power steam-driven machine. The only drawback was that it had been impossible to represent the true proportions of the heavenly bodies, their respective distances, and their real movements; but the pupils, being aware of these slight imperfections, were nonetheless helped to understand what was, by the representation of what was not.

A general museum completed these teaching methods at the high school of Sans-Pair. Samples of all natural materials and all products of human industry had been assembled there. What the child had learned once upon a time by living and by experience was here taught in an artificial situation: he had for reference the entire creation in numbered compartments. They showed him a sample of the ocean in a carafe; Niagara Falls in a fragment of rock; the gold mines of South America at the bottom of a sandy hollow. He studied agriculture in a large glazed cupboard; different industries in display cabinets; machines set out like little models on a cheese plate. The whole world had been reduced for his convenience to a cabinet of samples; he learned about it by playing at dolls' houses, while knowing nothing of the real thing.

Such were the principles of *instruction* adopted in this educational system in Sans-Pair; as for *education,* that rested on an even more ingenious principle.

Since the sole aim of education was to produce worthy citizens—that is to say, citizens with skills to enrich themselves—their system was based solely on the *pursuit of their personal interests.* Each child was trained from an early age in keeping a profit-and-loss account for every one of his actions. Every evening he calculated what he had earned by his conduct during the day: it was known as the examination of conscience. There was a graduated tariff for merits and faults: so much for patience, so much for amiability, so much for good character. Virtues earned allowances or privileges, provided that they were the virtues specified in the prospectus; for the educational system of the republic of *United Interests* showed in this respect a wise prudence: it encouraged only those qualities that would one day be profitable to their owner. Expensive virtues were treated like vices.

Therefore, to encourage the children even more to acquire riches, they initiated them from an early age into the cult of comfort, making it a habit, and immersing them in that stream of material pleasures that make the conscience more supple. Their college was a palace for which industry had exhausted all its marvels. There were riding schools, billiards, a casino for a reading room, and a theater next to the chapel. Every pupil had his own room and a tilbury with a groom for outings.

M. Atout wanted to show Maurice the accommodation for boys, and they found it occupied by a pupil of the sixth grade already completely initiated into the student life.

In other matters the pleasant did not exclude the useful. In the middle of the main courtyard was an Exchange where the pupils all came to-

*A ninth-grade pupil in his room*

gether in the mornings. There they haggled over seasonal fruits, white rabbits, and steel nibs. There, as in the big Exchange in Sans-Pair, there were clever or risky transactions, sudden ruin and sudden wealth. Falls were triggered on the basis of false information, and rises by a joint cornering of the market, so that pupils were trained from early childhood in the legal lie, and acquired the vital habit of trusting no one.

They also made use of the periodical press, writing for four journals that held different opinions, in which they could calumniate and harm one another just as efficiently as grown men do.

After the high school of Sans-Pair came the national college, where the courses were taken by students of any age or gender.

The professor of numismatics, whom Maurice wanted to hear, was that day giving a lecture on nineteenth-century cuisine, while the professor of political economy was examining the question of Mexican antiquities. As for the professor of philosophy, he was completely wrapped up in the study of his subject, and emerged only in order to insult his adversaries.

When they came out, M. Atout showed his guests the schools of law, medicine, industry, and the fine arts; but they did not go in. Their organization differed little from that of the high school, and a review of the doctrines taught there would have taken too long. However, Maurice was to discover later how these doctrines were applied in daily life by businessmen, artists, lawyers, and doctors.

They continued on until they came to the examination hall.

Each school had a special room in which each candidate could be tested without any need for the presence of an examiner. It was a sort of labyrinthine enclosure with a hundred little doors, on each one of which was written a question from the program, with twenty wrong answers mixed in with the right ones. If the candidate selected the correct one, the door opened of its own accord, and he passed on; if not, he stayed shut in like a rat in a trap. In this way, error and unfairness were impossible; the examiner had attained the perfect level of impartiality and detachment so long sought: there was no longer a man with his enthusiasms, his preferred approaches, his dislikes, but a machine immutable as truth. Candidates were no longer selected, but winnowed: here the pick of the wheat; there the bran. The professors no longer had any need to do anything about the examinations except pick up the salary for work they no longer had to do.

As they were leaving the last door of the college campus, M. Atout pointed out a second establishment for the instruction of young ladies. The organization was more or less the same as that for boys; but the knowledge acquired there was essentially different. The principal study was the mastery of the harmonium to accompany folk dancing.[4] The pupils devoted seven hours a day to it. The rest of their time was employed in lessons on mineralogy, architecture, and anatomy. In addition there was a class once a week in orthography, and sewing was an ongoing activity.

Their moral life was regulated by a catechism that served as a rule of conduct for young girls; it was a text that they had to learn by heart. There was a chapter on grooming, a chapter on balls and on visiting, a chapter on marriage.

*Question:* Should a woman desire marriage?
*Answer:* Yes, if she can marry well.
*Question:* How would you define a woman who marries well?
*Answer:* She who, having married an honorable man, takes advantage of that position and enjoys it.
*Question:* What do you mean by an honorable man?
*Answer:* I mean a man who is wealthy enough to be eligible.
*Question:* How should a woman love her husband?
*Answer:* In proportion to the allowance he gives her.
*Question:* Can you recite the litany of your hopes in marriage?
*Answer:* Oh! My God, I trust in your infinite goodness to provide me with a husband after my own heart; may he be rich enough to give me a carriage, a mansion, the best seats in the theater of Sans-Pair;

and may he, dear God, be bold enough to increase his fortune, so that I may have the pleasure of spending it.

Maurice read no further. He asked the Académicien if the two great educational institutions that he had been shown were the only public establishments for education in Sans-Pair.

"There are also institutions that serve industry in particular," replied M. Atout—"junior schools, boarding schools, high schools, teaching all known areas of knowledge by every method ever devised. But the most famous of all these establishments is that run by M. Hatif, who has found a way of employing the hothouse system in the instruction of children, and who produces *forced* scholars, just as gardeners used to obtain melons of the best quality. All he has to do is place the pupils in a greenhouse that serves to speed up their intellectual development, and to keep a careful watch on the thermometer which shows the degree of heat necessary for the maturation of their brains. In this way he always maintains, under bell jars, some hundred school children who are grown men at ten and children again at twenty.

"Moreover, his factory for prodigies is successful. It is his workshop that produces all those virtuosos who compose symphonies in the cradle, the great mathematicians who calculate the circumference of the Earth before they can talk, and the precocious poets who write their first elegies before cutting their first teeth."[5]

*Pupils raised under glass like vegetables*

# §VIII

*Expansion of emporia selling the latest things—Story of Mademoiselle Romain—
Picturesque view of the town of Sans-Pair—Illness of Milady Ennui, treated
by forty medical specialists, and cured by Maurice—Insurance company
aiming to lessen the grief felt by the living for the dead—Meeting
with the great philosopher, M. Philadelphe le Doux.*

While he was furnishing these details, the Académicien had reached his carriage, and was about to get into it when Milady Ennui declared that she would like to take Marthe to the new galleries of the *Good Shepherd.*

It was an emporium in which all the products of the known world had been brought together for the benefit of the customer. It covered an area of two hundred hectares, and employed twelve thousand assistants. In addition to the line of omnibuses serving the interior, provision for a file of vehicles had been arranged at each counter. Fabrics rolling round between immense cylinders passed before the eyes of the crowd like the moving curtains that represent waterfalls at the opera. There were enormous displays, decorated with gold and jewels, revolving automatically; there were shelves filled with crystal, carved ivory, precious ornaments, which came round and round on copper rails, and they seemed to captivate the shoppers. Finally, in the midst of all this brilliance, liveried servants circulated with platters, offering refreshments.

"As you see," said M. Atout, "trade has increased like everything else; it's just a perfect goldmine. Profits, which once allowed a hundred thousand families to live in moderate comfort, have created ten royal life styles with money for anything. Your age was still the era of little tradesmen. After an apprenticeship, one married and opened a shop with one's beloved and one's courage. But today, goodwill cannot be used for capital, and the first rule in setting up a business is not to know something about it; it is to be a millionaire."

At these words, the Académicien began adding up in a loud voice for Maurice's benefit the value of the goods piled up in the galleries they were passing through, while Milady Ennui drew Marthe's attention to their prodigious variety.

But Maurice and Marthe were no longer listening, for they had just caught sight of the sign over the monster hyperstore: THE GOOD SHEP-HERD. Immediately they exchanged glances; their lips simultaneously murmured the name of Mademoiselle Romain, and they became very thoughtful.

This was because the name had awakened in them the memory of another world: one of those memories that melt the heart like the sight of the old hearth, where you listened to the stories told by your nurse; the little garden where you planted sprigs of hawthorn; the boundary stone that served as a bench for the beggar with whom you shared the lunch you were taking to school. Mademoiselle Romain, however, was neither a relation nor a playmate; she was just an old neighbor, a haberdasher at the sign of THE GOOD SHEPHERD.

But what a neighbor! And how could one forget her? Who could possibly have seen her down in her little shop without remembering her high-backed chair on casters, her foot-warmer, her big knitting needles, the wrinkles on her face redeemed by a big smile.

For God, who had been hard on Mademoiselle Romain, had caused her to be born poor, sickly, and unfortunate. She would have had every right to complain about her lot, but she preferred to look for whatever hidden good could be found. Her poverty ruled out indulgence, and she accepted it as a safeguard against excess. There was no respite from her sufferings, and yet they were for her a lesson in patience. Her plainness robbed her of the hope of being loved, but she made up for it by loving others.

And yet God had not been entirely without pity. Instead of giving her good fortune, He gave her a great duty to perform.

Mademoiselle Romain had a father who was paralyzed and depended on her entirely. His body was useless, but his mind retained its faculties; his heart was strong. Although he was incapable of promoting his own well-being or protecting himself against misfortune, he was still capable of feeling happiness or pain.

His daughter understood this and resolved to make his life as happy as possible. She spent all she had on buying merchandise, and set up in business at THE GOOD SHEPHERD. The shop was small, and many of the shelves were empty; but this saintly young woman had the faith of the great-hearted. Ready to make any sacrifice for the one she had vowed to care for, she could not believe that Providence would let her down. Would that not be akin to thinking God less generous than ourselves? Sitting by the counter, knitting in hand, she stopped working only when a customer came in; and if that customer kept her waiting too long, or if anxiety or discouragement slowed the movement of her long wooden needles, she would look into the back shop and see the old cripple who relied on her so confidently and cheerfully, and the needles would click away more rapidly. Her earnings were undoubtedly meager, but who can say what miracles can be achieved through good housekeeping and dedication? All that Mademoiselle Romain earned was devoted to the well-being of the old man; he mistakenly thought her to be wealthier when she deprived herself, and enjoyed these sacrifices without ever knowing the painful truth. His daughter thanked heaven for his error, which she thought of as a blessing; and to make herself worthy of it, she took on new responsibilities.

A poor woman, whom she had occasionally employed, died, leaving a mentally retarded son. Mademoiselle Romain took him in initially, so that he need not stay in the same room as the coffin of his mother; but on the following day, when she intended to take him to the orphanage, her heart failed her. The child had already claimed his place by the hearth, leaning his head against the knees of the invalid, looking up and smiling at the one who had given him a home.

Her heart melting, she thought to herself: "He could have been my brother." And, looking again at the two unfortunate creatures whom God seemed to have consigned to her care, she said to herself: "He is my brother!"

*The paralytic and the idiot*

And the child never left her.

When Marthe and Maurice knew her, the old man and the idiot still lived with her, happy because of her efforts and her labor and her tender ministrations. The shop was still just as small, the shelves carried hardly any more stock, but everybody knew Mademoiselle Romain, and everybody bought from her. Old people made her their confidante; the young greeted her as if she were beautiful, and mothers taught their children to respect her. How many times had Maurice and Marthe passed the narrow window of her shop, hand in hand, just to see her?

"There's the good lady!" they would say in whispered tones, "the one we should try to be like."

And they called her name, and when she answered, they went proudly on their way, full of kind thoughts, and vowing to be like her.

Ah! What are all the riches piled up in the galleries of Sans-Pair compared with this humble little shop, the sight of which is a lesson in itself? What are all the thousands of attendants compared with the little woman whose courage alone had sustained two lives and saved two souls? Alas! If God had arranged for her to come into the world later, into a more enlightened society, she would have lived and hoped in vain. *Goodwill could no longer take the place of money!*

Before taking his two guests back home, the Académicien wanted to give them some idea of the magnificence of Sans-Pair; and so he took them to the fine Union Square.

It was the city square where all the roads in the capital converged; it was embellished with fifty drinking fountains and two hundred gas lamps. The museum, the library, the national theater, and the chamber of deputies surrounded it, their magnificent facades decorated with posters painted in oils. Streets radiated outward, forming seemingly endless straight lines, all fronted by quadrangular buildings that looked so much alike that they could only be distinguished by their house numbers. A forest of smoking chimneys crowned this charming perspective that one could take in at a single glance.

The twenty-four zones which made up the town were designated by the twenty-four letters of the alphabet, and each citizen was required to live in the quarter corresponding to the first letter of his profession.[1] This arrangement had the slight disadvantage of locating your boot maker sixty-eight kilometers from your tailor; but it gave a regularity to the town that would have done credit to a chessboard; and if everyday relationships suffered, at least the ideal of rationality was satisfied.

*Picturesque view of the capital of the civilized world in the year 3000*

However, this arrangement had recently been sharply criticized by a learned astronomer, M. de l'Empyrée, because it was based on the duo-decimal system long ago abandoned for everything else. For that reason he had proposed, in the interest of mathematical unity, the demolition of Sans-Pair, and its rebuilding in ten divisions, corresponding to the ten digits of the numbers table. Everyone would be allocated a place accord-ing to merit—that is, according to how much tax they paid. This pro-found concept had caused a great stir—enough to distract public atten-tion from the discoveries on the moon, attributable, as has already been mentioned, to the same learned gentleman.

Maurice noted that the houses, which were built of iron, could be dis-mantled like pieces of furniture. If the owner moved house, all he had to do was get in touch with a firm of household removers who would trans-port his dwelling to the new quarter assigned to him.

The servants' quarters posed even fewer problems: they consisted of a large machine-made box, which could be locked. When evening came, the box became a bedroom with alcove and washroom. There was no need for a kitchen since the invention of the headset stove that allowed each smoker to prepare three plates using the heat of his pipe, and the lighter-pressure cooker that allowed one to prepare a soup and two beef steaks using the flame of a single match.

On returning to the harbor, the young couple saw an island where vil-las that they had not previously noticed nestled in woodland groves. They learned from their guide that it was the great floating village, *The Cos-mopolitan*, arriving back from its world tour.[2]

This extraordinary ship was several kilometers in length. There was a cottage for every passenger, with flower border, farmyard, and vegetable patch. In the middle of the village was the church, and at one end the concert hall. One hundred and fifty engines of four hundred horsepower each drove *The Cosmopolitan*, which raced through the waves with the speed of a Leviathan. Its voyage round the world took eight days. It called at New Guinea, sailed through the canal cut through the Isthmus of Panama, crossed the Atlantic Ocean, came back through the Mediterranean, entered the Red Sea by the Strait of Suez, and returned to its home port across the Indian Ocean.

The passengers who had tired of life at sea disembarked at Cairo. There they joined the great Asian railway, which took them as far as Malacca in house cars. These were houses on wheels, complete with bedrooms, restaurant, billiards, tavern, and Russian baths.

An armada of other boats, all of which were flying streamers advertising their different destinations, rode the waves near *The Cosmopolitan*. Some were floating theaters that traversed the oceans and sailed up rivers, bringing to the most remote inhabitants the pleasures of vaudeville or the rather more serious fare of comic opera. Others, constructed as ballrooms, traveled to the five continents, teaching the inhabitants the quadrilles of the Musardians of Sans-Pair.[3] Finally, the smallest vessels containing dioramas, menageries, or reading rooms dropped anchor in every inlet in the inhabited world to make people acquainted with the beauties of nature, performing animals, and the novels of M. César Robinet.[4]

A little further on, our travelers came to the great dockyard where was brought the produce of all the world's known mines. A system of underground canals, fed by water from the mines, linked these together and so enabled all operations to work together as part of one system.

On the docks of Sans-Pair one could see arriving, from a thousand gloomy caverns, barges filled with different minerals dug from the earth and transported by men of every race and costume. Here it was the Chinese with lead and tin; there, Spaniards with mercury; further on, Sicilians were bringing sulfur from their volcanoes. The Americans brought treasures in gold; the English loads of black coal; Africans consignments of bitumen; and peoples from the North brought copper, iron, and platinum. The ease and speed of communication had brought all the nations together without the intervention of any other unifying body. Each group had lost its distinguishing characteristics, but had not acquired those of the others. Their vacant faces were like coins worn away by use, which had lost their imprint and only differed because they were made of different metals. Because they had come to regard the world as a great highway, they had all lost their sense of nationality: they no longer had a town, or a hearth; and, in consequence, they had no motherland. Places were no more than bases of operation to which individuals were briefly attached, like posters pasted on the wall of an inn.

Maurice was beginning to share his observations with his guide when he was interrupted by Milady Ennui, who felt exhausted and wanted to go home. So, they got back into their flying carriage and returned to the townhouse of the Académicien. But, although the journey was very rapid, it was enough to increase Madame Atout's indisposition. As soon as they arrived, she declared that she was worse and had to see a doctor.

The problem was to know which doctor, for the progress of knowledge had brought the division of labor even into the sciences. Doctors had divided up the human body which had traditionally been indivisible. Each one had his own specialty and claimed no expertise outside that. One took the head, another the stomach; to this one the liver; to that one the heart. If a number of organs were affected at the same time, you consulted a number of doctors; if all organs were affected, you consulted even more. Each doctor treated his own area of illness, and the patient was cured in bits, if he did not die all in one piece.

Since Milady Ennui was suffering from spasms in particular, it seemed a good idea to send for Doctor Hypertrophe.

The doctor explained first that, since life was maintained by the blood, and the blood was kept in circulation by the heart, every illness was necessarily caused by a failure to maintain equilibrium in a weak and flabby cardiac muscle. After examining the patient he declared that her indisposition was caused by too great a flow into the left auricle, and he prescribed an anti-phlogistic mixture of which he was the inventor.

But he had only just left when the pains of the invalid moved to another spot. M. Atout immediately called for Doctor Jecur, well known for his work on the bile ducts.

When he had examined Milady Ennui, he declared that the source of her illness was evidently in the liver, in a gland that was responsible for separating bile from the blood, and which—since it was the very principle of life itself—determined health or sickness. But his prescriptions were no more successful than those of his colleague, and after he had gone, the pain spread to her limbs.

At this point, the Académicien turned to Doctor Névretique, who specialized in illnesses that had no apparent cause.

This doctor bounded in, exclaiming:

"The nerves! the nerves! . . . organs of the will . . . of sensation . . . everything is there . . . nothing else counts!"

He walked three times round the bed of the invalid, prescribed dances and entertainments, with an infusion of orange leaves, and left.

However, the choking sensation suffered by Milady Ennui did not go away, and M. Atout continued to call on the knowledge of the various specialists in vain, until Maurice remembered the sort of padded suit of armor that encased milady. Rather hesitantly he had the suggestion passed on to her that she should get out of it, and the result was instantaneous. Madame Atout, who now found herself able to move freely, was suddenly cured. The cause of her illness was merely a breathing problem, and had she not consulted a lung specialist, she would inevitably have died of asphyxiation.

While giving her the necessary attention, the Académicien summoned a notary and witnesses in order to record the illness of Madame Atout. When she had recovered, he took the certificate they had drawn up and went off with Maurice to the office of the *Company of the Centenarians.*

There, one could insure not only one's life but also one's health; and one could receive compensation for the most trivial indisposition, just as once upon a time one could receive compensation from the Phoenix Company for a small fire. By this means, the illness of your parents allowed you to live, while you waited for them to die and enrich you. Self-interest kept affection in check: you consoled yourself for their suffering by calculating how much money their sufferings would bring. Their end, perceived as the supreme bonus, seemed less cruel, and arithmetic with its consoling figures eased the pain of broken hearts.

Thus, arithmetic had neutralized the sting of death . . . at least for the survivors.

As they came out, the Académicien saw a policyholder leaving the mortuary, and recognized M. Philadelphe le Doux, President of the *Humane Society* of Sans-Pair, and member of all the philanthropical societies of the inhabited world.

He was covered in bows of black crepe, signaling the number of cruel losses he had suffered, and a commissionaire followed him loaded with sacks of money that attested to the consolation offered by the company.

When M. Atout caught sight of him, that modestly contented smile of the prudent man who has done well for himself played about his lips; but as soon as he saw Maurice and his companion, his expression changed, and an air of melancholy immediately clouded his face.

*An heir who has just received the insurance money for his deceased relatives*

M. Atout stopped to speak to him and was anxious to know what had happened.

"Alas! As you can see," said the philanthropist, whose melancholy glance strayed from the mourning ribbons to the commissionaire, "Providence has grievously afflicted me! My brother . . . my uncle . . . my cousin!"

He stopped with a groan and dabbed his eyes with the bankers' orders clutched in his hand.

"Ah! It all comes back to me," said the Académicien, who seemed to be remembering something. "All three were aboard the flotilla of balloons that caught fire?"

"You should really say four," replied M. le Doux, " because my nephew was there too. . . . It is for him especially that I shed tears! . . . To die at twenty years of age! . . . and the directors of the company refuse compensation for this precious life! . . . They want me to supply positive proof of his death! Can you believe it? Me supply proof! . . . These wretches have no soul! . . . to say nothing of the fact that I have already conducted a vain search. But I will force them to honor their commitments . . . in the interests of the public. I shall accept this grievous burden."

At this point, the philanthropist turned his head again, as if to calculate what this heavy burden might add to that of the commissionaire. The Académicien took the opportunity to offer the customary condolences. After plagiarizing the ode of Malherbe to Duperrier, with many quotations from dead languages—a stratagem that always carries weight with those who know only living ones—he gave a statistical rundown of all the misfortunes that the four deceased had escaped in departing this life, and arrived at the conclusion that the only one to be pitied was their surviving heir.

M. le Doux seemed to find some consolation in this reiteration of his misfortune, and thanked M. Atout. Whatever his woes might be, he hoped to sweeten them through the noble exercise of philanthropy. The human race would be his family. Henceforward he wished to devote himself entirely to spreading the gospel of his society: *Look after yourself! Heaven will do nothing for you.*

He then reminded the Académicien that he had promised to subscribe to their work, and asked him to attend an exhibition by the wards of the society the next day.

# §IX

*Esplanade of Sans-Pair embellished with giant vegetables—Marriage bureau licensed by the government (no guarantees) —An arithmetical pastorale— A happy monster—Philosophical memoirs of King Extra.*

While they were discussing these matters, the two of them arrived at the gate of a public garden where crowds of people were walking. They went in with Maurice so that he could admire the plants.

The arrangement was entirely different from anything the young man had seen before. Along the principal avenues, colossal cabbages took the place of flowering chestnuts, and alternate rows of tree-sized lettuces replaced groves of acacia and sweet-smelling limes. As for the flowers, they had been replaced by tobacco, rice, and indigo.

M. le Doux drew Maurice's attention to these felicitous changes.

"You will see," he said, "that thanks to the efforts of economists and philanthropists, the face of the earth has so changed that God himself would not recognize it. Everything that was just for display has vanished. Leguminous plants, now enlarged and perfected, form the basis of our system of forestry. Where you had ridiculous oak trees that produced no more than acorns, we have the giant beetroot. In place of your rose trees, which were only of use to the perfume maker, we have planted forests of liquorice and an improved strain of radish. Thus everything has been tailored to the needs of man, who has reduced the whole of creation to the proportions of his stomach."

Maurice said nothing. His attention, initially focused on the plantings, had wandered toward some women who were walking along an alley way of enormous artichokes. At the entrance to the path was this inscription:

### MARRIAGE AVENUE

Each stroller had a sash round her, which gave her address and the amount of her dowry.

The avenue ended in a vast rotunda, under constant siege from crowds of people. It was the principal matrimonial agency of Sans-Pair. There, one could always find a complete assortment of lonely hearts, along with all the necessary information about age, character, fortune, and color of hair. The walls were covered with posters where the notices of the establishment were posted, and most of these were adorned with explanatory illustrations, the ingenuity of which Maurice found remarkable.

The first one to catch Maurice's attention was an enormous wallet stuffed with bank notes to the value of three million; and below it was this simple notice

## A GENTLEMAN SEEKS MARRIAGE.

Another notice presented a picture of a lady, taken from behind, with this statement :

# A WIDOW
### Who has already brought happiness to five husbands
### WOULD LIKE TO DO THE SAME FOR A SIXTH.
**For her dowry she will bring a graceful bearing and a tender heart**
## *Please write.*
*(Include a stamped addressed envelope.)*

A little further on there were the profiles of four women, linked by the chain of a purse; and underneath was written:

# THE FATHER OF A FAMILY

## The head of a house of several Daughters

### WISHES TO DISPOSE OF THEM BECAUSE HE IS MOVING

*There is one brunette, one blond, one redhead, and one of indeterminate color.*

## EACH ONE WILL RECEIVE ON MARRIAGE,

### A Sum of Sixty Thousand Francs.

*Please note: Only suitors who have been vaccinated*
*three times will be considered.*

While Maurice was engaged in perusing these unusual announcements, a kinswoman of M. le Doux arrived. She had just arranged the marriage of her son with the daughter of a wealthy attorney in Sans-Pair; she pointed out the two young people sitting a little way off, talking quietly to each other in a sequestered spot, while the families finished discussing the time and details of arrangements for the wedding. The philanthropist and the Académicien were invited to join the family council.

As for Maurice, once he had set eyes on the engaged couple, he could not look away. He knew the meaning of each gesture; guessed the reason for every smile. He understood without hearing what they said, simply by remembering his own experience.

This was because he too had lived through those enchanted hours that are the prelude to possession: delightful confidings in which a young girl, still bashful but without any sense of embarrassment, hesitantly begins this charmingly poetic exchange in which every phrase is a new beginning. She recalls all her doubts, fears, and hopes. Then, after all these doubts, comes the planning: an entire future to fill with anticipations, with visions, perhaps even with sufferings, but sufferings shared by the two of them; dangers to be faced with hands tightly clasped and hearts beating in unison to withstand whatever blows might be in store. Ah! Who can have known these first dreams of youth and then forget them? Even when they have disappeared, one still quivers at the mention of them, like the blind man lost in darkness who hopes to see once more through the eyes of others.

Without being aware of it, Maurice had yielded to his desire, and, while his companions were busy with their discussion, he had drawn near the young couple who, completely absorbed in their heart-to-heart talk, were oblivious to all around.

The young man was leaning close to his young fiancée, and she, her eyes lowered, was absentmindedly playing with the ribbon of her belt.

"Yes," he was murmuring in honeyed tones, "yes, you were the love of my childhood and my youth, or rather, I never dared to hope as much."

"And, no doubt, you said the same to many others," the young lady replied modestly.

"Who else could have so much to recommend her," said the young fiancé warmly: "A dowry of fifteen hundred thousand francs!"

"Not counting other hopeful expectations."

"Yes, I have heard about that. You have an uncle suffering from gout."

"And a cousin with dropsy."

"With no children?"

"And no relations."

"And from whom you will inherit before long?"

"The doctors have given up on both of them."

"Ah! You are an angel," said the husband-to-be, seizing the hand of the prospective heiress and kissing it with unfeigned delight.

Maurice did not want to hear any more, and hurried to rejoin his guide.

As they were walking down the last avenue, M. Atout stopped abruptly and pointed at a couple who were coming toward them. The woman was charming and young, and her companion was a dwarf of a man so hideous that one could hardly bear to look at him. But one monstrous feature made all the other unfortunate aspects of his appearance pale into insignificance. The annals of science record it only rarely. A bull's horn pro-

jected in the middle of his forehead, making his face grotesque and terrible at the same time.

Maurice's instinctive reaction was horror, and his second was pity.

"Do not feel sorry for him," said M. Atout, who had just greeted him:
"To that horn he owes his peace of mind, fortune, and fame—even the
pretty woman who married him!"

Maurice was dumbfounded.

"King Extra was for a long time like other men," the Académicien
went on, "and he shudders to recall that time. To hear the rest of the story
you should read his memoirs, which he published at the beginning of his
complete works."

"That's easy to arrange, since I have already bought them," observed
M. le Doux, presenting Maurice with a magnificently illustrated volume.

The young man opened it there and then, and since his two guides had
business with their banker, he asked if he could wait for them in the little
celery walk at the end of the esplanade.

In addition to his speeches to the Chamber of Deputies, King Extra's
book contained a number of philosophical treatises and elegies addressed
by him to the most beautiful women in the four corners of the world. At
the beginning there was the biographical preface to which M. Atout had
referred as his *Memoirs*. Maurice immediately began to read them.

### TO THE READER.

"On the 15th August 1971, the groans of a woman could be heard coming from one of the most humble dwellings in the tradesmen's quarter of
Sans-Pair. The groans, muted at first, then louder, then more desperate,
were suddenly interrupted by a thin piercing cry: a baby's cry! That baby
was me; that woman was my mother.

"I had just arrived in the world; all I had to do was live.

"To live! How many things that word encompasses! To live means to be
forever exploring the unknown, attempting the impossible, seeking the
infinite, making one's long and difficult journey in life!

"I began by cutting my teeth!

"Having cut my teeth, I went to school. There I outshone most of my
classmates, and every year I was crowned with laurels; but a rival, whom
fate had placed in close proximity, overshadowed me completely. This rival's name was Claude Mirmidon. He was scarcely three feet tall, but as
soon as he appeared, all eyes were turned on him, admiring his amiability
and marveling at his intelligence. Every laurel seemed twice as impressive

on his small brow: I was as tall as the next man, and the world was content to say: Well! He's all right!

"On leaving high school, I hoped to find a place in the administration and set to work making applications. Every day I sought audience with men of power and influence, in order that my presence would remind them that I was there, waiting; but no one noticed me: I was merely a face in the crowd. Mirmidon came in his turn, and from the very first moment he attracted attention. Everyone wanted to know all about him; they were fascinated by him; a few days later he was given the position I had been hoping for those last three years.

"Rejected by the powers that be, I turned to the world of letters. As is the common practice, I wrote a glossary in which I developed—under different letters of the alphabet—a series of philosophical, literary, and political ideas. My book should have secured a place for me among the elite of the writing fraternity; but unfortunately all the booksellers refused to read it on the grounds that it was my first book. One must make one's début with the second!

"'If only you had some other claim to fame,' the most affable of them objected. 'If only you were famous like Mr. Mirmidon, from whom I have just bought a volume of elegies. Everyone wants to know what kind of verse such a diminutive poet writes. But what sort of stir would a book written by someone of your size create?'

"I gave up in despair!

"My only consolation in the midst of all these woes was my love for a young kinswoman whom I was going to marry. Reflecting on the matter, I trembled lest my Lilliputian rival should rob me of this happiness. Like me, he was a welcome visitor at the home of Blondinette, whom he entertained with a thousand party pieces. He hid behind the stovepipe to sing romantic songs; he danced the polonaise on the chairs, and walked blindfolded through a maze covered with eggshells. At first, I scoffed at the childishness of these turns; but Blondinette, who enjoyed them, took offense at my remarks. Then I complained about the liberties she allowed Mirmidon to take, and she maintained that he was so small that he could not be treated like an ordinary person. Finally, I lost my temper and told her she must choose between me and the little man. She replied at once that her choice was made, and showed me the door. I stormed out, choking with rage.

"At this last setback, I was completely disheartened. Tired of aspiring in vain to fame, to position, to love, I decided to end it all. I bought the necessary poison, and having drunk it, I waited calmly, like Socrates, for *the vision of that day which has no yesterday and no tomorrow.*

"But I had reckoned without my druggist. The poison he sold me was adulterated and only managed to half-kill me. I hovered for a whole month between life and death, calling loudly for one, and perhaps less loudly for the other. However, my attempt had an immediate effect. A whole host of friends, who had neglected me when I was hale and hearty, wanted to see me when they heard I had tried to poison myself, and they brought all the toxicologists in Sans-Pair, one after the other to see me. The treatment lasted for a whole year. Finally, I could get up; but the poison had taken a terrible toll. I had undergone a complete transformation, and had become what you see now.

"When I looked at myself in the mirror, I was horrified. My first reaction was despair; my second, shame. I asked myself what abyss would be deep enough and dark enough to hide my ugliness, and I bemoaned the fact that I had not died.

"Mr. Blaguefort found me in very low spirits. He had only come, he said, to see me and assure himself that I was cured. However, after examining me very closely, he unhesitatingly proposed a hundred thousand écus for the commercial exploitation of the horn that I now bore. I thought he was mocking me, and ordered him out; but he came back that very evening and doubled his offer. I chased him out again. He sent me a letter proposing eight hundred thousand francs, then a million!

"My depression gradually changed to surprise—almost to elation! What I had regarded as an embarrassment became an unexpected source of wealth. I looked again in the mirror at the ornament on my forehead; and it seemed less odd than before. Evidently, prejudice had played a large part in my first reactions. Did not the primitive peoples of America once upon a time regard the antlers of the elk and the bison as the most graceful adornments for a warrior? Did not the knights of the Middle Ages top their helmets with crescents of steel; and were not the brilliant horns of Moses the sign of superhuman power?[1] Among the wise peoples of Greece, as among the warlike northern nations, the horn has always been regarded as a cornucopia—a symbol of power and plenty. A coarse joke from barbarous times has succeeded in making it an object of ridicule; but the day of its rehabilitation had come.

"After considering these rationalizations, and many others equally convincing, I found such a change in my ideas that, instead of despairing because I had a horn, I regretted having only one. Two horns would obviously have presented a more symmetrical and elegant appearance. For two horns, one could demand two million.

"For the time being, however, I was content with what I had got.

"My exhibition was a prodigious success. People came from all over the world to see King Extra—that was the name Blaguefort gave me. The most exalted personnages in the republic invited me to their receptions. I was lionized. Everyone wished to hear me, to converse with me; and the monster was recognized as a wit.

"Various kind-hearted ladies wrote to me, out of curiosity. I responded in courtly verse which made my fortune, and from then on I was the one to whom society turned for that style of writing. Every day my office was filled with albums, which I had to inscribe, and with letters begging for an answer. I wrote and wrote without stopping for rest; and in this manner I acquired universal fame. All the women who received a verse from my hands never tired of talking about the range of my knowledge, the profundity of my judgements, the range of my imagination. The old publishers who had turned down my philosophical manuscript came running to buy my madrigals.

"Their publication was quite an event. The great literary Panjandrum himself deigned to bang every drum to promote them. Having delivered a lengthy review of my book, while managing to say nothing about it, he exclaimed:

At last we have a new writer of undoubted style, and what style! Oh! What a beautifully pointed form to inspire the rest of us young scribblers who relish the bold approach. What a felicitous and charming prodigy whose very genius is monstrous!

"This important testimonial made the heads of government decide to make use of my great abilities. As I had been working in the fields of literature and the fine arts, naturally they put me in charge of stud farms. I was given the title of Guardian-in-Chief of the Stallions of the Republic.

*Perfect stallions*

"These new duties gave me a social position that gave me entry into political assemblies, temperance societies, and philanthropic clubs. My presence as a speaker brought in the crowds. My horn was a guarantee of my eloquence.

"Finally, election day arrived. The druggists' quarter had always been distinguished by its choice of deputies to the national assembly. They had sent one after the other the giant Pelion, who one day walked out carrying the rostrum on his shoulders, the mimic Perruchot, who was expert in imitating any voice and assuming any appearance, and finally the magician Souplet who created majorities by making ballot papers vanish from the box. To follow in the footsteps of such men, they had to find an equal talent. The honor of the electoral district was at stake. Someone mentioned my name. It was greeted with great applause, and I was chosen as the representative of the druggists at the National Assembly of the United Interests.

"These were not the only successes. There were others, less obvious perhaps, but more gratifying. Feminine curiosity had remained as strong as ever. Having seen what I knew about writing, the boldest ones among them wanted to find out what I knew about loving. The monster is as rare a creature as Antinoüs, and the experience was worth trying. In all probability, I came out of it not too badly, for my reputation grew and grew.

"These easy conquests, however, could not make me forget my cousin Blondinette. She was the only woman who, to my shame, had rejected me, and consequently the only one whose memory was precious to me; for there is always something contrary in love.

"She herself regretted her imprudence in breaking off our relationship. From that time on I had too great an advantage over Mirmidon to view him as a serious rival. I boldly went to see her, was received with emotion, and after a few days Blondinette had grown completely accustomed to my new appearance. As I told her the size of my income, my legs seemed to her more normal, my horn less obvious. At the first million she found me passable; at the second, she declared that I was charming.

"Our marriage was celebrated with all the pomp that such an occasion demands. The archbishop of Sans-Pair himself was eager to give us his blessing.

"Since that day, my happiness has known neither interruption nor diminution, and fortune has smiled on me so constantly that I am now known not just as *King Extra,* but as the *Happy Monster.*

"As for the readers who ask why I have recounted the story of my life at some length in the preface to this volume, I say it is to point a lesson. Here is that lesson: success depends less on your worth than on how you present yourself. The first requisite for success is not to *do* anything, but to make sure that everyone knows about you. It follows that genius can be useful, something absurd will occasionally do, something vicious will often suffice, but there is nothing like monstrosity."

# §X

*A high-society poisoner—Law Courts of Sans-Pair—Route map of legal
probity—Procedures for the development of eloquence in lawyers—
Tariffs for the seven deadly sins—The old beggar and his dog.*

Maurice had just finished his reading when his host and M. le Doux came
out from their meeting with the bankers. The philanthropist told them
that he was obliged to leave them to go to the Law Courts.

"Is there a big case going on at the moment?" asked M. Atout.

"What!" exclaimed M. le Doux. "You mean to say you haven't heard of
it? The day after tomorrow a judgement will be given in the famous poisoning case."

"Of Doctor Papaver?"

"Precisely. The accused has sent out invitations to all and sundry, but
he has forgotten about me! Can you believe it? Me, a former colleague! We
once served together as vice presidents of the *Humane Society.* But I must
stake my claim, especially since twenty or so ladies who knew I was a
friend of the doctor have asked to come. They say it's going to be magnificent: six hundred witnesses and sixty attorneys! The president has
arranged for cakes and lemonade to be available during the proceedings;
so one can have a little snack while the court is in recess."

"And this Doctor Papaver is accused of poisoning someone?" Maurice
inquired.

"A whole family," the philanthropist replied, "seven people whose perfectly preserved remains will be put on display. You'll see how these testify
to the effects of the poison, and be able to read letters that compromise
a lady from the highest circles. What's more, the doctor's six-year-old
daughter will testify against her father. It's the most interesting case to at-
tract attention these last ten years! Already the admission tickets are selling for two hundred francs."

M. Atout declared that he certainly had to get some, and he followed
the philanthropist into the court.

Over the main entrance stood a huge statue of Justice, blindfolded so
that there could be no doubt about her clear-sightedness. In her left hand
she carried a pair of scales, and in her right a sword, as if to show that she
cared less about weighing the evidence than about meting out retribution.
On the pediment were engraved these words:

## THE ADMINISTRATION OF JUSTICE IS FREE

And beneath one could read the list of charges for the various services without which one could not see justice done: so much for registration, so much for the clerk's office, so much for the stamp, so much for experts, so much for the solicitor, so much for the barrister. The whole came to a sum that permitted only the wealthy to go to court to safeguard their rights.

Happily, the poor were consoled by the maxim inscribed over each doorway:

## ALL CITIZENS ARE EQUAL BEFORE THE LAW

Maurice first passed through a room where the lawyers were submitting the statements of their expenses to a judge who was responsible for these matters. The size of the claim was fixed in advance.

*Measuring the size of the bill*

Thirty meters of the roll for short cases, a hundred for serious matters, a thousand for complex issues. When it came to filling the pages, the lawyers had devised a very simple method. It consisted of following each word with all the others that had any significant collocation with it, thereby allowing them to scan the dictionary for one phrase.

If, for instance, they had to issue a summons for a witness to appear in a week's time, they never failed to write:

"In consequence of the reasons given above, and of all others that we might find it expedient to issue at a later date:

"Without committing ourselves either implicitly or explicitly:

"Have named, called, summoned, served a writ upon—by means fixed, as much by usage and custom as by decrees, ordinances and laws—the undermentioned:

"To present himself and to appear in court, without putting forward any objection, any challenge, or any plea of nonreceipt:

"In order to reply truthfully, freely, categorically, and clearly, whether it be on information that he himself has, relative to the affair, whether it be on hearsay, whether it be on inference suggested by logic or analogy:

"Which subpoena and summons are served for an appearance in a week's time—that is to say on the eighth day following this day; or, to put it another way, so that there will be no room for doubt, or wrong interpretation, for the . . . February in the year . . . .

"Which day is duly appointed, except for any error in the date or the calculation of days."

This ingeniously long drawn-out document was written on paper bearing an official stamp, in letters eight millimeters high, with spaces between the lines and indented paragraphs. And all this that Justice might shine more clearly . . . and to bump up the expense account.

While M. Atout and the philanthropist were going down to the Public Prosecutor to get tickets, Maurice entered the hall of lost causes, where he found a crowd of legal gentlemen in their robes, all pursuing different branches of the law.[1]

First of all there were the lawyers in training, gathered round the old hands whose task it was to teach them the exact boundaries of the law. Their exposition was made simpler by the use of an immense synoptic table containing the whole body of legislation for the United Interests. Colored lines, similar to those on our geographical maps that mark the conquests of Alexander or the invasion of the Barbarians, indicated the permitted range of their operations. One could see the byways into which the most difficult matters could be diverted. There were poorly guarded passages down which one could elude pursuit, and unfrequented gorges where one could lie in wait for an adversary and assassinate him quite legally.

Another chart set out, in ordered sequence, a code of conduct for the legal practitioner. This showed him how, and to whom, he could be offensive; when he could lie, and for whom he could lie; at what inducement he could be embarrassed, at what higher inducement he could be irritated, and at what still stronger inducement he could weaken.

Then there were the formulas for the defense.

Was it a case in forensic medicine? One must speak of the inexactitude of the sciences. Was it a case of vindicating a thief? He must be portrayed as a victim of the police. Was it a case of saving the hide of a murderer? He must be presented as having been overcome by a fit of madness.

When it came to matters of eloquence, the guidelines conformed to a strict pattern. Should unctuousness be called for, then one proclaimed:

"Gentlemen, my client has nothing to fear, for he comes before you with a halo of innocence round his brow."

(A gesture indicated the head of the accused who thought they were disapproving of his hat and removed it.)

"He has sought the sanctuary of the law, protected by humanity and justice."

(The attorney's hand pointed to the two officers standing at the door.)

"Above all, he has before him the cross of the God of truth, who died to save us all."

(The counsel for the prosecution bowed respectfully.)

Should a dramatic touch be required in a different scenario?

"Yes, my client will face any tests. . . . If it is true that he struck the blow, let the victim rise from the dead and accuse him!"

(Here he struck a pose; the dead man did not appear.)

"Let him rise up and cry: 'That is the man who killed me.'"

(The attorney sat down, and the children's nurses exchanged glances, convinced of the innocence of the accused.)

Was audacity called for?

"If, despite every proof, calumny and hatred continue to pursue my client, he will resist no more. Confident in the judgment of posterity, he will be happy to offer his head to his enemies."

(The schoolboys in the audience signified their approval.)

Was pathos called for?

"Gentlemen! Having secured your intellectual conviction, I shall now appeal to your hearts. Think of the father of the accused, a noble old man on whose white head you would not wish to bring sorrow."

(The hearts of all the baldheaded jurors melted.)

"Think of his mother, who watched for so long over his cradle!"

(The fathers of families blew their noses.)

"Above all, think of his children, those innocent creatures to whom you will bequeath nothing but dishonor for their inheritance."

(General emotion; the porters who happened to be in the audience applauded.)

After the lawyers in training came those who had already made their names, and were now busily making their fortunes, talking all the time; always pleading, even in conversation; involved with great as well as little things; indispensable everywhere; serving no useful purpose anywhere. At their head were those old practitioners, grown fat on preferments, honors and riches—vultures with their talons worn down, who could never get enough of the prey offered to them, and who made the litigant wait humbly before deigning to devour him.

The procurators mingled with all these groups, and went from one to another like men whose duty it was to keep them fed. Then came the bailiffs, the lesser rodents, eating the crumbs that fell from the masters' tables.

*Bailiff, attorney, and lawyer*

Maurice walked about for some time in the midst of this crowd whose joviality was chilling. They made their living from troubles, crimes, and ruin, as doctors live on fevers and ulcers—sad physicians of the soul, with their hands forever in some moral wound, feeding on the unfortunate and the villainous for their livelihood.

Without realizing it, he had come to a courtroom, and finding the door open, he went in.

The walls were covered in inscriptions, borrowed from articles of the legal code, with the object of making known the penalties attached to every infringement. There you could find the tariff for yielding to your worst instincts; the seven deadly sins had a price against them in figures, like articles in a novelty shop.

The traditional image of Christ, his lacerated head hanging on his breast, appeared in the middle of these articles. Near that side from which the blood had flowed for the salvation of all mankind were written the words:

DEFENDANTS TOO POOR TO FIND BAIL WILL BE IMPRISONED.

And beneath that mouth that had proclaimed the equality and brotherhood of all mankind were engraved these words :

WE NEED ONLY SUPPORT OUR FOREBEARS AND DIRECT
DESCENDANTS TO THE SECOND GENERATION.

For seating, the judges had couches piled with soft cushions that were plumped up by the defendants, who knew very well that they would be judged more leniently if the members of the tribunal were comfortable. On the other hand, the crown prosecutor was seated on a chair with sharp angles that caused great discomfort and irritation, and were guaranteed to make him cantankerous. As for the barristers, they had hanging in front of their bench the price schedule of defense speeches, the sight of which sustained their eloquence.

*The beggar and his dog*

When Maurice went in, there was an old man in the dock. He was an old peasant, bent with age, whose white hair fell over a ragged cotton cape. His chin rested on his hands, which were supported by a staff, and his lips were parted in that vague half smile of the aged. He was looking down at a dog curled up at his feet, which, with head half raised, was watching him closely and gently wagging its tail. There was obviously between the two of them that bond of friendship and shared experience that needed no more than a look and a smile. The old master and the old servant understood each other.

This close bond was the subject of debate.

Too old and weak to work anymore for his living, the peasant had been forced to ask for public charity. After fifty years of honest, patient toil, society would have let him die in a ditch, like a useless and aged beast of burden; but philanthropy had come to his assistance. It had offered him a place in one of its refuges, where those who could no longer work were given a pallet of straw and black bread to eat while they waited for death.

Unfortunately, the old man had wanted to share his accommodation with his dog, and the management had refused his request. They had tried to take his old companion from him; he had resisted, and that resistance had brought him before the court.

The prosecuting attorney put the case for the management.

First of all he listed the services provided by the *Humane Society,* of which he had the honor to be a member. He drew attention to the growing number of their homes—an indisputable indicator of national prosperity —and announced, with considerable satisfaction, that the expenditure on their inmates had been cut by half, thanks to a course of action as simple as it was ingenious. All that had been necessary was to reduce the amount of food, to substitute pallets for mattresses, and to replace calico with a coarser material.

But these improvements would become ineffective if they were undermined by the prodigality of some of the privileged beneficiaries. And using this peroration to introduce the case of the peasant's dog, he declared that this dog was a scandal to humanity. He calculated what could be saved in bones chewed over, in bowls licked clean, in crumbs surreptitiously eaten, and found that the total would have nourished *three-fifths of one old person.*

Then, seeing that the judges were impressed with his argument, he maintained that, since the administration had agreed to pay for the care of the old peasant, it had the right to sell his dog; that it would be only a meager compensation for all its sacrifices—an example indispensable to morality and human dignity. He ended by calling upon the tribunal not to encourage this pauper in the luxury of a companion that was of no use whatsoever, but to let him get used to eating nothing but the economical soup of the refuge, seasoned with the sympathy of the philanthropists, his benefactors.

After this summing up, which the magistrates had listened to with obvious approval, the judge invited the old man to state the merits of his case; but the old man seemed not to hear him, and said nothing. He seemed lost in a melancholy contemplation, as he looked at the old friend lying by his feet.

No doubt the dog understood the emotionally charged silence, for he got up slowly, looked searchingly at his master, and made one of those plaintive little sounds that denote a bewildered plea.

The old peasant put his toilworn hand on the head of the animal that had brought joy into his life.

"You heard, did you not?" he said sadly and tenderly, without looking at the judges. "You heard that we have to part? Feeding you will ruin the republic. What reason can I give for keeping you? Shall I say that for fifteen years you have shared my bread and water and my small place in the sun, and I have grown used to hearing the sound of your breathing at my feet? Shall I say that you are the last living creature who needs me and loves me? A creature that can give only love is useless, old friend. They have just told you so. Ah! If we were living in a barbarous land, I would go out with you into the countryside. I would stop at cottage doors and, on seeing my white hair, the men would take off their caps, the children would come and stroke you, the women would give us bread and salt. We would both drink fresh water at the fountain; we would sleep in the shade of the rocks, keeping each other warm. We would walk on paths bright with little flowers, surrounded by woodland scents, by the songs of birds and the babbling of brooks. But we are living in a civilized land, and all roads are closed to us. To move the hearts of the fortunate ones to pity is forbidden; to sleep out under the sky is a crime. They have taken away the hopes of compassion with the difficulties that freedom brings, and the philanthropy of men has opened a prison for us, where each one has his allowance of bread, light, and air.

"But for you, my friend, there is no place! We may eat and sleep, but what use is love? Do the regulations ever suppose that man has something between his throat and his stomach called a heart? Go, my friend. I wanted to keep you with me so that I could feel there was one creature left for me; but *the regulations don't allow it*. Go and look for a new master, and may he make you forget the old."

With these words, the old man took the head of the dog in his trembling hands and held it against his heart. He kissed it and stayed some minutes without moving.

When he stood up, a small tear ran down each of his furrowed cheeks.

Maurice could not hold back an involuntary exclamation of pity.

"Ah! Let him keep the dog to love him!" he cried.

But the judges had been in consultation during this quiet farewell from the old man, and the edict of separation had been pronounced.

# §XI

*House of the Trappists — Moral reeducation of convicts by turning them into idiots; Maurice's first diatribe — The Pantagruelists; advantages of a criminal career — Maurice's second diatribe — M. le Doux says nothing.*

On leaving, Maurice met M. Philadelpe le Doux who had come to look for him. He had just remembered that it was time for his prison visit, and wanted to take the young man with him.

The prison of Sans-Pair, situated behind the law courts, was composed of two distinct establishments, and was managed under two quite different systems.

The first one that M. le Doux entered was called the *House of the Trappists,* and its dreary aspect completely justified the name.

No windows were to be seen, because daylight entered through apertures on the interior courtyards. The wooden flooring that surrounded it deadened the least sound, enveloping the building in a sinister silence. The main door itself slid noiselessly on smooth rails, and the heavy hangings in the corridors completely muffled the sound of footsteps. The walls were padded in such a way as to absorb every sound; the doors were covered with three layers of matting; and a notice, repeated at every intersection, warned visitors to speak in low voices.[1]

Daylight was just as carefully controlled as the sound. A kind of twilight reigned everywhere, exaggerating shapes and softening outlines. The air itself entered imperceptibly and noiselessly, with no sudden gusts.

The further Maurice advanced down these silent, gloomy corridors, the more his feeling of unease grew. He found the atmosphere, where neither the slightest sound nor glimmer of light penetrated, most oppressive; a chill struck his heart, and he shivered involuntarily.

"I find the stillness disturbing," he said, "the place feels like a tomb."

"And yet you are surrounded by ten thousand prisoners," observed M. le Doux. "Come along and see them."

He had drawn back a curtain, and Maurice found himself in a panopticon that was at the center of an enormous circle of cells that housed the prisoners. To see those lines of small cells, one on top of another, turning in a gigantic spiral, until they were lost to sight in the rafters, one would have said it was Dante's inferno in reverse—save that there were no cries, no groanings, no prayers to be heard: a chill silence lay over that strange hive of stone. One could see each prisoner moving soundlessly in his barred cell, like a dead man galvanized into activity in the tomb. All were pale and moved restlessly with dazed or haggard expressions. Sad and silent, they worked the levers of machines, without comprehending their purpose. The cells were so arranged that no prisoner could see his neighbors; and, in like manner, the guards too were hidden from sight. Surrounded by an incomprehensible surveillance system, they knew they were always watched without themselves being able to see anything.

M. le Doux explained to Maurice all the advantages of this perfect system of *solitary confinement.* In this way," he said, "we can weaken even the most resilient natures. Enclosed in a silent twilight, the captive resists at first, but he fights the system in vain: boredom, like stagnant water seeping below the surface, gradually undermines his will. He feels his muscles growing weak, his blood turning to ice. The inertia of everything around him ends by infiltrating his whole being. He is appalled by the void all around him; he looks out and sees nothing but the walls of his prison; he calls out, and hears nothing but the sound of his own voice. Some cannot endure this trial and become insane, but they are only a small number; the majority become passive and relapse into a state of torpor. Certain that their smallest movements are closely monitored, and no longer able to think for themselves, they give up. The regulations become their conscience; habit takes the place of positive desire to act. They even forget how to speak; they are merely domestic animals, instinctively obeying the rules of the house. Their memories have been obliterated, their passions extinguished, their hopes destroyed. The mind is a tabula rasa; we have achieved our objective. We have in effect turned them into zombies, and now all we have to do is instruct and reeducate them in new ways of thinking."

"Yes, alas! I see," said Maurice. "You have done for these men what the chatelaine of Valence wanted to do for her son. She was a pious lady, widowed, with an only child for whom she would have given up her own place in paradise. But the child, hot-blooded, and ever eager to taste the delights of the world outside, would often escape from the château, where the only sounds to be heard were bells and prayers. Gradually, he was so drawn to evil, that he was only unhappy when he could not be wicked enough. He was very familiar with the three chariots that carry human beings down to the abyss: the first is driven by pride, the second by impurity, the third by idleness, and he had taken his place successively in each one of these without so much as a glance at the frail chariot of repentance trundling along far behind.

"The pious mistress of the château, thinking that the damnation of her son was a certainty, prayed tearfully to the archangel Michael, patron saint of the family, and asked him to save the young man, even if it were to cost him his life. The archangel, who, ever since he saw Mary at the foot of the cross, had been moved by the tears of mothers, was filled with compassion and came down to earth to speak to her, saying:

"'Be of good heart; your son can still be saved. Our Savior has given him an allotted span of days, and only three hundred remain to him on earth. As long as they are without sin, all his old transgressions will be forgiven; and, at the appointed hour, I myself will come to take his soul to heaven.'

"This revelation gave great joy to the mistress of the château; there was still time for her son to aspire to the happiness of God's chosen ones. This thought made her accept, almost without distress, his approaching death; the Christian virtue of hope assuaged a mother's grief.

"But, in order to achieve this reward, the sinner would have to give up all his sins against God's law; and, alas! How could she ensure that he did that? She had already pleaded with him in vain, and the prayers of the church had not been any more effective. Her thoughts turned to an Arab doctor whose spells were reputed to exercise a powerful control over the will, and she went to his house to let him know what she hoped to do.

"After hearing what she had to say, the doctor went with her to see her son who was still fast asleep; and he began to pronounce the powerful incantations that would deliver him from the tyranny of the passions.

"First of all, he touched the sides of the sleeper, and his mother saw emerging from them a swarm of bold and fierce spirits. These were forcefulness, anger, and boldness, and along with them came courage and shrewdness.

"The Arab doctor then touched his forehead, and out sprang imagination, clothed in all the colors of the rainbow; reason armed with a double-edged sword; memory holding in her hand the golden chain that links the present to the past.

"Finally, he touched the heart, which immediately opened to let out a cloud of passionate desires, ever-changing enthusiasms, illusions on wings of azure—a foolish but charming company, which fled away with plaintive cries.

"When the young man came to himself a little later, he was completely transformed: all the ideas that his mother had fought against, all the inclinations that had so distressed her were gone. He had now no will other than hers, no tastes other than the ones she inspired. His spirit had become like the bark carried along by the waves, going wherever wind or the helmsman took it. His mother told him to walk, and he walked; to pray, and he prayed. Temptations had no effect on him; he watched them go like strangers, without a second glance or a greeting.

"In this way, the three hundred days passed for him in a kind of waking dream, and when the chatelaine saw the archangel Michael, she said:

"'The terms imposed have been fulfilled; he has earned his place in heaven; then come, master, and without further delay take his soul.'

"But the archangel shook his head sadly and said:

"'Alas! Poor mother, he no longer has a soul. You cannot remove the stones from a house without destroying it. What the Arab doctor took away from your son was the fabric of the soul itself. He made a gift of the soul to Satan, and left you only his body.'

"This legend could be read as an allegory for those who built your prison. Under the pretext of redeeming the sinner, you have robbed him of his soul. Since when can man be reformed by the destruction of his deepest feelings? If these unfortunate creatures have failed, it is because they have never been fully integrated into society, and you have condemned them to solitude; it is because the desire for good is more feeble than that for evil, and you have killed both these inclinations indiscriminately; it is because their rational self has never been ripened by the sun of experience and you condemn them to inaction. Centuries ago we rendered an enemy powerless by cutting the sinews of his limbs. But you have perfected your control technique: now you destroy the sinews of the soul with boredom, and because these restless ones have become apathetic, you declare that they are cured. But what is the use of a cure like this? What good are men who have lost their personality, who have forgotten how to feel passionately about anything—men reduced to the level of domestic animals, living under the eye of the master? Where you had men acting in ignorance, culpable maybe, you are now left with madmen, idiots, and hypocrites.

"No doubt solitary confinement can be employed to calm the initial turmoil of a rebellious heart: it acts like an ice-cold shower to calm the raging spirit. But you have made a regime out of what should be no more than a temporary remedy; you have followed the example of those English mothers who dose their children with opium in order to stop them

*Consequences of the cell system*

crying. And do not say that you have done this in the interests of the offenders in order to reform them. No, you have acted out of self-interest, so that the even tenor of your lives should not be disturbed. When the external forces that shape a man's life were taken into account, the task was difficult. It was necessary to discipline restless spirits, to soften hearts grown hard, above all to bring an ordered calm to tormented souls. You have chosen to wall them into a tomb. In my day we put bodies in chains, but left souls free. You reckoned that was a brutal thing to do, and asked: 'What good are these chains that bruise the flesh and jangle on the ear? Let us deliver the body from them and quietly kill the soul. The deed will go unnoticed; and once the soul is dead, the body will give no more trouble.' What Pharisees! Pretending not to know that brutalization is not regeneration! Oh! Men of little faith, you who cannot conceive how love and patience can touch even the most hardened criminals. Seek out the most obdurate heart, knock wherever you will, and a living spring will come forth from it. While a man lives, so long as he loves something in creation, God will never abandon him completely, and his soul will never be irretrievably lost."

M. Philadelphe le Doux had taken advantage of Maurice's spontaneous outburst to give M. Atout his annual report, drawing attention to the excellent results obtained through their system of separate cells, and to pencil in some notes on the need to remove room numbers *which could still distract the condemned men.* When he had finished, he raised his head and looked at the young man with the vague smile of people who want to give the impression of having listened, when they have not taken in anything at all.

"Ah! Very good," he said, "I see that you have made a study of the question. Nowadays, however, there are still two systems that between them regulate the prison population. We have seen the *House of the Trappists;* we must now pay a visit to the domain of the *Pantagruelists.* Go straight ahead please, then take the door on the left, and we shall arrive in time to see them at dinner."

Maurice followed the directions given and found himself walking across a courtyard and approaching the entrance to a building with a marble colonnade, surrounded by fountains and walks. It was the second prison of Sans-Pair, founded recently for the most hardened criminals.

The only sounds to be heard were music, singing, and loud laughter. The first room was a sort of parlor where the prisoners received visits. And here came great ladies, all very charming, drawn by a desire to converse with the elite of the criminal classes, or by the wish to get their autographs. There were artists working on the portraits of the most famous villains; men of letters working, for the edification of the public, on the intimate details of the lives of forgers and murderers. The prisoners were doing the honors among their visitors with the proud punctiliousness of men who are fully aware of their own importance.

*A famous criminal*

Close by was the concert hall, echoing to the sound of popular ditties, sung to the accompaniment of music arranged for clarinet and hurdy-gurdy. Then came the tavern, where the regulars, lolling on velvet divans, were smoking hookahs with amber mouthpieces. Next there was the billiard room furnished with cues for the game, and next to that a bar where the condemned men could get sorbets, mulled wine, or punch, Roman-style, all day long.

In the evening there were entertainments, followed by masked balls where there were no guards present.

Just as M. le Doux had indicated, the visitors found the *Pantagruelists* at table. They were sitting down to three courses: little trotters and spring vegetables, followed by dessert, coffee, and fine liqueurs.

"You can see," said the philanthropist with a smile, "the system of moral reeducation is quite different here. Over there we improve the convict by removing the basic necessities from him. Here we achieve the same result by letting him live in luxury. Each method has its advantages, and the results from each are equally satisfactory. With the *Trappists*, we secure submission by depriving a man of essentials; with the *Pantagruelists*, by indulging him in every way. The former has not energy enough to escape from captivity; the latter is held here by a life of pleasure. There is no recorded case of a *Pantagruelist* trying to escape, and most of them shed tears when they have to go. We also see to it that whenever a prisoner is freed, just to soften the blow, he receives a sum proportionate to the time he has spent in prison. That means that the really important crooks go out from here able to vote, and they are often eligible to stand for election themselves. There have been some complaints about this generosity toward convicts; but, as I have pointed out in my last report, these villains are still our brothers. *Homo sum et nihil humani a me alienum puto*. It is a maxim of philanthropy, and it is written on the hearts of all our members and at the head of all our correspondence. Doesn't that say it all? *Homo sum!* That is to say, I could myself be a thief, an arsonist, a murderer. *Nihil humani a me alienum puto*. So, I must regard all murderers, thieves, and arsonists as my brothers."

"Well, yes," said Maurice, "but what do you do for the virtuous who work hard, set a good example, and make an honest living? You, who are so indulgent towards poor criminals, will you show any compassion for poor honest folk? Philanthropy is much concerned with wrongdoers; it offers them shelter, provides them with resources, gives them support. But those who have resisted temptation, or have struggled to overcome it, are left without any help. In order to enjoy your protection, one must have a

*The brotherhood of man*

certificate of crime, just as in days gone by one had to have a certificate of civic virtue. Ah! by all means show mercy to the sinner; Christ pardoned the woman taken in adultery and raised up Mary Magdalen; but give a little thought to the innocent! Do it so that duty does not become too onerous. Do not wait until they have fallen to give them a helping hand; do not let them find that society makes greater efforts and greater sacrifices for its ungrateful children than it does for the virtuous sons. In short, do not kill all the fatted calves for the prodigal son, but keep some for his brothers who have not wasted your substance. What really astounds me is not that your *Pantagruelists* accept the kindness done to them, but that the hardworking and conscientious are resigned to the misery where you leave them to fend for themselves. To do the right thing in such difficult circumstances and with so little help, whatever anyone might say, must suggest that virtue should be made attractive. How many unfortunate creatures could feel envious of the daily bread, the woollen coat, the warm washroom of these prisoners and try desperately to understand why their own honesty keeps them so poor?"

"Your wishes have been anticipated," said M. le Doux, "for our beneficent care takes in the hardworking too. Since we are investigating the operation of philanthropy, I should like to show you the industrial community of our vice-president, the honorable Isaac Banqman. Not only is he a very wealthy man, and a man with considerable political influence, but there is no one in the republic more zealous for the improvement of machines and the laboring classes. We will take the train, and in three seconds we shall be at the door of his establishment."

# §XII

*M. Isaac Banqman's factory; superiority of machines over men — Maurice*
*remembers; the soldier Mathias — Wards of the Humane Society —*
*Human race improved by the English method of cross-breeding —*
*A woman punished for her maternal instinct and devotion.*

The Isaac Banqman factory was situated on the far side of a mountain
riddled with underground vaults, where the din of engines filled the air
and where wagons thundered through unceasingly. A hundred chimneys
belched clouds of smoke which hung in the air, condensed, and formed a
floating dome over the top of the hill. Huge wheels turned slowly at
rooftop height, while dull and heavy rumblings shook the mountain.

All this noise, all this activity, and all this smoke were the result of
making molds for buttons. These were the specialized product to which
Banqman owed both his fortune and his importance in politics.

To tell the truth, the celebrated industrialist had brought to the manufacturing process refinements that could not fail to enhance his importance. He had begun by ruining all the other manufacturers who, with
fewer resources than himself, had dared to set themselves up in competition. Then, in a single move, he had increased by 50 percent the selling
price of his products. Finally, thanks to his political influence, he had obtained from the minister an edict that required all public servants to wear
three buttons on their shorts.

Moreover, he had earned this preferential treatment by announcing
that he would supply, free of charge to the hospitals of Sans-Pair, all the
buttons that the sick, the deceased, and the babes in arms might need.

In addition, he had decided to establish in his own factory that commune of workers to which M. Philadelphe le Doux had referred in his conversation with Marthe and Maurice.

When they arrived at the factory, the philanthropist sent word to the
honorable M. Banqman who was in his office, absorbed in watching
goldfish in a bowl.

M. Banqman continued this interesting examination for the decent in-
terval an important man must always wait if he wishes to appear busy.
After half an hour he went down, excusing himself on the grounds of the
innumerable matters he had to attend to: the government came to him
with every difficult question; he was the victim of his reputation as a

practical man. They had come to understand the danger of consulting the theoreticians, the thinkers. Now they only wanted to hear those who, like himself, had studied the important principles of political economy as these applied to the manufacture of buttons. In consequence, he no longer had a minute to himself; his time was entirely at the disposal of the State and of Humanity.

M. le Doux interrupted him at that point to let him know the reason for their visit. M. Banqman was flattered and said he was ready to show them the model community, for he thought that if that system were to be adopted generally, it would one day inaugurate a golden age for the whole world.

So he took them on a tour of the factory, and explained as they went along the different functions of the machines of all shapes and sizes.

They watched immense arms moving slowly to lift great weights, their claws grasping objects like giant fingers, their thousand wheels turning, rolling, intersecting. Watching the precision of every movement, and hearing the thunderous rumblings of the steam and flames, one would have said that by his devilish art a magician had breathed a soul into these skeletons of steel. They no longer seemed mere material constructions, but looked like nameless blind monsters, bellowing deeply as they worked. Every now and again, blackened figures appeared in the midst of the swirling smoke. These were the mahouts for these mammoths of copper and steel, the menservants whose task it was to feed them water and fire; to mop the sweat from their bodies; to rub them down with oil, as was once the custom with athletes; to manage their brute strength at the risk of perishing, sooner or later, crushed in their workings or devoured by the flame of their breath.

Maurice gazed sadly at these victims of improved mechanization. Instinctively, he compared these wonderful machines—their limbs polished, gleaming, perfectly maintained—with the worn-out and haggard men who milled around them. Listening to the terrible concert of hissing steam, of iron grinding on iron, belching flames, bubbling water, bellows roaring like the wind, he was seized with a kind of terror. He searched in vain for life in the midst of this turmoil of mechanized matter. He could hear the noise perfectly, could see every movement, but it all looked like an imitation of the real thing: all this activity had no true life of its own. In its presence, however, far from feeling excitement, you felt yourself overwhelmed by a sense of torpor. The regular movements of these machines had nothing to say to you; there was no bond between you and them; they were blind and deaf monsters, possessed of a terrifying power.

All of a sudden, Maurice recalled the little workshop near his uncle's house—the sound of the various operations performed by children or young women; the constant laughter that drowned out the rasping sound of the needles; the songs that were taken up from bench to bench; the playful mischievousness and the whispered confidences. He remembered especially Mathias, the old soldier—a pleasant and happy memory, which conjured up again for him a picture from his youth.

For fifteen years Mathias had served with the colors all over Europe, often hungry, often under fire, every morning conquering at bayonet point the place where he would sleep at night. And Mathias had done all that for the sake of a word that he barely understood, but felt very deeply about. That word was France! That had been his life until the day when his country, defeated by force of numbers, had been forced to accept peace; and on that day Mathias, his heart swelling with sorrow and anger, had taken off the cockade that for fifteen years had meant a life of combat and suffering.

Back home in France, he remembered a sister, his only living relative, and made his way to the village where she lived.

There he learned that his sister had died, leaving a son and daughter whom a neighboring farmer had, out of charity, taken into his house.

But charity without love is like a loan with crippling interest; it enriches only the lender. When Mathias arrived at the farm, he found the two orphans on the doorstep fighting over a crust of bread, while the farmer, annoyed by their quarreling, shouted:

"These children can't stand each other!"

"You mean they can't stand being hungry," replied Mathias.

And taking the two famished children by the hand, he took them away with him.

It was a heavy responsibility for the old soldier, but he was not afraid to take it on. He remembered the maxim of his lieutenant that to complete even the longest march, you had only to put one foot after the other; and he had made it his guiding principle in life.

Once he had arrived in Paris, he worked to support them until the time when they could earn their daily bread. Mathias had found work for them both at the same factory. When work was finished, never a day went by when Mathias was not to be seen arriving, carrying the covered basket with their meal. When they saw him, the little boys shouldered arms and made a charge, while the little girls smiled and said to one another :

"It's Papa Mathias! Good day, Monsieur Mathias!"

For little girls and boys are both fond of those old lions that only roar against the strong.

When he had acknowledged them all with a gesture, a word, or a smile, the old man would sit down in a sheltered spot with Georgette and Julien; then they would take the cover off the basket. But not immediately! They first had to guess what Mathias had brought, and heaven alone knows what pains they took never to guess exactly, but to give him the pleasure of surprising them. Finally, when the children declared they could not possibly guess, the old soldier would lift the wicker lid, slowly take out the surprise dish, and present it to his guests.

"Ah! You never thought of that," he would exclaim. "Today is a feast day; we've got ribbons on the pot."

And in the kindness of his heart, he would spread out, on the basket that served as a little table, the poor dinner that was transformed into a feast by the goodwill of them all.

And how they talked when they were sitting down to eat! The children told him what was going on in the workshop, and Mathias always found an occasion in their stories to give them good advice. For, during those long nights encamped under the stars, when hunger and cold kept him awake, he had formulated a philosophy for himself that could be expressed in a few axioms that had stood him in good stead a dozen times in his life. Among these axioms there were four in particular that he was always quoting, since they encapsulated all the others:

1° You will be faithful to your flag till death;

2° You will think less of your own safety than of the victory of your regiment;

3° You will not make war against the defenseless;

4° When it rains, you will not ask to see the sun.

And, so that the orphans would understand these aphorisms, he explained to them that the flag, for them, was honor; that their regiment was the whole of mankind; that the poor and the weak were defenseless; that the rain and the sun were the path, difficult or easy, that God had ordained for us.

He included many valuable pieces of advice on perseverance, on pride, on relationships, and always ended by urging Georgette and Julien to work hard.

"The week," he told them, "is a carriage of provisions, drawn by seven horses. If you take one of them off, the carriage will still keep moving; two, and it will only proceed with difficulty; three, and it will stay where it stopped and leave the army without food."

The children listened religiously to the old soldier's homilies and kept them in their hearts. For three years Maurice had seen them coming back to the same place, obedient and happy. Mathias interpreted the world for them, and they were his future. While age was bowing his shoulders and ravaging his brow, the two children were growing up by his side, young and vital, like vigorous shoots springing from a withered trunk.

And often the other children from the factory came to sit next to the old soldier begging for stories of the battles he had fought, and they sat in on the lessons—the old man's spiritual legacy, which he was anxious to bequeath to them before he died. It was an ever-open school for all, by the hearth, or on the doorstep, where the one who was nearing the end of his life initiated his pupils into a life of courage, patience, and sacrifice.

Alas! Maurice looked in vain for anything like that little workshop of former days. Here there were no longer any tumbledown premises, no longer any faults in workmanship; but neither was there any laughter or singing. He tried but failed to find the likes of Papa Mathias, Georgette, or Julien. He saw only perfect machines and exhausted men.

When M. Banqman had shown and explained everything to his visitors, he brought them finally to the living quarters of the wards of this business.

The accommodation was in a series of lodges, each one constituting a household without children—for these had been separated from their parents at birth, to be contracted out. In this way, the woman was freed from the cares of motherhood, and she was also relieved of wifely duties. She did not have to prepare meals, see that clothes were washed and repaired, or do housework; the management took care of all that. She no longer had to manage her husband's earnings, since there was a house-keeper who took charge of salaries and expenditures; or to watch over his health, since there was a doctor who came round every morning; or to help him to live a virtuous life, since there was a chaplain who preached every week. The husband, for his part, no longer had to plan for the future, to protect his family, be courageous.

"In this way," said M. Banqman, "the worker remains under our care, well housed, well fed, well clothed, with no alternative but to be prudent, his good fortune handed to him on a plate. Not only do we regulate his actions, but we look to the future and decide what he should do.

In the past, the English perfected the breeding of domestic animals, with a view to their future use, and we have applied this system to all the human race, in order to improve it. Selective breeding, properly understood, has allowed us to produce a race of blacksmiths whose strength is entirely concentrated in their arms; a race of porters with no other muscular development apart from the small of their backs; a race of runners whose legs alone have developed; a race of town criers who are all mouth and lungs. In these lodges you can see the different types of proletariat to whom we have given the name *industrial hybrids.*"[1]

"And no less thought has been given to their education," added M. le Doux, who was tired of listening to explanations instead of giving them. "We have removed everything from the curriculum of the working classes

that has no immediate practical application. In the past, precious time was lost in reading the history of great deeds, in learning poetry that disturbed the feelings, in repeating maxims distilled from morality and religion. Instead of all that, we now have arithmetic and the Statute Book. All the factory's employees learn to read and write, but only just enough to read day-to-day prices and to keep a written note of expenses."

"And they submit willingly to this system?" Maurice asked.

"Some depraved natures resist our paternal guidance," replied M. Banqman. "You have an example there before you."

"Do you mean," Maurice asked, "the young woman whose expression suggests amiability but pride too?"

"Nothing can break her spirit," replied the manufacturer. "She claims that we have ruined her happiness by freeing her from the task of looking after her child. She says that we have deprived her of her greatest joy in not letting her look after her own home."

Maurice turned to look at the young woman, and he said to himself:

"Perhaps the voice of God is not yet entirely extinguished in all these hearts. Are there still some who have preserved a feeling for the most important principles? Keep up the opposition, brave woman! Keep on fighting against the enforced peace and quiet they have given you, because they come at the cost of your most sacred joys. Can they not see that the sleepless nights and the cares of a mother, the labor and household management of a wife are the most precious links in the family chain? Do they regard the union of man and wife as no more than a commercial association with profit as its chief end? Society is not built on money alone, but on patience, goodwill, and affection. They are the capital that must be invested if the community is to prosper. Ah! Let the woman keep her everyday chores, so that she will become every day more precious to man! Let her do her own work, even though a stranger might do it better, so that she can enjoy the reward without which she cannot live—the acknowledgment of her worth from those she loves! Why seek to improve the lot of the poor by freeing them from family duties? Do you not see that in them is the source of all that is good? Far from making these duties less onerous, make them appear more blessed by allowing the poor to look after themselves. Do not usurp the place of conscience, rather shine a light on it for them; above all, do not take over these struggling souls, but rather give them more freedom of action, more life. People are not spendthrifts incapable of managing their own affairs, but children to be guided and encouraged on their path to maturity."

Banqman and le Doux went on with their guided tour, showing the visitors the home for workers where they spent their last years, and the hall where their bodies were delivered over to the scalpels of medical students for an agreed price. Since parents were from the cradle no longer involved with their children, the children were no longer concerned about them after their deaths.

But Maurice looked without seeing, and listened without hearing. Oppressed by a sense of great sadness, and feeling deeply despondent, he returned to the house of M. Atout.

For her part Marthe had seen, more clearly than yesterday, the emptiness and wretchedness of home life here; and when Maurice told her what he had seen, she threw herself into his arms, her eyes brimming with tears.

"Ah! What have we done?" she sobbed. "In the world where we used to live, we had not yet abandoned the true God for the Golden Calf; the bonds that unite families were not everywhere broken; the heart's deepest feelings were not completely extinguished. Although we made light of evil, we still believed in the existence of good. But here, Maurice, all is irretrievably lost!"

"Why is that?" the young man asked, hoping against hope it was not true.

"Alas!" replied Marthe, "because they no longer know how to love."

*The sick awaiting permission to enter the hospital*

# THE SECOND DAY
# §XIII

*Principal hospital of Sans-Pair, built for the scientists, the doctors, and the
director. Fearing to admit people who are too healthy, it will only admit
them after death—Marthe reflects—The condition of mankind
according to Doctor Manomane—The insane in the year
three thousand—The zoo and the botanic gardens.*

The next day, when the young couple came down, they found their host with a kinsman of his, Doctor Minimum, who had heard of the indisposition of Milady Atout and had come on an unofficial visit to inquire about her health.

Doctor Minimum was the most renowned exponent of a new medical system. This entailed giving you an illness you did not already have, and then applying the hothouse treatment to encourage its development. As a result of

{ 109 }

these methods the patient would usually die on the second or third day, obviously saving time for him.

As for the doctor, he had but one aim: to make the illness sound worse so that he could take more credit for curing it. For instance, a cold became a pleurisy; a headache was soon brain fever; a dizzy spell turned into a stroke.

As the young couple came in, M. Minimum was telling his cousin about the marvelous results obtained by this method, and was urging him to visit the hospital where they applied his theories. M. Atout excused himself, but Maurice took up the offer, and, after making arrangements with his host to meet at the home of M. de l'Empyrée who was expecting them at about midday, he got into the doctor's carriage with Marthe.

The doctor took them to the principal hospital in Sans-Pair, which had been built on the edge of town.

The first glimpse they had was of elegant buildings surrounded by lawns and groves: these were built for the doctors. Next came a magnificent edifice, which rose amid banks of flowers: this was the home of the nursing sisters. Then came a palace, in front of which were gardens adorned with grottoes, water features, and shaded arbors. This was the home of the director.

It had cost the town twenty million, according to Doctor Minimum, to ensure that their hospital was a model establishment. Here doctors, senior nurses, and administrators were housed and fed at the republic's expense. Carriages, with horses already harnessed, awaited their orders, and their daughters received a dowry from the administration.

"But what about the patients?" Maurice asked.

"Ah! The patients are down there," said the doctor, pointing to a gloomy-looking building hidden at the bottom of a long walk, airless, and without any greenery around it. Because the sight of this complex was depressing—it would have spoiled the harmonious unity of the buildings —it had been hidden away. In effect only those buildings that constituted the real hospital—that is to say the homes of the top functionaries—were visible. Unfortunately, the builders had run out of space. When the garden for the doctors, the parterre for the nuns, and the park for the bursar had been allocated, there was only a tiny courtyard left for the convalescents. Since most of the patients did not survive, however, it was quite possible to do without an area for them to walk around and take the air.

"You don't take them in until they are on the point of death?" Marthe asked. "When we don't admit them until after death," replied Minimum. "Whoever wishes to be admitted to hospital must first of all get himself to the diagnostic center over on the other side of Sans-Pair, wait his turn, obtain a certificate, then travel eight leagues to get himself a bed. Thanks to these excellent precautions, we can be certain that we never admit people in good health. However, the sick can be allowed in after they have died: it is a slight disadvantage in the otherwise good system established by the governing body. In other respects, we have done everything possible to ensure that our principal hospital of Sans-Pair serves the progress of science. We have an experimental center, always in operation, where new theories can be tested. If the patient recovers, the treatment is adopted; if he succumbs, so much the worse for the system. In addition, there is a laboratory to study how many known elements are in each substance. There are kennels where dogs are raised to be poisoned or dismembered in the interests of human beings; dissecting theaters always stocked with selected cadavers, and a magnificent collection of skeletons in glass cases. There are still some things lacking, however. The gallery of monstrosities is not yet complete; we need to restock our jars of fetuses, and there has, for a long time, been a demand for specimens of different races properly preserved. But our director hopes to get all these improvements from *bonuses.*"

Maurice asked what these were.

"We give this name," replied the doctor, "to the economies made at the expense of the patients. Let the soup be a little less rich—we have a bonus; and the bread not quite so white, another bonus; if the wine is mixed with water, yet another bonus! We have perfected this method in order to make a bit out of the housekeeping money that provides for ten thousand meals. In this way institutions grow rich, and bursars earn gratitude and extra money. One can say that, in principle, a well-run hospital is one where the patients are uncomfortable enough to ensure that the institution makes some money out of them."

In the course of conversation, the doctor had arrived at the first room.

The floor was carefully polished, the beds elegant, the walls adorned with colored hangings, and the windows dressed with silk drapes; but this luxurious effect was spoiled by the items of surgical equipment, of all shapes and sizes, that stood about with steel arms poised. Where nursing care was concerned, the place was neither more caring nor more sensitive than in days gone by. The doctors conducted their examinations of patients in public—the same as ever—exposing each wound to the scrutiny of their students. They coldly discussed the patients' sufferings in loud voices, as they weighed their chances of survival. The groans of the dying terrified the wretched patient whose fate was under discussion; the sight of the dead body, with funeral pall draped over it, froze the smile of the convalescent who had felt he was on the mend.

Marthe, her heart deeply troubled, and eyes brimming with tears, turned to Maurice.

"Ah! This is not what I hoped for," she said in a low voice. "It is just as it used to be in our day. It's the old infirmary for the poor and abandoned. The floor may be more highly polished, the walls not so bare, the windows more expensively curtained; but what have they done for the relief of those who are suffering? Are they not still treated like cattle, delivered over to scientific experimentation, terrified by the sight of these instruments of torture? Ah! What I had hoped from a more enlightened civilization was a hospital that had lost its harsh character; a place where the sick would no longer be objects to be merely repaired. They would be suffering creatures whose pain could be controlled, whose fears would be recognized while they were offered support and encouragement. I had hoped that they would have found in this community something like the care they would have in their own families. What is the good of all that money poured out on equipment if nothing (alas!) has changed for human beings? Give every one of these unfortunate creatures a little room of their own, where the groans of the dying will not frighten them. Do not treat their suffering bodies as commodities they were forced to sign over to you on crossing the threshold of this institution. Do not let them feel that they are being cared for out of charity, or that they are completely in your hands not just because they are sick, but because they are poor and unfortunate. Their suffering makes them the masters, and you their servants. Have you never felt a redoubling of sympathy for members of your family who are in pain? Have you not noticed how their wishes become paramount as you forgive them everything? Have you not thought that you would gladly sacrifice some of your own well-being to make them better? Well, aren't the poor and neglected members of our wider family? Even the worst mothers still have some love left for a sick child. Why should society treat its children more heartlessly?"

"A beautiful sentiment," stated Doctor Minimum, who had heard the end of Marthe's speech. "I have always maintained that one must never economize on hospital services, and that our salaries should be doubled. But no one understands the real needs. All the resources of the republic are gobbled up by women and lawyers. Fortunately, we have the consolation of duty well done and of looking after our clientele. Mine grows by the day, thanks to the success I have had with my treatment here. I have called it the *method of the infinitesimal*, because I dispense only minute quantities: atoms of lime, atoms of orange flower, atoms of sugar candy. The less there is of these, the more their effect is assured. I take a molecule of some substance, something impalpable, tasteless, invisible—the thousandth part of nothing. I throw it into thirty liters of water, mix it, decant it, and prescribe it in teaspoons. Any illness that resists this medication is definitely incurable, and the death of the patient can only be attributed to his constitution."[1]

When the visitors had gone through some of the rooms, they emerged again at the far end of the hospital and found themselves in front of a second building given over to the care of the insane. At the request of his two companions, Doctor Minimum asked to see his colleague, Manomane, who was the doctor in charge.

The latter arrived with a look of alarm and looked closely at Marthe and Maurice, exclaiming:

"I see, I see . . . wary looks . . . furrowed brows . . . startled expressions! All the faculties have been concentrated on one particular obsession. The condition was classified some time ago, and can be cured."

"May God forgive me, he takes you for inmates!" Minimum exclaimed, interrupting him. "Please tell him yourselves that you have not come because you are ill, but because you are curious."

"Ah! A visitation," replied Manomane, who examined the two who had been restored to life with a very searching look. "A visit made out of curiosity! . . . We have another symptom here!"

And leaning toward his colleague, he added in a whisper, "Don't trust them . . . that calm appearance . . . that smile . . . we know all about that."

Then, when Minimum burst out laughing, he looked at him more attentively and muttered: "Inability to follow a line of reasoning . . . blind credulity . . . third type observed by Doctor Insanus, and classified as incurable!"

And thereupon, walking ahead of the doctor and his two companions, he brusquely told them to follow him.

Continuous contact with the sick had imperceptibly come to affect Doctor Manomane. He claimed that society had shut away certain madmen so that people would believe in the good sense of those left at liberty, but that in reality the world was filled with people who were all to some degree mad. The most sensible were, to say the least, on the way to being mad. He developed his views on these matters by enumerating the signs by which one could recognize aberrations. Do you think of one thing more often than another? Madness! Do you like someone else more than yourself? Madder still! Do you take delight in vague hopes? The height of madness!

Manomane had composed a litany of six hundred and thirty-three types of mental illness, comprising all flights of fancy and every impulse of the heart. At the same time he showed his three companions examples of these various derangements, in their different classifications like families of plants in a herbarium.

In the course of this demonstration, Maurice stopped in front of a man who had a calm and cheerful air.

"This man," said the doctor, "was one of our wealthiest businessmen. Unfortunately, everyone thought him eminently sane, until an old associate ruined by his father started proceedings against him for restitution. The judges decided in favor of our very wealthy friend. However, when the process had established the truth he refused to accept the judgment in his favor, and wanted to give up everything to his adversary. The only way to stop him making restitution was to forbid it absolutely and lock him away.

"As for the old man over there, we only know him by the name *Father of Men*. He has worked for fifty years on a social system under which all are to be rewarded according to their works. He claims that God gave all human beings an equal right to happiness, and that in a Christian society poverty should not be the result of chance, but the punishment for wrongdoing. Every evening and every morning he goes down on his knees, and with hands joined repeats this prayer:

"'Our Father, who art in heaven, thy kingdom come, thy will be done on earth as it is in heaven.'

"The authorities judged this to be dangerous madness and sent him to me."

They had arrived in front of a young man with a countenance at once thoughtful and fearless.

"Here you see an aimless traveler," said Manomane. "While others travel in civilized countries in the interests of research or work, his only wish is to find lost routes and unknown regions. On three occasions he disappeared into the immense spaces of the old continent with no other motive than to visit peoples in decline, to cross forgotten rivers, to sleep among nameless ruins. Ask him why he does it, and he replies: 'To understand!' You would ask in vain for any facts and figures, or about the geological formation of the countries where he has traveled so extensively. The wretched man has not brought back from his travels the least fragment of rock or the smallest scarab; the only things he has to show are his assessments and impressions. So, on his return, his family had him committed. We have been treating him for three months with showers and bleeding.

"To find out more, you may approach and speak to him; he is not vicious and will share his observations with you freely."

Maurice took advantage of that authorization to approach Pérégrinus and question him about what he had seen. The young traveler, who had journeyed widely in the old continents, gave him a quick sketch of the state of the world in the year three thousand. From him Maurice learned that Africa, once progress had been initiated, had finally adopted civilized ways. Constitutional government had been established in Guinea; the king of the Congo was preparing a constitution for his peoples; the Hottentots had set up the republic of Capricorn, and Central Africa was governed by an elected president. Pérégrinus singled out for praise the Polytechnic of Timbuktu and the Conservatory of Music of the Sahara. As for Senegambia, it was famed for its medicinal preparations, and supplied the druggists of the entire world.

Asia, on the other hand, had relapsed into a state of decline that grew deeper by the day. Pérégrinus had traveled everywhere in the area without finding any trace of its ancient splendor. Hindustan was inhabited by a race of fakirs whose only accomplishments were sword swallowing and snake charming. Persia was divided between two sects who murdered one another to establish whether it pleased God more if you put a tamarind seed in the left nostril or the right nostril; and the Chinese empire, dulled with opium, had nothing to offer but a nation of dazed sleepwalkers.

There was still Europe, and Maurice and his companion were very much interested in the changes there. Pérégrinus had stayed there a long time, and could describe it in detail.

In that continent the transformation was even more pronounced, because the passionate vitality of its peoples had propelled them more rapidly on their chosen paths. Elsewhere, nations had slipped unheeding toward their inevitable ends; but in Europe each nation had its own obsessions, riding them like horses from hell, urging them on with voice and spur. To see them in such headlong pursuit of their own perdition, overcome by their most dangerous instincts, they invited comparison with Alaric's barbarians. Panic-stricken in the moment of defeat, these men had hurled themselves in their chariots into the midst of their conquerors, believing they had them on the run, and had charged to their death as fast as their chariots could carry them. Pérégrinus had seen Russia come to grief in her hurried efforts at civilization—a giant raised by hand under emperors of genius, who had tried in vain to create a nation. Stripped of her distinctive character, without the will needed to forge another one, without strong government but not entirely barbaric, Russia had worn out fifty czars, forever aping neighboring civilizations, and sinking back into obscurity just as surely as the sun sinks below the horizon.

Germany had hardly ever been in a more contented state. Philosophizing with pipe and glass, the Germans had debated for a whole century the etymology of the word *liberty*, for another century the essential meaning of the word, for a century the limits of freedom, and again for a century the conclusions reached. Having arrived at that point, her kings had established a constitution that allowed complete freedom of thought, so long as people took care to say nothing; complete freedom of feeling, so long as they did not let those feelings show; and freedom to wish for anything they desired, so long as they did not seek to realize their ambitions. Then the Germans, with considerable self-satisfaction, had lit their pipes, replenished their glasses, and gone back to chanting patriotic songs while shaking a fist at France as they sang:

No, you will never have our German Rhine

In any event, France hardly ever dreamed of laying claim to the Rhine. Because of cheese-paring administrations, an honest electorate, and tents stolen from the emperor of Morocco, France had collapsed into a national

bankruptcy that was followed by private bankruptcies.[2] Thrown back into feudalism by the power of the bankers, driven from every ocean where she had once traded, with no other encouragement for her agriculture than the reports of scientific societies, and the money given to the directors of stud farms, her people had opted to console themselves with entertainments and masked balls. The French people, typified by the late Chicard and Pomaré, took to their deserted fields, empty ports, and ruined towns and danced a polka that had been banned by the prefect of police.[3] Some remnant of her former glory still survived, however, in that most intellectual of nations: France still supplied the world with milliners and chefs.

Belgium, the world center for infringing copyright in publications from all five continents, had ended up running out of space to store her documents in octodecimo and in trigesimo-segundo. They had to be used as building blocks for the construction of towns inhabited solely by paper manufacturers, compositors, bookbinders, and finishers, each one living like a rat in his piece of cheese. One day, however, a spark set fire to these mountains of printed paper, and Belgium went up in flames along with its puny inhabitants. When Pérégrinus passed that way, there was a search going on to find their remains in the ashes.

During the same period, Switzerland had been bought by a company

*Paris in the year 3000*

that enclosed it within a great wall, built with stones from the forti-
fications of Paris. This company was exploiting her scenery, her waterfalls
and glaciers. There was a pay station before every natural attraction, so
that it was impossible to admire the Rhine Falls without buying a ticket
and depositing your umbrella. This huge park had a dozen monumental
gates, and on the front of them the company had caused to be engraved
the old axiom: NO MONEY, NO SWITZERLAND.

Around this time, Italy had become a special domain, but it was closed
to the public in general. The Papal States had been bought by a Jewish
banker, who then went on to add to his wealth by expropriating the property of the King of Naples, the Emperor of Austria, and the Duke of Tus-
cany. He had given orders for the rebuilding of public monuments, and
the restoration of paintings and statues; but the people were still naked
and hungry.

The situation was quite different in Turkey. Throughout history the
European powers had seen that country as an ancient cloak of imperial
purple from which they all wanted a piece, and Turkey had remained
cross-legged and supine, letting the world go by. Every time a province
was seized, the Turks repeated: *God is great!* and had a sherbet. That situation continued until that day when the crows that were tearing strips
from her flesh turned upon one another and fought to decide which one of

them should have the best portion. After a war in which two or three million men perished, they all decided to accept what had before been unac-
ceptable. They agreed on an amicable division of the spoils; but when
they came to claim their allotted portions, they discovered that there was
nothing left. While the quarrel about possession was going on, the Turkish
nation had quietly expired; and where her invaders had hoped to secure
some populated areas, all they found were desert wastes where a few
bored old camels were sleeping.

The English had dreamed of making something out of that situation, if
only by selling the camels' hides, when a revolution suddenly brought an
end to their triumphant depredations. Up to that time their aristocracy
were warm and comfortable in their fine woollen garments, and lived well
on roast beef and sherry. They were as knowledgeable about the art of
boxing as about the art of government, and their poverty-stricken masses
were kept in subjection, dulled by the unhealthy air of the mills and a diet
of potatoes and gin. Their rulers had allowed the last glimmers of divine
light to die away in their souls. And then, when it was brought to their notice that these were also God's children, that they were men to be given a
place in the sun, and not relegated to the level of beasts, they replied:

"What good is that? The beast is a more patient worker!"

But one day that patience wore thin: the beast, grown desperate with
suffering, was transformed into a ferocious animal that flew at its master's
throat and ripped it out.

*England in the year 3000*

Once the violence had begun, the anger of the oppressed swept through England like a whirlwind. What could they have preserved, those who had never owned anything? Property was their enemy; for twenty centuries it had been their master. They were men, but they had been the slaves of inanimate things; so those things had to be destroyed, wiped out! Everything vanished in that first wave of destruction: palaces maintained by the sweat of their brows; mills where they languished like prisoners; machines whose steel arms had robbed them, mouthful by mouthful, of bread for their families; ships into which they were press-ganged and held by fear; ports, towns, arsenals, monuments to a glory paid for by their blood and tears. Oh! What cries of joy arose over these heaps of ruins and ashes. Those riches, that power, that glory were so many links in their chains that vengeance had broken. Did they have a flag, those who had no rights? Were they a nation, those who were not human beings? They wiped out the past, because it reminded them only of their humiliation and suffering. Then, when everything was razed to the ground, they danced around the ruins, like the savage round the stake where he has endured long torture.

But their unskilled hands could not build anything to replace what they had torn down. The kings of England had fallen, and power had gone with them. The conqueror, coarse and ignorant, did not even try to put the pieces together. He left the bramble to grow on the deserted roads, the weeds on the abandoned canals, the holly and the quick thorn in the barren fields. The revolution had not been a reform, but only a deliverance. His halter broken, the beast had gone back to the forests. When Pérégrinus saw the three kingdoms, the transformation was already accomplished. Instead of the energetic race, stubborn and proud, whose navigators had linked two continents, he had found only a savage people, living on piracy, perpetually at war, and eating their prisoners instead of the roast beef of old England. Some feeble remnants of the proscribed aristocracy were hiding in the mountains, constantly pursued by the descendants of John Bull who, in the absence of chamois, hunted lords.

Spain had also passed through this period of irregular warfare; but, thanks to the great improvement achieved in this kind of sport, the participants were soon decimated and destroyed. As the number of Spaniards diminished, the *Mesta* finished the work they had begun. As the numbers of human inhabitants dwindled, the numbers of sheep increased; and their enormous flocks, continually nibbling at the hedges, at the crops and meadows, ended up turning the kingdom into a great barren expanse in which the sole inhabitants were sheep.

*Spain in the year 3000*

While Maurice was listening to these accounts, Manomane had continued his perambulation with Marthe, and they had stopped in front of a young woman seated in a grove of cotton plants whose silky filaments floated on the breeze like petals from fully opened flowers. Dressed in a faded skirt, her breast half covered by a pale blue stole, she was leaning forward, and with a distracted air pulling the petals from flowers heaped up at her feet. A twig, pulled from the hawthorn hedge and full of sharp thorns, was entwined in her dark hair.

At the sound of footsteps she started and turned her head, blushed at the sight of strangers, and pulled the stole more closely about her.

But her eyes, lowered at first, were raised almost at once to Marthe with a timid but tender expression.

Marthe, feeling an instant sympathy, stopped. There was, in the smiles they exchanged, one of those instant communications of feeling that make any outpouring of words unnecessary. Then, with what seemed an involuntary movement, the young woman rose, and with a murmured exclamation held out her hands to Marthe.

"Upon my soul, our beautiful dreamer likes you!" said Manomane, his brusque manner softening slightly.

"Ah! . . . I thought . . . yes . . . her face reminded me of my mother!" the young woman stammered, with tears in her eyes.

Marthe took her hands, and held them in her own.

{ 121 }

**MISS RÊVEUSE**

*An image of madness in the year 3000*

"It's a rare honor, coming from our Miss Rêveuse," said the doctor with a smile. "She usually runs away at the approach of visitors."

"Why should I let them see the sad spectacle of my madness?" the young woman asked in gentle tones. "The wicked mock, and the good are distressed."

"But I?" asked Marthe, leaning toward her.

"You," said Miss Rêveuse, with a trusting and tender look. "You understand me!"

"Did you hear?" Manomane asked quietly, turning to his colleague. "The mad understand each other. Let's leave them together and you will see."

The men drew away, still continuing to observe them, while Marthe and the young woman started on one of those conversations where souls confide in each other about whatever the fancy dictates, like two children holding hands and skipping through the countryside.

Rêveuse spoke of her mother, whom she had hardly known, and the tears flowed; then she showed Marthe the flowers she was cultivating, and gave a little cry of joy to see them opening. She sighed when outlining her griefs, and smiled when describing her joys. Like the waves of the sea, her mood changed, sometimes in the depths, and sometimes bright in the sunshine of hope.

Marthe listened enchanted, following every movement of her spirit as one follows the movements of a restless child; she looked in vain for signs of madness, and found only the passing fancies of a young and unfettered imagination.

Rêveuse, however, averred that she knew she was mad: in her heart she knew it. She could not speak of it without the tears brimming under her long dark lashes. She crossed her hands over her breast with a touching childlike resignation, and all her yearnings and hopes were stifled abruptly by the cry:

"I am mad!"

"Mad?" repeated Marthe in disbelief. "Who told you so? What grounds have you for thinking so? Where is the proof?"

"Alas! My whole life!" replied Rêveuse. "My thoughts have never been like those of other people. I have shared neither their happiness nor their loves. When I was little, the most pleasurable thing in the world was to be with my mother; I would sit at her feet without saying a word, for it was happiness enough to feel the folds of her dress against my shoulder, and to know that her gaze rested on me. When she died, I wanted to be with her, knowing nothing of death except that it was a separation, and I did not want to live without my mother. I escaped from the house and ran to the graveyard; I went from tomb to tomb, spelling out the names, and when I found the one I was looking for, I sat there saying: 'Mother, it is me. Do not send me away.'

"The day passed and I never felt hungry. I cried because I was alone; then I gathered wild flowers to make a posy for my mother. Night fell; I said my prayers; I called good night to my dead mother, and went to sleep on her tomb.

"It was there that they found me the next day, and those who had come in search had to drag me away. When I arrived back at the house, I threw myself down on my knees, imploring them to restore my mother to me; I refused to eat; I wanted to die to be with her in the grave. That was the first time I heard them say: 'She is mad.'

"Time did assuage my grief, but did not banish it. I made it my custom never to leave the places dear to the one I could not forget, to do the things she did, to keep her tastes and habits alive. At first they were alarmed at the persistence of my love for her. Finally, they made fun of me. Their mockery confirmed me even more in the path I had chosen. However, I did not speak of it nor let it be seen, and I grew up always alone with my memories.

"That solitude gave me the taste for reading, for books are the consoling and faithful companions of the solitary. I opened the wasteland of my life to the old storytellers and the old poets. Their heroes became my friends, and I shared in their misfortunes and their triumphs as if they were living, breathing people. I would be found in transports of joy, or bathed in tears, without being able to give any reason except the happiness of the Primerose family or the death of Marguerite. I no longer lived in the company of the living but dwelt with shadows. These alone excited my admiration, love, and hatred. I no longer knew who our neighbors were, but I was very familiar with Childe Harold, Jocelyn, and Faust. Their names were forever on my lips, and those around me, full of pitying scorn, repeated more insistently:

"'She is mad.'

"But this madness was to grow even more pronounced, alas! By immersing myself in the delightful visions of the poets, I gradually began to live my life among them. Under their inspiration, my tastes were refined, and I aspired to a higher life. Having grown accustomed to such an intoxicating draught, I rejected everyday existence as an insipid drink. In my heart I built a mysterious temple where there was room only for the most noble and enchanting creatures of my imagination; I created for myself an ideal, and swore I would wait for it to become reality.

"In vain my family said that it was time for me to marry, and that wealthy suitors were seeking my hand. The only fiancé I would accept had been chosen long ago; but he only existed in my imagination. I was like one of those heroes of fairy tales who are dying of love for an unknown princess when they have seen only her portrait. At first I refused without giving a reason; then, when surprise turned to displeasure, and then to reproach, I thought to put a stop to it all by revealing my true aspirations. A single cry went up:

"'She is mad! She is mad!'

"I had to believe it, because no one understood me; no one felt as I did. I accepted being shut away, resigned myself to never finding a place in a world made for other hearts and minds, and told myself:

"'You are mad.' And I let them bring me here."

"And you will stay here?" Marthe exclaimed with tender concern, holding our dreamer's hands tightly in her own.

"Until that day when the doctor decides that I am a hopeless case and sends me to the Island for the Incurables. But here are some new visitors. Their curiosity only humiliates me, and I am afraid of the questions they will ask. Good-bye. Do not forget me."

She embraced Marthe affectionately and disappeared like a startled doe into the woodland groves.

Marthe rejoined her companions, from whom Manomane had just taken his leave, and the three of them walked along to the Observatory where M. Atout was waiting for them.

In passing they visited the Museum where they saw, among the representatives of vanished species, those domestic animals that found favor only by their devotion to man, and those wild beasts whose sole appeal was their beauty. The doctrine of utility had naturally removed from the animal kingdom anything that did not produce an appreciable and immediate benefit.

Again, the species preserved there had been very much improved through a program of crossbreeding that had changed their characteristic forms. They were no longer creatures governed by a law of proportion and harmony, but living things modified to give greater profits to the butchery business. Bulls, bred to put on a great deal of weight, had lost their bones; cows were no more than animated machines that turned grass into milk; pigs were no more than masses of flesh, growing larger before one's very eyes. It was all perfect and yet hideous. The animal kingdom, thus revised and corrected, had ceased to be a pleasure to look at, and had become simply a source of food. God Himself would not have recognized His creation. Most of the creatures made by Him no longer existed except in the form science had given them. His work of creation had been put in a flask with alcohol and handed over to the taxidermist.

In the Botanic Garden near the Museum, there was a complete collection of all the herbs, arranged by families, all with beautiful red labels giving their Latin names in case they should not be recognized. There were also greenhouses where plants from all five continents were cultivated to instruct and give pleasure to the public who never visited the place. Fortunately, our visitors met M. Vertèbre, whose acquaintance they had made on the *Dolphin*. For them he now opened doors normally kept locked. He showed them a seedling of a northern fir growing under a cloche, oak trees in pots, and a border of poplars fifteen centimeters high. These were specimens from the virgin forests of the ancient world. And then they marveled at cherries the size of melons, and bananas that had to be cut down like groves of tall trees.

When they left the greenhouses, M. Vertèbre led them to the little compartments reserved for the menagerie, where he showed them whale embryos he was feeding like goldfish in large bowls, bottle-fed baby seals, and polar bears not yet mature, which he wanted to introduce into the country and naturalize. Finally, since time was pressing, they took leave of the esteemed professor of zoology, who called them back to announce that one of the great Sauria of the West Indies was about to give birth, and to invite them to come again to see the new arrivals.

## M. VERTÈBRE

*Member of the Zoological Society in the year 3000*

# §XIV

*A fashionable cemetery — Vehicles built for visiting the dead —*
*Graveyard bazaars — System of taxes — Choice*
*of epitaphs — A funeral broker.*

When they left the Botanic Gardens, our visitors had to stop for a long file of people following a hearse. Blaguefort was among them and, recognizing Maurice, he left the cortege to speak to him. The young man wanted to know who was the person they were taking for burial.

"Good heavens! You know him," replied Blaguefort. "It's our old traveling companion, the Racahout man. The committee legally appointed to make him lose weight succeeded in confirming his identity, but the process killed him. It is a loss that will be deeply felt by his family, and especially by the company for whom he was a living advertisement. I am here because of the orthonasal prosthesis, which, as you know, he had ordered."

"So," said Maurice, "a gendarme's mistake has cost one man his life, ruined a family, and jeopardized many interests."

"Without their being able to claim compensation," said Blaguefort. "If a private individual makes a wrongful accusation, he is reviled as a slanderer. If there is proof that he acted in haste or imprudently, he is held responsible. But officialdom is in the privileged position of being allowed to make mistakes. If it is ignorant of a law, if it ruins an honest man, if it brings death and desolation to the innocent, it is enough for it to say: 'I made a mistake,' and that is deemed sufficient reparation. It is the same old story of the wolf who thinks the crane very lucky not to have been eaten:[1]

> Allez, vous êtes une ingrate,
> Ne tombez jamais sous ma patte!

While he was speaking, Blaguefort had approached the carriages again, and Maurice and Marthe, who had taken leave of Doctor Minimum, followed him.

They arrived at the cemetery, which was surrounded by a kind of bazaar.

"Here you have an example of a fashionable cemetery," said Blaguefort. "All those who live in style must arrange to be buried here, or else it would be considered bad form. In truth, the directors of this funerary establishment have done everything to preserve the reputations of the deceased. They are fully aware that the obsequies for the dead must be observed in a way that best suits the living; and so the cemetery is served by three lines of vehicles called *mourning cars*. The widow and orphan have only to pull the cord for the driver to stop for them at the grave of their loved one. You will find, too, special rooms for people who wish to mourn in private, and vendors of ointment for red eyes. The bazaar next to the cemetery stocks everything that might be needed in the service of those who have passed on and of their families, from wreaths of dried flowers arranged on ribs of whalebone to capons à la Marengo. There are even funeral orators who, in return for a modest fee, will undertake the task of pronouncing a eulogy for the dead, and of expressing the hope *that the earth will lie lightly upon him*. The person speaking at the moment, whom we cannot hear at this distance, is one of the most sought-after of these functionaries. A former auctioneer, he has brought to his new career all the tricks of his old trade. Depending on how much he is paid, he will augment or decrease by 30 percent the virtues of the deceased. But the ceremony is finished here, and all that remains for us is to take leave of the brother of the deceased who has been in charge of the funeral."

They tried to approach the latter, who had been saying good-bye to the assistants and was making his way to another entrance, but he was besieged by a great crowd of workers who were hoping to exploit his affection for the deceased. First there was the monumental mason offering smaller versions of funerary monuments in a range of prices and forms; the gravedigger soliciting a tip, holding out his cap on which was written: *It is forbidden to beg*; the gardener suggesting the planting of cypress and scarlet runners around the grave; the janitor waiting for the gratuity that every new tenant must pay to the church; the clerk for the *mourning cars*, offering a season ticket good for fifty trips; and finally, the sellers of everlasting flowers, angels in imitation stone, and porcelain funerary lamps, all offering their wares at cost price. Blaguefort shook his hand, then when he had walked some distance with his companions, said:

"They say the unfortunate man will be ruined. One could live for ten years in Sans-Pair on the sum one has to pay to die there. And that's not all. Here you see only the incidental expenses. There is also the money due to the tax man. Wherever the tear-stained black of mourning is seen, you will find the tax man who comes running with open mouth and sharpened claws. There is a tithe to pay on every inheritance. Like the vampires of Bohemia, the system grows fat on the dead. It may be that a woman has lost a husband who was everything to her; that a widow weeps for the son who supported her; that a child is overcome by the death of a father on whom he depended completely—the tax man arrives, and, in the name of society, takes away a slice of their inheritance, so that they may be allowed to hold on to the rest. Every death certificate is a bill of exchange written in favor of the tax man. In truth, these regulations bring in funds for the treasury and provide for the maintenance of thirty-two million civil servants, all occupied for eight hours a day in cutting quills for their pens and ruling lines on paper. It is one of the branches of that great tree that is always loaded with flowers and fruit that we call the tax system."

"No doubt there is a principle behind this system?" Maurice inquired.

"An admirable principle," replied Blaguefort. "It had long been observed that the poorest men had the most modest needs. Those who frame our laws concluded from that fact that the one at the bottom of the heap, who lived on nothing, must have, more than anyone else, abundant funds put by. Consequently, they made him support a double burden: provide double the amount of service and pay twice the taxes. Everything he consumed had been subjected to three or four taxes. But the intended aim was not easily achieved. For a long time the poor devil had struggled against this *distributive equality* of the law. A tax was imposed on food— he went without; on clothing—he went naked; on daylight—he blocked up his windows. Every attempt to find a tax that could not be circumvented came to nothing, until our minister of finance made the breakthrough: he created a tax on noses. From then on, whoever rejoiced in this extremity had to pay without giving any further information; the tax man needed neither age, nor profession, nor domicile, nor wealth: only the nose had to be declared. Some politicians wanted to make the tax proportionate to the size of the latter, saying it was sufficient to apply the metric measurement that showed the ratio of the nose of each citizen to the diameter of the earth; but those of the opposition party argued that all men are equal in the eyes of the law, and the proposition in favor of this nasal measurement was abandoned."

"However," Maurice objected, "men who have nothing cannot pay anything—beggars, for example."

"We have no beggars," Blaguefort replied.

"You have created homes for them then?"

"We have created signposts for them. The money that once went to the relief of the poor has been used to tell them that no more relief would be forthcoming. From then on, wherever they went, they encountered the familiar notice: BEGGING IS FORBIDDEN IN THIS DISTRICT. Thus, going from one signpost to another, from one prohibition to another, they inevitably ended in some ditch where they died from exhaustion and hunger. You would not believe how quickly this procedure brought about the disappearance of beggars. Some remained, however, helped by renegade citizens; but the government has just proposed legislation under which the givers of alms will receive the same punishment as the recipients. In this way we hope to root out completely the very concept of what they used to call charity. No one will rely on anyone else. All will be fully occupied in looking after themselves. There will be no more demands because there will be no more giving, and all men will get on quietly enjoying their good fortune . . . or their lack of it. But here we are at the entrance to the cemetery. Before we leave, would you not like to have a look round the city of the dead?"

At that, Maurice and his companion gazed around them. The graveyard was divided into three sections enclosed by railings and served by a concierge. The smallest contained the most famous names, and their graves could only be visited in the company of several attendants. The first guide pointed out the most illustrious warriors, received his gratuity, and passed you on to a second attendant, who, having shown you the great writers and obtained a second gratuity passed you on to a colleague who was in charge of deceased scientists. The fee always had to be negotiated before you reached a fourth guide who presided over famous artistes. Each guide had, in addition, a little sideline, such as a trade in cuttings from Napoleon's willow tree; locks of Voltaire's hair—fair or dark according to demand; pieces from the coffin of Héloïse and Abélard; the snuffbox of Lord Byron, who never took snuff; white roses gathered at the tomb of Robespierre, and aconites growing wild on the grave of M. de Talleyrand.

The second section was dedicated to bankers, members of the middle class, men of independent means, merchants, and civil servants. It was there that carved crosses of honor were to be found, busts under glass, and little stuffed dogs. As for the epitaphs, there were just three to choose from, always written under the names. The tomb of a head of a house bore the inscription:

HE WAS A GOOD HUSBAND, A GOOD FATHER,
GOOD FRIEND
AND ELECTOR OF HIS DISTRICT.

For the grave of a young woman :

HER LIFE WAS THAT OF THE ROSE
THAT BLOOMS FOR ONLY A DAY.
*REQUIESCAT IN PACE.*

For the tomb of a child :

ANOTHER ANGEL IN HEAVEN.
BURIAL PLOT HELD IN PERPETUITY.

The third area was dedicated to the poor. These leave no monuments save in the hearts of their families . . . when they leave any at all. At the very most some stones, some crosses of blackened wood on the path to the great communal trench into which were piled the generations born in poverty, who lived without hope, and were abandoned in death. There, no cross was to be found, no headstone, but in the distance children kneeling, women quietly weeping—living epitaphs for all the world to read: a more eloquent tribute than those engraved in marble and bronze.

Blaguefort and his companions were on their way to one of the exits when a funeral broker barred the way. He was a very thin giant of a man, dressed in a pair of black shorts embellished with teardrops and wearing a cloak of the same color embroidered with a skull and crossbones.

"These gentlemen have seen the cemetery," he said, with that relent-

less volubility of the market-stall trader accustomed to proclaiming his wares all day without pause. . . . These gentlemen can rest assured . . . it is the finest establishment in Sans-Pair, the only one where people can be buried in the proper style. . . . The plots of land get more expensive all the time, and people fight over them to be buried here. Before long, they will all be taken. Would these gentlemen not think it prudent to select in advance the place they would like to occupy one day? I can help them with this. I can arrange for three meters, six meters, nine meters, and no one can secure better terms. I enjoy the favor of the management. These gentlemen could design their plots . . . there are all types of planting schemes. . . . Would they like a willow . . . a cutting from that of Napoleon . . . guaranteed. . . . The willow is very well established. . . . I also can quote a fixed price for monuments—simple gravestones, ornamented headstones, mausoleums with statues and other appropriate furnishings. When it comes to embalming, I hold the permit to employ the Putridus method; I preserve bodies in all their original grace and vitality. Even their nearest and dearest would not be able to tell the difference between the subject I have worked on and the living person. In addition to all that, I supply original epitaphs; I prepare biographical articles; and, as a special favor, I obtain permission for the deceased to be interred in the area reserved for great men. . . . These gentlemen will not find anyone else who can manage these things as I can. For twenty years I have been taking care of the dead. I know everyone here; I am at home here. If these gentlemen ask for a discount, we could discuss it. There will never be a better time. The management is planning improvements and needs money; you can buy a grave site for next to nothing. . . . These gentlemen can be sure of getting a very good deal . . . If they do not wish to make use of the plot themselves, they can let someone else have it. There is no other property that one can dispose of so easily; it is a house that will never be short of tenants. . . . These gentlemen don't wish to commit themselves. . . . They will regret it. . . ."

Fortunately, Maurice had arrived at the entrance to the cemetery. The funeral broker stopped at the gate like a trader at the door of his shop, but the sound of his voice pursued the visitors for some time after they had set out for the observatory.

# §XV

*Observatory of Sans-Pair—How M. de l'Empyrée saw on the moon what was happening at home—Meeting of all the Academies—Usefulness of the urban guard for druggists, the soft furnishings industry, and wine merchants—What must be done to establish the right to a prize for virtue.*

The observatory of Sans-Pair was built in the middle of a very large public garden on a hill that commanded an uninterrupted view to the horizon. It was there that the chief astronomer of Sans-Pair maintained the state register of heavenly bodies, keeping a scrupulous record of their ages, their conjunctions and oppositions, and their deaths. But, since his latest discoveries, the moon occupied his entire attention. He searched for it by day, contemplated it by night, and, whether awake or asleep, talked about it all the time. Endymion himself had never shown so tender a preoccupation with his pale mistress.

M. Atout and his guests found him glued to his huge telescope in transports of joy. "I can still see them," he said to Blaguefort, who was standing right behind him, "and they are the same people that I saw yesterday."

"Who are they?" said the Académicien, coming closer.

"Who?" replied Blaguefort, quite carried away. "Upon my soul! A pair of lunar lovers whom our illustrious friend has been observing for a week. He has witnessed all the first steps in a love affair—signaling from windows, exchange of letters, scaling of walls."

He was interrupted by the astronomer. "See, here they come. Yes, I can make everything out, except the face of the veiled lady. . . . There is a large garden with a summer house . . . and alley ways of palm trees . . . and now they are about to sit down under a fig tree."

"What the devil! That's the tree where our first mother had her encounter with Satan," said M. Atout.

"The lady seems rather alarmed," the astronomer continued, without taking his eyes off the lens. . . . "She is looking behind her. . . ."

"Are there any husbands on the moon?" asked the commercial traveler. "Good heavens! I know now why she is making that crescent-shaped sign."

"Hold on a moment," said M. de l'Empyrée, "the lady has decided to sit down."

"Good."

"He takes her hand. . . ."

"And she permits it?"

"No, she resists. . . ."

"That's so that he will hold it more tightly."

"Yes, he holds it against his heart. . . ."

"Oh! goodness gracious!"

He falls on his knees. . . ."

"Ah, even that! But does that mean that up there they behave just like us down here?" murmured Blaguefort, in some surprise.

Maurice had been watching and saying nothing; but he now interrupted with a smile to say, "I think you will find their behavior the same in every way."

"Why is that?" asked Mr. Atout.

"Because the telescope is now in the horizontal position again, and instead of pointing at the moon, it is trained on your own garden."

M. de l'Empyrée leapt up.

"The garden," he echoed. "How on earth! . . . the palm trees! . . . the summer house! . . . the fig tree . . ."

"There they are, before our eyes."

The astronomer looked out in front of him.

"It's true," he said. "I hadn't noticed."

And leaping up again:

"But the lady," he exclaimed. "The lady whose veil has just been raised . . ."

He ran to the telescope, lowered it to look, then gave a cry. . . . It was Madame de l'Empyrée!

What he was looking for in the heavens was happening closer to home.

There was a moment of general embarrassment. Blaguefort and Atout gave each other a look; Maurice walked off a little way; M. de l'Empyrée sat down heavily in his chair, pale and distraught.

"It was not our moon," he finally stammered in dismay.

"It was your garden," said Blaguefort, whose stupefaction was just as great.

"It was not a lunar woman," the astronomer went on.

"It was your own wife," said the commercial traveler.

"And all this was going on a few steps away from us," the learned gentleman continued.

"And we have just set up a business for interplantary telegraphy," added the industrialist.

M. de l'Empyrée put his head in his hands.

"And so I haven't discovered anything," he cried in despairing tones.

"Allow me," Blaguefort interrupted, always the first to regain his composure. "What you have seen should not be dismissed so lightly. Some advantage may be gained from it. I would propose that you do not yet sell shares for your new business, since astronomical progress has not yet reached that point. But you could start legal proceedings and claim damages."

"What! For . . . ?"

"Precisely."

"But who will pay?"

"The lunar man, whom I recognized—in other words, our minister for ethics and religion, who is undoubtedly acting outside his calling at the moment."

"Ah! The traitor."

"You should say the unlucky one. You could claim from him what the law calls a consolation award—possibly hundreds of thousands of francs."

"Which I could use to perfect the telescope," said M. de l'Empyrée. "You are right! I must turn it to my advantage. Gentlemen, you all saw the insult; you must come with me to the public prosecutor's office to act as witnesses."

He got up to look for his cane and his hat. Maurice tried in vain to calm him down, but the prospect of damages had taken firm hold of the learned gentleman. He was already calculating all the improvements he could make to the instruments of his research. Thanks to the money to be supplied by the minister for religion, he would be certain to know, within three months, if husbands on the moon were entitled to the same consolation awards as those on earth.

The visitors would have been obliged to follow him to the Law Courts, where his complaint would have to be lodged, if M. Atout had not suddenly remembered that the annual general meeting of the Institute of Sans-Pair, of which both were members, was scheduled for that morning. They had just enough time to get there. M. de l'Empyrée resigned himself to postponing his deposition and accepted a seat in the Académicien's carriage, while Maurice and Marthe followed in Blaguefort's flying vehicle.

The latter, who had noticed the distress of the young couple when the astronomer made his discovery, hastened to reassure them.

"We are no longer living in the days," said he, "when the deceived husband demanded the conviction of the seducer, or even his blood; nowadays, he contents himself with his wallet. A wife's betrayal is an inconvenience for which the resulting monetary gain can be a compensation. Moreover, there is now no longer anything shameful about it for the husband—the money it brings in is like an indirect legacy, the munificence of which makes amends for its origin. Isn't it advantageous to stay with the woman who is a source of wealth? If the Jews had known about consolation awards, far from stoning the adulterous wife, they would have raised a statue in her honor next to the Golden Calf. Matrimonial infidelities are no longer a matter of sentiment but of arithmetic. At each new revelation, the husband buys a property in the country with the proceeds of his misfortune, or turns it into an annuity for life. There is no scandal, no gossip, just a simple statement at the outset. One says: *M. \*\*\* has been given an award*, rather as one might say he has been made churchwarden or lance corporal in the National Guard. It is an opportunity to acquire wealth effortlessly—to live the story of the man who for a long time sought riches unsuccessfully, and on returning home found them in his bed. To be fair, I have to confess that we got the idea from England, and that our own civilization has merely perfected it."

The doors of the Institute were guarded by a company of the National Guard. It was the first time that Maurice had seen this city militia, and he was struck by their appearance.

They had been allowed to wear arms and uniforms regarded as too impractical for the army, like children given cast-off military gear so that they could play at soldiers between classes. Each citizen grenadier wore a bearskin helmet three feet high to protect him from sunstroke, riding boots to protect him from chilblains, and an ammunition box full of marshmallows and sticks of barley sugar. Instead of a sword hanging at his side, there was a spectacle case.

"Here you see one of our finest institutions," said Blaguefort. "The National Guard of Sans-Pair has always covered itself with glory—witness the decorations worn by its men. You will find there are no more than two or three drummers who have no medals, and that is for want of influence. It is the guardian of our liberties, even though it is forbidden to express an opinion while under arms. And it is the mainstay of public order, although the municipality still appoints the police. It offers a legitimate career to ambitions that would otherwise be unfulfilled. Some licensed druggist would go to the grave without ever having held public office, if his neighbors had not elected him second lieutenant; some pork butcher would give up the ghost without ever having known social distinction if his position as lance corporal had not brought him three medals. The National Guard also brings profits to several businesses in our country—for instance, innkeepers and merchants of whitening and sandpaper. It ensures a steady stream of people with bad colds, rheumatic problems and aching bones, who swell the profits of doctors and producers of licorice. And finally it keeps alive in the country a military spirit all the more precious because it had almost been consigned to oblivion. When it comes to the services rendered by these citizens in arms, they are so obvious and numerous that I hardly need to enumerate them for you. First of all, they defend all the gates already defended by the police or the army; they guard public monuments from behind closed grilles; they go up and down the town with their boxes, their bearskins, their riding boots, and their blunderbusses, and their job is to apprehend thieves. They also serve a decorative purpose on public occasions, like the vignettes used by the printer to adorn announcements of marriages and notices of funerals.

The young couple found the Institute of Sans-Pair housed in a circular chamber with a gallery for the public. Each Académicien wore a pair of shorts embroidered with a garland of green laurels, and a sword suspended from a broad belt of everlasting flowers. Proceedings began with the reception of a member recently admitted to the Academy of Fine Language. Blaguefort explained to Maurice that nominations were the result of a competitive examination: the one who, in the given time, made the greatest number of visits was more favorably viewed than the other candidates. From this it followed that the surest way to succeed was not to have written a good book, but to possess a good carriage. The newly elected member had gained his place without any trouble. He was a great lord whose complete works consisted of two songs, three New Year's Day letters, and a madrigal.

The permanent secretary whose duty it was to explain the circumstances of the candidate's election, recalled the fame of one of his ancestors, who was a general in the cavalry. The great lord replied with a eulogy of his predecessor, the subject of his two songs. Then they moved on to the distribution of prizes for virtue, known according to ancient custom as the Montyon Prize.[1]

The chairman began by explaining this name, the origin of which was lost in the mists of time. It was made up originally of two words *mont,* or height, and *ione,* a precious stone—from which came *montione,* later corrupted to *montyon,* a symbolic expression that one could translate as *precious mountain,* virtue being essentially the most precious and most important thing in the world.

Then came the report on the candidates given awards by the Academy. The first was a man whose life's work had been to help the poor of his parish. After feeding and clothing them for twenty years, he himself came to be hungry and in rags. The Academy, through the agency of its chairman, had christened him the St. Vincent de Paul of the republic of United Interests and accorded him, by way of encouragement, three pounds of good chocolate and a special pair of ceremonial shorts.

The second candidate was a workman whose head had been crushed under a beam, and who had suffered a fractured skull in saving a family from a fire. They compared him to Mucius Scévola, and his reward was a cotton hat embroidered with a crown of laurels.

The third one, a woman, had lost her sight working every night in the service of her old master. She was given a pair of spectacles bearing the official stamp of the Institute.

The fourth was awarded a special pair of shoes for his achievement in saving twenty-two people from drowning.

Finally, many others, more or less impoverished or crippled through their dedication, received gratuities varying in value from fifty centimes to ten francs.

They made no distinction in award between a citizen soldier who had served for thirty years without missing a single tour of duty, a coach driver who had gone through seven wives and had used his whip only on his horses, an assistant clerk at the savings bank who was always polite, and a helpful employee at the library.

These last two prizewinners were the only ones whose qualifications seemed questionable, and who occasioned some murmurs of incredulity.

Then the proceedings moved on to the prizes for history, political economy, and poetry.

In history it was a case of deciding who was the greater genius, Hannibal or Alexander (the official line being that it must be Alexander).

The permanent secretary announced that none of the candidates had dealt with the question as he himself would have dealt with it, and that, in consequence, the prize would be withheld until next year.

The proposition put to the economists was to find a means of improving the lot of the most ignorant and poverty-stricken classes in society.

The chairman announced that all the candidates had come to grief in looking for the means, because there were none, and that the question had been taken out of the competition.

Finally, the theme set for the poetry competition was a description of spring, including an elegiac passage on the cultivation of early potatoes.

The commission appointed to judge the three thousand entries let it be known that all the poets had described spring in their own countryside, instead of painting a picture of *spring itself,* and that most of them had fallen into grievous error on the cultivation of solanaceous plants. In consequence, the prize was changed to an honorable mention accorded to entry number 940 by an anonymous author.

Here there was a break in proceedings. A group of Immortals left the room, and lemonade sellers circulated in the public galleries. Acquaintances exchanged greetings and small talk, information about absent friends, invitations to balls, what was happening on the Exchange, the current epidemic—every subject, in fact, except the proceedings just concluded. Only after an hour had passed did the president's bell announce the resumption of the sitting.

There now appeared on the agenda the communications received from other academies.

First came the reading of a paper that set out to determine whether the Shepherd Kings were black or simply dark-skinned; then a fable illustrating the following profound theme: *that the weak are more often oppressed than the strong;* finally, an archaeological dissertation on the subject of the spurs of Francis I.

But these were a mere prelude, a curtain-raiser before the main play. At last the bibliophile appeared at the rostrum with the first chapter of his famous treatise *The Manners and Customs of France in the Nineteenth Century.* The reading had been announced three months ago, and word had spread about how wonderful it was. All the people in the audience were leaning over the gallery rail in anticipation. There was complete and total silence. And then the Académicien began to speak in those solemn and cadenced tones that the bourgeoisie call *a beautiful voice.*

# §XVI

*Paper given by an Académicien of the year three thousand on the manners and customs of the French in the nineteenth century—How the French had no knowledge of machines, navigation, or statistics, and how they all died violent deaths according to the evidence of notaries—Government charged with composing epitaphs for famous courtesans— Dress worn by the kings of France when on horseback— Names of authors were allegorical—Remarkable language employed in conversation.*

"It has been said many times, gentlemen, that as long as there remain some traces of the literature and the arts of a nation, that nation is not dead. Research can fit the pieces together and make it live again like the antediluvian creatures reconstructed for us by the inductive reasoning of science.

"Are literature and the arts not, in effect, a faithful reflection of the customs and moral climate of an epoch? Do we not find there a picture of habits, beliefs, characters, and feelings? If we have only faulty information about people who lived in other times, we have only our own laziness to blame, since a serious study would have made the truth apparent.

"It is this kind of study we have attempted for the French in the nineteenth century.

"We have devoted fifteen years to visiting their monuments, examining their paintings and statues and, above all, studying their books—that immense gallery in which all the distinctive characteristics of an age are revealed.

"The work that we have the honor to submit to you is the result of these long years of research."

(Here the speaker paused, ostensibly to take a drink, and the public, taking the hint, applauded.)

"First of all, gentlemen, let us register a protest against the common prejudice that until now has regarded the French people as lightweight, fickle, and pleasure-seeking. That is far from the case. A careful study of what they have left behind tells us that there was a dark side—that they were passionate and bloodthirsty, with hands ever reaching to grasp sword or phial of poison. Their dramatists, their poets, their novelists, who have painted the customs of the age, leave no room for doubt on that score.

"To cite only one example, we have calculated from a reading of their works that seventeen-twentieths of legitimate unions ended in the death of one of the partners. The normal consequence of marriage was suicide or murder; it was exceptional for one spouse not take the life of the other.

"So common was this kind of behaviour that a husband strangled his wife on their wedding night, simply because he could not remember her name.[a]

"Lovers fared hardly any better: either the woman killed the man to teach him to be more careful,[b] or he killed her to avoid the reproaches of her husband,[c] or they killed themselves in a suicide pact, as we can read on any page of the newspapers of that time.

"In addition, there were all the little accidents: the hand that had to be amputated because it was caught in a door;[d] the eye put out by the one-eyed husband too eager for equality;[e] the branding iron applied to the

[a] See *La Confession* (J. Janin).
[b] See *Les Mémoires du Diable* (F. Soulié).
[c] See *Antony* (A. Dumas).
[d] See *La Grille du Château* (F.Soulié).
[e] See *Le Général Guillaume* (É. Souvestre).

forehead;[f] duels fought every year at the first sign of spring;[g] stones dropped deliberately from builders' scaffolding.[h]

"These accidents and a thousand others affected all classes and ages indiscriminately. One has only to read *LES MYSTÈRES DE PARIS*, that admirable picture of nineteenth-century society, to understand how difficult it was to avoid death by drowning, stabbing, poisoning, or being immured or strangled in the very heart of civilized France. Evidently, the ones who escaped assassination were set apart—social rarities who served no doubt to supply the ranks of the upper chamber, which, as everyone knows, was composed of old men, *pares ætate*, whence comes the name *peers*.

"This multiplicity of violent deaths was mainly the work of notaries, high-society ladies, millionaires, and doctors. Doctors disposed of their patients in order to inherit from them more quickly;[i] millionaires used their wealth to hire assassins to get rid of men, and to introduce poison into bouquets of flowers for women;[j] great ladies watched the murder of their rivals in their own homes;[k] and notaries maintained an account with poisoners, hired killers, and men who specialized in drowning accidents in Paris or the suburbs.

"The only resort for honest men in this general disorder came in the form of German princes, who left their country disguised as workmen to go to champion virtue in the bordellos of the rue Aux-Fèves,[l, 1] or escaped convicts who opened up a future for the impoverished young and discovered in a house of ill fame the woman who would make them happy.[m]

"Often the influence of these champions of virtue was counteracted by the famous Society of Jesus, with the assistance of trainers of wild animals from Germany, stranglers from India, and directors of mental homes in Paris.[n]

"You can well imagine, gentlemen, the morals of such a society. There were little French working girls living saintly lives among painters, solicitors' clerks, and shop assistants;[o] but well-born ladies had nothing to oc-

[f] See *Mathilde* (E. Sue).
[g] See *Rêve d'Amour* (F. Soulié).
[h] See *L'Histoire des Treize* (H. Balzac).
[i] See *Les Réprouvés et les Élus* (É. Souvestre).
[j] See *Mathilde* (E. Sue).
[k] See *L'Histoire des Treize* (H. de Balzac).
[l] See *Les Mystères de Paris* (E. Sue).
[m] See *Le Père Goriot* and the sequel (H. de Balzac).
[n] See *Le Juif Errant* (E. Sue).
[o] See *Les Mystères de Paris* (E. Sue).

cupy them but love affairs, and good fathers of families took it upon themselves to provide a little house where their married daughters could conveniently receive their lovers.[p] If by any chance a great lady remained chaste, she never failed to lament on her deathbed the wasted opportunities[q] and to sing in despairing tones the famous psalm:[2]

> Combien je regrette,
> Mon bras si dodu,
> Ma jambe bien faite,
> Et le temps perdu!

In truth, nothing was neglected that would turn women's thoughts in that direction. Art had no chisel, no pen, no paintbrush for anyone other than beautiful sinners; and the administration too showed a tender regard for them. The prefects themselves even built monuments to the most celebrated courtesans, with explanatory inscriptions for the instruction of young girls. The tomb of Agnes Sorel has recently been discovered on the banks of the Loire, and on it are inscribed these words:[3]

THE CANONS OF LOCHES, ENRICHED BY HER GIFTS,

PETITIONED LOUIS XI

TO REMOVE HER TOMB FROM THEIR CHANCEL.

"I GIVE MY CONSENT," HE SAID, "BUT RETURN HER DOWRY."

THE TOMB REMAINED.

AN ARCHBISHOP OF TOURS, LESS JUST,

HAD IT RELEGATED TO A CHAPEL.

WHEN THE REVOLUTION CAME IT WAS THERE DESTROYED.

COMPASSIONATE MEN GATHERED THE BONES OF AGNES,

AND GÉNÉRAL POMMEREUL, PRÉFET OF INDRE-ET-LOIRE,

REBUILT THE MAUSOLEUM FOR THE ONLY

MISTRESS OF OUR KINGS

WHO HAD SERVED HER COUNTRY WELL

IN DEMANDING AS THE PRICE FOR HER FAVORS

THE EXPULSION OF THE ENGLISH FROM FRANCE.

THIS RESTORATION WAS CARRIED OUT

IN THE YEAR M. DCCC. VI.

[p] See *Le Père Goriot* (H. de Balzac).
[q] See *Le Lys dans la Vallée* (H. de Balzac).

"Such were the moral sensibilities of the time, engraved in stone in 1845, and still to be seen at the château of Loches, to the great credit of *men of feeling* and of the French women who wanted to *expel the British from France*.

"The way to make one's fortune in that same era was no less extraordinary. Some grew rich on the legacy of the Wandering Jew; others acquired great wealth by importing gold coins into the towns where gold was scarce, and by planting poplars on the river banks;[r] others by becoming the henchmen of great lords and doing well for themselves in that way.[s]

"No matter how much money they had, all of them carried their riches with them—witness the plays of M. Scribe—and their money could be passed on without making a will. This practice had, it seems, been adopted because of the very understandable terror inspired by the legal profession.

"If we now move on from the moral attitudes of the nation to their ways of dressing, we shall find them no less singular and just as varied. Their apparel showed a wide range of bizarre features. While the deputies appeared in the chamber wearing nothing but a cloak—witness the tomb of Le Général Foy—military commanders, even on foot, wore buckskin trousers and high riding boots, as can be seen in the statue of Le Général Mortier.[4] There is even reason to believe that they strolled about clad in armor, for the author of *Méditations* states positively, when speaking of the emperor Napoleon:[5]

Rien d'humain ne battait sous son épaisse armure.

"This leads to the inevitable conclusion that he wore armor. The gray greatcoat mentioned by Bérenger was no doubt just his undress uniform.

"A good indication of female attire can be seen in the colossal statues found amid the rubble of the ancient Place de la Concorde. These have been shown to be representations, as we have formerly proved, of princesses of the blood royal. Their style of dress was obviously kinder to those with fine figures than to those with weak chests. Indeed, contemporary authors indicate that consumption was one of the commonest illnesses among French women in the nineteenth century.

"The lack of any common mode of dress, revealed in the various monuments created by artists in France, supports the conclusion that dress varied according to circumstance and occasion. To give just one example,

[r] See *Eugénie Grandet* (H. de Balzac).
[s] See *Le Chemin le Plus Court* (J. Janin).

a painting of Louis XIV on foot shows him wearing velvet breeches, a coat of brocade, silk stockings, and high-heeled shoes, while his equestrian statue shows him wearing nothing but his wig. The only possible conclusion is that, when they went riding, the kings of France wore nothing but the latter.

POLLET.

"As for science and engineering, to judge by the monuments that escaped destruction, the French in the nineteenth century were, at the very most, at the level of the ancients. In effect, we can see that, having succeeded in raising an obelisk—a feat performed by the Egyptians two thousand years earlier—one of their architects had engraved on the plinth a triumphal inscription, as if they had done something wonderful. Moreover, their navy was composed of nothing but triremes, as is proved by the medal struck to commemorate the victory of Navarino.

"The remains of a drinking fountain that have come to light recently, however, display a bas-relief with the representation of an unusual vessel. It carries four masts, one of which is positioned off the main axis of the ship, and a bowsprit at the stern. That arrangement, in the words of a rather witty gentleman, makes it look like a horse with its bridle at the tail. The wind blows its sails toward the stern, but that does not stop the prow cleaving the waves in the manner of a wheelbarrow that goes forward as it is impelled from behind.

"Can we really imagine that a ship so at odds with the laws of motion would be depicted on a public monument, if nineteenth-century France had been familiar with those laws? A nation would not allow the suggestion that it was so ignorant. With the enlightenment of science, its people do not permit misleading representations of a state of ignorance to be recorded permanently in iron and stone, especially when they have a minister of public works, a prefect for the Seine, and a director of fine arts. And I say nothing of the minister for the navy, who no doubt was too busy with ships that sail the salt seas to give a thought to those carved on fountains of fresh water.

"We have to recognize, gentlemen, that the French of the nineteenth century had no knowledge of these things. As for their military glory, I doubt if we can any longer take it seriously after the research of our illustrious colleague Mithophone. It furnishes evidence to prove that the expeditions of the so-called emperor Napoleon Bonaparte were only the modernized version of those of Bacchus, embellished by the same popular imagination that added, a little later, the symbolic incidents of Robert Macaire and Bertrand.[6] One cannot fail to recognize in those two characters the twin sons of Leda. The only warrior of any importance in the nineteenth century whose authenticity is incontestable seems to be Général Tom Pouce, in whose honor a medal—which has happily survived—was struck. The author of *Plutarch universel*, who has made a study in depth of the subject, tells us that he drove in triumph through the ancient and the new worlds. Crowds threw themselves in front of his chariot; even crowned heads came to pay homage, and women offered large sums to obtain one of his kisses.

"But we will leave all these details to the works quoted earlier, and content ourselves with looking at the literary record.

"We all know that the French of every epoch have been noted for their love of brilliance and display. To this trait they owe their first name of *Galli*, or *Coqs*, of which they were so proud that they did not hesitate, later on, to put on their flags the bird that gave them their name. A similar disposition must have gone into the making of a nation of journalists, lawyers, and men of letters. They excelled in these professions, and often pursued them simultaneously. But the nineteenth century will be remembered particularly for the fierce brilliance of its writers. They were the ones who invented those literary anthologies of brilliant airy nothings, which, placed side by side, seemed to create an important work. They created a tide of sonorous words that played about with ideas but never really engaged with them. Above all they possessed the art of letting their own personalities imbue everything they touched.

"The passion for the striking and the ingenious led them to abandon even their own names and assume invented ones; for my recent studies, gentlemen, have left me in no doubt of this. For some time it has been quite clear to me that the names by which we know French writers of the nineteenth century are merely symbols, intended to disclose the character, the genius, and the ambitions of the author.

"We can cite the hairdresser-poet Jasmin, whose perfumed name hints at two professions; the mason-versifier Poncy, with a sobriquet as stony and solid as his talent; the cobbler-writer Lapointe, whose ability to get through to the masses justifies his symbolic surname; the historian Laurent, so called in allusion to his hero, the emperor Napoleon who sizzled in the fiery furnace of St. Helena, as did St. Laurent on his griddle; the novelist Dumas—an abbreviation of Dumanoir, a warrior name that happily suggests the dashing and bold style of the writer; the double-barreled Pitre-Chevalier, who signed thus his fine book *Bretagne et Vendée* in order to pay homage in his title to two chivalrous lands, the setting for the great adventures he recounted.[7]

"We will not pursue these examples any further, gentlemen, for they must appear incontrovertible to any right-thinking man; but we cannot conclude without mentioning the curious language in use among the French during the historical epoch we are dealing with at the moment.

"It was marked by analysis and subtle nuances. If the intention was to paint a picture of a slightly bearded dark-haired lady, then the writer would say *'the faintest down could be seen on her cheeks and in the curve of her neck as it caught the light, giving it the sheen of silk.'*[t] If it was a question of the youthful freshness of her lips, then the writer would praise *'the lustrous scarlet of her dreaming lips'*;[u] if he wished to draw attention to her tiny and well-formed ears, he would declare they were the *'ears of a slave and a mother.'*[v] Finally, if he was speaking in the course of conversation of travels in Spain, he had to say: *'I have seen Madrid with its wrought-iron balconies; Barcelona holding out its arms to the sea like a swimmer about to take the plunge and held to the shore only by a ribbon; then in the heart of Spain, like a spray of flowers on a woman's breast, Andalusian Seville, the favorite of the sun.'*

"This language proves how little evidence there is to support the opinion of those who believe the French language to be the most lucid, the most concise, and the plainest of all the languages of Europe.

"I shall summarize my conclusions for you, gentlemen, by saying that

[t] H. de Balzac.
[u] H. de Balzac.
[v] Dumas.

the nineteenth century in France was a semibarbarous epoch, where subtle but ignorant individuals, tenacious and bloodthirsty, abandoned themselves to all the excesses of a superabundant vitality. My next paper will prove that it was also the century of fiercely held religious belief, as is indicated by a host of poets forever offering themselves as sacrificial victims; and a century of great devotion to political causes, as we can see from the utterances of ministers declaring that they only remained on their *bed of pain* in the interests of their native land.”

# §XVII

*Le Grand Pan, a journal with universal appeal, containing all the daily papers and a wealth of other things — Three articles with opposing views on a single truth — Organization of* Le Grand Pan — *M. César Robinet, entrepreneur for literature of every genre — Machines for creating serials — M. Prétorien, editor in chief of* Le Grand Pan — *A literary contest with prizes — Blaguefort obliged to buy the critique of the book he wants to publish.*

The moment the bibliophile sat down, the entire room erupted in applause. No praise was too great for the prodigious erudition that allowed him to pronounce, without hesitation, on the morals and customs of a people living twelve centuries ago.

Blaguefort had not heard the lecture, but he noted the impression it produced, and abruptly left his companions, promising to return soon.

Maurice thought he must be dreaming. He looked at Marthe in stupefaction, and the two of them burst out laughing.

“From now on we will know what constitutes a scientific investigation of history,” said Maurice, “and what we should think of *established truths*. I now understand why these truths change in each century. History is a tangle of threads that each scholar unwinds and weaves into his own interpretation. The thread is always the same, but the material and the pattern vary according to the workman.”

“So you have detected errors in the learned gentleman’s paper?” said M. Atout, who had just come in.

“Alas!” replied Maurice with a smile, “his picture of France in the year three thousand resembles the image of ancient Greece that we had in 1845. The result is like one of those monsters, with each part borrowed from a real animal, and the totality no more than a chimera. All is authentic—except the monster."

"And you could point to the principal errors?"

"If I could have a copy of the paper to analyze . . ."

"You shall have it," came the brisk interruption from the Académicien, lowering his voice. "We shall find it at the newspaper offices. Come along quickly. However painful it may be to reveal the errors of a colleague, one must sacrifice everything in the interests of truth. . . . We must have a crushing reply with some pointed allusions. I can furnish you with details all the more telling because the bibliophile is my friend. I know his weak points, and where to mount the attack."

They were approaching the great literary agency, which occupied an entire street and was run by a group of wealthy men who enjoyed the publishing monopoly in Sans-Pair.

To exploit this monopoly to the full, they had brought together newspapers representing different points of view, all under the direction of a single publication called *Le Grand Pan* which supported all of them in turn. *Le Grand Pan* did not appear on a particular day, nor at a particular hour. Printed on an endless roll of paper, it *appeared nonstop.*[1]

A battalion of journalists attached to the establishment sent squadrons of employees to advertise the paper and keep the presses rolling.

At the exit from the printing house an immense roll of newsprint delivered itself to individual homes on a system of large spools. You could see it snaking through the streets, climbing to the third floor, coming back down to ground level, passing cafés, shops, and reading rooms, hotly pursued by non-subscribers who hoped to snatch a little information as it went by. As it went whizzing along, it could be glimpsed by the impatient and perused at leisure by members of the bourgeoisie now enjoying retirement. It was relentless in its progress, forever bearing away over roof and wall the article you had not managed to finish.

Moreover, certain distinguishing signs, placed as headings to the articles, indicated their leanings and the color of their views, so that each subscriber would know at a glance what had been written with him in mind. If he were a monarchist, he would only read the piece under the sign of the crayfish; if he were a radical, he looked for the scales that gave equal weight to the millionaire and the beggar; if he were middle-of-the-road he would focus on some anodyne symbol; if he were a pious individual, he would stop at the bowl of the alms collector and the holy water sprinkler. The layout gave the paper an appearance that was both picturesque and literary, as can be seen here :

FRED HOMME.

# LE GRAND PAN

## THE PAPER THAT NEVER SLEEPS,

### PROVIDING SIX THOUSAND AND THIRTY-FIVE SQUARE METERS OF READING

*twenty-four hours a day.*

Subscription price: one year, 5 fr.; six months, 10 fr.; three months, 20 fr.; one month, 30 fr.

THE LIST OF ANNUAL SUBSCRIBERS BEING COMPLETE, ONLY MONTHLY SUBSCRIPTIONS WILL BE ACCEPTED.

"The new act before the chamber of the Republic of United Interests has been passed, in spite of the efforts of the opposition. This result, which seems at first like a victory for the minister, is in reality a defeat for him. Let us take a close look at what the result of the ballot means.

"There were 540 votes counted, and of these the minister received only five hundred. If you add to the forty blackballs those who were sick and the absentees—and, as everyone knows, they always vote with the opposition—you will find that the opposition could have collected 490 votes. In that

case the eleven votes of the monarchist group could have meant a defeat for the act.

"Nowadays all honest men agree that a majority depends entirely on those eleven votes, and that one way or another they could either assure success or prevent it. Such a state of affairs needs no comment. When we have reached the point where one view can decide affairs of state, that view will of necessity soon prevail."

---

"The republic is saved once more. The good sense of the Chamber has seen justice dispensed to those who were advancing specious and muddleheaded arguments, and to those ambitious characters who sought to plunge us back into a reign of terror. The minister has achieved not just a majority in the Chamber, but a unanimous endorsement. What are a mere forty deputies with blinkered views and petty preoccupations compared with five hundred citizens as remarkable for their enlightenment and wisdom as for their impartiality? As for the monarchist deputies, we shall say nothing, because they abstained from voting. When a party has arrived at the point of abdicating its responsibilities, one can confidently predict its imminent demise.

---

"The minister has carried the day! Excellent! We rejoice at his triumph! 'Another victory like this,' said Pyrrhus to Cineas after a battle against the Romans, 'and there will be nothing for us to do but leave Italy.' 'Another victory like this,' we shall say to the ministers, 'and there will be nothing for you to do but leave your mansions.' You claim to have a majority! Well! Unfortunately for you, that sounds your death knell! What, in effect, is this majority? Some hundreds of privileged men, grown fat on preferments, sinking under the weight of their allowances. Time servers of every kind, whose double-breasted coats cover wallets, not hearts. May those men support you as they are obliged to do, since they

accept your wages: they are your creatures. When times are difficult, however, who can rely on lackeys? Listen to the reliable advice of your faithful enemies: *the time foretold is at hand!* This minority that you secretly deride has the entire people behind it. It has only to stamp its foot to raise up legions. But, when we have justice and numbers on our side, there is no need to debate the issue: time will tell."

---

"The die is cast; the century staggers on in its blind way. Yet another impious law, inspired by that sterile philosophy that has produced nothing but wind and storm, *ventum et tempestates*. And the opposition is still not satisfied: it demands more liberty! Liberty, good God! As if it were not the case that liberty has meant the death of faith: *libertas mors Dei*. Liberty? Ah! Ask only for the kind and strong yoke that piety alone can impose through the hands of its ministers! But no! Sunk like the vile worm in the mire of your wickedness, and spreading over everything that is most holy the poisonous slime dripping from your silver tongues, you have lost the light of the spirit, moderation in judgment, and a proper regard for language, which is henceforth reserved for us alone."

---

In the first room M. Atout and Maurice found a crowd of people of all ages and conditions who were awaiting an audience with the editor of *Le Grand Pan*. The Académicien went up to several whom he knew and engaged them briefly in conversation. They one and all affected scorn for the powerful being to whom they had come to pay their respects; they all complained about his wickedness and corruption; they all declared themselves indifferent to his friendship or his enmity.

M. Atout, seeing that they would have to wait some time, proposed a quick visit to what were known as the offices of the paper.

When they had passed through several rooms, where thousands of employees were engaged in less important tasks, they arrived at the large editorial center, partitioned off into two hundred cubicles with grilles for the two hundred working journalists. Each one had his own distinct area of responsibility, indicated by the inscription on his cubicle. There was one writer to cover husbands who poisoned their wives, two to cover wives who poisoned their husbands, and three who dealt with those cases where husband and wife had poisoned each other—known as *assorted poisonings*—and so on. Then came the *puffers,* a select company whose work had to be treated with some caution. One specialized in fires in towns that no one had heard of, earthquakes in far-off lands, and the shipwreck of important personages referred to only by an initial. A second writer covered stories of bears devouring old campaigners and stories of sea serpents and tame crocodiles. A third was responsible for the vegetable kingdom, filled with marvelous things like white mustard and giant cabbages.

Each completed article was dispatched through a tube that delivered it to a machine where it was printed without the need for any typesetters—a proceeding that had, among other advantages, that of making journalists responsible for any spelling mistakes.

The second room was occupied by writers of advertisements, who spent all their time fabricating new catchphrases; the third was given over to correspondence conducted by means of the electric telegraph; and finally, the last rooms were dedicated to the production of serialized fiction.

This latter enterprise had been run for several years by the famous César Robinet who had bought up the rights to all the stories to be published in *Le Grand Pan* and the other papers in the republic. Several machines of his own invention turned out serials of every kind, at the rate of a hundred lines an hour.

First and foremost, there was the historical machine, into which they threw chronicles, biographies, memoirs. Out of it came novels in the style of Walter Scott.

Then there was the *miscellany* machine, which was stuffed full of *sketches*—legends, anecdotal accounts, collections of reminiscences. This one churned out travel stories like those of Sterne.

The *fantasy* machine took in all the old poets, the old tales, and forgotten dramas, and from them they manufactured new works like those of Bernardin de Saint-Pierre and Abbé Prévost.

Finally there was the *leftovers* machine, into which were thrown loads of literary odds and ends that could not be used anywhere else. This machine produced second-class Perrault and Berquin.

César Robinet did not read his books, but he signed them all. That meant that he was condemned to fourteen hours of forced labor a day. When Blaguefort arrived, he was signing the hundred and thirty-third volume of the adventures of Colonel Crakman—a charming story into which he had managed to introduce all the published material on the subject of Frederick the Great and his court.

All around him were sixty secretaries sorting out other peoples' books, which were about to undergo a metamorphosis and emerge as his own work.

Maurice was lost in wonder. The system of remodeling, once restricted to hats, had been extended to ideas. The secondhand business had taken over the republic of literature. The most ancient volumes were taken apart, carved up, set aside, and reconstituted, becoming sought-after originals: it needed only the signature of CÉSAR ROBINET to turn the old into the new.

Atout, thinking it was time for him to go to the reception, retraced his steps and went in to see the editor of *Le Grand Pan*.

In Sans-Pair M. Prétorien was the true begetter of the liberty of the press—that is to say, the freedom to oppress people. Since no one could refuse him anything with impunity, no one refused him anything at all. Pen poised over his paper like a sentinel guarding the camp, he alone decided who should be sent away or admitted. In brief, he was very good to his friends, sharing with them his profits, his power, his influence; and he was the best ruler in the world, provided that you were not one of his subjects.

At the moment when our visitors entered his offices, he was giving audience to all those whom Maurice had seen in the antechamber. Their scorn for journalism had given place to respect, their indifference to eagerness. It was a question of who could be the most meekly submissive, or the most friendly and familiar.

The first ones to pass him were twenty or so authors who had just offered their books bearing those sacred words: *with the compliments of the author.*

Then came painters, sculptors, musicians, who as proof of their talents bore letters of recommendation; alluringly perfumed actresses, undulating with a thousand caressing gestures like tame panthers, and not departing until they had made sure of leaving their addresses; solemn gentlemen bringing eulogies all prepared; and others more solemn still, bringing in addition diatribes against their adversaries.

But the arrival that struck Maurice most forcibly was that of Mlle. Virginie Spartacus, founder of the society of *sensible women*—a society composed of all those who could not live happily with their husbands.

Mlle. Spartacus, however, was an exception: she had proclaimed in her opening discourse, modestly borrowing an image from antiquity, that *no man had as yet untied her sash!*

Her hostility toward men was, therefore, uninfluenced by the recollection of any personal experiences: it was a metaphysical animosity; a virtuous determination, born of principle and maintained in the interests of humanity.

She had come to ask M. Prétorien to print several articles, for Mlle. Spartacus had a twofold claim to fame: as founder of the women's society and as a woman of letters. Even if she did not occupy the first rank among contemporary writers, the fault lay with men who were in league against her sex. But, as she pointed out, this tyranny was almost at an end. The day was coming when the masters would be forced to agree to the liberation of their slaves, and Mlle. Virginie had formulated in advance the nature of this freedom. The rights of women were as simple as they were clear: they consisted in not recognizing those of men.

M. Prétorien received the rebel queen politely, but refused the articles; and Mlle. Virginie departed, saying loudly that it was time to think seriously about the sanity of the human race.

When all the visitors had finally departed, the editor of *Le Grand Pan* approached M. Atout apologetically, holding out his hands in welcome.

"You see what my life is like," he said with a sort of rueful distaste. "It reminds me of those trees planted along our highways where every passerby thinks he has the right to carry off a branch or a leaf. I can protect neither myself nor my friends."

"And yet," said the Académicien in flattering tones, "you are equal to all occasions."

"I have just taken on another responsibility," said Prétorien with renewed animation: "a completely new venture."

"Yet another?"

"A huge one! And what's more, I must tell you all about the plan. . . . Sit yourself down; I should like to have your advice."

M. Atout knew the world too well not to realize this was code for "I want you to congratulate me on this." He resigned himself to admiration, determined to exact repayment at the first possible opportunity.

Prétorien, who had been searching through his papers, brought out a prospectus of the new publication. It gave information about a *general biography* to detail the public and private lives of all the citizens of Sans-Pair.

The heading of the prospectus carried the following philosophical maxim:

**SUBSCRIBERS ARE ENTITLED TO INDULGENCE.**
Nonsubscribers are only entitled to the truth.

Then came a system of free gifts so cleverly devised that the publisher would pay back at least a hundred and twenty times the price of each subscription and make a profit only on numbers.

The privileges attached to each category were clearly set out.

Each of the first thirty thousand subscribers had the right to a barouche bearing his own monogram, and drawn by a balloon. These were the comfortably well-to-do citizens of Sans-Pair.

The next forty thousand subscribers would receive season tickets (without time limits) for all the omnibuses of the republic, with connections to the five continents.

Finally, the last of the subscribers would receive a cup of café au lait and a small glass of rum or cognac at home every morning.

When he had listened to all the details of this literary enterprise, and had extolled the benefits that it would bring to civilization, M. Atout moved at last to the subject that had brought him there.

Prétorien immediately rang the stenographer's bell under the word ACADEMY, and a paper folded in four fell from the aperture over his desk: it was a résumé of the paper presented by the bibliophile.

M. Atout opened it and began to read it with Maurice, who stopped at every line to make some correction. Prétorien was delighted and declared that there would have to be an article written on it. That would cause a

**M. PRÉTORIEN**

*A journalist of the year 3000*

sensation—a scandal—and nothing was more beneficial to the health of any paper.

"Do not spare our bibliophile," he added resolutely. "It is always best to tell the truth, especially when it brings in subscribers. He refused to join us, and he who is not for us is against us. We must see that the paper on *The French in the Nineteenth Century* sinks under a wave of ridicule."

"What's that I hear?" said Blaguefort, putting his face round the open door. "Hold on a minute, my young friends. What the devil! You can't torpedo the merchandise of your friends."

"The merchandise!" echoed Prétorien. "Have you by any chance had any business dealings with this man?"

"For five papers from him."

"You have signed a contract?"

"And paid a hundred and twenty thousand francs in cash! You must understand that you cannot say nasty things about a book that has cost me a hundred and twenty thousand francs and is going to cost me four hundred louis to promote it."

"Good heavens! You do have a point," said Prétorien in some embarrassment.

"However," objected M. Atout, "I should like to point out that truth . . ."

"Is the art of the possible," interrupted Prétorien. "The ancients themselves said: *Amica veritas, sed magis amicus Blaguefort.*"

"So, you refuse to accept the objections of my guest?" said the Académicien, somewhat nettled.

"The reason being that it would cost me two hundred louis . . . and the friendship of Blaguefort, which means more to me."

"Ten times more," said the businessman. "I pay him more than fifty thousand francs every year for advertisements."

"Then M. Maurice will look elsewhere," said M. Atout gravely. "*Le Grand Pan* is not the only organ of publicity."

"That is true; you could try the *Serpent à sonnettes*," said Prétorien sarcastically.

"Or the *Chacal de l'ouest,*" added Blaguefort casually.

"Why not the *Maringouin*?" said Atout pleasantly.

The journalist bit his lips, and his friend appeared anxious. The *Maringouin* was one of those little papers that everyone treasured because of its reputation for malice. Its mischievous journalists were very amusing until the joke was at your expense. They could sling mud at all who came near without fear of reprisals, because mud never stuck to them. Although he occupied a very important position in the press, Prétorien feared the little paper just as the lion dreads the buzzing and the sting of the midges. As for Blaguefort, he knew exactly how the attacks of the *Maringouin* could make readers desert him; and so he at once assumed that frank and open countenance that businessmen display when they are setting a trap, and taking the arm of the Académicien who was about to depart, he said:

"We must not part like this. Good heavens, no! It will never be said that *The French in the Nineteenth Century* made me quarrel with the most illustrious writer in the republic of the United Interests."

M. Atout made as if to protest.

"With him whose brilliant imagination has extended the realm of poetry."

M. Atout demurred more vigorously.

"With that eloquent, universal genius who has assured us of superiority in every genre."

M. Atout was loud in his protestations.

"In short, with the greatest man of our age."

M. Atout shook Blaguefort by the hand, confessing that he had perhaps been getting carried away.

The latter, who had exhausted his supply of flattering remarks, appeared to give in reluctantly; but, fortified by the success of his flattering insinuations, he began to plant the seeds of alarm in the Académicien by suggesting the repercussions that might result from the proposed publication. It would make enemies, expose him to reprisals, and injure the reputation of the Academy, of which he was the guardian and crowning glory.

These were powerful arguments, but it is difficult to forego the pleasure of making a colleague appear ridiculous; the arts fraternity is descended in a direct line from that of Cain and Abel. Atout resisted the temptation, and, as ever, came up with an answer. He talked of the interests of science, of history, of matters of principle—all those considerations that are cited when someone does not want to tell the truth. He invoked especially the dictates of conscience, that mysterious idol that spoke or was silent, according to the will of the high priest.

Blaguefort, who had had enough of eloquence, suddenly gave a start, as if a great light had dawned.

"Now I understand," he said. "You don't want to let an opportunity slip; this critique of the work of our bibliophile will inevitably arouse curiosity, and one could sell as many copies of these articles as of the book itself."

"If not more," Atout added, "and then I have other reasons."

"I know, I know," Blaguefort interrupted, "science . . . principles . . . conscience. . . . I will buy the lot!"

The Académicien took a deep breath.

"A hundred and twenty thousand francs for the bibliophile's work, and a hundred and twenty thousand francs for the refutation," the great speculator went on. "That will take care of everything. I shall sell the first one as a masterpiece, then the second to prove that it is a work of the imagination. In that way, the public will get two studies, and I shall make a double profit. Very agreeable, don't you think? I will put the conditions in writing to avoid any misunderstanding."

Blaguefort took a seat at the table of M. Prétorien and drew up the contract. M. Atout signed, received a promissory note, and took leave of the editor of *Le Grand Pan*. In the meantime Prétorien, who was going to the museum, offered to take the young couple with him. They accepted his offer with alacrity, and M. Atout departed on his own.

# §XVIII

*The National Library and its catalog — Using the promenade — What constitutes*
*an artist in Sans-Pair — Portraits by the gross, with likeness guaranteed —*
*M. Illustrandini, sculptor to the whole world — M. Prestet,*
*government-appointed painter; equestrian or other*
*portraits — Views of Grelotin on painting.*

As they followed their guide, Maurice and Marthe came to a large, forbidding building guarded by soldiers. They would have mistaken it for a prison if they had not read over the entrance portal these words:

## NATIONAL LIBRARY

They said they would like to go in, but Prétorien told them it was closed.

"The name has deceived you," he said with a smile. "At Sans-Pair a National Library is not one that the public can enjoy, but one that they pay for. It is rather like the public highway, always closed off by the powers that be, because it is always under repair. Besides, what would there be to see? Mountains of books piled up higgledy-piggledy. All the zeal and the know-how of the librarians have failed to sort out the chaos. The funds necessary to do this have been appropriated by the sons-in-law and nephews of deputies, who are assigned special cultural missions to taste the wines of Tokai, investigate the oysters of Ostende, or study the Circassians of the Caucasus.

They have now been working on the catalog for three centuries. Every month they classify a hundred volumes and receive a thousand that remain unclassified. It's an ocean where new tides roll in every day, and these they try to drain off into lakes using only a cockleshell. The building would already have buckled under the ever growing weight of the books crammed in there, if the bookworms and the collectors had not been quietly working away to lighten the load. And then, the police guard the door with the utmost rigor: heavy shoes are forbidden because of the dust they bring in; parasols are absolutely proscribed, and hats must be left with the porter on entering. I might add that the library of Sans-Pair is everywhere cited as a model; and, except for the books, it is in perfect order."

Opposite the library was a public garden, which Prétorien crossed. There Maurice could continue the observations he had started earlier. All the people on the promenade were engaged in useful activities as they walked. Some were embroidering as they went along; others were making tapestries, weaving baskets, or making purses and homemade Christmas presents. The public playgrounds were equally productive. Every swing set in motion a mechanical mixer for making cakes; wooden horses turned a coffee grinder, and the popguns in the rifle ranges served to crack nuts.

Maurice was especially struck by a middle-aged man who had managed to make his walk profitable in three different ways : he read, knitted, and pulled behind him a fuel-efficient contraption that was cooking his dinner.

When they left the promenade, the young couple found themselves in a new quarter of town.

Here everything appeared quite different. The only people to be seen were bearded men and disheveled women, all wearing every imaginable costume known to man from the fig leaf of our first parents to the dressing gown of the nineteenth century. M. Prétorien informed them that this was the artists' quarter.

The most important and constant concern of the artists was not to dress like the bourgeoisie, not to furnish their homes like the bourgeoisie, and not to look like the bourgeoisie. In consequence, they were dressed in togas, breastplates, or knitted hose. They went about in Turkish-style slippers. They sat in great cumbersome armchairs that dated from the time of the Crusades; they drank from ancient, battered tankards and smoked strong tobacco through hookahs twelve feet long. It was all for art's sake, and because they despised the bourgeoisie.

It goes without saying that the whole world was bourgeois, except for themselves.

Apart from this great animosity, the artists of Sans-Pair adopted certain principles as a code of their society, and these can be summed up in six aphorisms:

ARTICLE 1. The sculptor believes that painting has ceased to exist.

ARTICLE 2. The painter believes that there is no longer any sculpture.

ARTICLE 3. Painters and sculptors acknowledge talent only in the dead; and it follows that they too will be famous one day.

ARTICLE 4. The best republic is the one where people buy the greatest number of statues and paintings.

ARTICLE 5. One has a duty always to help a brother artist, but no duty to admire him.

ARTICLE 6. The artist has three enemies: the dealer, the public, and his landlord.

First of all, Prétorien took his companions to see the school where young people with an aptitude for art were sent for instruction. It was adorned with statues and paintings retrieved from the ruins of Paris, which were recognized as masterpieces now that time had left its mark upon them. But the editor of *Le Grand Pan* gave Maurice no time to look at them. He had promised to take him to the most celebrated artists of Sans-Pair, and the first one he visited was M. Aimé Mignon, portrait painter to all the princes, all the bankers, and all the pretty women in the republic.

M. Aimé Mignon was the first artist to think of offering portraiture as a ready-made package. He had reduced all the various physiognomies to five types—the *serious*, the *cheerful*, the *rugged*, the *voluptuous*, the *unremarkable*—and he had painted in advance a collection of canvases appropriate to the different types but *without the face*. These canvases were on view in his studio, with the price calculated by the square inch, so that each sitter could choose his image ready-made, rather as one chooses an outfit. It only remained to add the head, and in that exercise M. Aimé Mignon always succeeded because he aimed to please the buyer. He himself explained his methods to Maurice.

"The role of the portrait painter," said he, "is not, as people used to think, to reproduce what he sees, but what should be there. Nature is generally ugly; our role is to improve on it. I would go so far as to say that it is our duty. After all, what do most people want when they sit for their portraits? To have proof that they are more handsome than they appear to be. If a portrait merely reproduces our ugliness, why go to all that expense? Isn't it enough to know that one is ugly? Do you think that a stammerer would pay good money to hear someone imitate his stammer? The portrait painter always has a way of knowing if, in fact, he has been successful. If the sitter declares it to be a good likeness, he must rub it out quickly. If he claims it is flattering, all is well; the work will be paid for without demur, and recommended to friends."

From M. Aimé Mignon, Marthe and Maurice went on to Signor Illustrandini, sculptor in ordinary to the five continents. To them he supplied with equal facility: statues of the Virgin Mary, with or without child; Venuses modest or not so modest; Christs dead or alive; full-length martyrs; pagans on pedestals; and important men of all shapes and sizes. Signor Illustrandini had marble quarries operating for him, foundries working all the time, and twelve hundred young men who modeled and carved for him.

Prétorien found him busy sending off sixty parcels of saints, as yet uncanonized, to a destination in Ireland, and a colossal statue of Incredulity commissioned by the Atheists' Club of Boston.

At the sight of the newspaperman he came forward with open arms.

"Here he comes," he cried, "our guardian angel, our guiding star, our sun! He's the one who has shown our ministers what they should do."

"What's all this?" asked Prétorien, who appeared not to understand.

"Don't you remember the commissions they wanted to distribute to all and sundry?" said Illustrandini.

"Well?"

"They gave them all to me."

"Ah! so they came round at last," said the journalist, betraying some self-satisfaction.

"Thanks to you," said Illustrandini, taking his hands. "Who would dare to stand against you? Are you not the leader of public opinion? But I can tell you that in doing me a service you have been no less useful to the cause of art. I shall be worthy of you, Master—all the more so since the first prices have been agreed . . . fifteen hundred thousand francs! How could one fail to create a masterpiece? Apart from that, since yesterday my brain has been on fire; I can visualize my statues; they walk, they see, they cry out. . . ."

Illustrandini had that uncritical enthusiasm peculiar to rather confused artists. Instead of drinking quietly and seriously at the sacred fountain, they plunge in up to their necks with loud cries. When he was speaking of art, he drew out the syllables in each word he pronounced; it was like the thunder you hear at the theater, something heavy and rumbling over a deep hollow. The heaviness was in the word, and the hollowness in the spirit.

However, these calculated distortions were well received by everyone. Since Illustrandini lacked all common sense, they thought he must be blessed with imagination.

A good marriage had given him a place in the world; he acquired a carriage and gave dinners and balls, and the fame of his guests eventually ensured the reputation of the artist.

Illustrandini was prepared for it, for he was, above all, a businessman. Once he was fashionable, he set to work to exploit his popularity with all the grim determination of the arriviste. A living advertisement for his own merits, he was to be seen everywhere, putting himself forward, urging, soliciting. Every piece of work given to another was in his eyes a theft. He trumpeted the loss to art, deplored the passing of the great eras of Napoleon and Louis-Philippe, and raised against his unfortunate rival a mob of his cronies and dupes. For him, having everything was not enough.

While he let these familiar outpourings sweep over him, Prétorien absentmindedly looked about him. Illustrandini stopped suddenly.

"Ah! You are contemplating my Minerva," he exclaimed.

"A Minerva," replied Prétorien, whose eyes had come to rest on a lump of clay.

"It is she, indeed," said Illustrandini complacently; "she sprang fully armed from my head as from that of Jupiter. I modeled her with such passion that the clay smoked beneath my fingers."

"Yet, it seems to me," said Prétorien, somewhat hesitantly, "that there is still much work to do there."

"For my pupils," Illustrandini finished the sentence for him. "Journeyman work: arms, legs, body! But what does that matter when the idea is already there? The idea is all-important. The goddess, leaning with one hand on her spear, is offering an olive branch with the other. That is the statue; the rest is mere detail and does not need the inspiration of the artist to complete it. Come back in a month's time; the veil that hides Minerva from you will have fallen, and you will see her in all her divinity."

Prétorien promised to return and moved on toward the studio of M. Prestet, who occupied the same position in the painting fraternity as Illustrandini held among the sculptors.

There was, however, nothing poetic or solemn about him. Far from it. Prestet sang the ditties popular in the workplace, cultivated the art of the pun, sounded the hunting horn, and imitated the calls of all kinds of animals. He was a carefree child, painting as he hunted and as he played billiards, with an offhand, casual insouciance. He worked in every genre. He had no marked preference for art; for him, it was a profession. He wrote down in a daybook the orders he had received, and worked on them in regular succession. And then it was reckoned that in order to complete them all, he would need to live to the age of twelve hundred, and that he would then have produced 745 kilometers of paintings in every genre.

It only remains to say that he had managed to cut down the time needed for work on the very large canvases destined for the Pantheon of Sans-Pair by painting them from a locomotive, using a pole with four brushes. For smaller paintings he made do with an ingenious device that allowed him to work on five at the same time.

He received our visitors without stopping work, excusing himself by saying that he had eight paintings to deliver that same evening, and he continued his work on three of them, talking all the time.

Maurice wanted to hear his views on painting, and M. Prestet outlined them for him with his customary ease and aplomb.

"Painting," he said, "is the art of depicting everything in the schedule to the satisfaction of the government and its distinguished circle. They give you an order for a battle—you show fighting men in uniform; a group of nymphs—you produce three scantily clad women; an ingenious machine—you design a contraption from which a pair of socks is emerging. If everyone recognizes an untitled work, you can say like the old Italian: '*I too am a painter,*' and the proof that you are is that you get commissions for paintings. People talk about the harmony of tone, vibrant color, composition. Madness! Painting can be summed up in a nutshell: copying what is in front of your eyes, in such a way that even the minister of fine arts can see that a bundle of sticks is not a counselor of state. Everything else is like the poetic notions of Grelotin, all very well for Grelotin, and worthy of Grelotin."[1]

Maurice wanted to know who Grelotin was.

"A near-idiot—a standing joke to our artists," Prétorien explained. "He studied art for twenty years; and, since he could never attain the ideal, he resigned himself to becoming custodian at the Museum. There he continues to work in his own way; for Grelotin has a system that will infallibly make him a great painter, or a great sculptor, depending on whether he chooses to paint or carve. You can hear more by asking him yourself when we come to the galleries."

They took leave of Prestet and made their way to the Museum.

All the schools, divided into groups like the different families of the same tribe, had been crammed into one room, so that the other rooms could be reserved for *national art*—the name given in Sans-Pair to the works of Illustrandini, Mignon, and Prestet.

Grelotin was standing at the door of the huge gallery, like a dragon before the treasure he guards.

He was a small man, of poor physique and almost bald. His lips trembled all the time, and he was forever looking about him with a gentle and distracted air.

Prétorien introduced Marthe and Maurice, telling him they were two people from olden days. Grelotin looked closely at them.

"Did they live in the time when men knew how to make paintings that sang?" he asked with eager curiosity.

The two of them looked at their guide.

"Yes, yes," Grelotin insisted, "there was a time when brush and chisel could endow their works with a melodious voice. I am sure of it, because I can hear it in this place."

"You can hear it?" said Marthe in some surprise.

"Every evening," Grelotin replied. "When the door of the gallery is closed, and when the setting sun bathes the walls in its brilliant rays, I run quickly down there, to the Italians, and I hear all the canvases singing in complete harmony, and with each voice clear and distinct. I recognize that of Raphael by its sublime sweetness, that of Correggio, rich and tender; that of Titian, which seems all-enveloping; that of Carracci, of Leonardo da Vinci, of Guido, of Guercino, of Andrea del Sarto, impassioned, smooth, eloquent, or tender by turns. Then come the Flemish, whose music is less celestial, but more vibrant: Rubens, whose powerful voice encompasses every tone; Van Dyck, profound and somber; the tuneful Jordaens; the delightful Teniers; Van-Ostade, Ruysdael; Berghem, Wouvermans, mingling their arcadian pastorals with the songs of Miéris and Gérard Dow. Then it is the turn of the Spaniards: Murillo with his tonal variety, the bold Ribera, the chivalrous Velázquez, the mystical Zurbarán. Finally, the old French painters—Poussin, Lesueur, Claude Lorrain, Watteau, Lancret—a choir of noble and enchanting voices that we would hear more clearly without their successors; for French painting has lost its way. Look at these last canvases. They no longer sing; they do not even speak; they only know how to make discordant sounds. You might say that they compete to see who can make the harshest sound. Every now and then some of them manage a melodious murmuring; but in the midst of the tumult they can scarcely be distinguished: they are like the voices of angels singing when chaos reigned."

"Fortunately, a new world has risen from this chaos," Prétorien observed.

"Yes," said Grelotin, shaking his head, "a silent world."

"But our national art? . . ."

"Has lost its voice," the idiot went on sadly. "Walk through these rooms, listen to these paintings and statues, and you will hear nothing. You think that what you are seeing is art, but it is merely a semblance of art. We no longer have any living art: canvas and marble have ceased to sing."

The newspaperman burst out laughing and took leave of the custodian; but Maurice had grown pensive. Of all those he had listened to, Grelotin was the only one whose words had touched his heart. The others exploited art; he felt deeply about it.

# §XIX

*Reform of the dramatic genre, thanks to which the play has become an incidental. —*
*Successive transformations of a historical drama — First performance —*
*A box at the front of the house — Examination of* Kléber en Égypte,
*a play in five acts, with several animals in the cast.*

At the exit from the Museum, Prétorien remembered that he was meant to be at the first performance of a play, and rumor had it in Sans-Pair that it was going to cause a sensation. It was entitled *Kléber en Égypte*, and, according to those in the know, it raised questions about learned historical studies.[1] The author had successfully placed his characters and his plot in the ancient and simple setting of the nineteenth century. However, he had not been able to put his play on the stage until a number of problems had been sorted out. The editor of the *Le Grand Pan* now launched into an account of these for the benefit of his companions.

"In former times," he told them, "in a piece for the theater, the play was the principal thing: the scenery, the costumes, and the actors were chosen to suit the play; the supremacy of the spirit over the dramatic trappings was recognized; the supremacy of the music over the instrument that played it. We have changed all these too facile ways of doing things. Today, the play is an incidental: the director reads it, with his stage scenery in mind and arranges it to suit his cast. He trims the beginning, draws out the ending, and pads it out in the middle. Every comic actor, instead of creating a character, plays himself. We no longer present plays; we present actors. The drama of *Kléber en Égypte* offers a striking example of the flexibility of our authors in adapting the theme to meet every eventuality. The play, which initially bore the title *La Jeune Esclave,* was written to launch the career of a charming actress, who unfortunately found herself unexpectedly in a position where she could no longer play virginal roles. In her place it was proposed to have a young man in love, with the title *Le Jeune Esclave.* It was merely an artistic modification, as the director wittily observed (since directors are allowed to be witty now that authors are not); but the young lover refused the part, objecting to the costume, which did not allow him to wear those long boots worn by dragoons. Those cavalry boots were his trademark and the occasion of all his triumphs. A writer of your time might well have given up after all these setbacks, but ours are more tenacious. The author of this new piece learned that a famous animal trainer had arrived in Sans-Pair, and the plot immediately underwent a transformation. Kléber was brought in to replace the great Sesostris, a bald eagle to replace the captain of the guard, and a very promising young cayman to take the place of the young lover. He is the big attraction we are going to see. They say that the part is admirably suited to his abilities, and is full of striking effects. It is not yet time for curtain-up, but it is almost dinnertime. Let us go to the *Boeuf de la Reine d'Angleterre*—a new restaurant opened by our society. Its shares are already trading at 80 percent above par. They accept anything in payment: bonnets, watch charms, cabriolet wheels. A poor devil can exchange his old boots there for a cutlet, or his suspenders for a bowl of soup. You will see quite a crowd there. However, diners who pay in cash are given a private room, and a choice of the best dishes.

They went into a large dining room where a dozen enormous tables were set up, and on each one was a whole animal. Near the entrance there was one with a whole bull on a bed of fried potatoes and sauerkraut; further on there were calves in aspic, sheep studded with cloves of garlic, pigs browned in the oven, mountains of plump chickens exuding an aroma of truffles, and lines of ducks swimming on rivers of turnip or garden peas. Enormous steam-driven knives did the carving at this Homeric feast.

"Perhaps you are surprised at the sight of a culinary exhibition like this," said Prétorien. "Its purpose, however, is to guard against fraud

on the part of restaurant owners. Here each guest can check the name and the part of the animal. What he eats is genuinely what he thinks he is eating. Like St. Thomas, he can see and touch. Let us sit down in front of this bull, whose body is still intact; the horns and skin have been retained for further authentication. Indicate which portion you would like, and it will be cut for you at once and served. If you want something to drink, go and look at the names on the barrels, and when you have chosen, simply turn the tap.

The young couple took their places at a table protected, in the English manner, by partitions that ensured for each diner the comfort of not having to look at his neighbors and of not having them looking at him. Each diner ate, like a horse, alone in his stall. He was saved from the necessity of having to speak to another guest or affording him those little courtesies that maintain the social fabric. He was alone, by himself, with no need to think about anyone else.

From the restaurant Prétorien went on to the large theater that was putting on the new play.

The peristyle was adorned with statues of Shakespeare, Schiller, Calderon, and Molière, placed at the entrance there, no doubt to indicate that their genius no longer had any place inside. The new arrivals came into a room in which lights blazed and many spectators had gathered. They made up a crowd of artistes, writers, and journalists invited to taste the first fruits of all those feasts of wit and spectacle. They came only to scoff at their host and and at the show—a coterie of the scornful and world-weary, who despised the pleasures set before them but were indignant if they were not invited.

As he walked along one of the corridors, Prétorien saw a group of people, among whom was M. Claqueville, who could ensure the success of any production.

M. Claqueville had white hair, the Cross of Honor, and three thousand six hundred and forty-three medals from the society of playwrights for that same number of plays that he had rescued from sinking into oblivion. In addition, he was the inventor of a whole host of refinements dedicated to transforming any works secured by the house into masterpieces. Not only did he have people engaged to laugh, others to cry, others to applaud wildly—all having their assigned places in the human menagerie of M. Banqman— he also maintained an army of supporters who had the task of working the audience: eight women who excelled in producing attacks of nerves and fainting fits; three old men who specialized in getting themselves crushed against the doors of theaters, to prove how many people wanted to get in; and finally, a squad of conjurors whose job was to remove whistles and rattles from pockets.

Just when Marthe and Maurice met him, he was completely surrounded by the squad leaders, to whom he was imparting his orders of the day.

"Attention, everybody," he cried, raising his cane like a commander's

sword. "The management has paid out six hundred thousand francs, so the play must bring the house down. Let me find myself carried away to the heights of the Great Pyramid in Egypt, of which you see a miniature version in our painted scenery. We must ensure three hundred perform-ances, my lambs. Those who applaud until they have blisters to show shall get a bonus, and those who shed enough tears to give themselves a head cold shall get a handsome gratuity. Above all—since he has given me tickets—give the entries of the crocodile the full treatment.

Prétorien opened the door to a box at the front of the house, in which he had recognized Madame Facile in the company of MM. Banqman, le Doux, and Blaguefort and Milord Cant, who was acknowledged in Sans-Pair as the king of fashion

Milord Cant merited this distinction in every respect: he kept the most handsome carriages and the most expensive mistresses, made the biggest bets, and took care to be seen wherever there was nothing useful going on. You would search in vain to find in his life any trace of dedication, any feeling of sympathy, even one hour of endeavor in a noble cause.

Milord Cant had never seen reason to distinguish between being proud of the good fortune that comes through luck and the success that is a result of one's own efforts; between that which comes from without and that which we achieve ourselves. For him, the most important thing was not how one lived but how one was perceived. His guiding principle was not the good but the expedient. His was a miserable egotism, puffed up with vanity, which has the same function in society as those huge golden figures stationed at the head of regiments on parade days for the admira-tion of old women and children.

At that moment when Prétorien appeared with his companions, he had put to his ear a little ivory horn that he managed to hold there by means of a particular muscular contraction. The ivory horn in Sans-Pair was the mark of supreme elegance; it had even outclassed the lorgnette for fashion. Society, having discovered that it was very stylish to be short-sighted, now realized it was even more stylish to be deaf. It was a proof of being even more useless.

Milord Cant had also allowed his nails to grow, following the example of the Chinese, in order to proclaim his leisured state. He wore a garment made of hemp cloth. This was regarded as a luxury item, since the mate-rial was scarcely ever produced; and instead of diamonds, which were now objects of ridicule because they could be manufactured like glass, he wore buttons of gun flint, much admired by all the ladies for their beauty.

Milord Cant and the newspaperman greeted each other like two kings,

**MILORD CANT**

*King of fashion in the year 3000*

of whom one has won his crown and the other was born to it—Prétorien
with a veiled irony, Milord Cant in a slightly disdainful offhand manner.

As for Madame Facile, she seemed delighted to see Marthe and Maurice. She made them sit next to her, wanted to hear their story, and marveled greatly at their plans, without showing any desire to be associated
with them.

"To know what the future of the world will be!" she exclaimed. "And you have traveled through all those centuries for that. What does the future matter to us who have only the present? Why should we care about those who will come after us? Why bother about anything we cannot see and touch? The future is the unknown, and the unknown is a void."

"Not for those who have hope," said Maurice. "The unknown is a field in which we sow our dreams and watch them germinating, growing, and flowering. And who would want to live without the consolation of the possibilities that may come to us in our misfortunes? What would life be without those horizons that recede for ever, and the clouds that veil the distant future? Without the unknown, the spirit would be a prisoner whose horizon was bounded by dungeon walls; it would forget the use of its wings. Ah! Do you never feel that impatience to look beyond each day and see what is to come? Do you not have that thirst to know, that aspiration toward the infinite, that horror of unknowing that cries unceasingly—'Onward!' Is today as dear to you as tomorrow? And what do your thoughts turn to when you are alone and when you look up into the heavens?"

He was interrupted at this point by Banqman, who burst out laughing. "What does she think about? Good heavens! She wonders what the weather is going to be like."

"For my part, I think about the meetings I have to go to," Ledoux added.

"Visits I have to make," said Milord Cant.

"My settlement dates," said Blaguefort.

"I don't think about anything," said Prétorien.

Maurice looked at them in astonishment.

"What! No dreams? No thought of the invisible world? Then why are you alive?"

"Ah! But . . . to live!" Banqman replied with a coarse laugh. And leaning toward Prétorien, he said under his breath: "It seems that our friend is slightly touched."

"No," replied Prétorien in a whisper. "He is a child."

Their conversation was interrupted by the bell that announced the beginning of the show. They all took their places, and all eyes were turned toward the stage. The curtain rose.

Here we are obliged to adopt the form of the review and to present our account like a Monday column. May God and our readers forgive us!

---

The scene represents the countryside on the banks of the Nile; in the distance Cairo appears, copied from an English illustration. On the right stands the house of Achmet, a minister in days gone by of the Egyptian Sultan, but long ago fallen into disgrace and recently deceased. His body lies in state on a palanquin at the gate of his house, and a crowd surrounds it in silent prayer. One or two extras, to complete the picture, make the sign of the cross.

One figure among them is particularly striking: that of Astarbé, the dead man's daughter, standing with her arms raised to heaven, while the crowd sings in chorus:

> The virtuous Achmet is gone!
> O God, your wisdom is great!
> His child has a lonely fate;
> Protect her, O God wise and strong.

When the orchestra has finished the instrumental refrain traditionally associated with public mourning, the crowd retires, leaving Astarbé alone with a stranger who, for several days, has been a guest of her father.

He has come to announce his departure to the orphaned girl. Hearing this news, she cannot restrain her tears. The stranger exclaims:

> She weeps! Oh, bliss! You weep. You must love me!

Astarbé lowers her eyes and does not reply. The speaker, who knows the old proverb, immediately proposes that she should go with him. Astarbé, who does not wish to be outdone in politeness, invites him to stay with her; but, at this request, the stranger looks round to make sure that there is no one to hear him except ten thousand spectators, and says:

THE STRANGER.
Listen . . . but you alone, my child . . . I have deceived you!
The costume I wear is borrowed, my name not my own.
ASTARBÉ.
Tell me quickly!
THE STRANGER.
Well, I . . . am not Egyptian!
ASTARBÉ.
O Heavens!
THE STRANGER.
I am French!

ASTARBÉ.
May Osiris help us!
What, then, is your name?
THE STRANGER.
Jean-Baptiste Kléber!

Astarbé, overcome at first, eventually yields to the joy of being loved by
the commander in chief of the French army. He has come to Cairo simply
to gather information about the forces of the Sultan; but now that his
mission is accomplished, he must return to his troops. Astarbé agrees to
follow him, provided that a marabout who lives nearby may bless their
union. Kléber, whose tolerance extends to priests of all nations, finds the
marabout acceptable, and goes out to hire him himself.

Astarbé, waiting alone, gives way to feelings of joy interspersed with
melancholy. She is taking leave of everything around her:

> Farewell,
> Land of brown maidens, paternal home;
> Life-giving river where crocodiles roam;
> Horizon where obelisks of stone meet the eye.
> Like heavenly pillars that hold up the sky;
> Oxen that other men eat we revere;
> Sphinx, haloed at dawn, in aspect severe;
> Lotus symbolic, and pensive Ibis;
> Crops three times blessed, and most holy papyrus,
> Delicate sheath of noble Nile reed,
> Which gives us the letters our children can read.
> Dear father, embalmed, judgment awaiting,
> Though happy to go, I leave you weeping;
> Where'er Kléber abides nought makes me blench;
> When the heart is French, the soul too will be French.

Then, sensing a movement among the bushes along the bank, she remembers the baby crocodile, hand-reared and tame, and exclaims:

> It is he, the cayman, grown gentle for us,
> Called by my voice and this plate of couscous.

At this point, all the brass in the orchestra rises to a great crescendo,
the drumroll assaults the ear, and between two clumps of tinplate reeds
the head of a crocodile appears.

His entry is greeted with applause from the whole audience. The creature puts his short legs on the painted board that represents the banks of the Nile, runs to the food Astarbé holds out to him, gobbles it up in an instant, then rolls over amorously on his back and rubs his scaly head against the young girl's feet.

More applause, and Astarbé starts on the simple tricks that she has taught Moses. Yes, that is the name of her crocodile.

At first she lets him play at knucklebones, then jump through a hoop, then dance a polonaise.

A loud noise coming from behind the stage puts an end to this fun. Moses goes back into his cardboard Nile, and Astarbé, much alarmed, returns to the back of the stage, where the arrival of the Sultan is announced.

He arrives with his guards, followed by the crowd that always appears when a chorus is indicated. The guards sing:

> Here is our master supreme,
> Fear not, he wants you to love him.
> Allah! Allah! God alone is great,
> And his prophet is the Sultan.

But the crowd have their own version that they sing in conspiratorial tones.

> Here is the master, pale and severe,
> He thinks we love him, because him we fear.
> Allah! Allah! God is great,
> But beware, beware the Sultan!

When the chorus has finished, the prince dismisses everyone except Astarbé. He announces that for three days now he has seen her bathing, has consequently fallen madly in love, and has decided to make her wife number five hundred and ninety-two.

Astarbé is appalled and tells him it cannot be. The king is going to carry her off by force, but Kléber arrives with the people who have come for the judgment of the dead, which Achmet must undergo before the rites of burial are accorded him. The Sultan, having too few men to stage an attack, pretends to observe the law; but, at the moment when the body of Achmet is to be committed to the tomb, he presents evidence of a debt that the old minister had been unable to repay, and claims, according to established custom, his body as security.

Astarbé throws herself at his feet in vain, pleading with him not to condemn the old man's spirit to wander without shelter on those gloomy banks. The Sultan replies in this implacable verse:

> Surrender yourself to the living, and the dead will be
> surrendered to you!

And he makes preparations to carry off the body of Achmet.

But Kléber is moved by the young girl's despair. He seizes one of the king's horses, leaps on it with Astarbé in his arms, spurs on the charger, and disappears at a gallop, followed by Moses carrying the body of Achmet.

Stupefaction guaranteed at this point.

"After him! Bring him back!" cries the Sultan when he has disap-

peared. The orchestra plays an air, ostensibly Egyptian, but which Maurice recognizes as "Va-t'en voir s'ils viennent, Jean."[2]

## SCENE TWO

The setting has changed. Sand made from chopped straw swirls about; two tame ostriches walk up and down with a bored air; gazelles run after biscuits, and a pyramid rises in the distance: it is the desert.

Kléber and Astarbé, and the aged Achmet (who, in his character of an embalmed corpse, is played by an actor who never speaks), arrive on their charger, which is limping. All three are exhausted. They halt, and Astarbé, slightly delirious, begins to murmur:

> Down there by the well why not rest,
> By the breeze from great palm trees caressed?
> There's a house where they give to guests without money
> Rice pudding sweet with a touch of honey;
> Where the modest woman always indoors
> Cares for her husband and looks to the chores.

### KLÉBER.
Astarbé! What's that you say?
See how the desert burns in the heat!
### ASTARBÉ.
I should like an iced sorbet to eat!
### KLÉBER.
Hear you not the approach of the simoom in its rage?
### ASTARBÉ.
Please give me a rose for my corsage.

Kléber tries to reach the shelter of the Great Pyramid; but the whirlwind of straw catches the horse and carries it away, leaving the dead and the living to proceed on foot.

In despair, Kléber calls on his army. He enumerates all his feats—always an agreeable task for a soldier—and does not pause until he hears the sound of horses. Thinking it must be his faithful camel corps, he gives a cry of joy; but almost immediately he recognizes the Sultan and his cavalry. He is ordered to surrender. He refuses and is about to perish with the woman he loves, when the Nile, which has reached its highest level of the month, overflows its banks in the nick of time and drowns the tyrant's guards.

Kléber seizes Astarbé, who has fainted, and carries her up the Great Pyramid, and as he is about to disappear into the dark opening to the tomb, he cries:

At last, I have saved her.

ASTARBÉ, *recovering her senses*

Ah! my father, my father!
If he is lost, I shall die!

KLÉBER, *with a cry of joy*

O happy fate!
Look where Moses comes swimming with him.

ASTARBÉ, *falling on her knees in pious exaltation.*

Ah! I will believe in a God who created the crocodile!

Final tableau shows the pyramid, Kléber, Astarbé, and the crocodile. Soft music suggesting inundation. The curtain falls.

### SCENE THREE.

Inside the Great Pyramid; Achmet has been placed among the illustrious mummies housed there. The only problems now are the ones that face the living.

Meanwhile Astarbé, who knows how to bring nobility to the work blessed by the gods of hearth and home, produces nourishing food for her commander in-chief, thanks to Moses, who brings her his catch in fish and meat every day. But, in spite of all this care, Kléber grows thinner; and, when the young woman, mystified, asks him tearfully,

What more can I do, my lord, what more do you need?

the Frenchman replies:

The black bread of glory! That's what I need!

At that moment the crocodile arrives with various provisions, among which there is a bottle of Bordeaux. But it contains nothing but scribbled messages thrown into the sea from a French vessel at the moment of shipwreck. The general discovers that the army, believing he is dead, is planning to re-embark. This news throws him into a transport of grief and rage.

> Where are my legions, glories untold,
> Over whose recitation pipes have gone cold.
> What now, old warrior, who accepts as his
> What fate has in store, and life as it is.
> That noble simplicity of times Homeric ,
> When oxen were roasted on spits esoteric!
> I shall swim (it may harm me!)
> In search of my army!

Astarbé tries in vain to calm him in his despair. Seeing that Kléber has decided to leave,

> . . . Aboard the ship of courage,

she recalls the existence of underground passages that connect the pyramids with the seacoast; but she cannot find them. Finally, when she has given up hope, she turns to her dead father, who knew the entrances to these passages.

The dead man, hearing her call him, slowly opens the mummy case, shows her the secret door, and returns to his box again.

Astarbé and Kléber hurry down into the tunnel, preceded by the crocodile, swishing his tail from side to side to signify his delight.


SCENE FOUR.

The scene is now an idyllic spot, with the sea in the background and an inaccessible island in the far distance. The Sultan is sitting in Turkish fashion under the shade of palm trees, and his slaves are trying desperately to entertain him. They bring him all kinds of delicacies, but he eats nothing; they sing songs of every description, but he does not hear them; they offer him odalisques of every color, but he does not notice them.

An officer arrives with dispatches concerning the French army; the Sultan puts them unread on the platter of sweetmeats; then an Ethiopian appears with a great bald eagle—the admiration of all the crowned heads of Africa—which he has come to offer as a present.

Among his other useful talents, the great eagle has learned to carry letters, turn the spit, and fish with rod and line.

Having watched these party pieces with a distracted air, the Sultan throws a purse of gold to the Ethiopian, sends everyone away, and when he is alone, pulls from his breast a slipper that he smothers with kisses.

He had found this slipper on the day when he saw Astarbé bathing. It belongs to the daughter of Achmet, and the sight of it inflames the Sultan.

After contemplating it for a long time, he puts it close to him, takes his guitar and sings the following words to a Coptic air, composed long ago by Mlle. Loïsa Puget.[3]

### TURKISH SLIPPER SONG

Too well, too well I know thee!
Slipper lying there
   At my feet
   Folded neat:
But were it your mistress,
What then? What then?

Slipper, when I kiss you,
There's a fire in my heart
   Through every sense
   A flame intense!
But were it your mistress,
What then? What then?

But some day, my enchantress,
As reward for my patience,
   After dread ennui,
   If I see
Astarbé face to face,
What then? What then?

Here the Coptic song with its guitar accompaniment has its effect, and the Sultan drops off to sleep. The orchestra plays very softly a soothing lullaby, and soon Kléber appears, leading Astarbé, who is riding on Moses.

All three, enchanted by the beauty of the place, want to stop and rest, until they catch sight of the Sultan. Moses, who in his character as a crocodile is somewhat voracious, opens his mouth to swallow him up, but Kléber intervenes, crying:

> Stop! Stop! the French fight their foe,
> But sleeping sultans—never so.

He allows Astarbé to retrieve her slipper, while he seizes the dispatches.

Moses, deprived of having the sleeper for his lunch, makes up for his loss as well as he can by eating the sweetmeats and then the platter.

But the general, who has opened the papers, learns that the French army is not very far off. Overjoyed, he exclaims:

> I return to share your woes.
> Come quickly grenadiers,
> Infantry, and camel corps.

Neither the infantry nor the camel corps come running; the Sultan wakes up; his guards arrive and surround Kléber, who seizes his sword to inspire Moses to do his duty and shows him the pyramid in the distance, saying:[4]

> From this great stone height twenty centuries look down on you.

The crocodile, eager to make a good impression on these spectators, performs miracles of bravery. For his part, Kléber repels all attackers. But the bald eagle, which has seen everything, takes wing, hovers a moment over his head, then, swooping with a savage cry, seizes his sword and carries it away. The Egyptians hurl themselves upon their now defenseless enemy.

Moses, now alone against them all, falls back to the sea and plunges into the water, carrying Astarbé to the island that can be seen in the distance.

The Sultan gives the order to pursue them but is told there is no boat. He makes a despairing gesture.

> THE SULTAN
> Can it be? Can it be?
> No crossing o'er the sea!
> What's to be done?
> What's to be done?

He remains deep in thought. Suddenly, the eagle reappears, holding Kléber's sword, which he drops at the Sultan's feet. The latter, with a flash of inspiration, cries:

Ah! we can reach her by air!

The eagle flaps its wings, the guards brandish their swords. Final chorus.

### SCENE FIVE

The scene opens to reveal a rock covered in large nests; it is the hometown of Moses, the capital city of the crocodiles.

The crocodiles are busy around their homes, attending to their domestic duties. The mothers are looking after small children; the fathers of families are going off hunting or fishing; the young males are going off with the young females. The scene is so perfectly arranged that it creates the illusion that you are watching a civilized people.

Away from all this bustle, Astarbé sits sadly at the edge of the rocks. Moses has just left her to go and visit his family. She is thinking of her husband, while she holds a miniature of him. She pours out a torrent of tears and poetic sentiments before wrapping herself in her burnoose, declaring that,

Seeing Kléber no more, there's nothing left for me to see!

The bald eagle appears among the clouds, glides down, seizes in his talons the four corners of the burnoose, and carries the young girl off through the air.

Moses, arriving at that moment, stands up on his tail, reaching up with his tear-stained paws; but Astarbé disappears into the clouds.

Here ensues a dramatic monologue in pantomime form in which the crocodile acts out his sadness by every means in his repertoire: he sighs deeply, holds his head in his scaly hands as if to tear out his hair, rolls on the ground, and finally lies there, overcome with grief.

But he is aroused from this swoon by the sound of a drum: it is the French army disembarking on Crocodile Island.

First the advance guard comes into view, led by the drum major. The crocodile runs to meet them and does his best, by his gestures, to induce the soldiers to follow him to the rescue of their general. But the French, who do not understand his language and are, from experience, wary of crocodiles, bar his way with their bayonets fixed. Moses desperately tries to escape; they conclude he is a traitor, and he is seized. At that very moment an officer sees the miniature that Astarbé has dropped, and says:

> The portrait of Kléber! . . . this monster has eaten
> —No possible doubt—our leader unbeaten.

The enraged soldiers clamor for his death, and Moses is taken away to be shot.

They march off to the tune *On va lui percer le flanc.*[5]


### SCENE SIX.

We are in the Sultan's palace; Kléber, a prisoner in a dungeon overlooking the river, is at work on a balloon that will provide the means of his escape.

In the midst of many thoughts about his own life, his labors lead to a more general reflection:

> O how potent scientific endeavor!
> The barbarian thinks I'm his prisoner for ever.
> But Montgolfier's art can the tyrant defy;
> Be he ever so clever, away I shall fly.

The noise of cannon fire breaks in on his scientific observation. He starts, for he has recognized the French artillery.

> Whose sound is the voice of glory itself.

The Sultan arrives in some alarm: the town is besieged and will fall if Kléber does not order his army to withdraw. Kléber refuses, in spite of being threatened with death by the Sultan. While they are arguing fiercely, the great bald eagle arrives and deposits Astarbé at their feet, still wrapped in her burnoose.

The daughter of Achmet throws herself into the French general's arms, declaring that she will die with him. The quarrel is taken up again, even more acrimoniously, descending to the personal.

Tremble!

says Kléber;

Tremble!

says Astarbé;

Tremble!

the Sultan replies.

And since he has just heard that the French are masters of the town, he draws his sword to kill the two lovers. Then Kléber runs to the window of the dungeon, pulls out one of the iron bars, and all the Egyptians take flight.

But at the grille of the door, now shut again, the Sultan repeats his terrible:

Tremble!

and adds, in a command to his slaves:

Neither pity nor pardon! The serpents!

And the slaves answer in chorus:

The serpents!

Terrified, Astarbé takes refuge in the arms of Kléber, who looks about him and shudders. . . . The orchestra plays a march with triangle and cymbals. A sound like the clickety-clack of scaley armor plates is heard; then a trapdoor is seen to open on the stage, and two monstrous boas rear their heads.

The lovers are rooted to the spot, frozen with horror and unable to speak, one hand extended in the direction of the reptiles. The two serpents uncoil themselves slowly for a frontal attack.

A memory surfaces in Kléber. He runs to his balloon, takes it to the window, helps Astarbé into the gondola . . . but he is already too late; the boas are only a few paces away; another lunge forward, and they reach their prey. The two of them give a low hiss of joy. It is answered by a terrible roar.

The two serpents pause; Moses has appeared at the dungeon window and hurls himself towards them.

They fall back slowly, surprised and uncertain. Kléber takes advantage of their retreat to get into the gondola himself, and the balloon takes off.

However, the boa constrictors have already regained their courage;

they return, and a fierce fight ensues. At first Moses has the advantage; twice he breaks out from the coils of his enemies; twice he forces them back; but finally, exhausted and caught yet again in their coils, he struggles ever more feebly, gives a low groan, and falls dying.

The victorious boas give a hiss of triumph, and return to their lair.

At that moment, the sound of armed men marching is heard. Astarbé reappears with Kléber at the head of a column of French soldiers; but they have come too late; the crocodile can only raise himself up, put a scaly hand on his heart, and fall back dead.

At that sight Astarbé is overcome with grief and faints, the general stands appalled, and every grenadier wipes away a tear.

Finally, Kleber is the first to regain the power of action. He takes the Cross of Honor that he wears on his lapel, and placing it on the dead body of Moses, he speaks these words with profound emotion:[6]

> Savage child of Nile, Ah! wear on your heart
> This reward for devotion, that sets you apart.
> Man or beast, does it matter who gains it?
> No matter the species; 'tis the spirit that earns it!

Tremendous success! They call for the crocodile, and he reappears, salutes three times and retires, covered in bouquets of flowers.

"You'll see that the play will run for three hundred performances," said Madame Facile. "The critics themselves will say nice things about it, because it has animals in it, and animals do not care if one says nasty things about them. Besides, it is the work of an unknown author, and you have no idea what a recommendation that is. The famous writer is odious not only to those who have come up with him, but also to those who are still on the way up. For the first, he is a rival; for the second, he is the top dog; and for all of them, he is their natural enemy. The unknown author, on the contrary, provokes neither fear nor jealousy. Those who aspire to fame applaud him as one of their own, and every famous man encourages him in the hope that he will take the place of one of his rivals in the celebrity business. They take up the cudgels for him against those who are already enjoying success; they raise sky-high his end of the seesaw, in order to put the other end down into the mud. It is very gratifying to speak well of a colleague, when it gives you the occasion to speak ill of others. The unknown are like the dead, and you know how fond we are of the dead, hating the living as we do. They will proclaim the author of *Kléber* a genius, if only to have the pleasure of treating his predecessors as imbeciles."[7]

"And there is another reason," added Prétorien; "the new poet is known to us all; he has asked our advice over every scene; tried out his verses on us couplet by couplet. There is something of all of us in his play; we believe it belongs to us all, and therefore it must be admirable. So we shall give it our unanimous support. There's a sort of tacit agreement entered into in advance by each one of us. Most authors come to us as unknowns with an offering of their inspired work for us to admire, and we regard it suspiciously, examine it in great detail, and judge it severely. There is nothing of that here: the muse who inspired *Kléber* is a sweet girl—a confidante. We can refuse her nothing. To admire and praise a woman, the guiding principle is not that she should be beautiful, but that she should be one of us." Here he was interrupted by Madame Facile:

"That's a singularly impertinent statement as far as the poor objects of your admiration are concerned."

"But why?" Prétorien asked. "Don't you know that to be one of us means to rule over us?"

"You choose to make a jest of it."

"Put it to the test. I offer myself as a guinea pig."

"And what would she who rules your destiny say?"

"She would say, like the rest of the world, that nothing can resist you."

"All the more reason why I should resist everyone."

"Ah! You think everything can be managed with a little wit?"

"Is that not the currency you use?"

{ 189 }

"I went through my fortune long ago."

"Then I will give you supper."

"This evening?"

"Yes, along with these gentlemen; and I hope that our young couple will come too, for there will be a meeting of the society of *Sensible Women*. Mlle. Spartacus is going to speak. Do come—it will be the little epilogue to the main play."

Prétorien accepted for himself and his companions, and they all went off to the home of Madame Facile.

# §XX

*An example of a select gathering—The grand critic, the medium critic, the little critic*
*—Why the man who has made the most widows and orphans is known*
*as a man of feeling—Marcellus the pietist—Conversation of the*
*well-born—Meeting of the Society of Sensible Women—*
*Speech of Mlle. Spartacus to proclaim*
*freedom for women.*

The house of Madame Facile was, everyone agreed, the most beautiful and palatial residence in Sans-Pair. It was the result of a sort of competition in gallantry among the principal members of the government. The minister of public works had arranged for it to be built with the stone taken from the demolished ancient church of the Virgin; the director of fine arts had embellished it with pictures and statues paid for out of the public purse; the inspector for the book trade had established there a library of volumes intended for the public libraries; the commissioner for stud farms had assembled in its stables the finest bloodlines purchased for the improvement of the equine race; and finally, the minister for religion had himself enriched the chapel with a complete altar.

Madame Facile showed her gratitude for all these gifts with certain services: she organized cavalcades with the provider of horses, arranged commissions for the inspector of books, received the ladies recommended by the minister for the arts, and worked to gain support for him at the ministry.

She had, moreover, friends in every class and every political party—an arrangement that kept her safe from any recriminations. Her house, open to any who wished to enter, provided a neutral ground where adversaries could meet. Every preoccupation other than that of enjoyment was left at

**Mme. FACILE**

*Fashionable lady in the year 3000*

the door. At her receptions, everyone made light of the sentiments they expressed elsewhere, and laughed openly at all and sundry, as well as at themselves. You could say it provided a peek behind the stage at the theater, where the actors made a parody of their true roles. It was there that the young generation of Sans-Pair learned that skeptical snigger, that freezing north wind that whistles across the flower-filled meadows of youth. It was there that irony halted the flight of innocent enthusiasms, ardent beliefs, fleeting hopes, ever-changing visions—poor butterflies in their dazzling colors—piercing them with her rapier of steel (laughing all the while), and exposing their agonies to the mockery of the crowd. Indifference to good or evil was labeled good sense, selfishness had become the mainspring of conduct, and men's scorn was regarded as merely a part of the experience of life. The art of corruption was regarded as the art of living. No longer was it necessary to raise a cross for the Christs of this world: they were given a bauble for a scepter, and for a crown the jester's cap and bells. There was no longer a passion for the sublime: it met with incomprehension and was the object of derision.

Maurice arrived shortly after Madame Facile and found a crowd of people gathered. Some were already known to him, and Prétorien pointed out to him a number of men well known in political life or in the arts for something they had achieved, and a much greater number known in the fashionable world because they had achieved nothing.

In the first group Maurice noticed in particular a thin, bored-looking man who was talking to everyone at large with an easy familiarity.

"That is M. Mauvais, our great critic," Prétorien informed him. "Since he is unable to create anything himself, he is dedicated to tearing to shreds any contemporary work—rather like those women who, unable to have children themselves, find other people's children insufferable. As long as he had only his talent to recommend him, nobody took any notice of him; but he then took to being malicious and spiteful, and today he is a famous man. His critical method is of the simplest: he selects three or four great names and uses their work as a touchstone for that of newcomers. In his manipulations, each ancient masterpiece becomes the cup of hemlock offered to poison young writers aspiring to glory. He judges each new book against an absolute standard by which it is damned, all the more completely since the standard has been invented precisely for that purpose. The method has been no less successful for himself—not with the general public who showed only a moderate interest in his pronouncements, but with his victims who writhed, yet craved his attentions; for there is always a little of the feminine in the artist. Better to be damned as mediocre than ignored. Our writers are like the marquises of the eighteenth century, who yearned for the honor of being dishonored by Richelieu. And that is why those who would subject themselves to the rigorous judgment of Master Mauvais queue up to be murdered by him."

"And this man is your only contemporary Aristarchus?"

"We have also a little jovial and lively character who has set himself up in the role of everyman's Triboulet in the interests of the public, and tries to keep everyone amused with epigrams or scandals.[1] This trade has given him a reputation made the greater by a couple of beatings, which he accepts as natural hazards in his line of work. He has even become founder of a school, and under his wing a whole phalanx of ordinary fools has gathered. Not having enough generosity of spirit to praise anything, they have taken to mocking everything. Their appointed task of killing off great works of human thought affords them some recognition: the man who holds the noose never looks like an ordinary person in the eyes of those to be hanged. These people are flattered, they are propitiated, and they become famous because of their power to harm and their dishonesty, just as others gain fame for their merits."

"And are there no exceptions?"

"They are rare, but they do exist. We still have some fair-minded critics who treat art as a flower with a perfume to be enjoyed, and not as prey on which to feed. These latter are great minds and noble hearts; but we rarely consult them. A newspaper is no more than a restaurant that caters to the intellectual appetite of the crowd, and the demand there is not so much for wholesome food as for spicy dishes."

From critics Prétorien went on to celebrities, who were to be found in great numbers at the house of Madame Facile. All of them were lionized for a speciality that endeared them to the fashionable world. It was either their gambling, or their packs of hounds, or their horses, or their mistresses. All this, incidentally, did not prevent them having serious occupations, such as kickboxing, baton fighting, and training horses.

Maurice noticed one among them to whom everyone seemed to show particular deference.

"That is the comte de Mortifer," said Prétorien, "the most fearsome assassin in the entire republic. He nearly always kills his adversary, and consequently he is treated with great circumspection. You overlook his impertinences and let his foolish remarks pass unnoticed in case he demands satisfaction."

At that moment, the count turned and came to meet Prétorien.

"Well, now, have you heard the news?" he asked without any preliminary greeting. "This clown Format has proposed in the Chamber a law forbidding dueling!"

"It is for his own protection," replied the newspaperman.

"And I say it is an insult," said Mortifer through clenched teeth. "The proposal is obviously directed against me, and I shall demand an explanation."

"From an attorney? He will dismiss the case."

"And you will allow such a law to be passed?" the count continued, addressing Banqman who had just joined them. "A law that will fine anyone who kills a man."

"Are you afraid of being ruined?" asked the industrialist with a smile.

"Good heavens! Who knows?" said Mortifer, obviously flattered. "After all, when one is a little sensitive on points of honor . . . I have fought sixty-four times, sir."

"Amazing!"

"And I have killed thirty-two of my adversaries."

"And that means you settled for 50 percent?" said Banqman pleasantly.

"And an ill-mannered cad like Format wants to deprive me of the liberty of continuing?" the indignant count went on. "No, that must never be! The duel is the last safeguard of morality and honor. Without it, all those folk who do not know how to handle a sword will brazenly tell you to your face what they are thinking. One would only have to be in the right to dare raise one's voice. We will never put up with such shame! The only way to preserve courtesy, justice, and loyalty among the bourgeoisie is to leave that duty to someone who feels himself insulted and is ready to put a bullet through the jaw of the offender or to run him through."

At these words, pronounced in solemn tones, Mortifer turned on his heels and went to join another group.

"You have just heard the views of all those who call themselves *men of feeling*," Prétorien said to his companion. "Slashing people's bodies or smashing their jaws make them smile all the more when they have a closely guarded monopoly on these activities. They contend that the duel is a necessary means of punishing crimes where the law is not effective. They do not add that, in this haphazard justice, it is often the one sinned against who dies and the guilty one who triumphs. They call it a guarantee against the insolence of the cowardly, but they do not say that it is, at the same time, an opportunity for the murderer."

There was an announcement that dinner was served, and the guests went into the dining room.

There they found a table covered with the most delicate dishes—that is to say, the most rare. Maurice was trying, without success, to recognize these new inventions of the cuisine of Sans-Pair, when he saw on the walls enormous enameled illustrations that presented the menu. They showed tarts made with pippins, soups made with the hearts of pigeons, compotes of partridge tongue, fried larks' livers. Our hero read no further. Evidently, this civilization was taking its cue from the fairies of ancient stories who required captive princesses to serve dishes of locusts' eyes or ants' nails. The unobtainable had become a necessity of life.

Moreover, the guests testified by their appetite how much everything was to their taste, and the wines flowed freely to reanimate any conversation that might be flagging.

Next to Maurice was a young man sporting the beard of a pasha, and a pair of spectacles, whom Prétorien had introduced as the most brilliant writer in the religious press. The great hopes reposing in him had earned him the nickname of Marcellus—an allusion to the young hero celebrated by Virgil: *Tu Marcellus eris.*[2]

His conversation was easy, and his faith all the stronger because it accommodated itself to all situations. He could be found by turns in the cafés where the celebrities congregated, and at vespers; at the sermons of the Abbé Gratias, and at masked balls; but he would be unfailingly orthodox, whether singing the *Dies Iræ* or dancing a lively polonaise.

Marcellus had at first applied his religious zeal to eating and drinking, but when he had fulfilled these all-important duties to his *prison* (that was the name he gave to his body), he began to take notice of his neighbor.

"So, you lived in the nineteenth century, sir?" he asked, wolfing down a tartlet and gazing fixedly at Maurice. "Then you will have known that

## M. MARCELLUS

*A New-Age Christian of the year 3000*

age of simple belief when man, untrammeled by less important desires, dreamt only of food for the soul."

He took another small tart.

"A happy epoch, gone for ever; strong and faithful generations, who were preparing themselves for the blessings of a better world, while quenching their thirst at the pure springs of faith."

He emptied his glass, smacked his lips, and sat motionless, with the pensive air of a devotee in meditation.

Meanwhile, conversation continued at the other end of the table, where Prétorien was telling the story of a lady of Sans-Pair. Among the cravings that afflict pregnant women, she had experienced a yearning to eat her husband.

"And did she eat him?" asked Blaguefort.

"Right down to the toes," replied the editor of *Le Grand Pan.*

"She was within her rights. The law declares that the husband must feed his wife."

"And the Church adds that the two must be one flesh."

"It was not enough to prevent her arrest by the crown prosecutor," said Prétorien.

"No doubt he was worried that she might set his own wife a bad example."

"Who the devil would want to eat a crown prosecutor?"

"Where a husband is concerned, there is no need to consult one's taste."

"But if perhaps the unfortunate lady could prove that she had been overcome by an irresistible craving?" queried Banqman.

"That it was a question of the life of the child in her womb?" said Mauvais.

"And that she had only eaten her husband to safeguard the life of his son?" Blaguefort went on.

"Is she at least young?" asked Count Mortifer.

"Twenty years old."

"And pretty?"

"Fresh as pink satin lined with swans' down."

"Then it is clear that the custom is a good one," Blaguefort interpolated, "and that our pretty women should adopt it."

"It is common knowledge that meat eaters enjoy the best health."

"Indubitably; the veritable Fountain of Youth is to be found at the abattoir."

"The very Hippocrene. Shakespeare was the son of a butcher."

"And it is thanks to this liking for roast beef that old England was named by Byron *a nest of swans.*"

Milord Cant interrupted them at this point. "Speaking of England, have you heard the news about the daughter of our ambassador?"

"She has been carried off by her father's secretary."

"And they have both run off to the Cape."

"That's ancient history."

"Yes, but the latest news is that our abductor ended up by finding Miss Confiance too sweet and too fair-haired."

"Then he made her dye her hair?"

"He proposed her as a stake at billiards for twenty points."

"Good gracious!"

"And he lost her?"

"The rascal was always a lucky gambler."

"Captain Malgache, who won, insisted on his rights."

"And the stake allowed herself to be handed over?"

"She threw herself out the window!"

"On the ground floor?"

"On the third floor!"

"Incredible! And her lover?"

"He gave her a decent burial, then embarked on the underwater steamer, and has just arrived in Sans-Pair."

"Ready to start all over again? A warning to innocent young maidens who *wish to reside in a foreign country.* There's a novel waiting to be written there, Robinet."

"That really is an idea," said the creator of serial novels, who was just finishing a kangaroo steak. "I shall speak to my copy editor."

"Will it be a moral or immoral tale ? Blaguefort asked.

"Whatever is required," said Robinet, between drinks. "We have a selection of four types of story: the genre known as Louis XV for hedonists; the genre known as German for papers catering to a melancholy readership; the genre known as commercial traveler for frivolous papers; and the genre known as virtuous for the papers that nobody reads. Every dish can be served up with one of these four sauces, according to the wishes of the consumer. All that is needed is to vary the spices and stir the pan."

"Then I recommend the story of the white boy of Martinique," said M. Banqman.

"Are there still Whites left in the West Indies?" Madame Facile asked in some surprise.

"Only one family who escaped extermination, and whom the Blacks take pleasure in torturing."

Philadelphe le Doux heaved a sigh: "Poor fellows," he muttered under his breath, "there's not much else in the way of entertainment for them."

"They have already caused the death of the father and his two sons."

"Simply out of ignorance."

"And drowned the grandfather."

"Without any ill will; they are simply children."

"Finally, the mother has been imprisoned until she can be ransomed for the sum of a hundred thousand piasters."

"A price that shows their high esteem for the Whites," said the philanthropist.

"That's why her son, who is only ten years old, has gone off to see if he can raise the money."

"Has he arrived in Sans-Pair?"

"After being shipwrecked twice."

"Now there's a model of filial piety," said Blaguefort, "I suggest that we give him public recognition for it."

"With an award of a hundred crowns."

"With an address from the mayor."

"He could hope for more," said Banqman. "We must organize a raffle for him, and a subscription ball, where he will be able to do a native dance."

"For the sake of his mother, who perhaps has already been strangled."

"Come now," exclaimed Blaguefort, "I'll bet that your little white boy from Martinique is a rascal who is taking his cut. It strikes me that the whole thing is a perfect little confidence trick on the side. You really are foolish to believe the stories of orphans. Besides, since it concerns a female slave, you should refer the affair to Mlle. Spartacus and her associates."

"Ah! I was forgetting," said Madame Facile. "I promised you a meeting of the Society of Sensible Women. . . ."

"Of which you are a member? asked Blaguefort.

"A free member!" Prétorien added.

"Which meets here," said Madame Facile, seeming not to notice the malice in that double interruption. "I have made available to Mlle. Spartacus the room where we play charades; but I have reserved the balcony for my own use, and we can go down there. The meeting will be open to the public." All the guests rose from the table and followed their hostess, to whom the minister for religion gave his arm.

When they arrived at the balcony reserved for them, the room was already full of women of all ages from thirty-six to sixty, and of all classes, from the widow of some senior army officer to the lady who looked after the reading room.

At the sight of the men accompanying Madame Facile, a great shout of disapproval was raised on all sides. The most vociferous cried: "String them up from the lamps!" although there was nothing more substantial there than candles. The more delicately brought up ladies were shaking their fists when Madame Facile made an imperious gesture for silence. Then, leaning toward the bonneted and howling crowd, she said in very confident tones:

"Sisters, I have brought you the chiefs of the enemy army, so that they may see your strength and your resolution. When they see the danger that threatens them, they will realize that resistance is futile, and that finally the day foretold in the Gospel has dawned: *The first shall be last,* which clearly signifies that from now on women will march in front and men will resign themselves to being mere train bearers."

A cheer from the assembled ladies greeted this short clarifying announcement; Madame Facile's guests took their seats, and a long pause ensued.

At last, a bell was heard; it heralded Mlle. Spartacus, arriving to take her place in the auditorium with other members of the committee.

When she appeared, there was some halfhearted applause. It was obvious that each of her colleagues believed that she had at least an equal right to preside over the assembly, and that her dominant role could be viewed as a usurpation.

This state of affairs was clear from the continued buzz of conversation, interspersed by the usual remarks.

"Well, now! Is that our president?"

"She is nothing to write home about."

"And her dress is badly made, don't you think?"

"And what a nose!"

"Well, speaking for myself, I should like to have a prettier general before I join the revolt."

"I believe she hates men; they really must hate her in return."

"Hush! She's opening her bag."

"We're going to get a lecture."

"What a bore that will be! Come on now, commandant, give us something worth listening to."

"We were told that there would be music and refreshments."

**Mlle. SPARTACUS**

*Defending the rights of women*

"It's always the same; on every agenda, they promise more butter than bread."

"Quiet! She's raising her arm—that's the starting signal."

Indeed, Mlle. Spartacus had arranged her papers, adjusted her glasses, and thrown back her head to give herself a more commanding air. The hubbub of voices in the audience died away, and the president of the Society of Sensible Women began to speak:

"Once again I am moved by the marks of kindness shown me so generously on every side, and find myself a little apprehensive at the thought of tackling the grave issue that has brought us together today. The agitation I feel in my heart almost overwhelms my mind; and, in spite of myself, I feel quite overcome by feelings of gratitude.

"But that very sense of gratitude brings into sharper focus the object of my mission; it strengthens me, kindles my hopes, and, after giving way to those natural feelings, I am once again ready to embark more steadfastly on the accomplishment of my project.

"You are already familiar with this project. I want to accomplish for our sex that great revolution that France accomplished once upon a time for all the classes in our society. Mirabeau proclaimed that there were no longer any commoners; I proclaim that there are no longer any wives!

"No, no more wives because man has, until this moment, condemned them to the abject cares of housekeeping and motherhood; no more wives because they are not allowed to manage workshops, or command the country's ships, or serve in the National Guard. No more wives because to men alone belongs the privilege of being killed or maimed in war, in travel, and in work.

"But how do we achieve this transformation, you will ask. That, indeed, is the question. An answer has been vainly sought for twenty centuries—no doubt would still be sought, if God had not sent me to free you.

"Yes ladies, married and unmarried, I come to complete the work begun by Christ; I come to break the last yoke left on earth; I come to place in your hands the scepter of the world!"

Here Mlle. Spartacus paused in order to prolong that moment of palpable interest in the audience; and her listeners took the opportunity to blow their noses.

Once the noses were quiet again (for in any audience the nose is always the most troublesome and rebellious element), the speaker raised her hand and continued:

"Such an outcome would be dazzling, no doubt; you are already thinking that it cannot be achieved without long and painful efforts; you are anticipating some new scheme as yet unknown. Discard that thought, amiable sex of which I rejoice to be a part! The method I have chosen was proposed two thousand years ago by a Greek poet named Aristophanes, but he was not aware of its full implications. It is based on nature and observation; it vanquishes man just as surely as hunger overcomes the horse that the ring master is training to tell the time; as the lack of sleep overpowers the dog learning to play dominoes; as opium and the rod of red-hot iron master the leopard who must become a circus performer. You are wondering what it can be? Ask yourselves what is in men the most ardent passion, the most universal, constant, and powerful impulse? Do you remember what it was that sent Troy up in flames, transformed Rome into a republic; what under kings of old supported the special position of noble families, or ennobled the families of the common people? And if I have not made myself sufficiently clear, read the explanation of the Greek poet himself, translated for those unfamiliar with the original. Here is a copy for each one of you."

Thereupon Mlle. Spartacus gave a signal, and the ladies of the committee took printed copies from a basket and tossed them into the crowd. In an instant the room filled with flying sheets of paper that were seized in mid-flight or passed from hand to hand.

Some of the sheets fell into the area occupied by Madame Facile and her guests, and Maurice recognized the translation of the third scene from *Lysistrata*. The method proposed by the president of the Society of Sensible Women was indeed very clear. It was a matter of reducing men through famine, not of the stomach, but of the heart, as the chevalier de Boufflers would say.[3] All the women were to sustain a sort of continental blockade (on the supposition that this word derives from continence), and their tyrants—now their victims—could not fail to surrender unconditionally, unless they resigned themselves to singing in solitude the refrain of Béranger:[4]

Finissons-en, le monde est assez vieux.

The translated passage was clearly enjoying considerable success in the assembly; all eyes were scanning it eagerly, and when the ladies had finished reading it, they started at the beginning again to get its message absolutely clear.

When Mlle. Spartacus deemed that the message had gone home, she took up her notes again and continued:

"You now all know, sisters and friends, the means that will assure our triumph, and none among you can doubt its power. On the day that women put it into action, man will be subjugated. *Victus et inermis drago!* that Latin quotation will not dismay you, ladies; once dominion has devolved on our sex, Latin will necessarily come within our domain, like fencing and little tots of spirits. I say again, *Victus et inermis drago!*

"Now, once our enemies are overthrown, we must take the opportunity to see that they never rise again, and the surest way to do that is to redraft the Bill of Human Rights.

The French Revolution proclaimed the rights of man; we will put in their place the rights of woman. And I have drawn them up in six articles, which from this moment on will be our law.

### RIGHTS OF LIBERATED WOMAN

"Article 1. God will henceforth be a woman, in view of her all-powerful nature and her perfection.

"Article 2. The rights of woman consist in not recognizing those of men.

"Article 3. All women alike will command, and all men alike will obey.

"Article 4. All important positions will be taken by the most interesting and frail sex, with the exception of the ones that women do not want. These will be the special responsibility of the ugliest and strongest sex.

"Article 5. All men will get married, and all women will remain chaste —that is to say that the first-named will be enslaved and will have only duties, while the second will be free and will have only rights.

"Article 6. Women alone will hold the purse strings, both public and private; men will have the privilege of keeping those purses filled."

Wild excitement greeted this six-part declaration that restored human equality in such an equitable way. Cries of *Long Live Our Liberator! Long Live Mademoiselle Spartacus!* rent the air with a thousand other exclamations of enthusiasm. Each listener was already formulating her claim. One wanted to be a préfette or major general; another attorney general to the royal court; a third inspector of remount establishments; a fourth chancellor of a university. It was a kind of lively carnival in which ambitions collided and jostled as in masked balls. Mlle. Spartacus, intoxicated by her triumph, had pushed her glasses up on her forehead, and was looking fondly at the twenty manuscripts that bulged in her velvet bag. In that bag reposed her campaign plan. She had first wanted to be sure of the favorable reaction of her audience; but the big question was to get approval for the contents of the package.

She started to speak again as soon as the enthusiasm of the crowd allowed her voice to be heard:

"I had anticipated these transports of joy, and I see here a new pledge of our certain triumph. Yes, dear co-conspirators, you will unite to vanquish the barbarity of that sex that repulses its adversaries with no consideration for their weakness, and does not even have the common decency to refrain from defending itself. But, in order to achieve this result it is essential that all women support our plan, that they understand its importance, that they are as clear about the means as the goal; and, for that, education is necessary.

"Now this system of instruction already exists, because for ten years I have devoted all my waking hours to formulating it, in novels, verses, philosophical treatises, travel accounts, entertainments. I have adopted every form in turn, explored every avenue. This bag holds the material for ninety-two octavo volumes, with no paragraphs and no spaces between lines—all of it directed to making the entire sex rally to our cause. It is a universal revolution in manuscript; and the only thing needed now is to raise the expenses for publication.

"But these expenses—a just return for the labors of the author— amount to one million two hundred thousand francs, and consequently can only be covered by the joint efforts of all concerned. I therefore have the honor to propose, in the name of the committee, an open subscription to be taken at the present meeting, in the interests of the cause, for the immediate publication of my entire works.

"The names of subscribers, and the amount they contribute will be recorded by my secretary, who will be waiting at the main door."

With these words Mlle. Spartacus readjusted her glasses, took her leave of the assembly, and went out with the members of the committee.

But no sound of applause was to be heard. The mention of subscription had frozen the hopes and cast a damper on even the boldest. Heads were shaken, and a murmur arose and rippled through the crowd, like a breeze over ears of corn.

"It's a trap," said several voices. "We have been lured into an ambush."

"All she wants is to use us to publish her outpourings."

"And to give her a private income, so that she can find a husband, in spite of her glasses and her large nose."

"She's a lunatic."

"A schemer."

"I shan't give anything."

"Nor I."

"Nor I."

"Nor I."

But, in spite of these protestations, all eyes were turned, with a certain unease in the direction of the main door, where the secretary (*female*) of Mlle. Spartacus was waiting. To pass by a subscription desk without giving anything is always a difficult thing to do, not so much because of the money, but because we are foolishly embarrassed. What will people think of us? Will they not accuse us of hard-heartedness, of meanness, of poverty? At that last thought we blush with embarrassment and put our hands in our pockets.

And this is what our sensible women would have done, although it went against the grain, when they caught sight of a concealed side door that would allow them to avoid the main entrance. They all made for it rapidly, while the secretary and Mlle. Spartacus, who had returned to join her, were still waiting patiently for subscriptions. Finally, a footman came to see if he might put out the lights. The room was empty.

The president felt she must see for herself. But, when there was no longer any doubt about it, she let her glasses fall and, hiding her face behind her lace gloves, she exclaimed, like Cato after the battle at Philippi:

"*Diutius vixi!*"

Which the secretary translated as: "I have too many manuscripts."

While all this was happening, Madame Facile and her little circle were leaving the gallery, laughing heartily and heading for the main salons again. Maurice and Marthe stayed behind alone, still sitting in the same place, holding hands and looking into each other's eyes.

"Always the same misguided views," Maurice said at length as, lost in thought, he sat leaning against Marthe's shoulder. "Ah! Why divide the children of God into two camps? Is Eve no longer Adam's flesh? Will they never understand that it is not the possession of rights that will cause servitude to disappear, but love alone? Are alliances cemented with recriminations and suspicions? Love wholeheartedly, and no one will desire the role of master, but only that of slave; be more loving and you will not even be aware who obeys and who commands, because two hearts will be one."

"Yes," said Marthe half turning toward him, her lips brushing against his hair, "that's the way we have lived, and will always live."

A tear hung on Maurice's eyelids. For a long time he held Marthe closely against his breast; then, making a great effort, he said:

"They will be coming to look for us, so let us go quickly. What would Madame Facile's guests think if they could see us and hear our conversation now? Alas! They would not even begin to understand, for understanding can only take flight on the wings of the soul. Left under the heavy weight of reality, it sinks to the lowest depths, and every day its horizon shrinks. Yesterday you wept over this new world because love had departed from it; but in departing she took her companion."

"And who was that companion?" Marthe asked.

"Poetry."

*The sensible women reading the Lysistrata*

*Authors outside the door of M. Atout*

# THIRD DAY
# §XXI

*General delivery of letters to M. Atout—Political system of the Republic of United Interests—Election circular of M. Banqman—Chamber of Deputies of the Republic of United Interests—Ministerial crisis over button molds —Magnificent speech of Banqman on the question of whether the army should or should not have knitted gloves— The assembly votes through every separate clause and rejects the act as a whole.*

The human spirit is so designed that only by facing difficulties can its enthusiasm be maintained. Passionate in pursuing the most trivial advantage if it threatens to be elusive, it is indifferent to anything that can be had without searching and without sacrifice. We have an endless desire for praise that has to be dragged out, while we receive with indifference a letter from an unknown admirer. We are eager to buy the books of a writer we have never met, but from the day he brings them round to us, we lose interest and they are never read again. We forever dream of making the acquaintance of a neighbor, and if the neighbor is the first to visit, we immediately become very reserved. We only have to see every day a man whom we hold in esteem for us to think no more of him. When we meet someone only once a year, we inquire about all his projects, his work, his ideas; but when we see him week in and week out, he ceases to be interesting to us, and we dismiss him from our minds.

What a strange makeup we have! We pursue only the people who elude us, love only the people who reject us, and regard with indifference all who seek us out.

M. Atout reflected on these things sitting at his desk littered with books, their pages still uncut even though the authors had presented them in person, free publications still in their wrappers, and stamped packages with seals still unbroken.

At the start of his career this kind of public recognition would have been received ecstatically; but, since those days, familiarity had taken the gilt off those golden opinions, and he now received them with nonchalant disdain. What stared him in the face was the need to reply to the three hundred contributions cluttering up his desk.

For M. Atout knew that punctiliousness is the courtesy of men of letters as well as of kings, and he always replied. He had three model letters prepared and ready. Only the address was wanting.

If, for instance, there was a volume of poetry with an accompanying wildly enthusiastic letter, he would use letter number 1, couched in these terms:

Sir,

You have a lyre in your heart! I have read . . . (here the title of the book) with emotion constantly renewed. Your muse is like those birds of other latitudes that make their nests in the long grass, sing amid the foliage of the woodlands, and soar through the clouds.

Keep on writing, sir, and the kind words you so generously say of me now will be applied with more justice to you yourself in the future.

If, on the contrary, it was a question of a periodical publication, then model number 2 would fit the bill:

Sir,

Your spirit is a two-edged sword. I have read with keenest interest your . . . (the name of the publication). The arguments you employ are like those weapons that cut equally well with both sides of the blade and with the point.

Keep it up, sir, and the high opinion you express of my work will be bestowed by the entire republic one day, and with more justice, on your journal.

Finally, if it was a matter of acknowledging receipt of a manuscript, then he had recourse to model number 3:

Sir,

Your imagination is an orchestra. I have read with rapt attention your . . . (here the title of the manuscript). The conceptions created by your genius resemble those symphonies where one hears in turn every strain and every tone.

Keep writing, sir, and the attention that the public accords, you say, to my voice will be accorded, with better reason, to yours.

The daily dispatch of these letters had enhanced prodigiously the popularity of the Académicien. All those men whose genius he acknowledged naturally extolled his discernment. How can we fail to support a famous person who writes to us? Do we not bathe in reflected glory? The more illustrious he is, the more his approbation honors us; we turn him into a great man, if only to increase the value of his autograph.

M. Atout knew that, and never neglected any means of enhancing his reputation, for it is the same in all human activity: luck sows the seed; it needs only skill to make it grow. Indeed many people are capable of making a reputation for themselves, but few understand the art of engineering it. It is essential to have the shrewdness to lay the foundations, the persistence to see it established, and the egotism to consolidate it. Above all, one must have plenty of vanity and little pride; for if vanity is a sail that we fill out ourselves to carry us along, pride is a rigid and tenacious anchor on which we float motionless. Flatter when necessary, be pliant when occasion demands, but always be seen everywhere. Believe in yourself as you want others to believe in you, for man is an imitator, even in his feelings. The esteem in which you hold your own merit will always be more or less contagious. Be careful, however, not to argue for your claims too seriously. Admiration cannot be forced; it can be obtained as a favor, but with difficulty as a right. Every man is a member, to a greater or lesser degree, of the family of Themistocles: the trophies of Miltiades gave him sleepless nights.

Write little rather than much. Do not imitate those men whose lust for glory is insatiable—those who are always to be found in the arena, their bodies glistening with oil, cestus in hand. Rest on your laurels; take your place among the famous dukes and glorious peers who are acclaimed to-day because of what they once were. In this way, it will be almost as if you are already dead—one of of those whom all the world honors because they are a threat to no one. Your idleness will be seen as restraint, your sterility as discretion; you will be respected for what you did not do, and you will have a place in that company of artists who prove their worth by knowing when to be silent.

We have already noted how this method had succeeded in the case of M. Atout. He occupied the highest position in literary circles in the United Interests without writing anything, and was in the first rank of professors without professing anything. Accordingly, he was resolved to continue in a way of life that allowed him to arrive without the trouble of walking. So he hastened to finish his regular correspondence, and then re-membering his guest, he went up to his apartment.

He found Maurice with a book in his hand and leaned over to see the title:

"What have you got there?" he said. "The history of the French Con-vention?"

"Yes," replied Maurice, "I was reading again the story of those brave and steadfast spirits, the least of whom died like Socrates. I was counting the silent sacrifices of the people of Decius, and discovering the secret of so much simple nobility in a single word: FAITH."

The Académicien nodded his head.

"Indeed," he said, with a grave air, "it was the motive power, the im-mortal soul of society. But time has brought enlightenment to men. We have brought patriotism to perfection, and have made it easier. Your motive power was like steam—an irresistible force but difficult to con-trol. Explosions were always leading to disaster. And so we have replaced it with a force that is more amenable, more manageable, and no less irresistible."

"And its name?"

"INTEREST. Our constitution has been so cleverly developed that the duties of the citizen have been reduced to the obligation to seek his own interest in all things. Moreover, your own constitutional government con-tained the germs of this wonderful reform—seeds guiltily hidden under-ground from the light of day; we have happily given them our legal bless-ing and encouraged them to take their place in the sun. Now, today, the political system of the United Interests responds to the needs of every truly civilized man.

"It is made up of the four powers that together form the social principles of our era.

"At the head there is the President of the Republic, or the Impeccable, so named because he can do no wrong; and he can do no wrong because he doesn't do anything. In fact, the Impeccable is neither man, woman, nor child, but what we call a government fiction: it is an empty chair under a baldachin. This chair is the legitimate head of government. Ministers may not speak except in its name, and their political statements are known as speeches from the chair.

"This happy arrangement has eliminated the trouble of choosing a president with a limited term of office, and has saved us from the disadvantages attaching to hereditary power. When the head of state is getting old, an upholsterer is summoned to make the chair like new again, and a dozen nails suffice to restore the status quo. In addition, there is no court, no civil list. The entire presidential establishment is reduced to a brush and a feather duster. There are no daughters to be provided with dowries or sons to be married off. We have nothing to fear from revolutions or usurpations: a chair is inevitably obliged to maintain the status quo. Finally, since it can do nothing, we have had the confidence to give it executive power.

"The second power in the land is the Chamber of Deputies, nominated by those who sleep on soft mattresses and drink aged wines.

"Legislators believed, in effect, that any citizen who slept comfortably and ate well must be a friend of good order—that is to say where bed and board are concerned—and that he would of necessity be knowledgeable about the ways of withholding those benefits from men who sleep on straw and live on black bread.

"However, since there was always the possibility of finding among the deputies certain muddleheaded gentlemen egotistic enough to prefer their principles to their interests, a counterweight was instituted in the form of a Chamber of Valetudinarians, made up of men who are agitated by any movement and exhausted by noise. To gain admission to it, you must prove that you are deaf or blind, gouty or asthmatic. Preference is given to those who suffer from multiple infirmities; with a little string pulling, however, pigheadedness and ignorance will suffice.

"Finally, the fourth power is composed of bankers who have made themselves purse holders to the republic, lending at high interest and making it their business to pass the public revenues through a sieve that allows the little coins to fall through but holds back the big ones. The state has gradually put into their hands as pledges the land, the rivers, the seas, the mines underground, and aerial transportation. In effect, they would be masters of all if the chair and the two chambers did not exist; but their power circumscribes that of the bankers, just as the power of the bankers circumscribes theirs. For there you have the crowning glory of our political organization: there is a complete system of checks and balances. The chariot of state is exactly like the one found in the ruins of the Arc de Triomphe in its great circle in Paris: pulled in different directions by four equally matched horses, it is inevitably kept in equilibrium—an arrangement that prevents it from tearing off over the horizon or sinking into a rut."

"But not from being torn into four pieces," said Maurice, "and sooner or later the chariot will be torn apart."

"If we did not have a magic kingpin that holds everything together," said the Académicien.

"And what might that be?"

"Fear! In former days men were passionate about politics, but today the progress of enlightenment has eliminated those men of *petite vertu* who stick to their own ideas and strive, at any cost, for the triumph of what they regard as the truth. Men no longer believe in what they defend, but in what they attack. Convictions are rented apartments from which you move out as soon as better ones are discovered. And then, there is more appearance than reality in our conflicts: we fight as in a theater, taking care not to get hurt, and only for the entertainment of the gallery. No one deals dangerous blows for fear of being on the receiving end of them. Enemies today will be allies tomorrow; the cockade we boo today is the one we will soon wear in our own hats. This expectation keeps a tight hold on indulgence, and if someone pulls in another direction it is with the halfheartedness of a cab horse paid by the hour."

"Now I understand," said Maurice. "You are protected from fierce political struggles, but who will save you from indifference?"

"As always, the constitution," replied M. Atout. "Do you think we are still living in those days when the voters were required to pay their representatives? We came to understand how such a requirement might put a damper on the enthusiasm of the voters. We have reversed the situation. Today it is the deputy who pays the voter. Each nomination is submitted to public auction, the candidates present their submissions, and the seat goes to the highest bidder. No more pitfalls, no more intrigues; everyone knows the terms and conditions. You should see the eagerness of the electors. Some of them are carried, at death's door, to the polling booths to vote and get their money. It's a good example of the thriving state of political life that supports institutions founded on the only true social principle: every man for himself. Somewhere I have on me the latest circular from M. Banqman, which will make you appreciate more than all my explanations the advantages of our system."

M. Atout went through his pockets, pulled out a large printed sheet of paper and gave it to his guest.

### M. BANQMAN, CANDIDATE FOR THE CHAMBER OF DEPUTIES
#### To the Electors of Quarter B
#### *OF THE TOWN OF SANS-PAIR*

Gentlemen!

If I had consulted my own interests, you would not see me here today soliciting your votes; I should have continued happily to enjoy a respected and comfortable position, far from the hurly-burly of politics. But the importunings of my friends have played havoc with my inclinations, and have made me decide to bid for my place as a deputy.

My policies are known to all, gentlemen. I desire the well-being of all citizens of the republic, and I will do all in my power to ensure that well-being. My vote will always be for the good and the true; I will champion only the cause that is right, and fight only the one that is wrong; I will not support ministers unless they support themselves, and, if they fall, I shall remember that the voice of the people is the voice of God.

So much for my thoughts on government. As to the grounds on which I may lay claim to your confidence, may I present them here. In an average year, I earn three million and fifty thousand francs—in other words, my affairs are in good order.

I have always refused to take on partners and to marry, because I love liberty.

I manufacture molds for buttons for all ages and all ranks in society—a labor that bears testimony to my respect for equality.

Finally, in all my dealings with human society I have always called men my brothers—an expression that proves my belief in brotherhood.

Now, when it comes to my profession of good faith, I shall be no less explicit.

I pledge myself to distribute button molds (seconds) to all the poor of the quarter.

I will give six balls and twelve dinners a year, to which all those who have voted for me will be invited.

All those who can muster ten votes for me will be entitled to a gift worth a thousand francs payable in horn trimmings from my factory, in small beer from the brewery to be built at Noukaiva, or in shares in the aerial telegraph.

Those who secure fifteen votes for me will receive in addition a bronze medal in an imitation leather case.

Finally, whoever can secure twenty votes for me will have an allowance in perpetuity of two liters of thick soup that he can obtain every morning from the Dutch company of Kamtschatka.

In addition, I shall cause to be distributed to my supporters, on the day of the ballot, slips with my name on them, in each of which will be wrapped a hundred-sou coin to give it more weight. Each person will put the slip in the ballot box and the coin in his pocket.

I dare to hope, gentlemen, that the frankness of my declaration will recommend me as a candidate, and that I shall soon be able to make known your wishes and your needs in the National Assembly.

BANQMAN


"And did this communication work with the voters?" asked Maurice, when he had read it.

"It succeeded so well that Banqman is now one of the most influential members in the Chamber of Deputies," replied M. Atout. "And he is going to put some devastating observations to the ministry this very morning."

"So he is already fighting the ministry?"

"Since the ministry authorized the introduction of foreign fasteners that threaten the production of his buttons."

"And is this sitting open to the public?"

"I was going to suggest that we should go along together."

Maurice accepted eagerly, and Milady Ennui, coming in just then with Marthe, said that she would go with them.

The debates in the Chamber of Deputies were open to the public—that is to say, that the public were only admitted by ticket. Fortunately, M. Atout knew the ambassador from the Congo and through his good offices secured entry to the diplomatic assembly.

Milady Ennui, happy to show off her machine-engineered corset on the front row of seats, leaned over the balcony eyeing the audience through her lorgnette, while M. Atout pointed out the politicians of Sans-Pair to the young visitors.

"The man you see across from you," he said, "the one busy examining the columns of figures, specializes in taking a fine-toothcomb to the budget; he spends his time checking the accounting figures and looking for reductions. In the last session he proposed economies of thirteen million, of which the chamber allowed him twenty-one francs and thirty centimes. A little further on you can see one of our colleagues, who has managed to have himself accepted by the Academy as a politician, and by the Chamber as a man of letters. Every year he gives the same speech against contemporary authors who are wrongheaded enough not to have given him a place, and a second one praising the ministry that gave him seven. At his side sits General Pataquès, known for his eloquence, his gold lace and clanking sword, and his barrack-room interventions. The old gentleman walking about down there is the famous Tacitus, a sort of Montesquieu in miniature, who has acquired the reputation of an excellent citizen by his abstentions, and of a profound thinker by tearing his colleagues to pieces. Behind him another jurist is engaged in conversation— M. Format. He regards the governance of the state as a matter of procedure, and would let the republic be sold, so long as it was sold according to the legal code. The man talking to him, Milord Grave, is a former minister, who was the first to introduce some austerity into corruption. On his other side is Dr. Traverse who speaks for government by the people, which he doesn't really want, in order to bring back the monarchy, which no one wants. Then, at the foot of the rostrum, is M. Omnivore, defender of the true interests of the republic, provided that they coincide with his own. All these deputies are the leaders of a number of groups that try to get along together when they cannot get rid of one another.

"The biggest group is that of the *Tightrope Walkers,* composed of men who know how to survive under any ministry, and whose opinion is formed by a salary slip. They are known as *Conservatives,* on account of their zeal to conserve their positions, appointments, and pensions.

"In opposition is the party of *Hopefuls,* composed of all those who were once ministers or aspire to become ministers.

"Between them float the *Indepen-*

*dents,* whose political program resembles the gait of a drunkard. When they have wandered to the Left, they return abruptly to the Right, for the sole purpose of proving that they are free spirits.

"Finally come a dozen factions, sometimes at loggerheads, sometimes united, parliamentary placemen who serve to overturn majorities, and thanks to whom the chamber reverses today its decisions of yesterday."

At this point, the Académicien was interrupted by the sound of a bugle playing the well-known air:[1]

> Du courage
> A l'ouvrage
> Les amis sont toujours là.

M. Atout told Maurice that this was the signal for the opening of the sitting. They had cleverly replaced the bell with a bugle, because it was easier to hear in the hubbub, and it spared the president the trouble of speaking. His interventions were transformed into familiar tunes. Did he, for example, wish to call an opposition member to order, he would play the refrain of the romance:

> Taisez-vous, je ne vous crois pas.

If it were a question of announcing that the minister for public education was about to speak, he would play in a minor key:

> Je suis Lindor, ma naissance est commune,
> Mes voeux sont ceux d'un simple bachelier.

If it were a matter of voting on the budget, he would announce it with the air:

> Quels dinés, quels dinés
> Les ministres m'ont donnés.

Then finally, if he were seeking leave for a marshal to rejoin his government, he would play:

> Malbroug s'en va-t-en guerre,
> Mironton ton ton Mirontaine;
> Malbroug s'en va-t-en guerre,
> Ne sais quand il viendra.

At his signal the deputies made their way to their seats, and a speaker mounted the platform to give them time to settle down and to blow their noses. Maurice recognized M. Omnivore. M. Atout explained to him that

## M. BANQMAN

*A deputy in the year 3000*

there were about a dozen minor players in the chamber whose duty it was to act as curtain-raisers, to do for the assembly what the glass of absinthe did before dinner, not because people liked it, but because it gave them an appetite.

They were followed by speakers of mediocre repute; these were the soup and the starters.

Finally, silence descended; the parliamentary feast was about to begin; M. Banqman had just appeared on the platform.

The illustrious manufacturer had his chin tucked into his cravat and his right hand behind his jabot—a sure indication of profundity. He let his eyes sweep the audience a couple of times, slowly raised his left hand, and started speaking in a voice that sounded like a cross between a trombone and clashing cymbals:

"Gentlemen,

"No matter how determined a man in politics may be to do his duty, there are circumstances when the accomplishment of that duty becomes a painful ordeal for him, and he inevitably envies the lot of those citizens with no responsibilities, who can subordinate their convictions to their inclinations and accord to friends they no longer approve of the favor of their silence!

"Unfortunately, we are not in that position. Charged with a public commission, we have a duty to our constituents, and we owe it to ourselves to be completely open about our views. We have waited for a long time in the hope that our government would be enlightened enough to recognize this duty, but our wait has been in vain, and to prolong it is no longer possible. The safety of the republic must be our overriding consideration, and we declare loud and clear, hand on heart, the moment has come to lose it or to save it."

*Murmuring from the center; applause from the fringes; prolonged excitement; the speaker drinks a glass of sugar and water.*

"Yes, gentlemen, the situation has never been more disturbing for the present or more perilous for the future!

"Whether we look at domestic or external affairs, the situation is appalling. The republic looks to us like a machine in unskilled hands—a machine that is shaken by contrary movements, a machine whose cogs are grinding together and threatening to disintegrate!"

*Profound sensation.*

"And it is in a situation like this that there is talk of imposing a new burden on the nation! They are asking for a loan of two hundred million, saying repeatedly that it is a vote of confidence. That may be, gentlemen; but let us first of all see if they have done anything to earn it."

*Differing reactions. The speaker, who is growing heated, drinks another glass of sugar and water.*

"I could advance many more criticisms, gentlemen, but I wish to impress upon you my moderation. I shall not go back over all the reproaches about the abuse of power; I shall content myself with looking at a single act, and that the most recent. It will be sufficient to give us the measure of the skill, the tact, and the justice of the men at the head of our government.

"When I speak in these terms, gentlemen, you must understand that my attacks are directed to those who can answer them, to the ministers present here, for they alone are blameworthy and can be held to account. There is a name that must remain outside the scope of our discussions; my remarks cannot enter that inviolate sphere where the head of state resides, calm and impeccable."

*General approbation.*

"But the agents of his administration are subject to our surveillance, and the constitution allows us to judge their acts."

*Total attention.*

"When I said that I intended to examine just one instance, you would all, no doubt, have understood that I wished to speak about the withdrawal of the provision of three pairs of gloves provided by the republic for its defenders—a withdrawal that has thrown the entire army into disarray."

GENERAL PATAQUÈS: "Yes, it's an idea that could only have come from civilians."

VOICES OF SEVERAL LAWYERS: "Civilians! It's an insult to the Chamber."

AN OLD APOTHECARY: "It's indecent."

CHORUS OF CITIZENS: "Order! Order!"

*General Pataquès puts his hat on sideways, shifts his weight to his left hip and drapes his mustaches over his ears; the shouting intensifies; and the president plays the tune:*

Grenadier, que tu m'affliges.[2]

*The general sits down again and the hubbub subsides; the speaker continues:*

"You might think, gentlemen, that this withdrawal would have been accomplished correctly, without violating the prerogatives of the chambers, that illegality would not have been added to ignorance! Well, it pains me to say it, but I must. This vitally important measure was taken by means of an edict."

*Profound sensation.*

M. FORMAT shouts loudly: "The act goes against all the rules of procedure . . . that is to say of the legislature."

MANY VOICES: "Yes, yes."

OTHER VOICES: "No, no."

*The ministers look at one another, anxiety written all over their faces; great agitation; the president plays the tune:*

Finissons-en, le monde est assez vieux.

*Banqman continues.*

"And what was your objective, ministers of the chair, in daring to gamble on such a coup d'état! Did it hurt your pride to see the hands that defend our native land wearing gloves like your own?"

M. TRAVERSE: "They are aristocrats."

M. BANQMAN: "And could you not, if it were reckoned absolutely necessary to carry through this inconceivable revolution, at least keep up appearances? Could you not, while denying gloves to the soldiers, let them still appear on the books; then no one would have been any the wiser, and national honor would have been safeguarded."

MILORD GRAVE (with a sign of approval): "That's what we must do."

M. BANQMAN: "But no, you have acted with your usual carelessness and effrontery, for those two characteristics are the mainspring of your political actions; to them you have owed your very successes, according to the admirable words of the profound thinker who said of you: 'They rose because they were empty.'"

*Agitation. All eyes turn toward M. Tacitus, who seems to be asleep; laughter and applause.*

"Consequently," the speaker continues, "I propose the following bill, a copy of which is on the president's desk:

"Article 1. The chamber rejects the measure that threatens the army, and decrees to each soldier six pairs of gloves instead of the three formerly accorded him.

"Article 2. These will be lisle gloves, knitted, with elastic at the wrist.

"Article 3. They must be distributed to every regiment three days after the promulgation of the present act.

"Article 4. The ministers in post, since they are unable to act impartially over this distribution, are requested to leave this duty to their successors."

*After the reading of these proposals, M. Banqman comes down from the platform to the congratulations of all the floating voters in the chamber—at this point the Independents. The minister of the interior goes towards the platform, but he is called back by his colleague for public works who wants to take his place; and he in turn is held back by the minister for foreign affairs. A lively discussion ensues; finally, there are shouts of: "Put it to the vote, put it to the vote!" The cries become so insistent that the president finds himself forced to proceed.*

*Article 1 is put to the vote:*

> *Number of voters* ........ 613
> *Blackballs* .............. 290
> *White balls* ............. 323

*The motion is approved!*

*The ministers quarrel more vociferously.*

*They pass to articles 2 and 3, which are also approved.*

*The ministers are about to come to blows; but the president reads out article 4, which has the immediate effect of calming them down; they go off to one side during the vote, and appear to be in consultation.*

*Article 4 is also adopted.*

*The only procedure remaining is to vote for the act in its entirety. The ministers, who have come to an agreement, pass a note to M. Banqman on which they have written: "The importation of foreign fasteners will be prohibited from tomorrow."*

*M. Banqman puts the note in his pocket along with the white ball and votes against the act. Another note informs M. Format that he has been appointed advocate general; a third makes the announcement to General Pataquès that he is now Marshal Pataquès; a fourth warns Milord Grave that the publication of letters to a certain countess, and her replies—a free translation of the correspondence of Héloïse and Abelard—is a distinct possibility; a fifth lets Tacitus know that his nephew will have a tax collector's post, and his cousin a tobacconist's shop.*

*A vote is then taken on the whole act.*

> *Number of voters* ........ 613
> *Blackballs* .............. 611
> *White balls* ............... 2

*The chamber rejects the act.*

The president plays the tune:

*Allons-nous-en gens de la noce.*
*And the sitting comes to an end.*[3]

# §XXII

*An English missionary—A ball for the public where dancing partners (female)*
*are provided—The institution known as the National Church—*
*M. Coulant explains his religion to Narcisse Soiffard.*

Marcellus had arranged to meet Maurice in the big room of the *Casino of
the Two Worlds.* He found him playing billiards with Georges Traveler, a
missionary of English birth who worked in three professions: as a dentist,
as a priest, and as a merchant in colonial goods. Georges Traveler had
journeyed through all the pagan countries of the earth on behalf of the
Society for the Propagation, and he had spared no effort to gain the
confidence of simple uncivilized people. Far from following the example of
those apostles for the Catholic faith who, with no weapon but prayer book
and crucifix, presented themselves in the midst of savage tribes as mes-
sengers from God, calling on them to renounce the error of their ways, the
honorable English missionary had found it convenient to participate in
their practices and had repeated the miracle of Alcibiades to the advantage of his faith and his business.[1]

So, it was noted that he had been by turns one of the circumcised in
Muscat, husband to a dozen women in the Mariana Islands, slave trader
in Zanzibar, and something of a cannibal in the Sandwich Islands; but all
this without his faith being shaken, and all accomplished on behalf of his
society.

Thanks to this innate flexibility, he had succeeded in distributing some
hundreds of sermons printed for the instruction of idolaters who could
not read, and he had off-loaded seventeen shiploads of rubbishy goods.

Although the doctor was not a member of his church, Marcellus was a
close friend of the man who had brought him hookahs and tobacco from
the Orient. When he was introduced to Maurice, he broke into an African
polka—one that was not licensed by the police.

This exhibition might have gone on indefinitely if Maurice had not reminded Marcellus of the promise he made the previous evening to tell him
about the new religion, known in Sans-Pair as the National Church. That
pious young man set off with him to show him the church of the Abbé
Coulant; but as they were crossing a square where public notices were displayed, he suddenly saw a huge billboard on a wall.

*An English missionary*

"God forgive me! The Eden is opening again!" he cried. "Please, please, let us get nearer so that I can make sure."

They crossed the square and read the notice, which covered the entire face of the building.

### EDEN HALL—MASKED BALLS.

SUNDAY EVENING,
GREAT ENTERTAINMENT: "THE WILD ONES."

*Two thousand pretty women members of the establishment*
WILL PERFORM DANCES IN CHARACTER.

Each man will receive on entering a number designating the dancer he must partner for the entire ball—in the interests of decorum changes are forbidden.

The dress will be that of the native inhabitants of America at the time of the discovery of the New World; but gloves must be worn.

There will be a cloakroom where umbrellas and shorts may be deposited.

---

Entry Price: 25 francs.

As soon as Marcellus set eyes on the notice, he made his excuses to Maurice, ran into the office, and emerged shortly with a ticket.

"Just in time," he exclaimed, "Another five minutes, and I would have been too late to find a partner; they could only give me number 1983 . . . a twenty-two-year-old brunette. I prefer blonds, but one must make sacrifices in a good cause. Please excuse me if I leave you; I must inform the president of the Society for Moral Standards—I was scheduled to hand in a paper to him the day after tomorrow—that unforeseen business is making me late with my work."

He told Maurice the address of the new church and left him to go on alone.

It was the first time that our young man had found himself alone in the streets of Sans-Pair, and he began to look about him more closely than he had done before.

He noticed that the inhabitants of each house had placed under their windows an inscription announcing their profession, in such a way that the whole town was a kind of directory of twenty-five thousand addresses. At every entrance, instead of a concierge, there was a huge mechanical revolving door, divided into compartments that each bore a name and a bell for the occupants. On arriving, the visitor sat down in the appropriate compartment, pulled the bell cord, and immediately the machine ascended and carried him to the very door of the person he wished to see.

Maurice saw too a dance floor where the feet of the dancers set in motion the wheels of a mill for grinding corn, and there were carts returning empty from the market that were turning a spinning wheel to spin cotton rejects.

Every now and then the streets were crossed by viaducts on which locomotives whistled as they were pushed along by steam or pulled along by a vacuum system. The wires of the electric telegraph criss-crossed through the air forming a tangled web; lightning conductors, reaching up into the clouds, continuously extracted the electricity to supply the needs of the gilders, the galvanizing operators, and the lighting company. Underneath each street ran a subterranean passage along which crawled,

like immense serpents, the thousand iron pipes for the distribution of water, heat, and light. Under his feet the young man heard the voices of
workmen punctuated by the roar of the wind, the lapping of the sewers,
the grinding of tools, and the hiss of flames. It was a second underground
city engaged in maintaining the life of the sunlit city above: a hidden machine that by turns supplied its needs and carried away its waste.

Maurice gazed on all these wonders of civilization with surprise tinged
with disappointment. In the midst of all these great improvements in material things he looked for the human being, and saw him just as poor, depraved, and disinherited. In vain he searched all those passing faces to see
if life had become easier to bear; but the faces were still worn with suffering and anxious care! Then the bitterness he felt in his heart prompted a
rational enquiry. He asked himself what good were all these industrial improvements if they did not result in greater happiness for everyone. He
sought to find what had happened to egality and fraternity for mankind
in the midst of all these miracles of engineering. He asked what had happened to true religion—the one that bound men to one another and
showed the way to heaven by a double ladder of love and devotion.

And then, at that very moment, his gaze was arrested by the facade of a
building where he saw written in letters of bronze: NATIONAL CHURCH.
He went in.

The National Church was an old auction room, repainted and refur-
bished in the service of the new religion. At the entrance was a hurdy-
gurdy in place of an organ, and a cubbyhole for umbrellas where a holy
water stoup might once have been.

The service was about to begin and the priest was at the altar.

Maurice did not need to listen for long to understand what it was all
about: the new religion consisted of reproducing in the vernacular what
Catholic priests intoned in Latin. So, instead of saying: *Introibo ad altare
Dei,* the National Church said: *I will go in unto the altar of God.* For the
words: *Ite Missa est,* it substituted these: *Go, the Mass is ended.* And instead of: *Amen!* it said: *So be it!*

After the mass the priest of the National Church went up into the pulpit and launched into a long diatribe against the ministers of other
churches, who were unable to embrace the new thinking and continued to
direct their prayers to God in a dead language. He quoted Cicero, Tacitus,
St. Augustine, and Tertullian to substantiate his claim that Latin should
be abandoned, and ended up with a national directive on the advantages
of growing rutabagas and cultivating the silk-worm.

The sermon over, the crowd of about thirty people dispersed, and Maurice was about to go himself when a laborer, who had listened with obvious impatience, abruptly approached the preacher as he left the pulpit, and barring his way, said: "One minute, Father," raising his hand to his bare head as if in salute, "you have just been talking about caterpillars and turnips, but I don't care about any of that. What I want to know is am I speaking to the founder of the National Church?"

"To himself in person, my friend," said the priest.

"Then," replied the workman, who had evidently taken plenty of liquid refreshment to fortify himself, "you must be the Abbé Coulant himself?"

"I am indeed."

The workman gave him a playful punch in the chest.

"You are the man I want to see," he said, "I've been looking for you. I have been into all the wine shops in the district this morning to find out the address of the National Church. Nobody had seen it; nobody had heard of it! It seems that your church is in rented rooms?"

The Abbé Coulant was apologetic.

"Nothing to be ashamed of," said the laborer, "me too. I'm in rented rooms and not so well lodged as your good God, what's more! I suppose we'll just have to make the best of it."

"Is there some matter you wish to speak to me about?" the Abbé asked.

"There are twenty," the laborer replied, "seeing as how I've been told you're a good lad; and me—I like good lads."

"So . . ."

"All in good time now! Before you get to the end, you have to begin at the beginning. So, to begin, good Father, I must tell you that my name is Narcisse Soiffard—a name that's as good as any man's—and that I have a twelve-year-old daughter, who helps her mother to card wool for mattresses. It seems to me there's nothing wrong with that."

"On the contrary. Work is a duty."

"That's what I always tell my daughter and her mother. Women have a duty to work, I tell them. . . . But, you see, her mother is religious, and wants her daughter to make her First Communion. Me, I've got nothing against it, because religion's like wine—there's nothing to compare with it. You have to respect those who've had too much, and leave them to stagger on. So much so that I went out to find our parish priest and told him about it."

"And what did he say?"

"Ah! now, there's a funny thing. He said that to take communion you have to understand what you're doing."

{ 227 }

"You mean to go to catechism classes?"

"That's it! To go for instruction just when she helps her mother. But I said to him, 'Father, do you want us to die of thirst? If the little one has to come to you, the work won't get done.' He told me she had to be instructed in her religion. 'I'm all for that, if she can do it while she's working on the mattresses,' I kept on saying. . . . It seemed to me clear as daylight. Well, he didn't understand."

The Abbé Coulant shrugged his shoulders.

"That's inevitable," he said. "The clergy know nothing about the needs of the people. Bring your daughter to me, and I will see that she makes her First Communion."

"Without any instruction?"

"What's the use of it? It is not knowledge that is pleasing to God. The National Church asks for no more than a good intention."

Soiffard clapped his hands together.

"That's the religion for me," he said. "No need for anything but a good intention. That won't ruin me. . . . You can enter me in your parish roll, Monsieur Coulant. I want you to be the one to bury my wife when she dies."

"All you need do is give your daughter her baptismal certificate," said the priest.

The workman looked at the priest, twisting his cap in his hands.

"Ah! Yes, her baptismal certificate," he repeated slowly; "you need to have that for communion?"

"Certainly."

"That's what I was going to tell you. . . . Me and her mother were always so busy . . . that the little one has never actually been baptized."

"You could make good that oversight."

"I won't say no, but it costs six francs, and for that I could buy eight bottles of wine a fortnight. But we've given her a name. She's called Rose."

"That will do then; she has a patron saint in the calendar. Well, let us see. It can all be arranged; the National Church is very accommodating."

"Well, that's the religion for me. Your hand, Monsieur Coulant, if it's no trouble."

"All right," replied the curé with a smile, "it will be enough if your wife brings a copy of your marriage certificate."

Soiffard scraped the floor with the toe of his shoe and spat.

"Ah! Is a marriage certificate necessary?" he said with some embarrassment.

"Absolutely."

The laborer scratched his head.

"Well . . . that will be a problem," he stammered. "That will be very difficult, Monsieur Coulant, seeing that we have moved about a lot, and that when you're moving, papers go missing . . . especially since me and my wife didn't go to the registry office when we were married."

"That's very difficult."

"It was just for reasons of economy—you must understand that. A marriage certificate costs more than a baptismal certificate, and in our condition in life you have to consider all these expenses: you have to make sacrifices."

"That's true," said the priest with a sigh. "After all, God pardoned the woman taken in adultery! Go on then, we'll shut our eyes to that, Master Soiffard. The National Church respects private life."

"True," cried Soiffard, "and that's the religion for me! Many thanks, Monsieur Coulant, you're a decent chap, and I'd like to buy you a drink."

The priest had much difficulty in avoiding the largesse of his new parishioner and making his escape to the sacristy.

Soiffard watched him go, then holding out his arm in the direction of the altar, with that solemn gravity of the drunkard, he said:

"It's true that religion annoyed me when it told me I mustn't drink, or beat up the bourgeoisie, or live as I pleased. But now that I have found a God who is a really good fellow, I shall take to it; and from today I declare that I, Narcisse Soiffard, and Madame Soiffard, and the little one will be members of this church forever."

With these words, he put on his cap and staggered off.

Maurice returned, pensive and discouraged. Marthe, who was waiting impatiently for him, was struck by his sadness.

"What is it you have seen?" she asked anxiously.

"What I should have been prepared for," Maurice replied, taking his wife's hands in his. "We have already looked in vain in this brave new world for love and for poetry; but there still remained faith, that universal consoler."

"Well?"

"Alas! That too is no more."

{ 229 }

# CONCLUSION

Marthe and Maurice were left sad at heart. The two of them wept over this world where man was now enslaved to the machine; where self-interest took the place of love; where civilization had tried to make the mystical triumph of Christianity accommodate the three passions that drag the soul down into the abyss. Burdened by these heavy thoughts they fell asleep.

But while they slept, they had a vision.

It seemed to them that God looked down on the earth, and at the sight of the world that human corruption had created for itself, He said:

"See how these creatures have forgotten the laws that I engraved on their hearts; their inner vision is troubled, and they no longer see anything beyond themselves. Because they have conquered the seas, imprisoned the air, and mastered fire, they said to themselves—We are the masters of the world, and no one can call us to account. But I shall teach them a hard lesson; for I shall break the chains of the waters, open the prison of the air, give back to fire its terrible power, and then these kings for a day will know their weakness."

And at that He made a sign: the three avenging angels took rapid flight toward earth where all was soon reduced to ruin and confusion. In the course of a long dream Maurice and Marthe saw porticoes crumble, rivers burst their banks, and waves of fire sweep the earth; and in this universal destruction, the human race fleeing in desolation.

But at the height of the destruction a voice cried out:

"Peace to men of good will. It is for them that the human race will be born again, and a new world will rise from the ruins."

*The mystic triangle*

# Notes

### Introduction, pp. xi–xxv

1. Eugène Lesbazeilles, *Notice sur la vie d'Émile Souvestre* (1857; 2nd ed., Paris: Michel Lévy Frères, 1859), v. Émile Souvestre, son of a civil engineer, was educated at the college of Pontivy with the intention of following his father's profession. On the death of his father in 1823, Souvestre turned to studying law at Rennes. His real interest, however, was in literature, and his first work as a writer was the unsuccessful tragedy, *Le Siège de Missolonghi*. For a time, he worked as a lawyer in Morlaix; he was later appointed to a professorship in rhetoric in the universities of Brest and Mulhouse. Success came in 1836; after he contributed some sketches of life in Brittany to the *Revue des Deux Mondes* Souvestre became the editor of *La Revue de Paris*, and enjoyed another success when his first novel, *L'Échelle de Femmes*, was well received. During the following eighteen years he produced some sixty books—fiction, essays, history, and drama—which sustained his popularity with French readers.

That popularity has continued in France: there have been frequent reprints; some four of his books are now in print; and a facsimile edition of *Le Monde tel qu'il sera* (Paris: Apex International, 2002) has appeared recently. In the United States the admirable Project Gutenberg has recently added a translation of Souvestre's *Un Philosophe sous les toits*, titled *An "Attic" Philosopher* to its digital holdings.

2. "JANUARY FIRST, A.D. 3000," *Harper's New Monthly Magazine* 12, no. 68 (January 1856): 145–58, available online at: http://cdl.library.cornell.edu/cgi-bin/moa/moa-cgi?notisid=ABK4014-0012-22. Whoever was responsible for this piece did not believe in fidelity to the original. The story is presented as a dialogue, much of the text is invented, and many passages are painfully facetious. One paragraph begins with "I can not tell you what became of France," and it goes on to report, "I have a general impression that it blew up in some way or other, in consequence of the discovery of some awfully-explosive substance by the Academy of Science."

3. Émile Souvestre, *Contes par Émile Souvestre*, ed. Augustus Jessop (London: David Nutt, 1868), ix.

4. The publishing history was as follows: *Le Monde tel qu'il sera*, illustré par M. M. Bertall, O. Penguilly et St-Germain (Paris: W. Coquebert, 1846); *Le Monde tel qu'il sera* (Paris: Michel-Lévy Frères, 1859), without illustrations; *Le Monde tel qu'il sera*, illustré par M. M. Bertall, O. Penguilly et St-Germain (Paris: Michel-Lévy Frères, 1871); *Le Monde tel qu'il sera* (Paris: Apex International, 2002 ); *O que ha de Ser o anno tres mil* por E. Souvestre accommodada ao gusto Portuguez por S. Ribeiro De Sa. (Lisbon, 1859); *El Mundo tal qual sera el año 3000*, 2 vols. (Lima, 1863).

5. Pierre Versins, *Encyclopédie de l'utopie, des voyages extraordinaires et de la science fiction* (Lausanne: L'Age d'Homme, 1972). For an excellent account of these early developments, see Paul K. Alkon, *Origins of Futuristic Fiction* (Athens: University of Georgia Press, 1987).

6. We are greatly indebted to Xavier Legrand Ferronière, editor of *Le Visage Vert*, for this information. He examined, and reported on, the very rare copy of the "Prospectus" in the Bibliothèque Nationale.

7. In 1832 Philipon introduced a daily paper, *Le Charivari*, which set an example for the British weekly, *Punch, or the London Charivari* (1841). By 1834 *La Caricature* had so enraged the politicians that it was suppressed. In 1838 Philipon revived *La Caricature* with the title *La Caricature provisoire*. There is an excellent account in David S. Kerr, *Caricature and French Political Culture, 1830–1848: Charles Philipon and the Illustrated Press* (Oxford: Clarendon Press, 2000).

8. Jean-Ignace-Isidore Gérard (1803–1847) was generally known by his adopted name of Grandville. A most gifted and original artist, remarkable for his ironic presentation of human beings with animal heads to show the best and worst in people. His principal works were *Les Métamorphoses du Jour* (1829), *Les Animaux* (1842), *Petites Misères de la vie humaine* (1843), and the splendid *Un Autre Monde* of 1844. Grandville is equally famous for his book illustrations, especially for his work on Balzac, La Fontaine, Swift, and *Robinson Crusoe*.

9. Alexis de Tocqueville, *Democracy in America*, trans. and ed. Harvey C. Mansfield and Delba Winthrop (Chicago: University of Chicago Press, 2000), 2:460.

10. Félix Bodin, *Le Roman de l'avenir* (Paris: Lecointe et Pougin, 1834), 16.

11. Julius Von Voss, *Ini: Ein Roman aus dem ein und zwanzigsten Jahrhundert* (Berlin: K. F. Amelang, 1810), 1.

12. Part 14 of *La Légende des Siècles, Plein Ciel* (in *Victor Hugo: Poésie*, ed. Bernard Leuilliot [Paris: Éditions du Seuil, 1972], 2:126.

13. Walt Whitman, *The Complete Poems*, ed. Francis Murphy (Harmondsworth: Penguin Books, 1986), 786.

14. David Goodman Croly, *Glimpses of the Future* (New York and London: G. P. Putnam's Sons, 1888), 153.

15. Edward Bulwer-Lytton, *The Coming Race* (London: George Routledge, 1871), 269.

16. J. A. Mitchell, *The Last American. A Fragment from the Journal of Khan-Li, Prince of Dimpf-You-Chur and Admiral in the Persian Navy*, illustrated (1889; 2nd ed., London: Gay and Bird, 1890), 21.

17. H. G. Wells, *The Time Machine* (1895; London: Ernest Benn, 1927), 52.

## Chapter I, pp. 1–12

1. These persons are, first: Julie d'Étange, the heroine of Rousseau's *Julie ou la Nouvelle Héloise* (1761). She was in love with the young Saint-Preux, but does her duty and marries the elderly M. de Wolmar. Later she reveals her love for Saint-Preux to her husband and he invites Saint-Preux to live with them as a brother. Second: Claire is the beloved of Comte Lamoral d'Egmont (1522–1568), a Flemish

general and statesman, who was beheaded during the Spanish repression of the Netherlands. Goethe used incidents in Egmont's life as the basis for his tragedy *Egmont* (1788), for which Beethoven wrote incidental music and the *Egmont* overture. Third, *la grande pastoure* is Joan of Arc, the shepherdess from Domrémy.

2. Alphonse Marie Bérenger (1785–1866), French lawyer, politician, and magistrate. Argued for a return to customary law and for the introduction of trial by jury.

3. Robert Owen (1771–1858), Welsh social reformer and industrialist. Pioneer Socialist who founded "model" communities at New Lanark in Scotland and at New Harmony in Indiana.

Saint-Simon (Claude Henri de Rouvroy, comte de Saint-Simon, 1760–1825). Most influential French social reformer and philosopher. Best known for his theory that the ideal organization of society is in an order directed by industrialists and inspired by scientists.

François Marie Charles Fourier (1772–1837), social philosopher who argued that there is a harmonious connection between humankind and God and that the best society would follow from the establishment of *phalanges*, communities of some sixteen thousand persons. He had his admirers in the United States, for a time, following on the proposals of Arthur Brisbane, Horace Greeley, and Park Godwin. The most famous community was Brook Farm.

Emmanuel Swedenborg (1688–1772), Swedish mystic and scientist whose strange dreams persuaded him that he was in communion with the spiritual world.

Victor Cousin (1792–1867), French philosopher and director of the École Normale. Best known for his thoughts in *Du vrai, du beau, et du bien* (1854).

4. Ryegrass (*Lolium perenne*), like the tares and cockle of the New Testament parable, is a contaminant in wheat and has to be removed in the milling process.

5. John Progrès has, of course, all the latest equipment. In 1823 Charles Mackintosh, a Scottish chemist, had begun manufacturing the protective clothing named after him: two layers of cloth held together by a solution of naphtha. In 1841 Charles Goodyear of New York improved on the original mackintosh with his oilskin: a form of rubberized cloth.

John Progrès sports a daguerreotype on his machine, a product of the recently invented process of "heliographic pictures"—the first form of photography revealed by Louis Jacques Daguerre to the French Academy of Sciences in 1833. Again, John Progrès travels by a steam-driven British contraption. The invention of the separate condenser by James Watt in 1764 delivered a most potent source of power. The first railway lines opened in 1830: the Manchester to Liverpool and the Baltimore to Ohio.

6. Asmodeus appears as a major devil in various demonologies: one of the seventy-two spirits of Solomon; or as a dragon-riding king; or as a teacher of invisibility and a guide to great treasure. In Le Sage's *Le Diable Boiteux* (1707) Asmodeus takes Don Cleophas on an aerial journey, removing the roofs to show what goes on in private. See Fred Gittings, *Dictionary of Demons* (London: Guild Publishing, 1988).

7. Pierre Jean de Béranger (1780–1857)—not to be confused with Alphonse

Marie Bérenger (see note 2)—was a gifted poet and a most popular writer of songs. He was a friend of Chateaubriand, Talleyrand, Lamartine. Stendhal considered him the greatest poet of the age.

8. Charles Maurice de Talleyrand (1754–1858) was certainly lucky. Appointed bishop of Autun in1788, he was an exile in England until after the Terror, then foreign minister under the Directory, later leader of the anti-Napoleonic faction, then foreign minister under Louis XVIII and negotiator at the Congress of Vienna, and finally French ambassador to the United Kingdom.

9. Souvestre here makes an oblique attack on the brave new-world-to-come by introducing mesmerism. Franz Anton Mesmer (1734–1815) was an Austrian physician who believed that the stars influence human health by means of an invisible fluid and that another mysterious force, animal magnetism, could cure maladies of every kind. Albert Robida has a similar send-up of mesmerists in his *La Guerre au Vingtième Siècle* (see chap. 5, *Opérations de Siège: Pompistes et Médiums*).

10. Jean Nicolas Gannal (1791–1852), French chemist, introduced the method of refining borax and developed a process of embalming by injecting a solution of aluminum salts into the arteries.

11. *L'Île du Noir-Animal.* "Noir-Animal" is a black carbon powder made from crushing dry, rotted bones. Webster says: "Bone black or bone char: the black substance containing chiefly tribasic calcium phosphate and carbon into which crushed defatted bones are converted by carbonization in closed vessels and which is used as a black pigment and as a decolorizing adsorbent. Also called 'animal black' or 'animal charcoal.'" We have translated this reference as "Charcoal Island."

### Chapter II, pp. 13–23

1. Charles Paul de Kock (1793–1871) was a French popular writer, famous for his sketches of Parisian life, especially in *André le Savoyard* (1825) and *Le Barbier de Paris* (1826). He was admired even more outside France. Souvestre here mines the contemporary joke that it was a scandal not to have read de Kock. The historical anachronisms are an early example of the game of mistaken identities, when the relics of the past lead to ludicrous conclusions.

Jean Nicolas Loriquet (1767–1845) was a Jesuit priest and historian whose *Histoire de France à l'usage de la jeunesse* (1820) was notorious: he made no mention of the French Revolution and Napoleon is absent from his narrative. Souvestre makes fun of Loriquet again (30) when a salesman says: "Here is a relic of Saint Loriquet, certain to inspire a real interest in history."

### Chapter III, pp. 23–35

1. Racahout, or "racahout des arabes" in its commercial form, was a drink much in vogue during the nineteenth century and greatly favored as nourishment for infants. It was a concoction of rice flour, potato, cocoa, sugar, vanilla and milk in varying proportions. In *Madame Bovary*, that great practitioner of realism Flaubert saw to it that the chemist's shop of Monsieur Homais reflected the everyday in the many advertisements that included: "Raspail's medicine, Ara-

bian racahout, Darcet's pastilles." Later, at the christening of Madame Bovary's daughter, Homais comes with presents that "were all articles out of his shop, to wit: six tins of jujubes, a whole jar of racahout. . . ."

2. Souvestre is here drawing on recollections, still vivid, of the Great Lunar Hoax of ten years earlier. Begun in the *New York Sun* on August 25, 1835, it concerned a serial account of the winged lunar inhabitants that Sir John Herschel was supposed to have seen during his astronomical observations at the Cape. The fabrication was the work of Richard Adams Locke, a Cambridge (U.K.) graduate and a recent immigrant to the United States. The will to believe was so strong that by August 28 the *Sun* had achieved the largest print run for any daily newspaper in 1835; there were instant editions and translations through the Northern Hemisphere; and in the United States the English bluestocking Harriet Martineau, then traveling through Massachusetts, found that the ladies of Springfield were collecting for funds to send a missionary to the moon.

### Chapter IV, pp. 43–47

1. Quai d'Orsai is a stretch on the left bank of the Seine, from the Eiffel Tower to the National Assembly in the Palais Bourbon. Best known as the location for the French Ministry of Foreign Affairs. Souvestre's comment comes direct from contemporary experience: building commenced in 1845, when *Le Monde tel qu'il sera* was appearing in parts, and continued under the direction of the architect Lacornée until completion in 1855. The remark about "no ornamentation" presumably reflects a dislike of the heavily ornamented style of the new building.

2. Marin Onfroi is the name given to a reputable cider made from apples originally grown in Normandy by Marin Onfroi.

### Chapter V, pp. 43–46

1. François Joseph Talma (1763–1826), celebrated French tragic actor, pioneered realism in scenery and in costume; a favorite of Napoleon who had him play *La Mort de César* before the kings of Europe at Erfurt in 1806.

As for Shakespeare: "To be or not to be, that is the question."

2. François Antoine Eugène de Planard (1784–1853) was a popular and prolific librettist, best known for his text for *L'Échelle de soie* (1808), used by Giuseppe Foppa in his libretto for Rossini's *La Scala di Seta* (1812). Did Baudelaire recall Planard's lines when he wrote *Sur l'Album de Mme. Émile Chevalet:* "Si toujours la nature embellit la beauté"?

> Au milieu de la foule, errantes, confondues,
> Gardant le souvenir précieux d'autrefois,
> Elles cherchent l'echo de leurs voix éperdues,
> Tristes, comme le soir, deux colombes perdues
>     Et qui s'appellent dans les bois.
> Je vis, et ton bouquet est de l'architecture:
> C'est donc lui la beauté, car c'est moi la nature;
> Si toujours la nature embellit la beauté,

Je fais valoir tes fleurs . . . me voilà trop flatté.

Charles F. Baudelaire, *Oeuvres complètes,* texte établi, présenté et annoté par Claude Pichois (Paris: Gallimard, 1975), 209.

3. These three lines record a climactic moment in La Fontaine's narration of "Le Diable en enfer" (*Les Contes libertins*):

> Which made a certain bodice
> Rise and fall, in spite of Alibech
> Who sought in vain to hold her breath.

The story of Alibech begins with Boccaccio (*Decamarone,* "3a Giornata") where she is first seen as "a simple girl of some fourteen years of age," who sets off to seek and serve God in the wilderness of the Thebaid. She comes upon a hermit, alone in his hut. Boccaccio goes on at some length to recount the agreeable way in which she learns how she can best serve God. The story supplied a congenial theme for La Fontaine in "Le Diable en enfer," one of the best of the entertainments in his *Contes libertins,* where he developed his talent for presenting outrageous topics in an urbane and seemingly frank manner. Souvestre clearly expected his readers to recognize the reference to Alibech and her encounter with the anchorite in "un bois sombre et dans ce bois elle trouve un vieillard."

### Chapter VI, pp. 48–54

1. Like Robida after him, Souvestre gave little thought to the probable advances in technology. Not for him the careful calculations behind the technological anticipations of Jules Verne. He recites the mantra of his age, "The skies, finally conquered," and fills the air with the most improbable flying machines, which seem to lack any means of propulsion.

2. Souvestre inverts the Lamarckien theory of organic evolution: all living organisms are dedicated to improving themselves, and acquired characteristics can be passed on to future generations.

### Chapter VII, pp. 54–65

1. In 1805, when William Wordsworth looked back on the France he had known in 1790, he recalled in memorable words "Bliss was it in that dawn to be alive." By 1793 the Republic was in crisis: on January 21 Louis XVI went to the guillotine; on February 1 the Convention declared war on Great Britain and Holland; and in July the Committee of Public Safety was reformed. The Terror had begun.

2. Souvestre selects two contemporary soldiers who would be well known to his readers for their exploits in colonial wars. Edward Law Ellenborough (1790–1871) was appointed governor general of India in 1841 and for three years, until his recall in June 1844, was involved in a series of wars in Afghanistan, Sind, and Gwalior.

Thomas Robert Bugeaud de la Piconnerie, duke of Isly (1784–1849), marshal of

France, distinguished himself with his flying columns in the Algerian campaign of 1836 and established the basis for French control of Algeria.

3. Brid'oison is a character in *Mariage de Figaro* (1784) by Beaumarchais: a judge, hiding his uncertainties behind a cult of appearances; bumbling, stuttering, ridiculous—the type of pompous, self-important social dignitary.

4. Souvestre liked to dwell on the recent and topical, even though his story came from the year 3000; and here he introduces the latest musical instrument. The harmonium, or *orgue expressif* (reed organ), was invented in about 1779 and proved so popular an instrument that it went through a rapid development: the Austrian physharmonica in 1818, the English seraphine in about 1830, and the French melophone in 1839. The 1840s and 1850s saw a craze for the instrument in France.

5. Souvestre seems to be joking with the knowledgeable reader when M. Atout talks about M. Hatif's use of a hothouse system to produce "forced scholars." Hatif appears in Arabic stories: a being that is heard but not seen, a warning voice, sometimes an oracular pronouncement.

### Chapter VIII, pp. 66–75

1. Here Souvestre uses his license to invent by making free with the world language of the year 3000. On arriving in the future, Maurice had discovered that "their language was a mixture of French, English, and German" (13). Then, revealing that the future alphabet has twenty-four letters (70), Souvestre demonstrates a world reshaped according to the duodecimal system that had been proposed by Georges Louis Leclerc, comte de Buffon, in his *Essai d'Arithmetique Morale* (1760). the scientists, who get all things wrong in Souvestre's scheme, want to return to the bad old days of the decimal system.

2. It is no accident that forty years after Souvestre's description of the *Cosmopolitan* island-village, Jules Verne described in his *L'Ile à hélice* (1895) a bigger and better floating island "four and a half miles long by three broad." Although Verne may have borrowed from Souvestre, it is far more likely that both writers had quarried in the great myth of progress—the dream of power that promised rapid transportation by submarines, flying machines, and land vehicles. In the beginning, this expectation was embedded in the revised 1786 edition of Sebastien Mercier's most influential *L'An 2440*. Taking a hint from the Montgolfier balloon ascents of 1783, Mercier added a new chapter to his utopia, *L'Aérostat*, in which he looked ahead to a regular air service between Beijing and Paris and a world joined in universal harmony by the still-to-be-invented flying machine. And so the dream has kept pace with the ever-growing powers of a technological society: a century ago Wells invented a machine for time travel, and rockets transported Wells's Martians to our planet. Today the world can see how warp drive makes distance disappear and the "Away Team" of the *Enterprise* beams down to strange planets.

3. Philippe Musard (1793–1859) was a violinist and conductor; he was a popular composer of dance music. He had frequent promenade concerts in Paris and London.

4. César Robinet (*robinet* = faucet) is another allegorical character.

## Chapter IX, pp. 75–84

1. The entry under "Horns of Moses' Face" in Brewer's *Dictionary of Phrase and Fable* records: "This is a mere blunder. The Hebrew *karan* means "to shoot out beams of light," but has by mistake been translated in some versions "to wear horns." Thus Moses is conventionally represented with horns."

## Chapter X, pp. 85–93

1. In this chapter Souvestre introduces what are apparently more detailed demonstrations of the calamitous condition of life in time-to-come, when his point of origin remains firmly fixed in the France of the 1840s. Like his contemporary Charles Dickens in *Oliver Twist* (1837) and *Bleak House* (1852), for example, he abominated the labyrinthine practices of the legal system in his time. As his own judge and jury, he condemned those "sad physicians of the soul, with their hands for ever in some moral wound, drawing on the unfortunate and the villainous for their livelihood." They were "lesser rodents," "vultures with their talons worn down."

## Chapter XI, pp. 93–100

1. The proper treatment of the imprisoned had been a growing concern of reformers like John Howard (1726–1790), a major influence in the United Kingdom and the United States, and of Cesare Beccaria (1738–1794) whose study, *Dei Delitti e delle pene* (1764), had great effect in Europe, especially in France. The French Code of Criminal Procedure in 1808 and the French Penal Code in 1810 incorporated his ideas. Tocqueville used the continuing interest in prison reform as a means that would allow him to go anywhere in the United States." The Americans took him at his word and on May 12, 1832, the *Mercantile Advertiser* reported: "We understand that two magistrates, Messrs. de Beaumont and de Tocqueville (*sic*) have arrived in the ship *Havre*, sent here by the order of the Minister of the Interior, to examine the various prisons in our country, and make a report on their return to France. To other countries, especially in Europe, a commission has also been sent, as the French Government have it in contemplation to improve their Penitentiary system, and take this means of obtaining all proper information" (André Jardin, *Tocqueville. A Biography* [London: Peter Halban, 1988], 108; first published in French as *Alexis de Tocqueville* [1805–1859; Paris: Hachette, 1984]).

## Chapter XII, pp. 101–108

1. A decade later Charles Dickens read from the same book of social reform in his *Hard Times* (1854), describing the appalling conditions of life in factory towns; insisting that the poor were entitled to the same justice, the same healthy conditions, the same freedom as the rich. Like Souvestre, Dickens went head-on against the materialism of what he saw as a profit-seeking society: "Fact, fact, fact, everywhere in the material aspect of the town; fact, fact, fact, everywhere in the immaterial. The M'Choakumchild school was all fact, and the school of design was all fact, and the relations between master and man were all fact, and every-

thing was fact between the lying-in hospital and the cemetery, and what you couldn't state in figures, or show to be purchasable in the cheapest market and saleable in the dearest, was not, and never should be, world without end, Amen."

### Chapter XIII, pp. 109–127

1. Souvestre's minimalist medical practice, "a molecule of some substance," ridicules the then new interest in homoeopathy promoted by the German physician Samuel Hahnemann (1755–1843). The phrase about "the thousandth part of nothing" is a layman's way of poking fun at the core theory of "the minimum dose."

2. Undoubtedly the most obscure sentence in the entire book. The "tents" refer to the war the emir Abd-el-kader fought against the French (1832–1847). Bernard Cazes, the distinguished historian of future-thinking, has suggested in a personal communication that: "Souvestre may have mixed up two things: 1. The capture in 1843 of Abd-el-kader's *Smala* (command post?) by the Duc d'Aumale, and 2. The defeat of the Moroccan army at the Isly river battle in 1844."

3. Souvestre here points to what many considered a reprehensible aspect of contemporary France. In 1830 Chicard invented (or named) the new cancan, based on the polka; and La Pomaré (Élise Sergent), a famous dancer, high-kicked her way to fame. Théodore de Banville celebrated the two of them in his *Bal Masqué:*

> Chicard danse dans les étoiles!
> Et son plumet tressaille encore
> Dans l'azur, et parmi les toiles
> De ce vertigineux décor.
>
> Pomaré, chaste en sa démence
> Dont jamais nous ne nous lassions,
> Danse un cavalier seul immense
> Avec les constellations.

### Chapter XIV, pp. 128–133

1. The last two lines in Jean de la Fontaine's famous fable of *Le Loup et la cicogne.* The greedy wolf swallows a bone and, as it begins to look like his last meal, a long-beaked stork responds to the wolf's signal of distress. Once the bone has been removed, the stork asks for her "salaire." The ungrateful wolf replies: "You're lucky I let you take your head unharmed out of my jaws."

### Chapter XV, pp. 134–141

1. Souvestre has his fun with contemporary events by projecting the Prix Montyon as an ancient tradition in the year 3000. In Souvestre's time, it was a new departure which became an important annual event. There were many prizes, including the esteemed Prix de Statistique. They began in 1836 after the death of Baron Antoine de Montyon (1733–1820), who gave large sums during his life to help the sick and left most of his fortune to continue his philanthropical enterprises.

**Chapter XVI,** pp. 141–149

1. The rue Aux-Fèves is an old area of Paris, notorious in the nineteenth century, where life was lived *à la Bohème*.

2. The refrain from "Ma Grand-Mère" by Pierre Jean de Béranger (1780–1857). It opens with

> Ma grand-mère un soir à sa fête
> De vin pur ayant bu deux doigts
> Nous disait en branlant la tête
> Que d'amoureux j'eus autre fois.
>
> *Refrain:* Combien je regrette
> Mon bras si dodu,
> Ma jambe bien faite,
> Et le temps perdu.

It was a popular song. Victor Hugo has an episode in *Les Misérables* (1862), in which Éponine hums the last three lines of the refrain (4.8.4).

3. Agnes Sorel (1422–1450) was in the service of Isabella of Lorraine and then of the queen of France, Mary of Anjou. In about 1444 she became the mistress of Charles VII. She died of dysentery after the birth of her fourth child in 1450.

4. General Maximilien Sebastien Foy (1775–1825) was a French general, originally opposed to Napoleon, but served as a divisional commander at Waterloo. Elected deputy in 1819, he consistently supported liberal policies.

Edouard Adolphe Mortier (1768–1835) was marshal of France, a corps commander in Spain, later French ambassador at St. Petersburg and minister of war 1834–1835. He was one of those killed on July 28, 1835, by the bomb thrown by G. G. Fieschi.

5. Souvestre quotes from "Bonaparte" which first appeared in the *Nouvelles Méditations* (1823) of Lamartine, precursor of romanticism:

> Rien d'humain ne battait sous ton épaisse armure
> Sans haine et sans amour, tu vivais pour penser
> Comme l'aigle régnant dans un ciel solitaire,
> Tu n'avais qu'un regard pour mesurer la terre,
> Et des serres pour l'embrasser!

6. *Le fripon* Robert Macaire, a total scoundrel, was, with his companion Bertrand, the creation of the great caricaturist, Honoré Daumier (1808–1879), a most effective means of holding up bourgeois society to ridicule. Their adventures began in *Charivari* in 1836 as the series *Les Cent et Un Robert Macaire*.

7. These were all contemporaries of Souvestre—minor writers, dramatists, novelists: Jacques Jasmin (1798–1864); Charles Poncy (1821–1891). Pitre-Chevalier (Pierre-Michel Chevalier, 1812–1863) was a well-known Breton author; his *Bretagne et Vendée* (1845) was a history of the French Revolution in the West.

## Chapter XVII, pp. 149–161

1. In his account of *Le Grand Pan* Souvestre develops an ingenious anticipation that stretches feasibility to the limit with his description of how " an immense roll of newsprint delivered itself to individual homes on a system of spools." This vision of advanced communications has been a constant element in conjectural literature: sometimes an exercise in prophecy, more often an incidental element in establishing the contours of a future society. An early projection of this kind appeared in the marvelous "glass prospective" and the "head of brass . . . that by art shall read philosophy" in Robert Greene's *Friar Bacon and Friar Bungay* (1590). The first appearance of a "future newspaper" can be examined in *Les Voyages de Kang-Hi* (1810) by the Duc de Levis. This had a double pullout at the front, "Journal du Déjeuner," which presented the news as it would appear on September 15, 1910. The first striking images were undoubtedly to be seen in Albert Robida's illustrations for *Le Vingtième Siècle* (1883), where the screens of "le grand téléphonoscope" display (in anticipation of CNN news reports) action pictures of the sack of Peking as it is happening. These fantasias of power reached their most sinister in Orwell's invention of Newspeak and their most marvelous in Ursula Le Guin's *ansible*, a necessary mode of instant space communications in the intergalactic age of the Hainish.

## Chapter XVIII, pp. 161–169

1. As an allegorical character Grelotin carries a supercharge, since the original Grelotin was a solitary sprite who had never hurt a soul. Our editor suggests that Souvestre may well have had in mind the root meaning of *grelotter* (to shiver, shake) and *grelot* (a tiny bell invariably associated with winter, sleigh bells, and Christmas) for Souvestre's character first appears in the story with trembling lips and "a gentle and distracted air" (255). The Grelotin of the fairy tale lived in a small, ruined village, and on a summer's day he went into the woods to gather strawberries. There in the manner of fairy stories, "il rencontra une vieille dame avec une canne qui semblait être une sorcière maléfique . . . elle prononça quelques mots et hop, Grelotin fut transformé en ver de terre" [he met an old woman with a cane who seemed to be a wicked witch . . . she said a few words and, pop!, Grelotin was transformed into an earthworm]. After many mishaps and challenges he is restored to his original form by the intervention, somewhat surprisingly, of Father Christmas: "Le Père Noël lui dit: 'Oui, mais ne me trahis jamais sinon tu seras plongé dans les profondes neiges.' Le lutin lui promit de ne jamais le trahir et ils furent heureux comme ils le sont encore aujourd'hui" [Father Christmas said to him: "Yes, but you must never betray me or you will be thrown into the deep snow." The elf promised never to betray him and they lived happily together as they are today].

## Chapter XIX, pp. 169–190

1. Jean-Baptiste Kléber (1753–1800) first saw service in the Austrian army; he joined the French revolutionary army in 1793. He was a divisional commander

during Napoleon's Egyptian campaign and was left in command of the French forces when Napoleon returned to France.

2. The refrain to the satirical poem *Les Raretés* by Antoine de Lamotte-Houdar (1674–1731), an admired writer in his day, famed for his odes:

> On dit qu'il arrive ici
> Une compagnie
> Meilleure de celle-ci
> Et bien mieux choisie.
> Va-t-en voir s'ils viennent, Jean,
> Va-t-en voir s'ils viennent.

3. Loïsa Puget (1810–1889) was a much admired French composer of romantic songs. Souvestre would have known one of her most popular compositions, the song *Je t'aime parceque je t'aime.*

4. Souvestre adapts the line from Napoleon's famous speech to the Army of Egypt before the battle of the Pyramids: "Soldats, songez que, du haut des ces pyramides, quarante siècles vous contemplent."

5. Opening line in the popular marching song *La Marche d'Austerlitz,* in which Souvestre makes one change to suit his theme:

> On va leur percer le flanc
> Ran tan plan tire lire au flanc
> On va leur percer le flanc.

6. Was the *Croix d'honneur* in Kléber's buttonhole invented by Souvestre? If he had the *Legion of Honor* in mind, that was instituted by Bonaparte in May 1802, two years after the death of Kléber.

7. Souvestre designed the entire play as a burlesque application of the themes and the elaborate stage effects of the new melodrama that dominated the French theater in the first half of the nineteenth century. His primary target must have been the extraordinary success of René Charles Guilbert de Pixerécourt (1773–1844). As "le père du mélodrame" he, more or less single-handedly, developed the new sentimental and romantic drama: he had some forty years of spectacular triumphs as an innovating régisseur and inventor of many stage techniques. He used large orchestras, mass choruses, even volcanoes and similar spectacles; and his play *Le Chien de Montargis* (1814) had a dog in the starring role. Did that suggest the use of a crocodile to Souvestre?

### Chapter XX, pp. 190–207

1. Triboulet (1479–1536) was the most famous of jesters, first at the court of Louis XII and then of François I, renowned for his instant wit. He was the inspiration for Verdi's *Rigoletto* (1851).

2. A celebrated line in Virgil's *Aeneid* (book 6), in which the poet introduces the funeral panegyric of the young Marcellus, son of Octavia and adopted son and chosen successor of Augustus. Dying young, he gave the world a potent image of great expectations that come to nothing.

Heu miserande puer! si qua fata aspera rumpas,
Tu Marcellus eris.

3. The gallant gentleman was Louis François, duc de Boufflers (1644–1711), marshal and peer of France. He was distinguished in the War of the Spanish Succession and for his defense of Lille against the duke of Marlborough.

4. An apt quotation from Béranger's "La Comète de 1832," which opens:

Dieu contre nous envoie une comète;
à ce grand choc nous n'échapperons pas.
Je sens déjà crouler notre planète;
l'observatoire y perdra ses compas.
Avec la table adieu tous les convives !
Pour peu de gens le banquet fut joyeux.
Vite à confesse allez, âmes craintives.
Finissons-en: le monde est assez vieux,
le monde est assez vieux.

## Chapter XXI, pp. 208–222

1. Souvestre here begins a series of apt quotations (330–332) that add a musical dimension to the narrative: arias and songs—from the nursery, army, and theater.

a. "Du courage / A l'ouvrage": From the first act of the opera *Il Duca d'Alba* (1842) by Gateano Donizetti (1797–1848). Again Souvestre forgets, or has his own way with, the original version:

Et Dieu disait dans ses décrets suprêmes
n'avez-vous donc d'espoir qu'en des secours divins
vos jours dépendent de vous-même
votre salut est dans vos mains!
Courage! . . . du courage
et pour braver l'orage
à l'ouvrage . . . à l'ouvrage!
Car le péril est là."

b. "Taisez-vous, je ne vous crois pas": source unknown.

c. "Je suis Lindor": Lindor was originally a character in Italian comedy: amorous, given to sighing and guitar playing beneath balconies. In the *Barbier de Séville* (1.6) by Beaumarchais, the comte Almaviva ("who sings as he walks about and plays his guitar") responds to Figaro's questioning by singing the Lindor quatrains. The second is

Je suis Lindor, ma naissance commune.
Mes voeux sont ceux d'un simple bachelier.
Que n'ai-je hélas d'un brillant chevalier.
A vous offrir le rang et la fortune.

d. "Quels dînés, quels dînés": The lines come from one of Béranger's most famous songs, "Le Ventru." The complete verse is

L'état n'a point dépéri:
Je reviens gras et fleuri.
Quels dînés,
Quels dînés
Les ministres m'ont donnés.

e. "Malbroug s'en va-t-en guerre": *Malbroug* is probably the most famous of eighteenth-century songs. John Churchill (1650–1722), duke of Marlborough, was the most successful general of his day, as his victories over the French at Blenheim, Ramillies, and Oudenaarde testify. The song aimed to cut Marlborough down to size: they misspell his name and report his death.

This sequence of artful quotations leads translator and editor to ask: Did Proust follow where Souvestre's bugler had gone before? In volume 1, *Swann's Way*, of Proust's *In Search of Lost Time* the narrator recalls the behavior of his grandfather when young Jewish friends came to visit: "And so whenever I brought a new friend home my grandfather seldom failed to start humming the 'O, God of our fathers' from *La Juive*, or else 'Israel break thy chains,' singing the tune alone, of course, to an 'um-ti tum-ti-tum, tra-la,'" . . . and so on, for four more variations on grandpa's theme (Marcel Proust, *In Search of Lost Time* [London: Folio Society, 2001], 1:88).

2. First verse of a popular marching song *Le Départ du Grenadier*. The correct version, according to the Web site of 1er Régiment de Grenadiers à Pied de la Garde, runs as follows:

Grenadier, que tu m'affliges, en m'apprenant ton départ.
Vas dire à ton Capitaine
Qu'il te laisse en qu'autant que j'en serais
Bien aisé, content, ravie t'avoir en garnison.

3. Yet another nugget from Souvestre's repertoire of appopriate allusions. This time from a popular nursery song, best known in the Midi version as:

Allez-vous en gens de la noce
Allez-vous en coucher chez vous!
No-o-o-tre fill' est mariée
Nous n'avons plus besoin de vous.

## Chapter XXII, pp. 223–232

1. The name of Alcibiades points to brilliant abilities and a total lack of principle. The Athenians, Thucydides wrote, "feared the extremes to which he carried his lawless self-indulgence."

# Bibliography

Alkon, Paul K. *Origins of Futuristic Fiction*. Athens and London: University of Georgia Press, 1987.

Bechtel, Edwin de Turck. *Freedom of the Press and L'Association mensuelle: Philipon versus Louis-Philippe*. New York: Grolier Club, 1952.

Béranger, Pierre Jean de. *Oeuvres complètes*. 3 vols. Paris: H. Fourner, 1836–1837.

Bloch, Ernst. *Das Prinzip Hoffnung*. 2 vols. Frankfurt am Main: Suhrkamp Verlag, 1959.

Bodin, Félix. *Le Roman de l'avenir*. Paris: Lecointe et Pougin, London: A. Richter, 1834.

Brooke-Rose, Christine. *A Rhetoric of the Unreal*. Cambridge and New York: Cambridge University Press, 1981.

Buckley, Jerome Hamilton. *The Triumphs of Time. A Study of the Victorian Concepts of Time, History, Progress, and Decadence*. Cambridge, Mass., and London: Harvard University Press, 1967.

Brunel, Pierre. *Mythe et Utopie: Leçons de Diamante*. Calabria: Istituto Italiano per gli Studi Filosofici, 1999.

Burmeister, Klaus, and Heinz Steinmüller. *Streifzüge ins Übermorgen*. Weinheim and Basel: Beltz Verlag, 1992.

Cazes, Bernard. *Histoire des futurs. Les figures de l'avenir de saint Augustin au XXIe siècle*. Paris: Seghers, 1986.

Crossley, Ceri. "Émile Souvestre's Anti-Utopia: *Le Monde tel qu'il sera*." *Nottingham French Studies* 24, no. 2 (October 1985): 31–40.

Champfleury. *Histoire de la caricature moderne*. Paris: E. Dentu, 1882.

Colombo, Arrigo, ed. *Utopia e Distopia*. Bari: Edizioni Dedalo, 1993.

Condorcet, M. J. A. N. de. *Sketch for the Historical Picture of the Progress of Human Mind*. Translated by June Barraclough. 1793; London: Weidenfeld and Nicolson, 1955.

Duveau, Georges. *Sociologie de l'utopie*. Paris: Presses Universitaires de France, 1961.

Escholier, Raymond. *Daumier et son monde*. Paris: Berger-Levrault, 1965.

Fortunati, Vita, and Raymond Trousson. *Dictionary of Literary Utopias*. Paris: Honoré Champion, 2000.

Goizet, J. *Dictionnaire universel du théâtre en France et du théâtre français à l'étranger: Alphabétique, biographique et bibliographique, depuis l'origine du théâtre jusqu'à nos jours par M. J. Goizet; avec biographies de tous les auteurs et des principaux artistes de toutes les époques par M. A. Burtal*. Paris: Chez les auteurs, 1867.

Gore, Keith. *L'idée de progrès dans la pensée de Renan*. Paris: Editions A.-G. Nizet, 1970.

Gozzi, Francesco, and Anthony L. Johnson. *Scienza e Immaginario.* Pisa: Edizioni ETS, 1997.

Hemmings, F. W. J. *Culture and Society in France, 1789–1848.* Leicester: Leicester University Press, 1987.

Kerr, David S. *Caricature and French Political Culture, 1830–1848.* Oxford: Clarendon Press, 2000.

Manuel, Frank E., ed. *Utopias and Utopian Thought.* London: Souvenir Press, 1973.

Melzer, Arthur M., Jerry Weinberger, and Richard M. Zinman. *History and the Idea of Progress.* Ithaca: Cornell University Press, 1995.

Moylan, Tom. *Scraps of the Untainted Sky: Science Fiction, Utopia, Dystopia.* Boulder, Colo.: Westview Press, 2000.

Mucchielli, Roger. *Le Mythe de la cité idéale.* Paris: Presses Universitaires de France, 1960.

Murray, Philippe. *Le 19e siècle à travers les âges.* Paris: Denöel, 1984.

Philippe, Robert. *Political Graphics: Art as a Political Weapon.* Oxford: Phaidon Press, 1982.

Pilbeam, Pamela. *French Socialists before Marx.* Montreal and Kingston: McGill-Queen's University Press, 2000.

Refort, Lucien. *La Caricature littéraire.* Paris: A. Colin, 1932.

Renonciat, Annie. *La Vie et l'oeuvre de J. J. Grandville.* Paris: ACR, 1985.

Restany, Pierre, ed. *Un Autre Monde par Grandville.* Reproduction en fac-similé de l'édition originale de 1844. Paris: Libraires Associés, 1977.

Ruyer, Raymond. *L'Utopie et les Utopies.* Paris: Presses Universitaires de France, 1950.

Schöndorfer, Dr. Ulrich, ed. *Der Forschrittsglaube Sinn und Gefahren,* Graz, Vienna, and Cologne: Verlag Styria, 1966.

Tsanoff, Radoslav A. *Civilization and Progress.* Lexington: University of Kentucky Press, 1971.

Versins, Pierre. *Encyclopédie de l'utopie, des voyages extraordinaires et de la science-fiction.* Lausanne: L'Age d'Homme, 1972.

Vincent, Howard P. *Daumier and His World.* Evanston: Northwestern University Press, 1968.

Watson, Janell. *Literature and Material Culture from Balzac to Proust.* Cambridge: Cambridge University Press, 1999.

## ABOUT THE AUTHOR

French novelist Émile Souvestre (1806–1864) was a contemporary of Balzac and a well-known writer of his day. Lauded by the French Academy for the moral tone of his work, Souvestre was awarded the Prix Lambert posthumously. His most popular work was *Un Philosophe sous les toits*, published in 1850.

## ABOUT THE TRANSLATOR AND EDITOR

Ian Clarke is a noted British science fiction historian and author of many books, including *The Tale of the Next Great War, 1871–1914: Fictions of Future Warfare and of Battles Still-to-Come* (Liverpool: Liverpool University Press; New York: Syracuse University Press, 1996), *The Pattern of Expectation, 1664–2001* (London: Jonathan Cape, 1979), and *Voices Prophesying War, 1763–1749* (London and New York: Oxford University Press, 1992). Ian and Margaret Clarke have collaborated on various projects, including the Wesleyan edition of *The Last Man* by Jean-Baptiste Cousin de Grainville. Ian Clarke was the Foundation Professor of English Studies at Strathclyde University, and Margaret Clarke was lecturer in English at Notre Dame College of Education in Glasgow. Both are now retired and live in England.